Safe Harbor, Safe Heart

Lynn Jenssen

Cover design by StanzAloneDesign
stanzalonedesign@yahoo.com

Dedication

To my husband, Bill. My safe harbor. Thank you for always understanding and always being there for me. I love you.
To my family – my sons, daughters-in-law, and grandchildren. You are my joy daily.

To Mom. I miss you.

Acknowledgements

This book has been a long time coming and is the product of many people's help and support.

I'd like to thank my "across the table, across the phone line and internet" writing sister, Christine Mazurk. She's the best friend anyone could ever want. Thank you!

Thank you to my dear friends at RIRW, many of whom have proofread, critiqued, brainstormed, and supported.

A huge thank you to Lyn Stanzione for the cover. She saw my vision.

Other books by
Lynn Jenssen

Sisters of Spirit Anthology:New View
Written with
Annette Blair
Christine Mazurk
Jeanine Duval Spikes

Safe Harbor, Safe Heart

Chapter 1
The Beacon

Annie breathed in the briny tang of salt spray. Home, as much a part of her as the air she breathed. Island girl. And now where had she come? Back to the island, back to the pounding surf. The lighthouse's rhythmic beam triggered the memory of flashing emergency vehicle lights helter-skelter along the highway. The gulls' screams echoed through her like the sirens on that awful night.

Pain. Loneliness, sorrow, loss. No solace found walking the rocky shore. The nightmare etched in her heart couldn't be washed away by the relentless surf or whisked free by the battering winds. The storm brewing offshore could not compare to the tempest thundering within.

The lighthouse beacon sliced through the dusk, focused and clear, the beam rotating past her. If only that light could refocus her life and reveal her path now that all happiness had been ripped away.

She stepped from rock to rock, one foot settling on a flat stone. It shifted. Her body twisted and fell as if in slow motion, her foot wedged tightly; hot pain seared up her leg. Her scream was lost among the cry of the gulls and swallowed by the thunderous surf.

The spearing flash in her head made it easy to embrace the encroaching darkness like the closing of a casket.

***

The plaintive moan of the foghorn reflected Eric's mood as he walked the rocky island shore. The angry surf crashed as the rhythmic warning light flashed. The wind in its natural fury could not tear away the mood that enveloped him.

He wanted the wind to obliterate his despair, the waves to pound away his loneliness. How could he live without her?

1

As he hiked through the stormy October dusk, a dark form caught his attention. It didn't have the long lines of logs washed ashore or the square angles of a lobster pot snapped from its run by an angry sea.

Leaving the waterline, he hurried toward the figure on the rocks. His emergency medical training kicked in. A body?

"Oh my God…it's a woman."

She lay twisted on the rocks, unmoving but not soaked as if she'd washed ashore. Her light blonde hair fanned over her pale cheeks. Checking for a pulse, he breathed a sigh of relief.

"Are you all right; are you all right?"

No response.

Without moving her, he searched for obvious injuries and discovered a lump on the back of her head. He pried free her ankle, twisted at an unnatural angle, from between two larger rocks. As he straightened her leg, she groaned, and made a weak attempt to push him away.

"Why couldn't I have died?" she sobbed as she regained consciousness.

Her anguish stabbed his heart. He recognized it as one who knew it well. "It's okay. You're going to be all right. Tell me where you're hurt."

"My head—I must've hit it when I fell. And my ankle—it's throbbing."

"Easy. Be careful." He reached to help her sit up. "Take it slow."

"My head feels like it's about to fall off." Her delicate fingers tested the spot. "Ouch"

Eric saw her blood-covered fingers and moved her hand away to take a closer look. A gash as well as a lump.

"We need to get you to the doctor's office," he said, gentling his voice. "You'll need stitches. You could have a concussion and a broken ankle."

"Oh swell—no pun intended. Just what I need."

"I'm going to carry you to my SUV rather than call 911. It's getting nasty out here and it'd take too long for the ambulance to get here."

A slight slip of a thing, he lifted her with ease. She moaned, settling her head on his shoulder. She shivered as he held her close, blocking her from the pummeling wind. Protectiveness surged, surprising him as he crossed the beach. God, he'd missed the warmth of a woman's body. That realization shook him.

"You okay?" he whispered into the softness of her hair. "I don't want to hurt you further."

"You aren't hurting me. Why did I have to wake up?" She turned her head into the nook of his shoulder.

"Your injuries aren't serious. The doctor will make you comfortable." His pulse quickened as her breath warmed his neck, her silky hair brushed against his face.

He rushed along the sand, only crossing the band of rocks to reach his car. As he settled her into the passenger seat, the sky erupted with pelting rain and lightning.

He sped to the small building that served as both clinic and home for the island doctor. She rested with her head back and turned away. He'd heard the pain in her voice. He didn't want to disturb her, but he needed answers to at least some of his questions. "We're almost there. What's your name? Is there anyone on the island I should call?"

"My name is Annie...Annie Gee. I'm staying with my mother but she's off island. She doesn't need a call about this. I'll be all right...unfortunately." Again the pain in her voice.

"Why do you keep saying that? I don't understand but I'd like to."

She looked at him through teary blue eyes set in a square face. "Of course you don't. No one does." She turned her head away.

Eric felt the rebuff like a slap on the face. What drew him to this woman? Why did he care?

Arriving at the clinic, he parked close to the front door. Though she objected, he lifted her from the car and carried her inside. Doc Stephenson must have seen their headlights and opened the door. Thank God.

Doc seemed surprised to see him with a woman in his

arms.

"Doc, glad you're here. I found her unconscious on the rocks at South Beach. Her name is Annie." Eric made his report as he carried Annie into the examining room, settling her on the table. She lay back cradling her head. He waited as Doc x-rayed Annie's ankle. Not broken, just badly sprained. The gash on her head took seven stitches.

She'd be going back to an empty house. She didn't seem in a good state – either physically or mentally – to handle that. He still couldn't handle being alone. Responsibility for this woman settled on his heart and surprised him. Where'd that come from? He could barely take care of himself. Maybe he needed to be needed. Nonetheless, he'd hang around and give her a ride home.

He stood in the doorway of the examining room. Doc talked to her. "You should call and let your mother know about this little mishap of yours. There'll be hell to pay if she comes back here and sees your chart out. A call from you would keep me off the hook."

Annie made a face. "I'll call her tomorrow. I don't want her to worry and come home early. I need to be left alone…and she'll fuss. Let her enjoy fussing over that new baby."

Doc asked Eric to grab an ice pack in the outer room while he got pain medication. Eric motioned Doc farther down the hall out of earshot.

"Listen, Doc, she made some desperate remarks when I found her. I'm more concerned about her mental state than her physical injuries. She said things like, 'Why'd I have to wake up.' Figured I better mention it."

Doc nodded. "I know. Annie is Sara Burdick's daughter. She'd moved off the island before you and Cara came. Sara and I talk when it's quiet in the office, and she's shared what's been going on in Annie's life. She's having a hard time. She's moved back to her mom's house. You know what it's like to suffer a grievous loss."

Gut punch to the middle. He blew out a breath. "Yeah, I know about loss."

Hard to believe someone else could be feeling this same pain and emptiness. As he drove her to her mother's house, she remained quiet until he pulled into the gravel driveway and parked close to the wood-shingled Cape.

"I suppose I should thank you." Annie spoke without emotion.

"You're welcome, but let's get you inside and settled. The weather is getting worse, and you shouldn't use crutches for the first time on a slippery walk. Hold the crutches, and I'll carry you into the house."

Eric lifted her from the passenger seat. She turned her head into his shoulder, avoiding the pelting rain and wind. Again, her body against his created a warmth he struggled to deny. On the porch, she turned the knob, swinging the door open for them. He set her down on the large blue overstuffed couch in the living room, and then leaned over to turn on the brass floor lamp next to her. She sat with her head back against the cushion. She made no move to take off her jacket or play the hostess, and Eric felt awkward.

"Are you gonna be okay? Is there anything you want me to get for you?" A flash of sympathy filled him. He studied her as she lay back with her eyes closed—an attractive honey blonde with freckles sprinkled over her nose, evidence of an outdoor lifestyle. Her light features etched with sadness contrasted with the dark circles under her eyes. From his brief conversation with Doc, he knew an emotional kinship connected them.

Eric flashed to the bouts of complete loneliness and hopelessness he'd experienced over the last ten months. He now wanted to live more than he wanted to die. Maybe he should tell her it gets better. No. He didn't want her to know he'd talked to Doc about her. No words helped him . . . only time.

He found the portable telephone and the TV remote and set them on the coffee table by Annie. In the large kitchen he poured a glass of water so she could take her meds. He noticed a list of telephone numbers tacked by the phone. Should he call her mother? No, he'd leave that decision to Doc.

5

She hadn't moved when he returned to the living room.

"Annie? Let me help you get out of your wet jacket, and we can prop that ankle up on the couch. Come on. Let's get you settled. Then I'll leave you alone. Okay?"

At last she opened her eyes and looked at him. She groaned as she leaned forward to take off her coat. She reached up to put her hand over the wound. "It hurts."

"I know." Eric helped remove her wet jacket, then adjusted the couch pillows so she could lie down and elevate her foot.

"Whoa—I'm dizzy." Annie held onto the back of the couch with one hand and her head with the other.

"I don't think it's a good idea to leave you by yourself. You aren't looking great. You probably have a concussion and shouldn't fall asleep for a while. When is your mother coming back from the mainland?"

"Mom's not due back for several days." Annie laid her hand on her forehead. "I don't want her to know about this until she gets back. She's having too much fun. She'll read my chart at Doc's office anyway." Her sad eyes stared up at him. "I'll be fine."

"Why don't I hang around to make sure you don't fall asleep? Then if you need anything, I'll be here to help you."

Annie raised herself up on her elbow to look at him. "Don't you have anything better to do than haunt beaches picking up unconscious blobs—saving those who don't want to be saved?" She sank back against the cushions, wincing when she tried to shake her head.

Taken aback by the sarcasm in her voice, he watched as the lines furrowing her brow deepened.

"I don't think I'll be leaving you alone. You're not sounding too rational right now." But he identified with her feelings. "I think I know where you're coming from. But my life isn't over, and neither is yours." Yeah, he'd stick around for a while.

"My name is Eric Nordsen. I own *Shore Delights* here on the island. I'm not in the business of rescuing soggy blobs, as you describe yourself, but it seemed like a good idea tonight.

And since no one is expecting me home, I'll stay here and make sure you're okay. So…what's on TV?" Eric's spunky retort provoked Annie to raise her eyebrows and toss him the TV remote.

"Suit yourself."

"Thank you. I will." He took off his wet jacket with a small sense of victory, hung it in the front hall, and made himself comfortable in the recliner with the remote.

Annie closed her eyes while he flipped the channels. He found a movie, *Back to the Future*, and paused.

"How about this? I've seen it before but it's entertaining."

"Whatever."

He glanced around the living room. Sara Burdick's house. He'd known Sara as the office manager for Doc Stephenson, but he'd never been in her home. The couch and recliner faced the oak entertainment center, with a flowered rocker set to the side looking out the picture window. A bookmarked novel and a pair of glasses lay on a side table.

Several travel magazines on the coffee table caught his attention, reminding him of the many travel adventures Sara shared during his frequent visits to the doctor's office with Cara. Pictures of two young blonde girls sat atop the entertainment center. The room portrayed Sara's comfortable practicality.

Eric settled back, surreptitiously watching Annie. She lay with her hand on her forehead. An emotional connection formed with this prickly, yet delicate, woman. Though he didn't know the details, he knew they both struggled with loss.

His Cara had been so full of life, so full of fun, with a smile for everyone that helped you laugh away a bad mood. God, he missed her smile. He looked over at Annie. What would she look like smiling? Instead, the pinched paleness and sunken eyes showed the sorrow haunting her… that same gaunt look that stared at him in the mirror every morning.

She hadn't fallen asleep yet she didn't watch the television, her eyes staring into space. He remembered feeling nothing, staring off for hours. He knew, but how could he help her? "Annie? How are you feeling?"

She turned her head but looked through him.

"How do I feel? I feel numb. Numb and nothing. That sums it up." She turned toward the television cutting off any further conversation.

Despite her attempts to push him away, he recognized her anguish, her despair, her numbness as she called it. He wanted to help her through it. He wanted to hold her in his arms again and comfort her.

Damn. Where'd that come from? He stood.

"I have to go."

***

Annie let him help her upstairs. If she knew watching TV would get rid of him, she'd have tried it sooner. To be fair, someone helping her comforted her, but he wasn't Mike. It would never be Mike again. The familiar scalding tears prodded her to take a deep breath. Think of something else. Crying wouldn't help her head, and she was so damned tired of being sad.

She stood on one foot, leaning on the crutches and studied her reflection in the vanity mirror. Dark circles, puffy wrinkle lines around her eyes—probably from all the crying over the last few months. God, she looked awful. If Mike could see her now, he wouldn't recognize her.

She needed to pull her life together. She needed a plan—a new plan—since the old one *happily married freelance writer with a family on the way* died with her husband.

Chapter 2
Return Voyage

Sara Burdick returned to the island and stopped to see Doc once she checked on Annie. He'd give her more of the story than her dear daughter. She found Doc on his back porch inspecting the paraphernalia in his tackle box.

"Hi, Sara. I didn't expect you back until after the weekend. How's Annie?" Doc Stephenson closed his tackle box with a snap. His tall form straightened to its full six feet. The sun lit the red in his gray-streaked auburn hair. More than aware of his rugged good looks, Sara struggled to focus on the topic of her daughter.

"She keeps telling me not to worry. If only she knew!" Sara sat on the picnic bench and ran her hand through her hair. "I wish she would share more. She isn't talking to anyone about her loss. She should be, but every time I suggest anything like that, I'm met with strong resistance, to say the least! She's always been so damn independent. What am I going to do?"

Doc sat on the bench and put his arm around her shoulders.

"Be patient. She's still grieving. Just be there for her, and let her know you love her."

"You're a good friend, Doc Stephenson." Somehow he always made her smile.

"I try, Mrs. Burdick." Doc's smile turned tender as he stroked her cheek with the back of his fingers.

A blush blossomed along with the tingle his touch created.

"I'm glad to be back. Even though I love to travel, and I spoiled my first grandchild, I missed you."

"I missed you too. We haven't had much time to talk lately. Do you think we could plan one of our impromptu dinners?"

A tingle shot through her. "Plan an impromptu dinner? Sounds wonderful!"

Yes, definitely happy to be home.

Chapter 3
Troubled Waters

"What the hell am I supposed to do now, Cara?"

No answer. Of course, no answer.

Eric swiped his hand through his hair. The end of October. With his summer help returned to college, and now his two remaining waitresses giving notice, what could he do? Close the doors for the season, maybe shut down for good? His stomach hurt at the thought of closing their restaurant. Their baby. All he had left of her.

Eric took a piece of paper and a large red marker out of the desk drawer and printed "HELP WANTED". How could he make it sound urgent? Who'd be looking for a job this time of the year? If he found someone, he'd have to ramp up the training.

The full burden of Shore Delights weighed down his shoulders—he and Cara opened it together four years ago. A teenager came in to wash dishes and help in the kitchen, but Jimmy couldn't wait tables. Eric shook his head at that picture.

Immediately—underlined. One more word added to the sign. It sounded desperate. Well, hell. He was desperate. "Ya gotta help me out on this one, Cara."

He blew out a deep breath to rid himself of the anger pricking at him. She figured out this stuff. He took care of the kitchen and the cooking; she managed the dining room and the staff. They'd been a great partnership—in so many ways. But now . . . the responsibility belonged to him. Him alone.

He taped the sign on the door window, and went to order the week's supplies. A partial list in front of him, his thoughts drifted to Annie and the night he found her on the rocks. Cold and wet, yet as he gathered her into his arms, soft and warm. He kept going back to that... her warmth in his arms. Guilt

11

followed. How could he think about someone, anyone besides Cara? He strode to the work counter to prep for the lunch rush; he needed to keep busy.

He wanted to protect Annie from the hurt so obvious in her demeanor, to get at her thoughts, to hold her again. Even after a week he felt her warmth. She haunted his thoughts.

The bell above the door jingled; he looked up to see Sara Burdick, Annie's mother, entering. Relief filled him knowing Annie was not alone. Sara smiled at him and approached the counter, reaching out her hand to shake his.

"I want to thank you for everything you did for my Annie. She told me you took good care of her last week. I'm so thankful you found her." Sara slid onto one of the wooden stools at the counter.

"I'm glad I could help. It was a pretty nasty night." He busied himself behind the counter, wiping down the workspace. "How is she? I stopped by the next day, but she said she felt fine." Disappointment had surprised him when he couldn't find an excuse to spend time with her.

"Her stitches came out this morning, and her ankle isn't as swollen. She's still wrapping it and limping a bit. Physically, I'd say she's fine. It's everything else I'm worried about." She rubbed her fingers from the bridge of her nose across her forehead. "Doc mentioned your concern about Annie's mental state." Her brow furrowed. "Grief is a tough thing...I don't need to tell you that. How are you doin'?" She looked up at him, her square face and light blue eyes similar to the darker pair haunting him this past week.

"Some days are better than others, Mrs. Burdick. I tried walking off a mood that night down on the shore. That's how I found Annie. It's taking time, but I'm getting through."

***

Sara Burdick knew Eric still hurt. Even the most casual bystander could tell. And she'd witnessed his suffering along with his lovely wife's through all their trips to the doctor. "It does take time, and you'll always miss her. I lost my Johnny ten years ago, and I still miss him. But hang onto the good memories. It helps. You go on."

She sighed. "I'll change the subject now. Can I get two of those delicious seafood salad pockets you make? I'll take them home to surprise Annie." She smiled. Such a kind man.

"Sure thing. It'll just take me a minute or two to put them together." He took out the fixings for the sandwiches and worked at the large cutting board counter facing the takeout area. He seemed comfortable there, his tall body graceful as he moved around the small workspace. He talked as he worked.

"Annie was angry with me for rescuing her. She said I should have let her die right there. Hearing those words from her tugged at something inside me. I'll admit to the same black thoughts after Cara died...but it shocked me to hear someone else speak them." He paused from scooping the seafood salad into the pockets. "Is she getting help from anyone? My talks with Doc certainly helped me."

"Doc Stephenson is a great listener and a good man." She smiled to herself at the understatement. "I wish Annie had someone to talk to. She's always been fiercely independent, and she's not sharing her feelings with me. She doesn't want me to worry, but that's a mother's job. Why won't she let me in?" She fidgeted on the stool. It devastated her to watch her vivacious, outgoing daughter morph into a withdrawn, silent shell.

"She tried staying on the mainland. By the end of the summer, she needed to get away. So she came here to me, but she isn't talking. Oh, I do worry." She shook her head, another grand understatement.

Eric finished wrapping the sandwiches, packed them in a bag with napkins. On the top napkin, he took a pen and jotted something. Smiling, he placed it in the bag.

"She's lucky to have your love and support. It'll help her get through it all." Eric passed the bag of sandwiches to her.

"How much do I owe you?" She opened her wallet.

"That's eleven fifty."

She handed him the money and turned for the door. "Thank you again, Eric. You take care."

"You too, Mrs. Burdick. If there's anything I can do for

Annie, just let me know."

As she left Shore Delights, she noticed the help-wanted sign. Eric needed help. Annie needed help. Maybe they could help each other. She drove home the long way—along the shore road. How could she put that idea into her Annie's head? Maybe if Annie started working there, she'd open up to Eric since he'd been through the same kind of loss.

She carried the mail and groceries into the house and found Annie writing at the dining room table. Though Annie had taken time off as a freelance writer for a women's magazine after Mike's death, Sara thought it a good sign to see her at the laptop again. Annie closed it while Sara took off her jacket.

Annie pulled out the two sandwiches. "What's this?" Annie asked as she continued looking through the bag, taking out the napkin with writing on it.

"I decided we needed a little treat, so I stopped by Shore Delights to get those great seafood pockets they make. I thanked Eric for helping you. He asked about you. What does the note say?"

Annie slid it across the table.

"Annie, hope you're feeling better. Enjoy the sandwich. Eric. Nice." Sara watched her daughter restlessly flip through the mail. No reaction to the note on the napkin. Her old Annie would have smiled. Instead, this deadpan shadow found the piece of mail she searched for—perhaps the settlement from the life insurance company.

Annie opened the single sheet of paper and quickly scanned it. Her face fell. Her skin blanched. She dropped into the ladder-back chair.

What could it possibly be now? Sara laid her hand on Annie's shoulder.

"Annie? What's wrong? What does it say?" Sara sank into the chair next to her.

"I'm not sure. There's some kind of complication holding up the processing of the insurance settlement. I don't understand what's going on." She put her head in her hands, elbows on the table, and stared at the letter. "I can't deal with this. You know Mom, my life sucks! I can't write…I don't have an idea in my head. My husband died in a car accident—not his fault—but the insurance company won't pay. I have no money and no prospect for it coming in anytime soon." She flicked the letter onto the table. "That guy should have left me on the rocks. That's where my life is anyway!" She buried her face in her arms.

Sara's stomach tensed as the reality of what her daughter suggested hit. She closed her eyes and tried to steady her frayed emotions. Okay, at least she'd shared.

"Annie. I know you're hurting; I do understand. It's to be expected with all you've been through." Fear for her daughter's emotional well-being twisted her stomach into knots. "You've never been a self-destructive person. Let's see if we can come up with another way to deal with all this. You need to take a few deep breaths and calm down. Go splash some cold water on your face and get yourself together, and then let's talk over lunch. Okay?" Sara reached over and smoothed her daughter's hair to soften the response. She watched as Annie reached for the letter and folded it, blew out a deep breath, and then rolled her shoulders to relieve the tension.

"You're right, but I'm so frustrated. I tried to write all morning with no luck. Now this. Let me get cleaned up, and I'll come down in a better frame of mind." Annie's tears moistened Sara's cheek when she leaned over to kiss her mom.

Five minutes later, she returned, her cheeks reddened from a cold-water splash. Back straight, head up, jaw set. Change in attitude complete. "This is good. You look more like my old Annie. I've never been so relieved."

"I'm sorry if I upset you, Mom. I don't really mean that…about not being rescued on the rocks. But I'm so overwhelmed and frustrated with things right now. I feel like a disappointment to you." She lowered her head as she spoke quietly.

The tension in Sara's stomach knotted. "Whoa, whoa! What are you talking about, a disappointment to me? Let's go sit in the living room and talk."

Sara reached for Annie's hand as they sat facing each other on the sofa. "Now what did you mean that you're a disappointment? I've never been anything but proud of you since the day you were born. How do you not know that?"

"Mom, I remember how brave you were after Dad died. Nancy and I fell apart when he went into the hospital; then he died, and you stayed so strong. You watched out for us and talked to us. You were so solid." Tears slid down her cheeks. Sara wanted to hold her daughter, but held back to let her finish.

"And I can't do it. I'm not strong and brave like you. I'm trying to hold it all together like you did, but it seems like all I ever do is cry." More tears flowed as Annie tried to wipe them with the back of her hands.

Sara handed her the box of tissues from the side table.

"Annie, when your father died, you were seventeen, Nancy fourteen. Strong and brave? No, but I couldn't let you see my fear. I had to figure out how to go on, emotionally and financially, without your father. And I worried about you two. I didn't want you to see what a wreck I was. I tried to be strong around you, but so many nights I cried myself to sleep." Sara reached over and rubbed Annie's shoulder.

"Listen. You've suffered a loss. It's okay to be sad and scared and uncertain. Grief is all of those things. But it gets better. Easier, more certain, less scary. You absolutely are not, and never have been, a disappointment to me. I love you, and I hurt with you through all of this. I know how hard it is. But let's see what we can do to work on some of your worries. You've always been a creative problem-solver. Let's see what we can think of." She continued to massage Annie's shoulder and neck. The physical contact seemed to help Annie relax.

"I'm starting to deal with Mike's death. I miss him, and I always will, but that's the way it is. It's the details of daily life that are getting to me. I'm worried about the house on the mainland and the mortgage payments. What am I going to do with that?" Annie ran her fingers through her long blonde hair

16

and pulled it into a ponytail. It reminded Sara of how young Annie had been when she'd lost her father. She looked like that young ponytailed girl now.

"Okay. But you don't have to make those big decisions right away. What are your options? Make a list."

"I know. You're right. Putting it on paper will help." Annie nodded. She seemed to be mulling some of the options in her mind. "Mom, what am I going to do about this insurance mess?"

"Well, tell me what is going on with that. You just looked at the letter earlier and lost it. I need the details."

Annie got off of the couch and went to the dining room returning with the letter. She handed it to Sara. With apprehension, Sara unfolded it and skimmed through it. The disheartening legalese confused her too. "Annie, I don't really know what this means, but I have an idea. Eric Nordsen is an insurance agent for a company on the mainland. He handles a lot of the businesses and personal accounts here on the island. Maybe he could help you understand the problem."

"I don't know, Mom. I don't see how he could like me. I was pretty harsh with him last week." Annie shook her head as she remembered that night.

"He seemed genuinely concerned about you today when I stopped in there. Give it a try. Ask him your insurance questions. Maybe he can help get it straightened out." She tried to remain positive in spite of Annie's objections. Annie needed something to go her way.

"I'll think about it. Mom?" Annie looked into her eyes with a steady gaze. "Thank you for listening."

" Annie." Sara gathered her daughter into her arms. She held her, rubbing her back, speaking softly into her hair. "Thank you for talking to me! I have been so worried about you. You don't have to be brave for me; just be you. It's going to be okay. We'll keep talking things through. Okay?" Sara felt Annie's nod against her shoulder. She held her close for one more moment. "Come on. Let's go eat."

Chapter 4

Surf Casting

By mid-afternoon, Sara decided to swing into the doctor's office to finish up some paperwork. Doc's forest green Chevy pickup sat in the driveway. As her good friend, he'd encouraged her to keep talking to Annie. He would be thrilled to hear about their conversation. She hurried up the walk and let herself in. Doc stood at the drug cabinet in his office down the short hallway.

"Hi, Doc. I wanted to finish up that paperwork so the insurance claims can go out in the Monday morning mail."

"We sure had a busy morning. I decided to put together the drug order so we can call that in on Monday too. Then I'm going fishing. The blues are running off the south side." Doc smiled as he continued taking pill bottles out of the cabinet.

"Oh, that sounds so relaxing. I used to fish with my Dad. Johnny never liked it much so I haven't been in a long time." Sara paused remembering the excitement of reeling in a fighting bluefish from the surf.

"I have some positive news. You've been so wonderful about listening to my worries you should get to hear the good stuff too." She walked over to the doorway of Doc's small but tidy office.

"Great, I like good news. What's up?" Doc stopped taking bottles out of the cabinet and leaned on the counter watching her as she spoke.

She told him about the letter from the insurance company that had been the catalyst to opening the discussion about Annie's worries, and her feelings.

"But Doc, the exciting part is that she's started talking to me. She's been trying to be brave for me. Today, she listened. She started problem solving; my Annie is beginning to come back." Hope for her daughter's future filled Sara for the first time in months.

Doc reached out and touched her shoulder. "I know how hard it's been for you. I've seen the toll your worries have taken on you, but you know what? It's so good to see you smiling! It's gonna work out." Doc's hand lingered on her shoulder, its warmth wrapping around her.

She nodded. "I am so relieved." She smiled into his golden brown eyes.

Doc gave a quick squeeze to Sara's shoulder and then pulled away.

"Hey listen. I have a great idea. You finish up the paperwork, I'll get this order written, and then we'll go fishing together. You said you used to enjoy it. I have an extra pole and loads of tackle. What do you think?"

Sara laughed. "I think you're a nut, but you're a good friend...and I'd love to catch a bluefish! Come on; let's get to work so we can go play!"

Sara pulled out her insurance folder; Doc worked at the medication cabinet, and within three quarters of an hour, they had both finished their various chores. Thankful she'd changed into jeans and a sweater after lunch, Sara helped Doc collect his two fishing poles and tackle box, load everything into his old Chevy, and head off to the shore to try their luck at surf casting.

They bumped along the dirt road leading to the ocean. Whatever had possessed her to agree to this? She couldn't remember the last time she'd gone fishing...or done anything on the spur of the moment. The adventure made her feel young, carefree, and happy. Maybe she'd even catch fresh fish for dinner. This could be kind of fun—what could it hurt?

Chapter 5
Ebb and Flow

During the quiet morning hours at Shore Delights, Eric took care of the restaurant business as well as his insurance accounts. He stood looking across the dining room, the morning sun reflecting across the glass-smooth inlet. Cara had loved it; she'd marveled at every sunrise and admired the harbor in all its moods. As if she were standing with him, serenity settled over him as he looked out over the placid view. He absorbed the calm, despite his worry over the waitress situation.

The jingle of the bell over the front door disrupted the quiet. He came to the archway between the dining room and the lunchroom to see who entered. The sight of Annie, dressed in black, surprised him. Her blonde hair pulled into a ponytail, her face gaunt and pale; his pulse quickened at the sight of her.

"Hello, Mr. Nordsen. I hope I'm not disturbing you. My mother thought you'd be here." Annie glanced around.

How did she see his establishment? Whoa, why did that matter?

"I wonder if I could talk to you." She fidgeted with her purse. "Do you have a few minutes?"

"Sure. Come on in. It's good to see you. How are you feeling?" Eric guided her into his office and motioned to the navy blue chair near his desk; his pulse raced at her light fresh scent.

"Oh, I'm fine. The ankle is still sore but better and my hard head...well, that's healing too. Thank you for helping me that night. I'm sorry I acted awful toward you."

"I'm glad I could help, and happy to hear that you're mending. What can I do for you?" He leaned against the front of his desk.

"Well, I know you aren't my insurance agent, but I got this letter in the mail yesterday, and I don't really know what it means, or what I have to do. I wondered if you could give me a hand figuring it out. My husband died in a car accident while driving a company vehicle—caused by a drunk driver." Her voice caught, as though the words jammed in her throat. She closed her eyes, took a deep breath as if to pull herself back from a horrific memory. "There seems to be a problem at the insurance company. I don't really understand it." Annie took an envelope out of her bag and handed it to him. She sat on the edge of the chair as he read through the letter.

"I'm sorry for your loss." He spoke quietly, knowing nothing he said would take away her pain. "Do you mind if I copy this and make a few calls? I don't think it's a problem, but I'll check and see what the holdup is and how long before you can expect a settlement check. Is that okay?" The protective urge he'd struggled with a week ago returned, and he wanted to make this right for her.

"That would be great." The relief in her voice warmed him.

He ran the letter through the copier as she spoke.

"Thank you so much, Mr. Nordsen. The little savings we had set aside is getting eaten up quickly by the mortgage and car payment. I need to decide what to do about the house, but I can't deal with that yet." Annie shrugged her shoulders. "I hoped for a little cushion. I guess this is what they call a cash flow problem."

"Annie, call me Eric. Everyone does, and it makes me feel old when you call me Mr. Nordsen. That's my father's name." He smiled as he handed the letter back. "What kind of work do you do?" he asked gently. He sat on the edge of his desk facing her. She looked into his eyes, as though searching for something—his help, his approval?

"I'm a freelance writer for a women's magazine. I've always wanted to work full time on the staff, but this is my foot in the door. I stopped writing when Mike died, and now I'm having a hard time getting back to it." Annie focused on her hands, as though she didn't want to meet his gaze.

"It's tough, but you have to give yourself the time you need to heal. It takes a long time. I lost my wife ten months ago, and I'm still trying to get myself together."

Annie's eyes filled with concern and understanding as she stared into his. "You lost your wife? I didn't realize…"

Eric cut her off. He didn't want to talk about his grief. She didn't need to hear his details while so deeply immersed in her own. "Listen, I have an idea about your cash flow concerns. How do you feel about waiting on tables?"

Annie chuckled. What a sensuous bubbling sound. Thunderbolt. The transformation in Annie hit him in the chest like a body blow. Her eyes sparkled; pink tinged her cheeks, and the worry lines disappeared from her brow. Eric sat in the desk chair to steady himself.

"I worked my way through college waiting tables. I saw the sign on the door and decided to ask about it after we talked about this insurance stuff. You need help, and I need some income." Annie relaxed, sitting back in the chair, setting her purse on the floor.

"It sounds like we have a deal!" Eric smiled at the prospect of solving his latest headache. He stored the copy of her letter in a folder and rose from his desk. "Why don't I go put on a pot of coffee and we can figure out a schedule, when you can start - all that kind of stuff. Are you up for a cup of coffee?"

"Sure." She followed him out of his office to the lunchroom where she slid onto a wooden stool at the counter. He felt her watching him as he put the grounds into the filter and pushed the button.

As he worked, he explained the business set up for this time of year. The formal dining room with windows overlooking the sheltered harbor stood separate from the open lunch area adjoining the work counter and kitchen space. Simple sandwich prep took place at the counter; the kitchen proper stood to the right partitioned off by a half wall.

"This is probably asking too much, but could you come back in a few hours to meet with Sue? She's working this afternoon and evening, and could show you the ropes. She's been in charge of the dining room, and I'd like you to train with her. Is that too soon?" Whoa, that sounded desperate. Had he pushed too hard? And yet, seeing Annie every day might satisfy his cursed preoccupation with her.

"I don't think that would be a problem. No pressing appointments—and my writing schedule's flexible right now. I'll be here. What time?"

Eric finished preparing the coffee and shifted to get two mugs down from the shelf. "Why don't we say three o'clock? The lunch rush will be over; you can spend some time learning the set up, and dinner customers start coming in around four-thirty to five." He breathed a sigh of relief at the prospect of solving his staffing dilemma.

Eric poured the freshly brewed coffee into the two mugs and carried them to a small oak table by a window overlooking the harbor. Blue paper placemats and small pewter hurricane lamps decorated the tables in the lunchroom.

"I can't come close to replacing your income from the magazine, but at least it'll be something to help with expenses. We stay open through New Year's Day. Then we close and reopen in late April. Hopefully, by the end of December that insurance check should come through." Eric stirred his coffee as he watched her face, the expressions changing subtly as she listened.

"This is going to help so much. I really appreciate the job. It seems you're rescuing me again." The sincerity in Annie's eyes belied a different attitude than after the first rescue. Perhaps the healing had begun for her.

"This time you're rescuing me too. Within two weeks, both of my waitresses will be gone. I'll keep the sign up and see if I can pick up more help, but as of right now, you've got all the hours you can stand."

Annie's smile lit up her face. Again the transformation awed him. Color came back into her cheeks, and the freckles dusting the bridge of her nose glowed. His chest tightened and his heart pounded with a sudden awareness. What a puzzling, beautiful woman.

"Thank you, Eric. I'm going to run now. I told Mom I'd stop by the doctor's office to let her know about the insurance stuff, and she'll want to hear about my new job." Annie picked up her coffee cup and put it on the counter as she got ready to leave. " See you this afternoon."

Eric watched as she left with a spring in her step despite the slight limp and it made him smile. Looking around his restaurant, he wondered how Annie saw it. Light oak tables and mate chairs were placed about, most with a view of the deck and sheltered harbor beyond. In the formal dining room, picture windows dominated the north and east walls looking out at both the harbor and the view of the mainland across the sound.

He thought of her again—the Annie who left with a smile on her lips, a purpose in her stride. What a difference from the sullen woman he'd found on the beach. Something to do every day might help her get through her grief. Keeping busy helped him through the worst of his.

A splinter of guilt shot to his gut. "Is this your way of working it out for me, Cara?" He waited for a response. Nothing concrete, but a broad shaft of sunlight shone on the harbor through the shifting white clouds. It was enough.

Later that afternoon, Annie returned to *Shore Delights* with an optimism she hadn't felt in months. Dressed in black slacks and a white blouse, ready to learn the ins and outs of the Shore Delights dining room, she entered the front door with a cheery hello. Eric looked up and paused behind the counter before he came around to greet her and introduce her to a young woman refilling sugar containers at the end of the counter.

"Annie, this is Sue. She's been with us from the beginning.. I'm going to leave you in her very capable hands. She can tell you where everything is much better than I can." Eric looked pleased as they exchanged greetings and moved off to the dining room to talk.

Looking around, Annie found it elegant yet comfortable. The light oak wood of the chairs and wainscot paneling, tables covered with cream linens and green cloth napkins created a tasteful atmosphere fostered a warm casual feeling.

As she and Sue went through the different areas of the restaurant, she learned where the silverware and napkins were stored, the water goblets and pitchers shelved, and the general system within the dining room. Annie knew Eric watched them. She didn't want to let him down, but how would she remember everything crowding in her head? How intimidating to think in two weeks, she'd be in charge of the dining room.

Momentarily distracted, Annie watched Eric move to the prep area behind the counter. His blond head bent to look into the ovens as he expertly maneuvered dishes. His tall muscular physique seemed large for the narrow kitchen area, but he moved in it with a sure competence that impressed her.

The first customers came in and Sue let Annie have the tables. Her nerves quickly settled as she became acclimated to the routine. As business picked up, Sue took several tables and the two women worked side by side with an easy sense of camaraderie. Eric hurried to keep things running smoothly in the kitchen, and by the end of the evening, all three of them were tired. Strangely invigorated by physical exhaustion, she realized she enjoyed interacting with the customers tonight. Aching lower back, sore feet, tired arm muscles—who would have thought it could feel good? Even her securely wrapped ankle didn't ache much.

"Pretty busy even for a Friday night. How you feelin'?" Eric asked as he locked the door behind the last departing customers.

"I'm pretty tired. I forgot how busy it can get, but I liked meeting different people and waiting on tables. My feet will just have to get used to it." Annie smiled as she sat at the counter, wiggling her injured foot to get rid of its stiffness.

"Any problems?" Eric seemed concerned for her comfort.

"No, Sue did a great job filling me in this afternoon. I'd say things went very smoothly for my first night." Annie nodded in Sue's direction.

"I'm glad you were here. It would have been too busy for one person to handle. I'll keep that sign up, so we can get someone to help, at least on weekends." Eric finished wiping down the last counter and stood with his hands on his hips.

"Do you have any idea when Barbara is going to stop working?" Sue asked as she sat down at the lunch counter next to Annie.

"End of this month, she thought," Eric grimaced. "That doesn't give me much time to find someone else...put the word out around town, will ya?"

"Sure. I'm headin' out, Eric. I'm pretty exhausted. Packing all day and waiting tables all night... makes for a long day." Sue took her jacket off the hook and swung it on.

Annie touched Sue's arm. "Take care, Sue. Thanks for all your help. You really made my first night go well."

"You're welcome. See you both tomorrow." Sue waved at them as she closed the door behind her.

"I think I'm going to head home too. Mom will be anxious to hear how my first night went. She went over to Doc's for a bluefish dinner, but she should be home by now. I'll sleep well tonight, I think," she said as Eric turned off the lights in the dining room.

"I'll see you tomorrow then?" Eric asked as she put on her jacket and gathered up her bag.

"I'll be here by eleven. That's what we said this morning, right? Gosh, it seems like so long ago." It felt like a different decade in terms of her outlook on life. Between the talk with her mother yesterday and the positive action she'd taken this morning to get help with the insurance, and her new job, things had taken a turn for the positive. Annie smiled.

"That'll be great. Barbara'll be in for the evening shift, it'll be good for you to see the lunch business. It's different than dinner." Eric continued to close things up for the night as he talked with her. Funny, but he seemed to prolong their conversation. Did he not want her to go?

Finally, with the restaurant put to bed, they walked out

together. They stood between their cars in the cool autumn night air.

"I'm glad things worked out today. You're saving me. I can't run the kitchen and the dining room too. Thanks." Eric murmured, and the smile on his lips touched his dark blue eyes as well.

"We could call ourselves a mutual aid society." Annie smiled in return. She opened her car door, and got in. For the first time since Mike's death, she could say she had a good day. Amazing.

As promised, Annie arrived at the restaurant at eleven the next morning. She helped Eric in the kitchen with some prep work, put the coffee on to brew, and made sure all the condiment bottles were filled. She felt Eric watching as she worked.

Customers hadn't started arriving yet. Eric put his hand on her shoulder. His light touch warmed her. "Annie, great job. I'm so impressed with how you've jumped right in. You find things that need to be done, and take care of them. It's like you've worked here forever."

"I'm enjoying it." She meant it. His praise created a glow that buoyed her spirit. She watched him prepare for the lunch rush behind the counter. He moved about with ease, deftly slicing tomatoes for sandwiches. He prepped sandwich vegetables while overseeing bacon cook on the grill. Impressive. Lunch customers started to arrive, and she quickly shifted her attention to them. By mid-afternoon when the rush died down, Eric suggested she go home for a few hours and rest her feet. She could come back around five-thirty before it got busy.

"I think I will. My feet are sore from last night. Maybe I can actually put them up and take a little nap." Annie headed for the back room to pick up her jacket. "Eric, listen. This job is helping me, financially definitely, but emotionally too. It's given me something to look forward to, and kept me busy. I appreciate it." Only fair he knew how she felt. Eric put his hand on Annie's shoulder. The touch comforted, stirred, and ended too soon.

"You're welcome, Annie"

She drove home filled with warmth, hopeful about her new job and the direction her life had turned.

Eric stood behind the counter as she left. He'd watched her, unable to take his eyes off her. She seemed better, no repeat of her dark thoughts of a week ago. She smiled at customers, talked and laughed with Sue. Maybe this job would help her heal. He knew firsthand about that long unsteady path.

Afternoons like this were the toughest. If Cara were still alive, they'd go for a walk on the beach or snuggle down to watch an old movie. The sharp stabbing grief he'd first experienced had been replaced by soul deep loneliness. So often, he turned to tell Cara something or talk to her. And he still told her. Crazy? Maybe. Anyone hearing him might think so. Would this too pass?

When Annie returned three hours later, he introduced her to Barbara, who would be working the dining room with her. A very pregnant Barbara announced next weekend would be her last. No surprise.

Barbara chattered about her pregnancy, Annie listened with what seemed feigned interest. He couldn't help watching from behind the work counter. She was quiet tonight, but he had no idea what happened between two and five o'clock to so drastically change her state of mind. Talk about mood swings. Though he knew about the ups and downs these last ten months. Cut her some slack, Eric.

Business picked up and all three of them swung into action. As usual, Saturday business boomed and the evening passed quickly. By ten o'clock the tables were cleared and reset. Annie collapsed on a stool at the counter. Barbara collected her coat, and Eric finished the cleanup in the kitchen.

"Whoa, I'm exhausted. My feet, my back...ugh. Good thing next week's the last." Barbara slid her jacket on and pulled it over her large belly. "My feet are swelling. I can't wait for this little one to be born." She rubbed her stomach as though soothing the baby within. "You ever thought of having children?"

"Not in the near future. Not married." Annie almost snapped out the reply as she turned her head away.

"Oh! Sorry. I saw your ring. Thought you were married. I need to get home and get these feet up. I'll probably see you during the week. Nice working with you. Take care, Annie. Bye, Eric." Barbara waddled out the door.

Annie took her time getting her things to leave. Stalling? She looked tired from the two long days on the job. Emotionally drained too? The bounce in her step from the afternoon was gone, and the spark in her eye dimmed. As she came to say good night, he decided to ask.

"How'd things go tonight?"

"Fine. I'm just tired I guess. I'll see you Tuesday." Annie turned toward the door.

"Annie, sure everything's okay?" Eric asked.

"Just leave it alone Eric." Annie lowered her head, a tone of defeat in her voice. "I said I'm okay. Let's leave it there."

Where'd that come from? Should he push more, or let it go like she wanted?

"Okay. I'll see you on Tuesday then. Have a nice weekend."

"Yeah. You too." And she left.

He watched out the front window. She trudged with her head down and her shoulders drooped. What happened? He wondered as he closed up...and he continued thinking about her long into the night.

Chapter 6
The Beach Rose

Rosa regosa— the beach rose—beautiful, fragile-looking pink or white flower protected by prickly thorns. Despite its fragile appearance, it is able to withstand the harsh conditions of the upper beach habitat.

Annie sat on a large silvered log washed up onto the rocky shore. In spite of her effort to quiet the turmoil in her stomach, angry sobs escaped as she stared out to sea. The thoughts swirling in her head only added to the misery enshrouding her despite the bright sunny Sunday morning.

Until last night, she thought she was getting better. Two good days in a row. The positive steps to straighten out her finances and deal with the insurance company. Her new job. But then, the smallest little thing sent her into tears. A cherished memory, an odd phrase, a special song… a question from an unknowing stranger. That's what opened the floodgates this time. Barbara's question about children.

How stupid. Why couldn't she handle a question like that? She needed tougher skin. Barbara had no way of knowing what she'd been through.

Annie watched the waves break on the shore, breathing in the salty air, listening to the call of the gulls. This rocky shore, always her haven, helped wash away her darker moods.

Last night, she'd fallen into bed exhausted after the busy night at the restaurant. The exhaustion complete –both physical and emotional. But the emotional roller coaster—the high of working and meeting people and the low of being reminded of her double loss—caused her to cry until the fatigue finally overtook her.

This morning she awoke with her hands over her empty

abdomen as she remembered Barbara gushing over her pregnancy and feeling the baby move and blah, blah, blah. Loneliness and being unpregnant pushed her to get out of bed. She needed a quick glass of orange juice, a bagel, and a walk to get rid of the ache inside her heart.

As she came downstairs, she heard her mom on the phone with her younger sister, the new mother. The baby had been awake all night, and Mom offered baby advice and moral support via the phone.

Annie skipped the quick breakfast and got out of the house.

Babies, babies, babies...

That's all that filled her head as she walked to the beach.

She waited for the wind and waves to whip away this mood. She breathed in the clear sea air. She listened to the ebb and flow of the surf on the shore, the small rocks sounding an applause as the waves caressed them.

Not happening. The mood remained. She scanned the horizon. No ships. The lighthouse sat quiet; no fog on this cool, crisp, fall morning.

As she followed the flight of two terns skimming over the top of the water, she spotted a figure down the beach walking toward her.

Aargh. Someone else on her beach. No peace. She struggled to pull herself together. She took several deep calming breaths. She checked her pocket for a tissue to wipe the tears off her cheeks. She looked again at the figure on the beach. Closer now, she recognized Eric.

The memory of her departure from the restaurant last night assailed her. Guilt added to her bleak mood. Her heart pounded; her cheeks heated to a blush. She owed him an apology...he'd tried to help her last night. But then she'd have to explain what happened. A knot formed in the pit of her stomach.

"Hi." She raised her head, trying not to meet his gaze.

"Hi, yourself. I don't usually see anyone out here this early on Sunday morning. I figure everyone is either getting ready for church or sleeping in on the weekend." Eric stood quietly in front of her, looking at her face. She shifted uncomfortably, knowing she had to apologize…to explain.

"I'm an early riser and needed to get out for a walk."

"You seemed upset when you left last night. I hope you're not thinking of quitting." Eric sat down next to Annie and turned to face her, his hands tucked in his pockets, his expression full of concern. Guilt pricked at her. He thought it was about the job. She had to explain, but would he think she's a moody witch…a neurotic mess? What could she say to make him understand?

"No, I wouldn't quit. I like working there. It's just me. I have to get myself under control—not be so emotional."

Eric's eyebrows rose forming the silhouette of a gull in flight. "Annie, you're allowed to be emotional. You've lost your husband. People understand. It's okay." Compassion filled his eyes.

"Not everyone around here knows about Mike. We didn't live here, and except for a few I knew when I was growing up, I don't know many people on the island anymore."

"What happened last night?" Eric studied her face.

Annie took a deep breath. "I have to apologize for the way I treated you last night. You were kind, but I wasn't nice in return. I'm sorry."

"That's fine. Your apology's accepted. You needed space and let me know that. No problem. What happened to upset you?"

Another deep breath and exhale. She closed her eyes and made up her mind. She needed to start talking to someone.

"I need to get over some things. I'm having a hard time dealing with Mike's death, so sudden and unexpected. One day we were happy, had life plans, everything on track. The next day, it's all gone—the happiness, the life plan, everything totally derailed. I can't seem to get myself back on track."

"I know what you're going through. Even when the death of someone you love is not a total surprise, it feels like everything is in complete turmoil and you wonder if life will ever be normal again."

Annie wiped away the tear that slid down her cheek. She looked Eric in the eyes and took another deep breath. More explanation.

"Mike and I were expecting. After we decorated the nursery, I miscarried. Six months ago—before Mike died." She lowered her head. "It devastated both of us." The memory, the loss, the failure—still close to the surface. Another tear escaped.

"And now, I'm inundated with talk about pregnancies and babies. My mom was on the phone giving baby advice to my sister this morning. I needed to get out of the house. Last night Barbara talked about her pregnancy and her hopes about her baby. She asked me if I wanted kids, and it was more than I could take. A double death—not only Mike, but hope for the family we wanted." She couldn't stop the tears now streaming down her cheeks.

Eric reached out and pulled her close. The contact, the shoulder to lean on comforted her as she let herself feel the sadness.

"I know." Eric held her, gently rubbing her back as she cried freely now. He rested his cheek on the top of her head, his warm breath on her hair, as she worked to stop the tears. The warmth of his body, his quiet embrace calmed her. She raised her head to look him in the eyes.

"You really understand." She didn't want to ask, though she saw pain in his eyes that matched the feeling in her gut. Annie pulled away from his shoulder and tried to wipe the tears away. It felt too good, too comforting, being in this man's arms.

"I'm so sorry to be crying all over you. You've been nothing but good to me and I'm repaying you like this!" She needed to move away from him.

"Annie, it's okay. I went through a similar experience. It's important to talk about it. Somehow it helps you work through the pain. I'm glad you talked to me." Eric gave her back one last rub and stood up. "Okay? How about a walk down the beach...that helps too." He extended his hand to pull her off the log.

A shaky laugh escaped her lips. "Last time I walked on the beach, I cracked this thick head of mine and had to be rescued by a dark mysterious figure coming out of nowhere."

"You do have a writer's imagination if that's how you saw it." He smiled at her, a twinkle in his eye.

"I didn't see any of it, remember. I was unconscious. Thank you for rescuing me, by the way. I never properly thanked you."

"You're welcome. You were a little prickly about being rescued. You pretty much wanted to be left on the rocks. Unfortunately, I'm not one to leave a beautiful woman in a storm in need of rescuing." Eric cocked a crooked smile at her. Then he looked down and murmured, "Besides, I identified with that feeling too. I've often walked this beach wondering why Cara died. Why not me?"

His confession shocked her. He understood. He'd been there too.

As they walked along the shore, Eric reached for her hand, partially to help her balance on the rocks, but truthfully, for the contact. Simple human contact. Something stirred inside him as he'd held her in his arms. He felt it again when he held her hand. What was it about this woman?

"You haven't told me anything about your wife and how she died. I feel like I've been unloading on you. It's your turn." Annie looked at Eric with sincere concern in her eyes. Eric's stomach tightened with anxiety, nerves. He had purposely not shared any of the details of Cara's illness and death with Annie. Yet he wanted her to trust him enough to talk to him...and trust went both ways. He paused a long moment to consider his words.

"We'd been married for nine years. Cara taught at the high school and helped me with the restaurant. We decided to start a family, and when Cara started feeling bad, we thought it was morning sickness that lasted most of the day. Then we got the results…not pregnant, tests showed ovarian cancer. We were devastated, scared." He paused, this time remembering the call from Cara's doctor. Cara's face had blanched as she grabbed the chair to sit. The long series of treatments and doctor visits began immediately after that call.

His hand in his pocket, he wrapped his fingers around the small silver sand dollar paperweight she gave him when they opened the restaurant. He carried it with him always.

"But, she fought. She gave it everything she had. In the end, the cancer still won. She died in my arms last January. So I know. Two blows in one." He bowed his head as he remembered the pain and loss, remembered both Cara and the family they'd dreamed of.

"Oh Eric, I'm sorry." Annie paused. "I didn't realize…. I didn't mean to open wounds for you again. Annie shook her head. "I feel so guilty and mean about the way I reacted to this whole baby thing. How do you get through it all?"

Annie stopped walking and turned to face him, looking up into his eyes. His stomach twisted from the remembered loss, the look of tenderness in her eyes… or something else?

"I can only tell you to keep going. It gets better." Eric turned and they continued strolling, hand in hand. "It helps to talk to a friend. I've spent many evenings talking with Doc. I'd come here to walk the beach and see his study light on. He's never minded me stopping in. He's a good friend."

He looked over at her, wondering what her reaction would be to his next statement. "You can talk to me anytime you need to. Okay?" He offered because he knew it would help her, and he felt connected to this fragile woman—no, this strong woman. A sixth sense nudged at him. Strong and independent. She's tougher than she gives herself credit for. She's a survivor, this beach rose.

"I may take you up on that offer." Annie gifted him with one of her transforming smiles. "You've helped me already. You carried me out of the storm, helped me home that night, gave me a job, and you're untangling my insurance mess. How am I ever going to repay you?"

"Don't forget, you're rescuing me too. I'd be scurrying back and forth waiting on tables and cooking, or closing down altogether, if you weren't running the dining room for me." Annie continued to smile and Eric basked in the warmth surrounding him.

Chapter 7
Past Voyages

The memory of Saturday with Doc ran through Sara's mind as she drove into work, anxious about his reaction this morning. They'd spent most of Saturday afternoon surf casting, of all things. They'd shared the catch that evening at his house, laughing together as they grilled the bluefish Doc caught and steamed some fresh vegetables Sara brought back from the mainland.

She'd seen a different Doc—relaxed, looking younger than his fifty-five years as he'd cast into the surf repeatedly, and watched the gulls working offshore to see where the fish were running. His broad shoulders flexed as he worked the fishing pole.

Things between them had shifted from all business to mostly business, some play, to what now? Something more personal still. Would he acknowledge their spontaneous outing and dinner together? Or would it be business as usual? Surprised at the turn of her thoughts, she parked the car. Gathering her purse, a folder of papers, and courage to face the unknown, she headed up the walk.

As she stepped into the office foyer, the smell of coffee drifted in from Doc's kitchen behind the adjoining door to his living area. Sara turned the thermostat up a few notches in the waiting room to banish the weekend chill. She neatened the magazines on the small white wicker table and adjusted the flowered cushions in the matching wicker chairs.

Leaving the door open into the receptionist's office so patients could check in, she turned on the computer and set about getting organized for the morning. As she put her jacket and purse into the closet, she turned to see Doc standing in the office doorway, a mug of coffee in each hand. He sipped on

37

one, smiled at her, and offered the other to her without a word.

She smiled. "Thanks. I need a second cup this morning." She watched Doc for some clue of his thoughts about the weekend. His tanned face held a relaxed countenance, his brown eyes twinkling with amusement.

"Too much playing this weekend, Mrs. Burdick?" A smile twitched at the corner of his mouth.

She should have known...Doc handled all but the most serious situations with humor. Well, she could give as well as get.

"You know what they say… all work and no play…" Sara teased right back.

"I had a nice time this weekend." Doc lost the teasing tone in his voice and with sincerity in his eyes said, "Thank you."

She dropped the eye contact, slightly uncomfortable with the sudden change in mood. That happened more often recently—teasing and then getting serious and quiet. The rules were changing between them, but to what?

"Me too. I told you, it's been years since I did any fishing. I'm afraid it showed too. You caught dinner."

"Practice makes perfect. I'll call you when I hear the blues are running again. Maybe you can catch dinner next time." The twinkle returned in his eyes. An unexpected thrill surprised her at the thought of a next time.

The sound of the front door opening and an elderly woman and her daughter entering the waiting area interrupted their banter. Before going to greet his first patients of the day, he turned to her, "Okay, off to the business of healing. We'll have to swap more fish tales later."

Sara laughed and shook her head. He did like to play with words.

The morning sped by with a steady stream of patients, keeping them both busy. As the lunch hour approached and the last patient left, Doc finished cleaning up and came to stand by the reception counter putting the last of the patient folders on Sara's desk. She looked up from her computer screen and smiled.

"What a busy morning."

"It sure was. I didn't even get to finish that cup of coffee I started. Things went right from Mrs. Frank's heart palpitations to Mr. Stuart's strained back muscles to Little Sammy Polk's strep throat…"

Sara shook her head as she finished counting the patients listed in the book they kept on the counter. "We saw fifteen this morning. That's almost as many as peak summer hours. What's going on?"

"I guess word's gotten out about the excellent service we offer." Doc smiled and walked into the receptionist area, sitting down in the second office chair.

"So, how was Annie's first weekend working at Shore Delights?" Doc surprised Sara with the change of subject, but she knew it would lead to something.

"She'd already gone to bed when I got home Saturday night, and then she got up early and went banging out of the house Sunday morning, but she came back in a better frame of mind." Sara turned and fidgeted with the already neat stack of folders on her desk. "It's so hard. I never know how much I should ask about, how much to offer. Her moods are so up and down. I know it's been hard for her."

"It takes time to work through all the phases of grief. Keep talking and offering your support and advice." Doc picked up a pen and played with it, weaving it through his long fingers. "She'll take it in and process it, use what she's ready for. Look at the result of your last talk. She's gotten a job and is getting out of the house. That's good progress."

"Yes, and I need to remember how difficult it is to get back on your feet. It took me a long time after John died, but I worried about the girls so that gave me a focus." Sara gazed out the window at the bare maples on the hill behind the office, remembering the uncertainty and loss from ten years ago, feeling again the emptiness and panic in her stomach.

"I see how this experience changed Annie. I've always been so proud of her. She's such a positive, happy, secure person. Outgoing, successful." She rubbed her forehead with

39

her fingers, trying to release the worry building there. "Since Mike's death, she's turned inward, is quiet...distracted. It's only in the last few days, that she's started to talk a little, been more positive ... more like my old Annie." She looked up into Doc's eyes to see understanding.

"I had an interesting conversation about Annie yesterday." Doc seemed to be struggling with something.

"Really?"

"Eric Nordsen stopped by. Sometimes he needs someone to listen, and he's a great guy. Apparently he ran into Annie walking the beach on Sunday."

Sara nodded. That made sense. That's where Annie went when she needed to work out things.

"It seems Annie's found a friend in Eric. I guess they've shared some of their common experiences." Doc tipped back in the office chair, his hands steepled together.

"That makes me feel better. At least she's started talking."

"I think it's good for Eric too. I had concerns about him not being able to form another relationship after his wife's death. It's a heart wrenching thing to watch the woman you love die in your arms."

Something in the way Doc stared off made her wonder if he spoke from personal experience, not professional observation.

He seemed to pull himself back to the present. She waited for him to continue.

"It takes a while, but life goes on. It's important to get back into things, stay involved."

"I always think it's so sad to see people who just exist after a loss. I hope that won't be the case with Annie," Sara whispered.

Doc puzzled her. Did he want to tell her something? What in his past brought this situation so close to home for him? How could she ask?

As she pondered a way to steer the conversation, the phone rang. Doc sat up and grabbed the phone.

Sara listened as he talked to the mother of a toddler with

what sounded like an ear infection. Doc told her to bring the child in, even though office hours were over. He smiled at Sara and rolled his eyes as he made all the right noises on the phone. Sara smiled back. Not at all unusual for him to see people after hours.

A wink and wave told her to leave before this rather talkative mother arrived with her child. Sara finished putting on her jacket and headed for the office door. Catching Doc's eye, Sara mouthed, "See you tomorrow," and walked out.

Chapter 8
Flotsam

"flotsam-debris washed ashore after a wreck"

Annie worked every day the next week, except Sunday and Monday. At night she arrived home exhausted but contented. She enjoyed the work, meeting the people of the island, and staying busy. And she liked the time with Eric during the afternoon lull, perhaps more than she should.

Monday, Annie walked the rocky shore. By early November the winter beach had started to arrive. It amazed her that each year, for some mysterious natural reason, the sandy beach washed out to sea, leaving a stripped down rocky shore. Then in the spring, the sand returned and the beach became glorious for summer.

As she walked the exposed rocks, she chastised herself. Always independent and decisive, the self-doubt that filled her now rivaled her impatience with herself. Her indecision and fear of a future without Mike only compounded her tenuous financial situation.

Her pay from the restaurant covered the car payment and living expenses. The little savings they'd banked would cover the November and December mortgage payment, but after the first of the year…she didn't want to consider selling the house, but what other option did she have?

Things were just too tight. If only she could get back to writing, but the writer's block since Mike's death loomed heavy and large.

She sat on a huge rock flattened on the top to form a natural, although hard, seat. Her mind jumped from problem to problem, not focusing on one in particular, unable to solve any. She took a deep breath trying to clear the thoughts muddled together in her head. Closing her eyes, she let the late fall ocean breeze flow around her. She forced her shoulder muscles to relax, to let the tension they carried flow away with the wind.

She sat with her eyes closed, mind wandering as the waves rhythmically washed ashore. The sound of the water, the wind, and the gulls calmed her state of mind.

She opened her eyes, scanning the horizon. A lone figure walked the rocks toward her. She sat leaning against the large rock. She watched as he approached, engulfed in his own thoughts. She wondered how he got through his sorrow. He appeared more together than she felt but she'd watched him in quiet moments, gazing off, a deep sadness filling his eyes. How does anyone survive?

As Eric walked closer to her end of the beach, she raised her arm and waved. He smiled as he waved back, walked a little faster, and headed toward her.

"We seem to meet here often." Eric casually climbed on the rock next to her.

"This is my favorite place in the whole world," Annie said. "Ever since I was young, it's been the place I come to for solace, quiet, peace. I missed it when I moved away." She looked out to the horizon.

"I think I've worn a path along those rocks within the last ten months. But…it helped. It gives me time to think without interruption, focus on what I need to do, and focus on working through it all." He sat with his fingers laced, resting on his knees.

"It's still near the surface for you too, isn't it?" Annie asked, watching Eric's face as he gazed out to sea.

"It gets better. The holidays will be hard, but I don't have to tell you that." Eric turned and looked at her.

"I haven't even thought that far ahead. I'm trying to figure out what to do about my house. I don't need to make decisions immediately, but financially, I can't afford to pay the mortgage and not live there." She swept her hand through her long blond hair, pulling it away from her face. "But I'm not ready to live there alone either. So many memories..." Images, like an emotional mental collage, of Mike working in his basement shop, rolling with her on their bed, standing at the refrigerator looking for a quick drink, churned through her mind. She shook her head to clear it.

"Where exactly on the mainland?" Eric asked. "Maybe there's a rental market for it." Annie pulled herself away from the memories and focused on the here and now. She took a deep breath.

"There is a college in town, but I'm not sure about renting to students. I hadn't really thought about it." Annie raised her brow and paused to consider the possibility. "How would I do that? I'd have to clean things out...that would be tough but if I had a reason..."

"You could get a real estate agent...which college?"

"Stratford College. It's not big but it's a good school." Annie thought fondly of the campus on the hill up the road from their brick-faced Cape.

"Really? That's where Natalie goes to school. She's one of the college kids who worked for me during the summer. Nice kid. I could see if she knows anyone interested in renting. A personal referral is better than renting to someone through an agency, I'd think."

"True. I need to think about this. Then I'll have to screw up my courage to go clean it out... I'll let you know." Annie smiled. "You're rescuing me again."

"Habit, I guess." Eric smiled back. He reached over and took Annie's hand in his. The warmth of his hand holding hers radiated throughout her. Deeper than a physical warmth, it touched her mending spirit.

They sat, looking out over the water, watching the waves, soaking up the quiet.

"Eric? How...what...have you cleaned out your wife's things?" Unsure how to broach the subject, she looked at him tentatively.

He blew out a breath, and paused for a long moment. He

let go of her hand putting his hands in his pockets. Annie felt the distance.

"Cara made me promise if she died, I would pack up her clothes and give them to the homeless shelter on the mainland. She told me I shouldn't keep things that would make me feel morose. That was the word she used. I could only keep things that would remind me of happy times, good thoughts, love."

Eric shook his head, again gazing out to the horizon. "She... was... remarkable. It took me a while to be able to do that, but after a false start or two, that's what I finally did. Packed up all her clothes and made a delivery to the shelter. They appreciated it, and it helped me. I gave some of her special jewelry to her sister and mom. I kept pictures, mementos, some special things." He pulled a silver sand dollar paperweight from his pocket. "Like this. It's one of the few things I've kept for sentimental value. It's helped me move on, I think."

Annie watched him speak, in awe of how he'd handled this part of the grieving process.

"I should think about at least checking the house... see what I have to pack up." Annie took a deep breath. "Maybe I'll go check it out next Monday when I have the whole day."

"Are you gonna be okay by yourself? I have a meeting at the insurance company for an hour or so in the morning, but I could go with you after that if you want." He put the sand dollar back in his pocket, then folded his hands together on his knees. "It's up to you. If you think it will help, I'd be happy to go with you." Eric reached for her hand again, giving it a little squeeze.

"You're a good friend." The warmth returned.

After a moment, Annie turned to Eric, decision made, confidence returned.

"Yes. I'm going next Monday. Yes, I'd really appreciate your help. And yes, I'd like you to call your waitress who goes to Stratford College. How great if I could find some nice coeds to rent it. It'd help finances, and I wouldn't worry about an empty house through the winter."

Annie let out a deep breath. She'd made a decision. Progress... dealing with one thing at a time; maybe she was getting stronger.

The next day, Eric told her Natalie expressed interest in moving off campus for the spring semester.

On Wednesday, Annie arrived at Shore Delights smiling. She slipped behind the work counter where Eric prepped for the lunch crowd.

"Eric, I talked with Natalie. She sounds perfect. She and a friend are interested in renting the house, and are meeting me on Monday." She bubbled with excitement as she filled Eric in on the conversation.

"She sounds wonderful. Eric, this is working out so well." She hugged him. Meant to be a quick friendly hug, it surprised her as she felt his arms around her and something inside her quickened. So real, so solid.

Eric murmured in her ear. "I'm glad it's working out." He took his arms from around her, an odd look in his eye.

Annie wondered at the look.

***

Eric walked the shore that night. How he could be such a jerk? He loved Cara with all his heart. How could he be feeling something for another woman? His stomach twisted, bile rising as though he may lose what little dinner he'd been able to eat. Guilt. He thought often about another woman. Unfaithful. A woman who dazzled him with her smile and filled him with warmth at a mere touch. A woman who was not his wife. And no matter how late into the night he walked the shore, the waves and the wind could not whip away the lustful feelings, the guilt, or the loneliness.

By the end of the week, his very dark mood made him unfit to be with anyone, let alone be at Shore Delights dealing with the public. Fortunately, Thursday night was quiet, and they closed up by eight-thirty. Annie sensed his mood, and gave him space. He felt her watching him. It added to his frustration and guilt. Now he'd let her down too?

As he finished cleaning the kitchen for the night, Annie came up behind him and laid a hand on his shoulder. He turned.

"Eric? Is everything okay? Do you want to talk?"

He turned back to the sink not wanting to see the concern in her eyes.

"No. I've got a lot on my mind."

"A walk on the beach helps. I'd be happy to listen if you want." Her hand on his shoulder burned a brand. He moved away from her touch. Self-preservation or guilt?

"I've got things to do in my office before the meeting on Monday. The weekend's busy, so I planned to stay late tonight to get it done." He made the mistake of turning around to face Annie. He saw the hurt in her eyes though she tried to cover. "But thanks anyway," he added.

"Okay." Annie looked at him in a funny way. "Just remember you have a friend too."

What the hell had he done? "I know."

He watched as Annie put on her teal blue jacket, the color highlighting the blue of her eyes, the blond of her hair. His heart thudded in his chest. He had to get out of here, but he couldn't go to the beach—he'd told Annie no.

She said a quick good-bye and left.

Alone. What a jerk. How can he feel things for her and he's just lost Cara? And Annie's still reeling from the loss of her husband. That's good Eric...chasing after the weak and helpless. Nice guy.

Remember you have a friend too. Annie's words came back to him. Maybe he would go see his friend. He'd helped him work through his darker moments. Maybe he could help tonight.

Eric turned off the lights, locked the door, and drove toward Doc's to see if the study light shone through the window.

He knocked on the door, wondering again. What would his good friend think of him now? He'd see the truth—he was a jerk...slime. Eric scowled. The door opened and Doc seemed surprised to see him.

"Eric! Come on in. I haven't seen you in a while." Doc acted funny.

"Let me get off the telephone, and I'll be right back. Come on in and make yourself comfortable." Doc hurried into the small kitchen, picked up the wall extension, and stepped around the corner.

Eric looked around. He'd spent numerous hours over the last year talking in Doc's living room. A comfortable room, definitely a room for a guy. A dark brown leather couch faced a stone fireplace with two hunter green wing back chairs and a small mahogany side table next to the hearth. The only electronic gadget was an entertainment center containing a large TV. Several prints of sailing scenes, oceans and sailboats hung on the off-white walls.

He thought about the style of the room. Cara talked about art and decorating styles. He could only scowl as he sat on the leather couch.

Doc came out of the kitchen smiling, two beers in one hand, a bowl of pretzels in the other.

"How're you doing? You haven't stopped by for an evening visit in a long time. Everything okay?" Doc seemed to know otherwise. He offered Eric a beer.

"Yes and no." Eric opened the bottle and took a quick drink, trying to figure out where to start.

"That's usually how it goes. What's going well?"

Eric recognized the approach Doc used.

"Business is going well. I've found someone to wait on tables and have another person coming for an interview. The insurance business is steady and working fine without going to the mainland office often. Professionally, things are good."

"Good! Okay, here's the question. What's not going well?"

Eric took a deep breath and blew it out, wondering where to begin.

"I'm almost afraid to tell you. I stood outside your door thinking what a jerk I am…the slime of the earth…and if I tell you, what will you think of me?"

"You're being pretty hard on yourself. I can't imagine a situation where anyone would think of you as slime of the earth. Why are you beating yourself up?" Doc sat back in his chair, took a sip of beer and waited.

"Cara died ten months ago."

Doc nodded.

"I loved her so totally." He felt the need to convince Doc. Doc nodded and waited, saying nothing.

"I think I have feelings for someone else. I don't know if I can call it love, but it could be. Or am I using her as a replacement? How big of a jerk am I? It's disrespectful to Cara...and it's wrong for this other person."

"I know how much you loved Cara. And I know you've mourned her, and will continue to mourn her for a long time. The good news is that you can still feel good things for another person. It's okay to fall in love again...if that's what this is." Doc shifted forward in his seat, putting his elbows on his knees, staring at Eric.

"Some people shut down emotionally after the death of a spouse; others take a long time to allow themselves to make that kind of connection again. Others, like you I suspect, are more emotionally open. You are a caring, compassionate person. It's good someone is meaning something to you. You haven't shut down the ability to care. Give this relationship time to grow and be comfortable."

"I'm being unfaithful to Cara," Eric almost whispered. He could talk to Doc like no one else...well, he'd talked to Annie about some very personal things too, but this was about Annie.

"That's the part of you that's still accepting Cara's death, the fact that she's really gone." Doc paused and watched as Eric took another swig of beer. He sat back and had some, too.

"You're right. My brain knows she's gone and not coming back. But sometimes my heart still thinks she's here. That's when I feel guilty." Eric looked to the older man for understanding. Doc nodded.

***

The sight of this young guy on his couch confessing feelings of guilt hit Doc close to home. He'd fought similar emotions for the past month. In fact, he'd just gotten off the phone with the source of his emotional dilemma. His feelings for Sara had grown to become much more than professional colleagues or casual friends. And it shocked him. He'd shut down that part of his life, his heart, many years ago. He thought he'd shut it down for good, but now...

"Cara will always be with you. She's an important part of your life, and her memory and the memory of your time together will always be with you. But would she want you to close off your life to other relationships? I don't think so."

Doc had the oddest feeling that there were more people in on this conversation than just the two of them. It felt as though he counseled not only the young man sitting on the couch, but also a young emergency room physician hidden deep within his own psyche. Physician, heal thyself? Something to think about in the late evening hours.

"No. She talked about that. I got angry with her because I didn't want to think about life without her, but she made me hear it." Eric's sad smile eased the worry lines on his forehead. "She knew me well, didn't she?"

"Listen to her now, and cut yourself a break. Take it slow, but follow your heart." Doc paused to grab a handful of pretzels, watching Eric for a reaction to the next statement. "Besides, she's healing too, if I'm not mistaken."

Eric glanced up into Doc's eyes. Bullseye. He'd guessed right.

"Yes, and that's the other thing I'm wrestling with. She needs me as a friend. Am I taking advantage of that by wanting more?" Without saying her name, Eric confirmed Doc's suspicions. Annie.

"Well, that's another reason to take it slow. Talk to each other. Listen to each other. If it feels okay, keep going. But give yourself some credit, Eric. Don't doubt your feelings or your motives. You're a good person with good instincts. Trust them."

Doc sat back in his chair and sipped his beer. He'd finished counseling for tonight. Doc knew from past conversations with Eric that he'd go and mull over what they'd talked about, and come back with questions or feedback when ready. Now if he could just get his own head straightened out. Well, not his head, his heart.

Chapter 9
Hidden Dangers

What had he gotten into? Annie needed help, both emotional and physical, to clean out her house, but why did he feel like he should be the one? He'd like to be the one, okay. The one to hold her in his arms and feel her body press against his, the one to run his fingers through her soft golden hair. He'd like to be the one. He shook his head trying to rattle the thoughts of Annie out of his mind. He knew that was as likely to work as anything else he tried this whole week. And Monday approached quickly.

Eric chopped vegetables for the salads with a vengeance as he worked through his conflicting feelings. He'd come in early to get paperwork done and set up for the weekend. He couldn't get Annie out of his mind.

She drove him mad with her feather touches...her fingers warm through his shirt sleeve as she spoke to him, her hand splayed on his back as she passed behind him at the work counter. Each little touch lightning'd to his core—his heart raced, pulse pounded in his ears, mouth dry and unable to form words, mind flashed to the desires, fantasies, dreams that plagued him of late. All from a single touch. And he couldn't say anything to her.

He'd go insane if he didn't put some distance between them. Ten months? What a jerk! He loved Cara, and all he mourned for her was ten months before he's struck by a lightning bolt again. Pitiful...totally pitiful. Acting worse than a horny teenager.

Eric put away the salad mix and started preparing the soup of the day, New England clam chowder. He cubed potatoes by rote, as he continued his lecture to himself.

Doc is right. He needs to back off with Annie and be good

friends. They both need to take this slow and heal. Recover from their losses. Develop a friendship and maybe it'll become more...when they're both ready. If he could stop remembering her soft curves against him...stop it, Eric. Just friends. Could he curb his wayward thoughts with Annie always so close?

The bell above the door rang as Annie came in for the lunch shift. Eric imagined it as the bell tolling for a sinking ship, his resolve sinking as he watched her jaunty step, her warm smile.

Annie moved around the work area behind the counter. Eric made an effort to stay away from her. Once the lunch rush slowed, he hid in his office, finding paperwork to occupy him. A fine line existed between remaining friendly and withdrawing a bit. And he didn't think he saw the line clearly.

Maybe it wasn't just Annie. Maybe it was that he hadn't been near a woman in ten months. The college girls that waited tables this summer were cute but he could never think of them in that way. A deep sigh of frustration escaped his lips as his mind drifted yet again to Annie. He could hear her chatting with someone who had just entered the restaurant.

"Eric, this is Agnes. Sue told her to come in and talk to you about a job." Annie stood in the doorway of his office, her smile spearing him.

He rose from his desk, crossed the small office to shake the attractive young woman's hand, and invite her into his office to talk. Her long dark hair and dark olive complexion topped a voluptuous body to form an exotic look. The lunch crew would certainly enjoy Agnes.

"You can call me Aggie, Eric."

She worked as a waitress for years on the mainland. New to the island, he hired her on the spot. Stepping out of his office, he called to Annie as she prepared for the Friday evening crowd.

"Annie, can you set up some training time for Agnes and work out a schedule with her? I've got a few things to finish up."

"Oh, I hoped you'd show me the ropes." Agnes rested her

hand on his arm, her eagerness obvious.

"Well, you'll be working with Annie, and she runs the dining room for me. I'm sure you two will get along fine." Eric nodded to Annie to take his cue.

Good! Maybe this would help. Annie wouldn't be working so much. It would give him a little space, although the new girl seemed quite forward. She was a knockout, but didn't have the attraction Annie did. So it wasn't just anyone. It was Annie. Filled with relief, disappointment, and the ever-present guilt, he left the two women together to figure out a schedule.

***

Distress filled Annie's mind as she tried to focus on a schedule with Agnes. She'd watched as Aggie came on to Eric. He seemed oblivious but he'd been particularly distant today, although he hadn't been talkative all week. Maybe he was interested in the new girl. A pang struck her at the thought. Or maybe she did something to upset him.

Mentally reviewing the week, she searched her memory for the cause of his mood. Once Aggie left, Annie searched for Eric. She found him in his office with paperwork on the desk, though he sat gazing out the window. He stood up from the desk when Annie entered. Hands in his pockets, he shifted from foot to foot, glancing at his desk rather than looking at her.

"We're all set with a training schedule. Agnes will come back for the dinner shift and we'll work it together tonight. I don't think it'll take her too long to get the hang of things. She's waited table before," Annie reported to Eric. No eye contact. What was going on anyway?

"I'm glad we found someone else. Otherwise you'd burn out with all the hours. Now you'll have some time for your writing." Eric removed one hand from his pocket to neaten the piles on his desk as he spoke.

"It's not really a matter of not having enough time to write; it's more that I don't have the focus necessary, or the drive, or something. I need to give it time. I sit and try to write, but it's not a pretty picture. Maybe after things get settled with the

54

house, I can focus more." Annie watched Eric as she spoke. He seemed preoccupied.

"Well, maybe after Monday. Aggie will be picking up hours, and hopefully things will be more settled on the mainland house."

The bell above the door rang. Eric shifted to leave the office; Annie followed him out. Several workmen had stopped in to order grinders to go. Annie finished straightening the lunchroom while Eric fixed the sandwiches and cashed out the order. She couldn't stop thinking about the odd vibrations from Eric. It made her more determined to talk about what bothered him.

Eric had tidied up, and started working on the evening specials.

She pulled up a stool next to the work counter.

"Can I do anything to help?" Unsure how to start the conversation, Annie tried to ease into it but Eric wasn't being helpful.

"No, I'm all set. I'm fixing this for tonight's special. I'll figure out what I'm doing for a dessert. It's quiet here. You can head home for a couple hours." Eric finished dicing vegetables to add to a large pot on the stove. He stirred the contents intently, not looking up. He seemed anxious for her to leave.

"Well, while it's quiet, I wondered if I could talk to you," Annie looked at him questioningly, waiting for a response, eye contact, something.

"I've got a lot on my mind right now, Annie. Is this something that could wait?" Eric looked quickly at Annie, then back to his work.

Annie raised her eyebrows at the response. He clearly wanted to get rid of her. Her heart beat fast, the pounding in her ears made her voice sound odd to her.

"Sure. It's no big deal. Maybe later. I'll be back around five o'clock. That's when Aggie is coming in too." Annie shoved away from the counter and flipped her jacket over her shoulders. She left quickly before she said anything she might regret.

"Bye"

"See you tonight, Annie."

And she was out the door.

That's the way he wanted to be, just fine. He'd moped around all day, avoiding her. She had no idea but the whole thing started with the conversation about her house.

Annie got into her car and slammed the door.

Maybe he didn't want to go with her and now felt trapped. She'd tell him tonight that he didn't need to go with her. Maybe that would help.

She stewed as she drove the winding road back home. The trees stood leafless and gray against an angry sky, mirroring her mood. Hurt and irritation plagued her. Why wouldn't he share his worries with her? Lord knew, he'd listened to hers.

She viewed their friendship as more two-way than this. She loved their chats, their serious conversations, even the conversations about Cara and Mike. He helped her in so many ways. So why shut her out now?

***

Though busy with the dinner shift, Eric watched from the kitchen as Aggie learned the routine quickly, Annie happy to have her help. He stayed clear, even after things slowed down. He let Jimmy go home, and as he finished up the dishes, Annie came into the kitchen.

"If it's okay with you, I'm going to tell Aggie she can leave now. She's worked out well. There's only one table left and everything is set for tomorrow."

"That's good. Sure, she can go. I let Jimmy go too. We were busy for a while there but it quieted down quickly." He wiped down the counter as he spoke.

"I'll tell Aggie. I wanted to check first." He turned and watched as Annie left the kitchen. She moved with an easy grace, her blonde braid swinging as she walked. Eric shook his head to clear it of the thoughts that came into it...holding that long graceful body against him, feeling her silky hair brush against his cheek, her slender fingers running over his back...What was he doing? Get yourself together man.

He snapped his mind back to work, focused on the pots and pans, tomorrow's specials, his meeting on Monday—anything to get his mind off the invading fantasies.

Annie said good night to the last customers, then the clatter and chink of dishes signaled she had cleared and reset for tomorrow's lunch. He finished in the kitchen and sat at his desk in his office trying to be busy. He sensed her presence in the doorway without looking up.

"Eric, I can go to the house by myself on Monday. You don't have to go with me. You've got your own stuff to do, and I don't want to be a bother."

Her clipped tone alerted him. What was this about?

She shifted on her feet. "I can handle it. I'm supposed to meet Natalie and her friend at one o'clock, so that'll take some time. You don't have to be there." Though she tried to sound positive and upbeat, her eyes didn't reflect the same emotion—sad, haunted almost.

It didn't add up.

Puzzled by the conflicting emotions, he sighed and ran his fingers through his hair and stretched himself back in his desk chair.

"I don't understand what's going on. I thought it would be easier for you if someone was with you. It's not a problem for me."

Annie sat down in the blue chair in front of his desk. He watched, trying to read her mind. His stomach twisted at the look in her eyes. "The only thing I have to do over there is that meeting first thing in the morning. I'd like to be there to help at your house. It isn't a bother." He tried to curb the frustration he heard in his own voice.

"I've picked up some weird vibes from you lately. They started after we talked about my house and going over on Monday." Annie looked down at her hands. "I thought it bothered you, so I'm giving you an out. What's going on anyway, Eric?" She raised her eyes to meet his, tears glistening. "You can't share with me, the way I shared with you? I thought we'd become friends."

The hurt in Annie's voice, the tears in her eyes ran a spear through Eric's gut. His heart hammered in his chest, and his stomach turned like he would be sick.

Good goin' jerk. He took a deep breath, trying to calm his churning stomach.

"Annie, I want to help with your house." He gentled his voice, hoping it would get rid of the hurt in her eyes. "I'm sorry you felt like I'm not sharing. There are lots of things on my plate right now, some to do with the restaurant, some with Monday's meeting ...I'm sorry. I'm still set for Monday, if you are. Okay?" He hoped that worked. He moved around the desk, standing near Annie. He couldn't tell her about his preoccupation with her. He needed to stop thinking about her all the time.

"If you're sure. I don't want to be someone you have to rescue. I'd like it if we could be there for each other. I am getting stronger, and I want to help you."

"I know, Annie. Let's keep the plan for Monday then." He smiled and held out his hand to take hers. He gave it a quick squeeze, then let go.

"Okay. I'll see you tomorrow then. Aggie's coming in for the evening shift. I'll be here before the lunch rush starts." Annie turned to leave.

"Good night Annie."

"Good night Eric. Don't stay here too late." And she left, closing the office door behind her.

He didn't stay late. Instead, he put on his heavy jacket and drove to the south shore where the ocean met the island—not in the gentle lapping of harbor waves, but with the rhythmic ebb and flow of waves blown across the open ocean. Even without the wind howling and a storm brewing, the ocean waves held a power that released as they crashed on shore. He needed that pounding to help release what he'd pent up inside him—guilt, self-doubt, disgust... lust.

***

Annie entered the house, wondering if her mother had gone to bed early, the house dark, except for the porch light.

She peeked into her mother's room. Bed made, no sign of Mom. Her car sat in the driveway but the house was empty. Weird. Maybe she'd gone to a meeting?

Annie changed out of her work clothes and into a comfortable blue sweat suit. Downstairs she flipped on the television and clicked through the stations. Nothing. She took her laptop into the living room to write in her journal. Maybe that would calm the churning thoughts going through her head. Her house worries, her finances, her career, Eric and her concerns about their friendship.

Annie heard the crunch of tires on the gravel driveway and looked up to see a pair of headlights swing into the driveway. Someone dropped off Mom?

The door opened and Sara rushed in, cheeks rosy, hair windblown and her winter jacket zipped up tight.

"Annie, you're home early. I didn't expect you until ten-thirty or so." Sara took off her coat and hung it up.

"Things were busy early in the evening but slowed down so we closed early. Where were you? " Annie waited the long moment it took for Sara to answer.

Turning on the brass lamp near the glider, Sara wrapped an afghan around her shoulders and settled into the chair.

"A friend wanted me to go for dinner, and then we took a walk on the beach. It's a beautiful clear night, and the tide's low so there's more beach than rocks. It was nice."

"Oh. Who was the friend? Why didn't you take your car?"

"Well, Doc and I were joking about things today and well…it's a long story and I guess you had to be there, but he came and picked me up for a picnic dinner…I know it's November but we roasted hot dogs on the beach." Annie listened as her mother tried to explain the obvious to Annie…her mother had gone on a date!

"So… you and Doc have been doing a lot of things together." Annie shut down her laptop, way more interested in this than her journal full of concerns.

"Yes…" Sara seemed to be choosing her words carefully. It amused Annie to hear her mother hedging like a teenager caught past curfew. "We enjoy doing things like fishing and having dinner together. We like a lot of the same things."

"That's great, Mom. It's nice to see you having a good time. Why didn't you mention it before?"

"Annie, you were wrapped up in your own troubles and I didn't need to add anything else for you to think about. Your mother's social life isn't really so noteworthy compared to the things you're dealing with. It didn't seem necessary."

"So, are you a couple, an item?" Annie kept her tone purposely light, but she wondered. Something about her mom's face—the rosy cheeks, the slight blush—said it involved more than friendship.

"We enjoy each other's company."

Okay, the tone said no more questions on this front.

"Well, that's good. Listen, on another topic. I'm going over to the mainland on Monday, to check on the house, and meet with some girls who want to rent it. Eric's coming with me to help clear some of the stuff out. Is there anything you want me to get while I'm over there?" Annie wanted to let her mother know her schedule, but couldn't handle a full-blown discussion of her mental state about clearing out the house.

Sometimes she needed to feel like she was getting through what she needed to get through.

"Do you want me to go with you?" Annie saw the concern in her mother's eyes.

"No, Eric's going with me, and if I stay focused on renting it out to these girls, I won't get too emotional. I am getting stronger, Mom. I want to try this."

"Good. I'm proud of you, Annie. You seem to be doing better with everything." Sara snuggled deeper into the afghan.

"Thanks, Mom. I am. I'm going up to bed. Do you want me to get you a cup of tea before I go?"

"No, I'm going to watch a little television, warm up a little in the afghan, and then I'll go upstairs too."

Annie put her laptop in its case as Sara switched on the TV.

"Good night Mom."

"Good night dear."

***

Sara watched her daughter go up the stairs. She'd made progress. Working, dealing with her finances, figuring out her life without a husband. She'll be all right. Sara hoped Annie didn't get involved with someone else too soon. She needed to heal and be herself.

Sara thought of her own life, and the hard times she'd gone through after her husband John died of a heart attack. They'd married young, and she stayed home with the girls until they were well into elementary school. The part time secretarial job she'd taken once the girls started school had supplemented John's income. He'd been the main breadwinner, the head of the family, the focus of her life. And then he died.

Sara rested her head back on the chair, gliding back and forth, closing her eyes. The remembered squeal of a small blonde thrown into the air only to be caught by her father's loving arms, the loud booming voice cheering the girls on at swimming races and basketball games, the look of pride as daddy's girl came downstairs dressed for her first dance…John had been a good loving father, and her beloved husband. Then gone.

It took her years to start thinking about what she wanted. How she wanted to do things, where she wanted to go with her life. As much as she missed her husband, and she did, Sara had become accustomed to making her own plans, and doing things that interested her. Like fishing. Johnny had never been a fisherman; he preferred to play golf or tennis. Sara had always loved fishing with her dad and brothers. And now, she enjoyed it again. She smiled as she remembered the fishing expeditions with Doc, picturing his long lean silhouette as he stood casting out into the surf. And his silly fish jokes. He always made her laugh.

Johnny had never cared for traveling. He'd rather stay at home and be comfortable than travel to someone else's house or stay at a hotel and not get a good night's sleep.

Recalling the weekend jaunts she'd started taking, Sara

61

shook her head at Johnny's loss. She loved seeing new sights, meeting people from different places. And she liked trying new foods, new experiences. She'd finally started to live and enjoy her life. That's what she hoped for her daughter. Be your own person. Do the things you love. But how did she tell Annie all she'd learned from hard experience?

Chapter 10
Nor'easter

Annie fidgeted in her car as she waited at the ferry dock for Eric on Monday morning. She hated the thought of being at the house without Mike. Was she strong enough to do this? She needed to stay focused on clearing it out for renters.

She picked at paint stains on her old work jeans. "I hope I can do this without breaking down. I miss him so much." She fought the burn of tears at the back of her eyes. Taking a deep breath to steady herself, she looked around for Eric. It wasn't like him to be late.

She jumped at the knock on the passenger window. The door opened and Eric put a navy blue gym bag and a black leather briefcase in the back. He climbed into the car, smelling of aftershave lotion, shampoo, and fresh male. The scents assailed Annie, making her all too aware of him in the seat next to her.

"Hi. How are you this morning?"

He watched her. Did he expect her to be falling apart already? It irritated her that he almost caught her.

"I'm fine." She started pulling the car forward at the hand signals of the crew loading cars onto the ferry. Maybe if she concentrated on backing onto the ferry, he wouldn't see the moisture in her eyes. Damn.

He settled in, waiting for her to finish backing into a spot in the bow of the boat. Annie took a deep breath as she turned off the car.

"Do you want to sit down in the car or would you rather go up to the cabin?" Eric asked.

"I'm dressed for cleaning the house. I'd rather stay down here, but you can go up if you'd like." Annie hoped he'd stay, even though she hadn't started out being too nice. "I'm sorry if

I was short with you before. You caught me at a bad moment."
Annie saw understanding in his eyes.

"I'll go get the tickets and some coffee. Don't worry about it. I'll be right back." Eric patted her leg and swung himself out of the car.

How could he be so nice to her when she was so witchy to him? She watched him weave around the other cars on the ferry toward the stairs. His navy pin-striped suit fit across his broad shoulders as if tailored for him. The cut of his suit pants accented his long legs and lean waist. The wind blew the front wisp of hair out of place, but it was the only imperfection in his otherwise perfect appearance.

She mentally chastised herself for admiring his physique. Again the tears sprang out of nowhere. She shook her head and wiped the corners of her eyes, trying to wipe away the thoughts that plagued her.

"Damn it Mike. Why did you have to die?"

Concentrate on cleaning things out. They needed to get at least one load of stuff to the homeless shelter. That would be good progress.

Eric returned with the ferry tickets and coffee. Annie wrapped her hands around the warm paper cup inhaling the fresh coffee scent.

"Thanks Eric. It's just what I needed."

Eric smiled. "Me too. I didn't get to have my usual two cups this morning before I left."

The wind and waves buffeted the ferry as it made the forty-five minute trip through the open ocean. The anticipation of her day cleaning out Mike's things and the anxiety of whether she could handle it caused her stomach to churn; the rough ride only intensified her discomfort. They talked on the ride over, but Annie barely stayed focused on the conversation.

.

"Annie? You okay?" Concern filled Eric's eyes as he watched her.

Annie took a deep breath and exhaled.

"I'm scared, Eric. I don't know if I can do this, but I have to keep moving on, work to get my life together. I just hope I'm strong enough. Don't pay any attention to me if I snap at you or start crying...my nerves are close to the edge." Annie looked into Eric's eyes, understanding and... something else gazed back at her.

"I'm here to help. We both know it'll be tough, but I do know you can do it. I've seen you trying to get back on your feet. I understand, Annie. That's all you need to remember. I understand."

"Okay." Annie felt her shoulder muscles relax, as though a burden lifted from them.

"While you're at your meeting, I'll run over to the mall. I want to get a cute little outfit for my new niece and pick out a bunch of cards. What time will you be finished?" Annie pulled her car forward and followed the signals of the crewmember to unload the car on the mainland.

"The client is supposed to be there at nine-fifteen. I can't imagine that the meeting will go any longer than an hour. Why don't I keep an eye out for you around ten-fifteen."

"Okay. I'll just park outside though. I don't want to come into the office dressed like this." She handed the purser their tickets.

"You look fine, but if that's what you are more comfortable with, that's okay too."

"I wasn't sure what we would be doing later this morning, but I didn't think my suit will be the correct attire." Eric smiled. "I threw some jeans, a T-shirt, and a pair of sneakers in the gym bag."

"I'm not sure what we'll be doing all day either. I'm going to play it all by ear. I don't know how I'm going to react, but I've come ready to work. I'm not forming any expectations about how much we get done."

"That's smart. It may take several trips, especially to get it ready to rent."

"We'll see how it goes." Annie pulled into traffic, trying to stay focused on driving and not thinking about the day ahead.

She followed Eric's directions to his office in an old

residential building converted during a renewal project. The nearby buildings housed lawyers, CPAs, and a florist shop. A quaint upscale area. Eric grabbed his briefcase from the back seat.

"See you in an hour or so," he waved as he closed the car door and headed into the brick building.

"Have a good meeting." Annie watched as he disappeared through the front door. Again the fit of the suit caught her attention, sending tingles throughout her body. An urge to smooth her hand over his broad shoulders overwhelmed her with its intensity. Where'd that come from?

Annie thought about Eric as she turned into traffic and drove to the mall. Things between them were a little better since they talked the other night, though she still didn't know what bothered him. She certainly didn't believe the line about this meeting and restaurant business. She could only hope he would trust her with his troubles. Look at all he'd done for her.

She remembered her state of mind that first night on the beach. She wanted so desperately to end the hurt, end the missing.

Though her life had changed forever, she'd started making progress, getting back to some order, thanks to Eric. She started to redefine it. He showed her by example that there is life after the death of a loved one. It's okay to take time…time to grieve, time to cry, time to heal. Going to the house today represented another step through grief toward healing. She hoped.

Locating the baby section in the department store at the mall presented no problem for Annie. Guilt over her lack of attention to her sister and the new baby pricked her conscience. Another sign of her healing heart showed itself in her concern for others in her family. She'd been unfair to her sister and her niece. Not their fault she miscarried…no one's fault. Maybe someday she would have a child… just not in the near future.

She let herself enjoy looking at baby girl outfits, finding a cute one-piece snuggly suit with pink hearts and bows on a white background. She knew Nancy would love it. Annie paid for the outfit, and then wandered to the jewelry section.

In the past on special occasions, Annie contributed to Nancy's collection of bangle bracelets. The birth of her first child certainly qualified as a special occasion. Annie wanted to acknowledge it with a gift for her sister. She picked out a silver bangle that looked like three separate strands braided together and had it gift-wrapped.

Feeling pleased with her purchases, Annie stopped in a card shop to select cards for several family birthdays.

Holiday cards lined the racks. Could she ever manage sending out cards to their friends and family? It would be the first Christmas since... Her eyes stung with threatening tears. She closed them and took a deep breath. She had to try. If she really couldn't do it, she'd save the cards for next year. Annie picked out several boxes. She passed through the section of friendship cards and decided to pick out a card for one particular friend on her mind almost too much lately. She smiled as she thought of him in his pin-stripe suit.

Annie paid for her selections and walked out to her car. As she pulled up in front of the office, The Wedding Song floated over the airwaves.

Tears filled her eyes. Her heart squeezed in her chest. Their wedding song. Every time they heard it, Mike had winked at her, or squeezed her hand, or somehow made her feel his love for her. Tears streamed down her cheeks. God, she missed him. Sobs escaped ...beyond her control.

***

Finished with his business meeting, Eric saw Annie's car pull up, and hurried out to meet her. He took one look at Annie's face, and knew, even as she wiped away the tears and changed the radio station to classical music.

"Do you want me to drive?" he asked quietly.

"No. Just a quick little crying jag caused by a special song. It's okay." Annie tried a tentative smile.

"Good girl," Eric patted her leg as she turned to focus on getting back into traffic.

"So...how was your meeting?" her watery voice wavered

67

but obviously she wanted to change the subject.

"It went well. Every once in a while I need to meet with this client to update his business coverage. He's a great old guy, friend of my dad's, and likes to get together to chat I think. I certainly don't mind. So, we updated his policy in about ten minutes and spent the rest of the time visiting. It gave me time to check in with my boss too." Eric watched her surreptitiously as she maneuvered toward the highway.

"It's great the way you can do most of your business on the island and have the restaurant as well."

"I am very fortunate that the partners let me try it this way. It's worked out well, and I've increased their business on the island too, just by being there."

Once on the highway, it didn't take long to get to her house. Situated on a quiet tree-lined residential street with college buildings in view further up the hill, the brick Cape sat empty with shades drawn.

Annie pulled into the driveway, stopping in front of an attached garage. She turned off the car and took a deep breath before looking at Eric.

"Okay. Here we go." Her face pale, she put on a brave front. His stomach churned as he remembered cleaning out Cara's bureau and closet.

He saw Annie gathering her resolve. She deserved a lot of credit. He knew how hard it had been for him to even be in the cottage after Cara died. And it took several attempts before he finally cleaned out her clothes. How many days had he sat on the bed with her things all around him?

Annie gathered her cleaning supplies, and Eric grabbed his gym bag and a stack of collapsed boxes. She let them in through the front door, put her armful of things down on the dining room table, and stood looking around. Eric watched her, standing back but nearby.

"There's a bathroom off the kitchen, toward the garage door, if you want to change. I'm going to put a pot of coffee on." She directed Eric to the kitchen. He heard her start the coffee then wander through the downstairs rooms. He quickly changed, wanting to be with her to help.

Pictures of Annie and Mike lined the mantel of the large stone fireplace that took up one wall of the living room. Others stood atop the entertainment center. Eric stood in the kitchen doorway, watching Annie gently run her fingers over a picture, pick up a frame and stare at it, then set it carefully back on the mantle. Tears streamed down her cheeks unchecked.

Should he go to her and take her in his arms the way he wanted, or should he leave her alone to have some time? He slipped back into the kitchen, looking around at the place that had once been her home.

The efficient looking kitchen filled with new stainless steel appliances and granite countertops caught his eye. Through the other doorway he could see the dining room where they'd left the cleaning supplies and boxes on the large oak table. He walked past the table, through the foyer area to the doorway leading back to the living room, still looking at the pictures. Oh man, it was harder watching her go through this than he thought it would be. How could he help her?

He approached her quietly, going toward her on gut reaction. She turned and fell into his arms, sobbing into his shoulder. He held her as her body shook, his shirt becoming damp with tears.

"Shh, it's okay. Let it all out. You've been working so hard to be brave. I know how it hurts." Tears stung his eyes as he held her, stroking her hair, caressing her back. Feeling her loss, feeling his loss.

***

Annie knew what she would do with Mike's tools, his clothes. Tools to his brother, his clothes to the homeless shelter. She liked that idea from Eric. But the pictures surprised her. She and Mike posing on the beach in Bermuda—their honeymoon. The candid of them kissing at her sister's Christmas party... Mike and his brother working on Tom's deck two summers ago...the close-up candid of his lopsided smile and the twinkle of an untold joke in his eyes. So much for making it through the day without tears...Oh God, could she do this?

Then Eric appeared, his arms around her, his comfort filling her. Keepsakes, but not ready to have them out and around at her mom's. She'd pack those up later.

"I think I need to get busy. I've had my cry, hopefully we won't have a repeat performance but no guarantees today." She tried a weak smile as she moved out of Eric's arms. "Thank you." Looking into his eyes, she took a deep breath and squared her shoulders. Eric watched her.

"Okay, here's where I think we need to start." Annie outlined her plan of attack. She wanted to clean out Mike's clothes and take them to the homeless shelter. That would make a dent in what needed to be done.

"Bring the box of garbage bags. Here we go." Annie led the way upstairs, her resolve showing in her stride. Once she got started, she felt better. They had filled several bags with clothes when Annie remembered the coffee.

"Do you want a coffee? I put some on while you changed clothes."

"I'll get it. You keep working. You can make more progress than I can." Eric carried the two full bags downstairs with him.

Annie sat on the bed with a pile of clothes on hangers next to her, Mike's favorite sports jacket on top. She smoothed her hand over the brown tweed. She picked it up and held it against her face, the remnants of Mike's scent filling her nostrils, squeezing her heart. Gone, but still here... all around her. She gently laid the jacket on the side, not sure she could get rid of everything of Mike's. She'd managed to fill half of another bag by the time Eric returned with two mugs.

Eric stayed all business. He kept things moving along so she wouldn't get sentimental. She knew...and was thankful for his presence and his quiet understanding.

By noon they'd emptied the tallboy in the master bedroom, as well as taken all of Mike's things out of the closet.

"We've got a lot of stuff here. We should make a run to the shelter before Natalie and her friend get here. Do you know how to get there from here?" Annie asked.

"I think so, but why don't we go together and stop somewhere for lunch?"

"Okay, we could get something to take out. I don't want to miss the girls."

Her emotions frayed, she needed a break.

***

Eric grabbed two large bags and started loading the car. He wanted to get her out of the house. So far she had one little meltdown and he wanted the rest of the experience to be uneventful. She needed to feel in control.

She'd shown she was tougher than she gave herself credit for. Eric remembered the feeling of uncertainty as he doubted everything he did after Cara died. He'd felt better once he started making decisions, taking action. And that's where Annie stood now; starting to make decisions, take action.

He loaded up the sports car with all the bags. They filled the trunk and the back seat. When Annie came out of the house carrying a bag of her things to get rid of, she laughed. The soft sensual sound shot straight to his core.

"I'll have to hold this on my lap!" Annie laughed as she piled herself and the huge garbage bag into the front passenger seat.

Lucky bag of clothes! He jumped into the driver's seat and started the car.

"Do you think we should go to the shelter first, or maybe we should do a fast food drive through...there's so much room up front for the food!" Eric tried to keep it light, but his heart hammered at her close proximity, her scent, her laugh. He took a deep breath as he pulled out of the driveway.

By the time they returned with burgers, fries, and drinks, the wind was whipping the nearby trees, and ominous clouds started spitting large drops of rain.

***

Annie watched from the living room as two young women sat parked in an older model station wagon looking up at the front of the house, pointing around the yard and bobbing their

71

heads up and down smiling. When the doorbell rang, Annie's stomach fluttered with nerves. The enormity of the decision to rent her house, their home with all its memories, suddenly hit her like the brick face of the house.

Take a deep breath and get over it. She had to do this, and they came highly recommended. She worked to set her shoulders back and adjust her frame of mind. Eric went to the door, giving her another moment to collect herself. Somehow he always knew when she needed him.

"Annie, I'd like you to meet Natalie. She's worked for me for the last three summers. She can zip those trays of chowder out faster than anyone I've seen!" Eric winked at Natalie and turned a smile on Annie, setting her at ease.

Annie smiled at all of them, silently sending a thank you to Eric with her eyes.

"It's nice to meet you, Natalie. And this must be your friend Liz that you told me about." Annie shook the girls' hands. "Come on in. It's getting worse out." They moved into the dining room, and Annie anxiously watched the girls look around.

"Annie, this is a beautiful place, and so close to school." Natalie's genuine smile calmed the flutters in Annie's stomach.

"Thank you. Let me show you around." As they walked and talked, the two girls' maturity impressed Annie. Not the giddy co-eds she'd feared but sensible young women working toward life goals. They took their studies seriously based on the complaints about the noise of dorm life.

Once they'd finished looking at the house, Annie reviewed a few concerns.

"My husband was a stickler about cleaning the chimney and the fireplace, but I'd feel better if you didn't use it."

"Certainly, Mrs. Gee. We're happy to be able to move off campus." Liz smiled as she spoke.

"I'd like to keep one room upstairs where I'll move all of my personal stuff, but I plan to leave all the kitchen stuff out for you to use if you'd like."

"Thank you so much. That's fantastic. Wow, that'll save

us set-up money too," Natalie spoke with enthusiasm.

"And it's going to be helpful for me too. I need someone living here for the winter but I'm not up to that yet. I really appreciate finding someone I can trust to be here." Annie felt Eric's hand on her back. The warmth of his hand radiated through her, and the support it offered warmed her heart as well.

"I'll draw up a lease, finish clearing the master bedroom, and put away things from downstairs. It'll be ready before next semester starts if you want to move in early. We can work something out."

"Annie, thank you so much. This is going to be great. It's close to campus and it'll be quiet."

"It's going to work for me too."

The girls left after three o'clock. The wind continued to blow and rain pelted against the side of the house. Just after they waved good-bye to Natalie and Liz the telephone rang, and Annie ran to the kitchen to answer it.

"Hello, Annie? It's Mom. I just heard that they're cancelling the evening ferry. There's a Nor'easter coming. The seas are running high and it's high tide besides. They think docking will be a problem with the strong winds and all. Are you going to be okay over there?"

"Um, yeah, we should be okay. Thanks for calling. Now I'll have a chance to run to the store and pick up a few things to eat. Any idea how long the storm is supposed to last?" Annie made a face at Eric, who came into the kitchen and heard Annie's end of the conversation.

"I haven't heard, but you should call the ferry tomorrow before you leave the house. What will Eric do about the restaurant? Does he want me to go put a sign on the door?"

"Let me ask." Annie took the phone away from her mouth and asked Eric about the restaurant.

"Can she put up a sign saying that I'm off the island and the restaurant will reopen as soon as the ferry starts running again?"

Annie relayed the message.

"Annie, are you going to be okay staying at the house tonight? If you want to go stay at a hotel..."

"I'll be okay Mom. I've been doing better than I thought all day, and it'll help to have Eric here with me. I'll call tomorrow and let you know what's going on."

Annie got off the phone and filled Eric in on the ferry cancellation. The wind howled outside as the rain ricocheted off the side of the house.

"Let's run to the supermarket before the weather gets any worse. We can get food for dinner tonight and something for tomorrow morning as well."

"How are you doing with all this?" Eric asked as they returned from shopping. "Are you going to be alright staying at the house tonight?"

She paused, trying to think how to say what she wanted to say. She knew Eric would understand, but she wondered if it would sound dumb. "I don't know if I can stay upstairs in the master bedroom. After Mike died, I couldn't sleep in our bed. I slept down on the sofa or in the small bedroom. It was just too hard." She rubbed her hands over her arms, a sudden chill settling over her.

Eric's hand massaged her shoulder, and she looked into his eyes. "I know. I had the same problem. Some nights I still move out to the couch. I did get a smaller bed. I couldn't stand to be in our big king size all by myself...without Cara."

Annie's heart hurt for Eric's pain as well as her own. "We'll figure something out for tonight."

They sprinted into the house, quickly dried off, and started putting away the groceries. Annie flipped on the television and turned to the weather channel. Gale force winds buffeted the coastal areas already as the storm intensified offshore.

"Wow. I hadn't heard anything about this storm. I wouldn't have come over if I'd known. Eric, I'm sorry for getting you into this. Will the restaurant be okay?" Annie worried that her lack of forethought cost Eric a day of business at the restaurant.

"I'd heard there was a storm coming, but it sounds like it's intensifying more than expected. People on the island know about getting stuck on the mainland. Not a problem. We'll be back by tomorrow night at the latest. I did close the storm shutters before I left this morning. That's why I was a little late getting to the ferry." He followed her into the kitchen to finish unpacking the groceries.

"I'm going to start getting dinner ready. We'll plan on eating around six-thirty, okay?"

"That sounds fine. Is there anything you want me to do? What about if I make dinner, then you can work on things around the house?" Eric stopped her from moving around the kitchen by placing his hand on her arm. It calmed her fidgety stomach.

"Probably more productive. Okay. Feel free to poke around in the cabinets to find what you need, or holler. I'm going to put away the pictures and things in the living room. I'll keep an eye on the weather too." Her nerves pulsed close to the surface. One moment edgy, the next close to tears, then calm. The maelstrom within her swirled worse than the storm outside. At least she knew what to expect from the weather.

***

Eric rolled up his sleeves and started dinner. While he worked he kept an eye on Annie. She seemed to be getting through most of it, but he'd seen several times where she'd taken a deep breath and pushed her shoulders back. He'd watch so he could be there if she needed.

She assembled several of the collapsed boxes and grabbed a roll of paper towels to cushion breakables, wrapping the first couple of knickknacks without a problem. It appeared harder when she got to several pictures taken on their honeymoon. She lingered over them just as she had earlier in the afternoon. She and Mike snuggled together smiling for the camera with a beautiful Bermuda beach in the background. Pictures of Mike with his brother, Mike and Annie in the backyard barbecuing. Tears slid down her cheeks. She wrapped the pictures, wiped her eyes, and took a deep breath. Annie packed up two boxes while Eric cooked and watched.

"Okay. Dinner's cooking. Do you want me to take these

75

upstairs for you?" he asked as he walked into the living room. She nodded. She looked drained, her face pale, her eyes red and damp. He wanted to take her in his arms and comfort her, but she was working so hard to be strong, and she needed to feel that strength now more than his comfort.

They sat down to eat dinner in front of the TV to watch the news report on the worsening storm. No sooner settled when the lights and the TV went off.

No power.

Chapter 11
The Undertow

Undertow: a strong current beneath the surface that sets seaward or along the beach when waves are breaking along the shore. It can pull unsuspecting swimmers away from shore or underwater.

Sara taped the makeshift sign securely to the front window on Shore Delights and darted back to her small red SUV. Soaked. The heater blew at full blast, the wipers flipped back and forth as fast as mechanically possible as she directed the car not toward her quiet Cape, but toward the center of town and Doc's house.

The wind pushed the little car along the road, making it sway to the weather's whim. She must be crazy to be out in this. She should go right home, but she didn't want to be alone.

Sara parked as close to the doctor's office as she could, jumped out, and ran for the door. She fumbled with the key and by the time she actually got the door open, she was drenched. Doc opened the inner residence door looking all business as if expecting a patient.

His smile lit up his tan angular face.

"Sara, you look like a fisherman gone overboard. You're soaked!"

"I put a sign on Eric's restaurant. He and Annie are stranded on the mainland and will be back when the ferry runs again. I didn't want to be alone in the house, and since I was out anyway, I decided to stop by here. Do you mind some company?"

"Not at all. But let's get you something dry to change into. You've made a puddle!" Doc chuckled at the double meaning of his statement as Sara looked at the floor.

She couldn't help laughing. "You're terrible." Doc laughed back as he reached to help her get out of the dripping yellow rain coat.

Sara shrugged her shoulders, trying to free herself from the jacket. "Maybe this wasn't such a great idea. My pants and feet are soaked clear through. I can't believe how it's coming down out there."

"Here, leave your coat. Take off your shoes and socks and bring them next to the fireplace. I'll go get something for you to change into and get warm." Doc brought her into the living room where the fire roared in the fireplace.

"I'm sorry Doc. I didn't mean to be any trouble." Doc disappeared around the corner and upstairs. She shook her head, guilty at feeling more impulsive the older she got.

"Doc, I shouldn't have come. I'll put these wet shoes back on and head home." Sara yelled up the stairs. Second thoughts and misgivings crowded through her head.

Doc descended the stairs with a pair of warm thermal socks and a navy blue pair of sweatpants.

"Nonsense. We'll have fun. I'm glad you stopped by. I'm not terribly fond of storms; why not weather it out together... hmm, get it...weather it out?"

Sara shook her head. "I get it. You're a nut. Okay, let me go change, then we'll have fun." Sara chuckled as she caught the sweatpants and socks he tossed to her. She quickly tiptoed to the small bathroom down the hallway.

"Do you want coffee or would you rather have a glass of wine?" Doc yelled to her through the bathroom door. She hurried to strip out of her jeans—cold, wet, and stuck to her legs.

"A glass of wine sounds wonderful, but don't go to any trouble. If you'd rather have coffee..."

"Actually, I hoped you'd say wine. I have a good bottle of Chardonnay chilled in the fridge. I'll go open it and see what else is out there." She heard Doc go whistling into the kitchen.

She hung her jeans over the shower rod and ran her fingers through her damp hair. Oh well, the fire's going—it'll dry...it just won't look so great! Giving her auburn hair one more flounce with her hands, she opened the bathroom door. The sight of Doc arranging several large pillows near the fireplace greeted her as she walked into the living room. Two glasses of wine sat on the low mahogany coffee table with a plate of crackers and cheese in the center.

"Wow, pretty fast work." She smiled as he handed her a glass.

"I thought it would be warmer here by the fire." He helped her settle on several pillows and dropped down next to her, picking up his glass. "To two good friends weathering the storm together." His voice gentled, sending tingles up Sara's spine. Deep, husky, and oh, so sexy. Sara couldn't remember how to breath, never mind think of something to say, so she clinked her glass to his, smiled and took a sip.

"Mmm. Good wine." She took another sip, warmth spreading through her…from the wine, the fire, the man.

"So Eric and Annie are stranded? I didn't know they cancelled the ferry but it's not a surprise. Did you talk to Annie?" Doc swirled his wine as he spoke.

"I called as soon as I heard about the ferry. Fortunately I caught them before they left the house. I hope she'll be all right. She had a hard time before. That's why she moved back home." Sara closed her eyes and tried to rub away the worry gathered between her eyebrows.

"Annie will be fine, especially with Eric there. He's been through a lot but he has a good head on his shoulders, and he genuinely cares about Annie. I hope they can find each other."

"What do you mean?" Sara puzzled over his words. She'd gotten the feeling before that sometimes Doc spoke with his past memories in mind, rather than the obvious present situation. She wondered about his past.

"Well, this healing thing is tough enough when the wound is physical, but it's even harder and less predictable when the wound is emotional. Some people are able to bounce back more quickly than others. Some go on to live their life with gusto, figuring life is short. Others take a long time to heal the wound, and some never do." Again he swirled his drink, looking into it, talking in vague terms, not the concrete specifics, like Sara usually heard from him. Something else was in that head of his. But what?

"Everyone finds their own way to deal with hurt and loss. Eric seems to be working through Cara's death. Annie's told me that Eric's become a good friend, listening, understanding. I'm glad she finally started sharing things with someone. I worry about her." Her fingers continued massaging the center of her forehead trying to relax the tension.

"Do you have a headache?" Doc watched her hands.

"No. It's a nervous habit when I'm worried." Sara pulled her hand away from her forehead and took another sip of wine.

"Here, give me your drink." Doc took it and put it on the table. "Close your eyes." Sara wondered, but she closed her eyes. She heard him shift near her, his gentle touch to her head and brow soothing the tension gathered there. His fingers circled, stroked, kneaded—gentle touches smoothed out the muscular ropes in her neck, her scalp, her face. She relaxed against the pillows as he worked his magic. How wonderful his ministrations felt to her... far more intimate than she could have ever thought.

As his fingers stroked her, she wondered if he had any idea how sensual this was for her. He's a doctor, for Pete's sakes, Sara. He's offering comfort, not trying to turn you on. Get a grip!

Both of his hands massaged the back of her neck and shoulders. A moan, a sigh...it felt so good. She felt his hands weave up into her hair, shifting to hold both sides of her head, and his lips gently touched hers, caressing, shifting, asking for more.

She responded without thought, without plan, with total abandon, parting her lips, deepening the kiss. He shifted next to her, one hand continuing to hold her head, the other caressing her cheek, her neck, her hair. Another moan, another sigh... her or him? His hand traveled down her back, encircling her, pulling her close against him. Her arms had somehow moved around him, the warmth of his muscular back against her palms.

It had been years since she'd been touched by a man. The sensation rocketed to her core, heightening the feel of his warm firm body next to hers. She wanted it closer still. Emotions, new all over again overwhelmed her with feeling, making her senseless with wanting, but afraid too.

"I've wanted to kiss you like that for a long time." Doc looked into Sara's eyes.

Surprised by his statement, she managed not to blurt out...why haven't you? She'd kept her feelings for Doc buried for so long...perhaps she had done too good a job.

"Sara, I'm starting to fall for you."

"Well, Doc, I'm falling for you too." She was being truthful, sort of...except she'd fallen a long time ago, but said it in a flippant tone so that Doc wouldn't know just how serious she was. What was going on here? What had changed and why?

He caressed her face lightly. "No Sara, listen to me. I'm falling in love with you...and it's scaring me to death."

***

"Oh wonderful! Not only are we stuck on the mainland but now we're without power." Annie put her head back against the couch and closed her eyes. She opened them again quickly. "Wait right where you are. I know where there are some matches." The frustration of the situation pushed her into action.

She impressed Eric. She was problem solving—not losing it as he'd feared. Good girl Annie. You're stronger than you think.

Annie carefully navigated in the dark around the coffee table toward the hearth. She located the fireplace matches and lit one of the fat berry-scented candles on the stone mantle. He watched as she brought it down to the coffee table, awed by what the candlelight did to her face.

"I wonder how long we'll be without power. Bet the phone's out too." Annie picked up the receiver and held it up to her ear. "Nothing."

"Maybe a tree limb took down the lines. It sure is blowing out there. Is that fireplace in working order?" Eric moved off the couch toward the fireplace.

"Yes. Mike was a stickler for things like that. We have wood in the garage too. It's stacked against the back wall. We should probably go bring in enough for tonight anyway, just in case the power's out that long. It could be a while." Annie rubbed her arms even though the house was not cold.

"Do you have any flashlights?" Eric turned to see her standing by the coffee table, again the candlelight lit her face … just the sight of her quickened his heartbeat, the sound of his own pulse deafened him. He reminded himself to breathe.

"Let's go look in the kitchen. I think there may be a couple of lights in the utility drawer." Annie picked up the candle and her dinner plate and turned, waiting for Eric to follow.

Together they searched through the kitchen drawers for flashlights. They managed to find only one with working batteries. Eric handed it to Annie to hold so he could carry in several armfuls of wood. In the garage, Annie grabbed an armload of kindling, while Eric loaded bigger pieces into his arms. They made several trips and filled the wood box next to the hearth.

He spent some time building the fire, thinking about their predicament, while Annie located several more candles placing them around the room. She'd gotten quiet; he wondered what she was thinking.

"We should probably sleep down here tonight. It'll get cold upstairs if the power is off all night." She turned and pointed toward the stairs.

He recognized her apprehension. She didn't want to sleep in her old bedroom. He understood. He'd had to make changes too.

She continued, as though convincing Eric. "I think there are sleeping bags in the closet upstairs. Let's see what we can find." Annie picked up the flashlight and headed for the stairs. Eric sensed her determination to avoid sleeping in her bedroom, avoid the memories, and fight the loneliness. He could identify only too well.

He read her body language—it screamed stressed. He followed her, wondering how to help her relax. Together they dug two sleeping bags out of the hall closet, grabbing a couple of extra pillows as well.

"It's been a while since I've been camping, and I don't think I've ever camped in a Nor'easter!" Eric joked as they hauled their bundles down the stairs. They piled them on the floor and went back to the couch.

"We can't watch TV or listen to music. Maybe we should roast marshmallows over the fire...this is a camp-out...or camp-in." He attempted to lighten the mood.

"Wait—I know what we can do. Stay here." Annie took the flashlight and disappeared into the kitchen. Her mood lightened once they'd found the sleeping bags and settled the sleeping arrangements. She seemed better—calmer. He heard her opening cupboards and drawers in the kitchen. Several minutes later, she carried two wine glasses, a bottle of Merlot, a deck of playing cards, and a cork screw into the living room.

"How's this. Merlot and gin rummy or pitch or poker. I picked the wine, you pick the game," Annie joked as she set the wine and glasses down on the coffee table.

"This could be an entertaining evening. I haven't played cards in a long time. Let's try poker." Eric picked up the deck shuffling them from hand to hand.

"I'll pour some wine, you shuffle and deal." Annie wound the corkscrew into the bottle and popped the cork.

"Don't you want to cut for the deal?"

Annie raised her eyebrows and glanced at him. "Hmm, haven't played in a while? Sounds like this could get serious. No wagers or gambling allowed."

"Right. We wouldn't want the police to bust up our little gambling ring here," Eric laughed.

She poured the wine and handed him his glass. Her eyes got serious as she looked into his.

"I want to make a toast." Annie held her glass up. "To a good friend, with my sincere thanks for all that you've done for me and mean to me." Annie clinked her glass to his and they each took a sip.

Annie's sincerity touched him. "You don't know how much you've helped me. I've kept the shop open because of your help. And your friendship means a lot to me. It's nice to have someone to talk to and share things with ... even the daily little things. Thank you." Eric clinked his glass to hers and they each took another sip of wine. As he watched her over his wineglass, he could see her mood shift as a playful twinkle came into her eyes.

"Okay, come on. Let's play poker." Annie laughed and picked up the top part of the deck to cut the cards. Eric did likewise.

"You deal." He shifted to face Annie on the couch.

Two rowdy, cutthroat games and a bottle of wine later, they threw the cards into a pile between them.

"Whew! You play a mean game of poker. We're tied—one to one. Do ya wanna break the tie for bragging rights?"

"I'm pretty exhausted. Let's call it a tie. We can have a rematch another time." Annie finished the last of the wine in her glass. "We should probably stoke the fire for the night and get the sleeping bags fixed. I'm ready to turn in soon. That wine mellowed me out."

"Sounds like a plan." Eric refueled the fire, banking the embers and adding a few large chunks of wood for the night. He heard Annie carry the glasses into the kitchen. When he'd finished stoking the fire, he turned and saw Annie spreading the sleeping bags out on the floor, side by side, unzipped and folded down.

They settled into the sleeping bags, listening to the soothing pop and crackle of the wood in the fireplace. Although the rest of the house cooled, the fire kept the living room at a comfortable temperature. The wind continued to batter the house, driving the rain in heavy sheets against the windows.

"That is quite a storm out there. I wonder if we'll be able to get back tomorrow." Annie shivered and snuggled deeper into her sleeping bag.

"I like hearing the fury of a good storm, especially if I feel safe inside. Sometimes I even like to walk the beach in a good windstorm. Something about the natural power...it puts me in awe."

"Eric, thank you for coming with me today." Annie took his hand in hers. "I don't know if I could have faced this by myself. You've made today easier to handle. Knowing you've been through all this helps me know I can get through it too. Does that make any sense?"

"Of course it does. You've been very strong, even tonight while I made dinner, and you put away the pictures." Eric shifted in his sleeping bag to face Annie. "That was the hardest thing for me. But I had to put them away for a while. It's too hard to have Cara looking at me from all around the house. I'm sure someday I'll be ready to bring them out again...after a little more time." He brought his other hand up to their joined hands, enclosing hers with his.

"That's what I was thinking too. Gone, but not forgotten. Do you ever have conversations with Cara? I mean in your head?" She looked at him tentatively, like she needed reassurance that she wasn't nuts. He frequently doubted his own sanity.

"I talk to her out loud around the house. I don't do it as much lately, only when there's a crisis or something I'm thinking about a lot." Eric laughed. "You should have heard the conversation I launched into when I found out that both of my waitresses would be gone within two weeks." He looked into Annie's eyes amazed at what the firelight did to them. "And then you came in and asked about the job. It's like Cara sent you to bail me out. The weirdest thing, but it worked out for both of us."

"Mmm...it has." Her eyelids fluttered against her cheeks.

"Let's try to get some sleep. You look exhausted."

Mmm...I am. It's been such an emotional day. And it feels so good to lie here. Good night Eric."

"Good night Annie." He let go of her hand, and the feeling

of engulfing loneliness shocked him.

Eric lay awake for a long time. He couldn't relax with Annie sleeping so close to him. He wanted to gather her up in his arms, hold and comfort her, taste her lips, feel her body against his. And his next thought would be of Cara, accompanied by a desperate guilt for feeling something for someone else so soon after she died.

Back and forth, Annie and Cara...the wind outside and the fire in the hearth... He rolled one way and he could see Annie sleeping so peacefully, he turned the other way and he could hear her breathing...add a little more guilt.

Eric finally lapsed into a fitful sleep. Images of Cara and Annie floated through his sleep-laden mind.

Cara walked the wave-beaten shore toward him. The wind blew her hair and her white gown whipped around her legs and torso. Yet she calmly approached him...floated toward him. She smiled at him, taking his face in her hands.

"My precious Eric... I am fine... now it's time for you to be fine again. You have mourned me with all your heart... I'm gone but not forgotten... but now it's time for you to find happiness again... I want you to be happy, my love...

Cara faded into the blowing wind—her diaphanous gown becoming the white frothy waves breaking ashore, and Eric saw a figure slumped on the rocks. He looked down at it. It rolled over and was Annie, reaching to him, asking him for help. He gathered her into his arms, carrying her as the wind blew and the waves crashed.

Eric awoke with a start. The crash of waves in his dream translated to a real crash, outside the house, near the garage. He sat up and got his bearings. Annie stirred in her sleep but apparently hadn't heard the noise through her exhaustion.

Eric found the flashlight on the floor next to him and got up. He went through the kitchen to the garage door, carefully opening it. He didn't see any damage immediately, however, when he crossed the garage and looked out the side window, he saw a large tree limb leaning up against the garage wall. He checked the interior garage wall. It looked fine, but he decided not to venture out into the storm to check the outside. It could wait until morning, and hopefully better weather.

He went back into the house, into the living room, and stood near the hearth to warm up. He stirred the fire, adding another log, then sat on the hearth letting the warmth penetrate his body. He watched Annie sleep. So beautiful. The ever-present worry line between her eyes disappeared in her sleep. Her blonde hair spread on the pillow behind her. He thought about the dream that had awaken him.

He knew what the dream meant. Cara wanted him to move on with his life. But could he?

***

Annie woke. Her eyes fluttered open, and focused on Eric sitting on the hearth, pensively staring into space. She closed her eyes for a moment, remembering the odd dream she'd just had. Maybe it wasn't really a dream, just a memory of her fall on the shore when Eric rescued her. She remembered the feeling of being gathered up in his arms. A sudden longing to be there again filled her.

She opened her eyes to find Eric looking at her. Could he read her mind?

"Hi. Is it morning?" Annie sat up looking toward the window. Still dark.

"No. I woke to a crash and went to investigate. A big limb came down near the garage, but I don't think it did any damage. We can check in the morning. It's still really howling out there, raining too."

"Ugh...the joys of home ownership. I'll have to hire someone to cut up the tree and haul it away now."

"Maybe we can take care of it before we go back. I noticed a chain saw out in the garage."

"We need to get back to open the restaurant. We can't be messing around with wood." It surprised Annie how nonchalant Eric was about opening on Tuesday. She wanted to make the morning ferry back to the island.

"Annie, listen to that wind. I don't want to ride the ferry even if they do run it in this weather. I have a pretty hardy constitution, but my stomach isn't made of cast iron. I really doubt they'll run the morning ferry. Maybe a noon one, if the wind lets up a little." He moved back to his sleeping bag, as she laid back down in hers.

"I'm anxious to get back to the island. I did pretty well all day, and even into the evening, but I'm starting to have a hard time being here. As long as I have something to do I'm okay."

Annie turned in her sleeping bag to face Eric. She decided to share an idea that had come to her in the afternoon. "I had an idea for an article while I cleaned out Mike's clothes. It actually was good thinking time. I want to do an article on death and dealing with loss. It sounds morbid maybe, but you and I have both experienced it. It doesn't just strike when you're old. And almost everyone has been touched by the death of someone close to them."

"I think it's a great idea. Are you sure you're ready to tackle such a personal topic?" The concern in his eyes touched Annie.

"I am tackling it…living it…just by being here."

"That's true." Eric scooted his sleeping bag closer to Annie. He'd seemed pensive and quiet since she'd woken up. Maybe watching her deal with cleaning out the house brought it all back for him too. She hadn't even thought about that.

"Eric, I know I said this before, but I can't say it enough. Thank you for helping me get through this. I'm sure it hasn't been easy for you either. It means more than I can tell you." Her eyes pricked with tears at the thought of how much he had done for her and what it cost him emotionally.

"Come here." Eric put his arm out to encircle Annie. She moved into his arms, feeling his warmth. This was right… just what she needed. He laid his head against hers, turning to lightly kiss her hair.

"Just stay here next to me tonight, okay?"

Annie relaxed against Eric feeling his warm breath against her head.

"Okay." She closed her eyes, secure and safe in his arms.

Chapter 12
Choppy Waters

Doc wanted to die. Why didn't she say something? He'd totally blown it. Maybe she isn't interested in a deeper relationship...maybe she isn't interested in him? No, he could discount that last nudging doubt. Sara's passion, evident even to him, spiraled close to out of control. Touching her, massaging her temples, her neck, stroking away the tension had been his undoing. His repressed feelings morphed into a force of their own, taking control when he lost it. Taken control of his mouth...disconnected the "think before you speak" nerve.

And now she sat there stunned.

"No, listen to me Sara. I'm falling in love with you...and it's scaring me to death." Why add that last little phrase? Say something Sara.

He watched the pulse in her neck race, looked into her eyes for the answer, felt her shallow breaths on his cheek.

"Doc, I don't know what to say..."

He pulled away from her, swallowed hard to get his composure back. "It's okay. You don't have to say anything. I can tell by your reaction that I'm just a friend...right?"

He'd cut her off before she could say the rest of it...something about being friends, working together...blah, blah, blah. No. That's not what he wanted to hear. What an idiot...he should've just kept his mouth shut...and away from hers.

The deepening scowl on Sara's face set off his internal warning system... fairly certain he'd done or said something wrong.

"How dare you insinuate that I would kiss any man like that and consider him just a friend!" She shoved him further away with a push to his chest. "If you hadn't been so damn busy keeping the walls you've erected around you in good repair, you might have noticed that I've had feelings for you for quite a while…although after this, I'm seriously wondering why!" Sara launched herself off the pillows and moved away from him…across the living room to the window. She stood with her back to him, arms crossed in front of her, head held high. Her body language said stay away—but he couldn't.

He was up in a second, across the room to stand behind her, wanting to turn her and take her in his arms. Fear and uncertainty paralyzed him. He put his hands on her shoulders, rubbing gently, kneading the tension, needing the contact.

"Sara, you've had feelings for me? Why?" His turn to be stunned. Had he heard her right?

Her shoulders relaxed, she lowered her head shaking it. Turning toward him, around into his arms, Sara looked up into his eyes.

"Why?" Her tone incredulous. "Do you want a list?" She smiled, still shaking her head. "You don't get it! You're a kind, compassionate man with a wonderful sense of humor—though a little warped at times. You have a special way of listening to me that makes me feel I'm the only person in the world. But you haven't been ready to hear about my feelings. You don't share yourself the way you encourage others to share with you."

"I'm sorry if I hurt you before. You didn't say anything and seemed so shocked. I panicked. I'd gone out on a limb telling you…You're right…I'm not as good at sharing as I am at listening. I'm sorry."

He pulled her to him, closed his eyes, absorbed her warmth, hoping for forgiveness. Her arms came around him, slowly moving up and down his back, her warm breath again on his neck. He moved away just enough to lower his lips to hers. Forgiveness, understanding, passion waited there for him in her kiss.

After a long glorious moment, she moved away from him and gently took his hand. "Come sit and tell me why I scare you to death. I'm not as big and bad as you think." She smiled at him as she led him to the couch. He willingly let her lead him—to the ends of the earth if that's what she wanted. He just wanted her in his arms again. He pulled her close on the couch.

"Why do I scare you?" Sara stroked her hand down his cheek as she spoke quietly, looking up at him.

"I've seen too many awful things in my life, been part of some of them. That wall insulates me from the hurt; helps me survive the horror. But I had to punch a hole in it to let you in. That's what scared me, still scares me—letting someone get close."

The hammering within his chest warned him of the buried images that flashed through his mind's eye. Images he longed to erase, fought to forget—with little success.

"Doc, why? What awful things have you seen? Where were you before you came here? I thought you lived in Florida." Sara shifted so she could gently massage Doc's shoulder muscles. He relaxed and closed his eyes. He needed to share with her. Let her in.

"I've been around. Army medic, Red Cross doctor, inner-city ER. Man's inhumanity to man...war and terrorists, street gangs and city violence. I gave up practicing medicine for a while and escaped it all to the Florida Keys. Then I saw the advertisement for this position. It's what I needed. It gave me time to heal." He opened his eyes and watched her face as her fingers reached around to stroke his shoulders, his neck. He couldn't tell her more. He'd given her something, all he could do for now. If only he could forget...

"I'm glad you're here, and that I'm here with you." Her quiet whisper sent lightning flashes of heat throughout his body. He pulled her toward him, into his arms. Her arms circled his shoulders and their lips met again, not tentatively, but with the passion of two ready to begin again.

***

Annie awoke wrapped in security, comfort, and love. She lay with her eyes closed. As the fog of sleep cleared from her mind, she realized where she was—in Eric's arms and on her living room floor. Although she enjoyed the warmth of his arms around her, guilt at her reaction to another man so soon after Mike's death chilled her.

Her relationship with Mike had always been a very physical one, touching often, holding hands, snuggling together on the couch. She not only missed Mike emotionally, but physically too. She eased herself away from Eric, sitting up in her sleeping bag. She took a deep breath and slowly blew it out. What was she doing? Using Eric as a substitute for Mike? The chill in the room surrounded her. She so wanted warmth back in her life again.

***

Eric felt Annie move away. Even though it surprised him that they'd slept in each other's arms, he wanted to keep her close, but he let her go. She seemed to move away emotionally too. Body language told him what he already knew.

Take it slow...but it felt so right holding her in his arms, sleeping next to her.

He opened his eyes to see Annie's back. She sat up, stretching like a cat waking from a nap. He looked toward the window. The rain still battered against the side of the house, the wind howling.

"It doesn't seem like the storm's let up much. That wind is still whipping around out there." He startled her, though he spoke quietly. Had she tried to move away from him before he woke?

"Power's still out too. We should get the fire going again. We only have hot coals left." Annie rose quickly and started toward the fireplace. She seemed uptight but he didn't know why.

Hell, they spent the night together in the home with all her married memories. The storm raged outside, the power's out...no wonder she's uptight. Keep things light and easy. They'd get through it.

"No problem...did I ever tell you about my days as a Boy Scout? I can start a fire with one match. Hot coals will be no problem at all! I won't even need the match." He threw in a swagger of his head, trying to lighten the mood by goofing.

"Well I was a Girl Scout so I've been trained for cooking

92

over an open fire...although I'm not too sure about coffee. I'll see what I can figure out for that!"

Relief filled him as she stood with her hands on her hips smiling at him. They worked together to build the fire up, taking the chill off the living room. Whatever bothered her receded and she went searching the kitchen for a pan to heat water. They managed to cook scrambled eggs and toast over the fire, and made instant coffee with the boiling water. Breakfast tasted wonderful to him despite the rough conditions.

"What do you think we should do about getting back to the island? The phone is still out so we can't call to see if the ferry is running yet. I don't think we should venture out in this. It's still looking pretty bad out there." Annie fidgeted with her napkin as she glanced out the living room windows at the torrential downpour. He could hear the anxiety in her voice.

"True, and you never know about downed power lines. I think we stay put. We can check out that limb that came down last night."

"What are you going to do about the restaurant?"

He finished the last of his coffee. She was more concerned about the restaurant than he was. He felt her tension level rising; but what could he do to help her?

"Well, there isn't anything I can do about it. Your mom put a sign on the door, and people won't be coming out in this mess anyway. It's okay. It'll be fine."

Nervous energy pushed her as she cleared their plates and added them to the dinner dishes in the dishwasher. He needed to distract her.

"Do you have any rain slickers around? I'm going to take a look at that tree." Eric followed her into the kitchen with their coffee mugs.

"I'll come out with you." Annie went to the hall closet and took out two yellow slickers.

Together they ventured into the raging storm to inspect the downed branch. The limb had grazed the outer wall of the garage, scrapping the paint but not damaging the shingles. Luckily, it completely missed Annie's car parked in the driveway.

"Thank goodness it didn't do more damage. Just paint. I can handle that." Annie smiled as they entered the garage through the side door. They hung the wet slickers on several pegs near the kitchen door.

"Let's bring in some more wood while we're out here." Eric began loading wood into his arms, and Annie picked out some of the smaller logs and built a load in her arms as well.

"That's good. Don't take too big a load. I can come and get more if we need it." Eric watched in amazement as this slight figure of a woman hefted a sizeable load of wood into the house.

"It's alright. I'm used to doing this. Builds muscles!" Annie's cheeks were rosy from the weather outside, and the fire inside. Her smile nearly caused him to lose his load of wood. Fighting his wobbly knees, he took a deep breath, and managed to get the load safely into the house.

***

Annie watched Eric as she wandered around the living room, neatening, straightening. His patience struck her as he gently blew the embers back to life. Mike had never been patient in restarting the fire. He'd make sure he had a good bit of paper and extra matches to get it going. It occurred to her that Eric was patient with her too. He understood her feelings, her moods, maybe because he'd experienced them too, maybe because it was his way. Mike had listened to her feelings, not really understanding them, but at least accepting them. Her moods...well, he'd tried.

She paced around the living room as Eric loaded more wood into the fire. Hands fidgeting, heart pounding, mind whirling, anxiety filled her. Anxious for the storm to be over, anxious to leave the house, anxious to be alone to figure out her feelings. It felt too good waking up in Eric's arms this morning. She didn't want to hurt him. He had plenty of pain in the last ten months.

And she wanted to be out of this house. Memories of Mike assailed her everywhere. Every room held his presence. Even the wood Mike had so diligently stacked for winter use reminded her of her loss.

Her stomach was in a knot, her emotions in turmoil, she missed Mike. Yet something had been there this morning with Eric. She was thankful he'd been there for her, yet afraid of the feelings that seemed to be developing. That only kindled the unease, the guilt. How would she ever survive this day?

She'd cleaned out the master bedroom. That had been tough. Mike's scent lingered on his clothes. She'd kept several of his sweatshirts to wear when she needed to wrap herself in his arms. She'd taken down all the personal knick-knacks and pictures around the downstairs, storing them away until she felt able to have them out as reminders of happy times, not reminders of her loneliness without him.

The house was move-in ready for the two girls. Now if she could just find something to occupy herself for the rest of the day. She paced, poking here and there.

***

As Eric worked on the fire, he watched Annie out of the corner of his eye. She fidgeted, and moved around, but did nothing. She must be mulling something over. He knew she liked to walk when she had something to think through. That's how they kept running into each other at the beach—they both walked to calm themselves.

Eric put several pieces of wood on the fire and turned to sit on the hearth, still watching Annie.

"Annie, is everything okay?" He spoke quietly and watched her for a reaction. He got it.

"Everything's just great. I wish this damn storm would end." Annie snapped back at him. He raised his eyebrows, but said nothing.

"I'm tired of being cooped up here. I want to get back to the island. I'm overwhelmed with memories here…I need to keep busy, and I don't know what else we can do." Annie muttered to herself, not really talking to him. But Eric heard more than Annie's words. He recognized her anxiety. He understood the anger, the guilt, the uncertainty. He had his

95

memories too.

"Well, we worked upstairs yesterday and things are set downstairs. Is there anything in the basement we should check on?" He consciously used a calm tone of voice, hoping it would smooth out Annie's nerves.

"The laundry is downstairs, and Mike's workshop." She looked pensive. "I can't believe he's gone." Her eyes shone with unshed tears. She took a deep steadying breath. His heart broke for her. He knew.

"Sometimes I still expect to turn around and see Cara come through the door after school. It's hard. But it gets easier."

She sat on the couch. He let her be. He puttered around, stirring the fire, checking things in the kitchen, hoping she would gather her reserves. When he came back into the living room, she'd rolled up the two sleeping bags and stacked everything at the bottom of the stairs to take back to the closet.

"I know what you can help me with today," she said.

"What's that?" The spark of determination in Annie's eyes hadn't been there only minutes earlier.

Good for you, Annie.

"I want to bring my computer back to the island, and the filing cabinet that has all my work in it. Do you think we'll be able to fit it all in my little car?"

"How big is the filing cabinet?" Eric mentally tried to estimate the size of Annie's trunk.

"It's the two drawer size. There are a couple of boxes I should bring back too."

"We'll be able to fit it all in. Let's bring this stuff up and take a look at what we're talking about." Eric picked up a sleeping bag and tossed the two pillows to Annie.

She laughed, and threw the second sleeping bag at him. He dashed to catch it. After storing them away in the hall closet, she showed him the small bedroom that served as her office. Quiet again, she looked at him with shiny eyes.

"These two rooms represent my dreams in life. That room was supposed to be the nursery; this room is my office for writing. We had it all figured out, you know. I'd be able to work here in this office, and the baby's room would be right across the hall. Now they're just empty rooms ready for renters. Empty dreams." He put his arm around her shoulder.

"Why don't you show me what we need to do in here?" He tried to redirect her thoughts. He remembered how hard this was. It took him days, and many false starts to take care of Cara's things. That she related it to her personal dreams only made it more emotionally devastating.

Annie pointed out the items she wanted to take back with her. With a little arranging, it would all fit into the back of her car. He would make this happen. She needed this distraction.

While she sorted papers, he took apart the various components of the computer. He carried it downstairs, placing it by the front door. The file cabinet should be packed first.

"What's in this thing anyway…family secrets?" Eric joked as they wrestled the file cabinet down the stairs.

"Not family secrets…just mine."

Eric smiled as Annie grabbed the slickers from the hooks.

It took most of the morning to pack up and load her office into the car, but keeping busy helped her cope. He saw her anxiety level decrease, no more fidgeting, pacing, or staring off into space. He kept an eye on her nonetheless.

As they came in from packing the car, the refrigerator hummed, the weather blared on the noon news, and the lights in the living room glowed. Power was restored, and the storm moved out to sea. The rain came down in occasional spits and sprinkles, and the wind still blustered but not nearly the gale forces they'd experienced throughout the night.

He helped Annie close the house. Time to leave.

***

As Eric concentrated on driving, Annie gazed out the passenger window, lost in thought. All day her thoughts returned to Eric, despite her attempts to the contrary. Waking next to him, his arms surrounding her with his warmth, strength, and gentleness.

She scolded herself. She missed Mike. Being at the house

97

with all his things around, all the memories…it brought her emotions close to the surface. That had to be it…she missed Mike. But she wasn't being fair to Eric. She wanted time to sort out her emotions.

Eric pulled into the line of cars to be loaded onto the ferry. The activity on the boat and loading zone indicated that the ferry would be leaving soon.

"I'll see what time they expect to leave. I'll be right back." Eric looked at her.

"Okay." She watched him stride to the ferry office. What did he think about waking up in each other's arms this morning? She couldn't stop thinking about it. Good grief, what had she done? Why does she feel so comfortable in Eric's arms? She needed to be stronger…and stop thinking about him.

***

Sara, soft and warm, cuddled next to Doc as he woke with the morning's first light. Glancing at the clock out of habit and seeing no red numbers lit, he rolled further into the arms that had surrounded him as he slept…the most peaceful sleep in many years.

Physician heal thyself… I think I've found the cure.

He feathered light kisses along her jaw, down her neck, her softness so inviting. How had he been blind to this woman for so long? Small gasps escaped her as he continued his journey back to her lips.

"Sara…last night…was it okay?"

"It was nothing, we were more than okay. We were unbelievable." A smile slowly crept to those lips as she opened her eyes slowly. "Don't you agree? You seemed in full agreement last night." Her voice, husky with the night's rest, sparked electric pulses through his body.

"Unbelievable doesn't begin to do justice to it…to us…as far as I'm concerned. I wanted to make sure you're okay with all this." Oh, he'd fallen. How could he have broken the promise he'd made to himself all those years ago?

"We lost power and I stayed here instead of traveling in that awful storm…I'm fine with that." The Mona Lisa smile she graced him with had him scrambling to figure her out. What exactly did she mean? Did she stay over just because of the storm? That didn't sound right. He'd have to look foolish and ask. This was too important for him to misunderstand.

"That's not the only reason you stayed last night, is it?" Doc didn't feel as cool as he tried to sound. His heart banged in his chest cavity, and he didn't need a blood pressure cuff to know his blood pressure was elevated too.

His hand idly stroked her bare back as he watched her face, her eyes closed again. She opened them looking directly into his, the twinkle warning him of something she planned. The onslaught of her mouth on his, her soft curves against him, her arms tightening to pull him closer still, overwhelmed him with the intensity of her passion. Nope, storm wasn't the only reason...you're a bright one Doc. All conscious thought faded as he gave himself over to this seductress in his bed.

Chapter 13
A Rough Ride

Eric and Annie sat downstairs on the lower deck of the ferry in Annie's car. Although the storm had passed through, the waters remained rough, and the ferry was battered by wind and waves as it crossed the sound toward the island. The ride that normally took forty-five minutes lasted twice as long.

Despite the rough seas, relief filled Annie. Happy to be away from her house, an odd reaction since she and Mike were so happy there. But now it just held memories, reminders of what she'd lost. What she wanted most right now — a shower, aspirin for her sore muscles, and her own bed. And time to sort out her feelings. She couldn't wait to get back to her mother's house.

Eric went to get their tickets. She admired his long legs, broad shoulders, his blond hair whipped untidy by the wind as he headed for the stairs. He held his jacket tightly around his body. The memory of waking up against that body—strong, firm, yet comfortable and gentle—heated her. She closed her eyes and remembered the scent of him, spicy and male.

What was she doing? How could she be so... so what? Disrespectful, pitiful, despicable? Weak.

Eric returned with the tickets and two cups of hot coffee before she'd finished scolding herself. The aroma of freshly brewed coffee filled the car. It tasted wonderful, though memories of the coffee they'd made in the fireplace filled her thoughts. She sipped the coffee and listened to his deep voice, musical almost, as he repeated what he'd heard upstairs about the conditions on the island during the storm. The high tides flooded over several roads on the east end. They'd evacuated some of the low-lying houses. She tried to concentrate on his words, but her mind kept slipping back to this morning before she'd opened her eyes and fully awakened. Would she ever get that out of her head?

Once the boat finally docked, Eric picked up his car and followed Annie back to her mother's house to carry in the computer, filing cabinet, and boxes she'd brought back with her. They deposited it all in a pile in the corner of her bedroom.

"Eric, thank you for all your help, not just now, but yesterday and last night too. I can't imagine being stranded there by myself. It couldn't have been very easy for you either." Annie touched his arm. Odd that she'd spent all that time with him but now didn't want him to leave.

"I'm glad I could help. And don't worry about me, I'm fine. Happy to have a nor'easter adventure." He laughed and winked at Annie. Butterflies battered her stomach.

"Listen, I'm not going to worry about opening for the rest of the afternoon," he continued, "but how do you feel about working tonight?" The eagerness in his tone made Annie wonder.

"I'll be there." She smiled at him. He seemed different today. A little quiet, almost a little shy with her. Was he thinking about waking up together this morning? She needed time to straighten out her thoughts.

After Eric left, she wandered the house, trying to settle her mood. The digital clock on the microwave blinked, as did the clock on the oven. Annie looked at her watch and reset them both for one-thirty, and then looked through the other rooms to see what else needed to be reset. They must have lost power this morning, after Mom went to work.

Annie returned to her room and started organizing an office area in the corner. She stood the filing cabinet next to the desk she'd used as a child. Maybe if it felt like an office, she'd work in it like an office. She'd try anything to feel like a writer again. She took the glass heart from her bag, the one Mike had given her on their first Valentine's Day. The one she'd always kept on her desk. Mike. Not forgotten. Always loved.

She sat cross-legged on the floor, took a stack of papers from one of the boxes and flipped through the pages of an old novel she'd started years ago. First chapter...not so bad. She'd play around with it. It'd be a good escape. She set it aside.

A little later Sara arrived home. She popped into Annie's room.

"Hi! I'm glad you made it back. How was the ride?" Sara crossed the room to sit on Annie's bed. She surveyed the boxes and paraphernalia on the floor around the small student desk where Annie sat.

"Rough, but it's good to be back. I'm glad I got things cleaned out though. I feel better now that it's finished." Annie sighed as her eyes met her mother's.

"I know how tough it is. And I'm proud of you. I worried when I heard they cancelled the ferry last night." Sara smoothed the bedspread next to her.

"We lost power around seven o'clock, right as we were sitting down to dinner but it was okay. We started a fire in the fireplace to stay warm and played cards to keep busy." Annie smiled at her mom. She'd only omitted a few details…like the bottle of wine and where they slept. "But we got everything done and it's ready for the girls to move in. A little closure, a step forward." That realization had just come to her. It felt good—forward progress.

Her mother nodded and smiled, but gazed off, distracted.

"Everything okay, Mom?"

"Oh yes, dear. Everything's fine. I'm just looking at all this stuff you brought back. Why did you bring your computer? You have your laptop." Sara looked up quickly at her like she'd missed something. Had her mother been daydreaming?

"I decided this morning that I wanted to set up this corner of my bedroom as an office. I brought back all of my writing files. I've got an idea for a new project and want to get started on it. I thought this would help me be structured about my writing time."

"There's an old table down in the basement you can bring up. That student desk is a little small for the computer and printer." Sara rose from the bed. "I'm going to change and then I'll help you carry it up if you think it'll work."

"I'll go check it out, but that sounds perfect. I didn't

remember how small this desk was." Annie ran her hand across the desktop, her fingers tracing all the dents and dings from her many hours at that desk.

"That's always been your writing space, hasn't it?" Sara smiled as she started for the door. "I'll be back in a few minutes to help you add to your office."

Annie watched as her mother left the room with a spring in her step.

***

Eric spent the afternoon going through the motions of preparing for the dinner rush. Memories of Annie in his arms as they woke, her laugh as they played cards and drank wine, her smile lighting up her whole face, distracted him so that even the simplest task took twice as long to accomplish.

When she entered the restaurant, ponytail swinging, smile on her face, Eric felt his heart thunder. It banged, it skipped a beat; he wondered if it would return to normal rhythm. He took a deep breath and hid behind the counter trying to look busy. He struggled to get himself under control. Take it slow. Regaining his emotional balance, he just barely smiled and acted normal when she greeted him.

Business was light all evening. Eric figured people were glad to stay home and let the storm blow out to sea. The rain had stopped but the wind still blustered as the last customers paid their bill and left the restaurant around eight o'clock. Annie turned off the dining room lights and sat on the counter stool, sighing and wiggling her feet, while he got the kitchen set up for the next day. She was beautiful even at the end of a long day.

"I may go down to the shore tonight. Would you like to come along?"

"Sure. That sounds like a nice idea." Her quiet invitation set his mind racing but he needed to be out in the wind and weather. Maybe that would help the tug-of-war he felt inside.

They drove in silence to the beach. The tide ran high and waves crashed on the rocks, spewing spray and foam into the

103

wind.

Annie got out of the car and walked over to sit on a log beached on the rocks. She closed her eyes and put her head back, taking in a deep cleansing breath. Her hair loose to the wind, her delicate features turned to the sky—her beauty gut-punched him as he watched her, pretending to look out to sea.

Annie sighed aloud. "Ah…this helps. I don't know why. Nothing's changed in my life from ten minutes ago but just sitting here with the wind in my hair, the ocean tang, waves crashing ashore… it's humbling… relaxing… rejuvenating."

As Annie tried to explain, Eric walked toward the log, his hands stuffed in his pockets, fingers wrapped around Cara's sand dollar so they wouldn't reach for Annie on their own. So beautiful. He wanted to hold her again. He couldn't say that of course.

"I know exactly what you mean. It helps clear your mind, heal your soul. I know." He looked at Annie. He wanted to kiss her. Instead, he sat next to her, taking her hand. They sat together letting the wind and waves work their magic.

How could he tell her what he felt for her? He didn't understand it himself; so how could he make her understand?

A sigh escaped her lips.

"Thanksgiving is just a week away. Do you have any plans?" She looked at him, anxiety in her eyes. His stomach churned.

"The holidays are going to be hard…for both of us, I'm sure. My dad called this past weekend. I'm going there and we'll go out for Thanksgiving dinner." He rubbed his thumb over her hand in his. It was small and soft. "Cara always made Thanksgiving dinner here so it'll be good that it's something totally different. And it'll be nice to be with my dad. I know he worries. He calls more frequently than he used to." He smiled as he thought about the support he'd received over the past year. "What about you?" He looked into Annie's eyes. They began to tear up. She seemed so fragile all of a sudden.

He heard another deep breath and watched as she straightened her back, set her shoulders back. Strong again.

"We always have Thanksgiving dinner here on the island. That won't change. My sister and her husband will come with the baby. I think Mom's sister is coming this year. But things will be different, too."

She looked down at their joined hands, placing her other hand over them. Warmth flooded through his hands to his core. "Mike's parents called and wanted me to come down to Florida but since we always came here, I kind of begged off. I think that would be too hard. It'll be hard enough without Mike, and then there is still the whole baby thing...I hope I can deal with it all."

"You don't give yourself enough credit. Annie, you're a strong person. You've had a lot to deal with, and you've done just fine. You don't see how much progress you've made since I met you...here as a matter of fact." He pointed down the beach to where he'd first found her lying on the rocks.

Annie smiled. "You've been a good friend to me, Eric Nordsen. Thank you." She squeezed his hand and looked into his eyes.

"And you've been a good friend to me. Come on, let's head back to the restaurant so you can get your car and go home. You're shivering." Eric pulled her up from the log and continued holding her hand as they crossed the rocks toward his car.

Before Annie could reach for the door handle, Eric turned her toward him and gathered her into his arms. Slowly he lowered his mouth to hers, tasting the sea breeze and something uniquely Annie. Her soft, pliable lips moved under his, accepting him, kissing him back. It felt so right.

***

Annie fought herself. Her lips responded of their own will to his mouth on hers. She had to pull away, but she didn't want to. As she slowly eased out of the kiss, she laid her head on his shoulder. His warmth filled her, heated her. Like this morning. Her heartbeat thudded in her ears. She wondered—was it beating like crazy because of the kiss, or because of the guilt she felt for liking it, wanting more?

105

"We probably shouldn't be doing this..." Annie looked up into Eric's eyes, trying to read his thoughts.

"Why shouldn't we?" his tone curious. He moved a strand of wind-blown hair from her face. His touch sent shivers through her body.

"With everything we're both dealing with, we don't need to complicate things between us. I think we should be friends, good friends. What do you think?" She moved a little more out of his embrace. The chill of the evening air hit her.

"I think we need to go slow, and keep talking. I've wanted to kiss you, and it seemed like a good idea."

He watched her face; could he read her mind? *Does he know I want him to kiss me again?*

"Well, I liked it, but I like the idea of going slow even better. Right now, that's the only speed I think I'm capable of." She smiled, hoping he understood her reserve; but also hoping he would ignore her words, and read her mind. *Kiss me again.*

She had a lot to think about, not the least of which was how she felt about Eric, how he made her feel. Her mind returned to the fear that she used him as a substitute. Transferring her feelings or reacting to him physically? How would she ever know? This writer's block spread to a total brain block... everything confused and muddled.

It was quiet on the ride back to her car. The feelings Eric evoked from her were more than friendship, yet the ever-present guilt plagued her too.

"Annie, do I need to apologize? I don't want to do anything to jeopardize our friendship." Eric parked next to her car and she reached for the door handle. He put his hand on her arm to stop her. Sparks tingled up her arm to her heart.

"It's all right, Eric. We're friends, let's leave it at that, okay?" She tried to stay calm, use a quiet voice.

"I'm okay with that for now if you are."

"We're friends. I'll see you tomorrow at eleven. Have a good night." She smiled as she got out, and closed the car door. We're so much more than friends, I fear.

***

Annie and Agnes were both on duty the next night; the school theatre group was gearing up for their annual performance over Thanksgiving weekend, and Cara had started the tradition of a cast supper at the restaurant before final dress rehearsal. Even though Cara was gone, the woman who had been her assistant had come to Eric saying the kids really wanted to continue that tradition and so did he.

Agnes waited the cast tables, Annie took the walk-ins, and they both hustled back and forth between kitchen and dining room serving meals and clearing tables. For a weeknight, business was brisk.

Eric's strength awed Annie. It had to be hard for him with Cara's theatre group. But he left the kitchen. She watched his tall lean frame casually move from table to table, talking to the students about the show and their parts. Very impressive. *He is so strong. I couldn't do that.*

Finally, the cast left for rehearsal and the regulars began to leave; Annie and Agnes chatted as they reset the empty tables.

"Quite some storm the other night. I heard you got stranded on the other side." Agnes seemed to be aware of everything happening on the island.

"I went over to do some errands and didn't even know that a storm was coming. I don't watch the news or weather at night since I'm working here."

"Was there some emergency at the doctor's office? I saw your mom's car there at six the next morning, when I walked the dog. Great thing about dogs, gotta walk 'em even in a storm," Agnes laughed as she shrugged her shoulders.

"I don't know. She didn't mention anything about an emergency, but she's pretty careful about confidentiality so she doesn't always talk about work."

"Oh. Right. Well that's good to know, I guess. Did you lose power on the mainland? We lost it here right as my favorite show came on at nine—they just played the theme song for CSI and blink, the power's off. What a pain." Agnes chattered on, but Annie lost track. She tried to figure out the blinking clocks at her mom's house. The power went out at nine at night, but they were still blinking when she came in after noontime.

"When did the power come back on here on the island?" Annie tried to sound nonchalant.

"It wasn't out too long. I'd say it came back on around ten-thirty or eleven— just long enough to miss the whole show."

"Oh. It was out all night and came on mid-morning where I was." *That's weird. Why were all the clocks still blinking when I got home the next day? Mom wasn't home all night? How am I going to ask her about that?*

Annie tried to keep things light and joking with Eric for the several days before Thanksgiving. No evening strolls along the shore, no nor'easter sleepovers. She worked hard at smiling and joking with him, but carefully left as soon after closing as possible to decrease the possibility of anything happening again. She thought of that kiss... too often for her comfort, but she couldn't control that, try as she might.

***

Memories of that kiss and how Annie felt against him plagued Eric. He needed to keep things platonic between them. He sensed a bit of panic in her, or confusion, or something that she tried to work out. He reminded himself frequently to give her space, just be a friend. But it wasn't easy. He felt more and more for Annie. Good that he would get away for Thanksgiving—give them both a little space. He was becoming too attached, too dependent on her smile to brighten his day. What if something happened to her, like with all the other women in his life? He'd barely survived the loss of his mother and then the loss of his wife. He couldn't allow himself to get that close to someone again.

Eric ran his hand through his hair and blew out a frustrated breath. They were closing on Wednesday night, and he left for the mainland on the first ferry in the morning. With the restaurant closed Thursday and Friday for Thanksgiving and Agnes working on Saturday, he wouldn't see Annie until Tuesday, almost a week away.

"Annie, I'll be back Friday evening. I know you took Saturday off so you could be with your family, but call me if you need to, okay? Here's my dad's number. Just as a friend, okay?" Eric didn't want to push, but he wanted her to know he'd be there for her if she needed him. He handed her the number written on the back of a blank table check.

"Thank you Eric. I'm really touched." Annie looked at him with what looked like tears in her eyes. "I'm hoping everything will go well. I heard what you were saying the other night about being stronger than I give myself credit for. I'm trying. But I might call to say hi," Annie added with a smile that hit him in the gut.

"I'd like that." Eric smiled back. We're friends, just good friends.

Before Eric left for the night he swung into his office to pack up a few papers to work on at his dad's. A yellow envelope sat in the middle of his desk. He recognized Annie's handwriting, and opened the card.

I'm thankful for many things, but I'm most thankful that you are in my life." Underneath the commercial print, Annie had written her own note to Eric. *Thank you for being such a good friend. Love Annie.*

Unexpected tears sprang to Eric's eyes.

Chapter 14
Changing Tides

The most adorable baby ever lay in her sister's arms. The moment Nancy sat down next to her, Annie fell in love with Kelly Marie. She wondered at her state of mind. How could she have had such a problem accepting the birth of her beautiful new niece?

"Can I hold her? Nancy, she's beautiful…and she's so happy!" Annie cooed at the baby who gurgled and waved her arms in the air.

"Of course you can. In fact, I'm going upstairs to help Phil set up the port-a-crib. We're both new at it so you'll probably have her for a while, okay?"

Annie took the newborn into her arms, the fresh baby scent surrounding her as she cuddled the soft bundle against her.

"I don't mind at all. We have to get to know each other, Miss Kelly Marie and Aunt Annie. We'll be fine!" Annie stroked the newborn's cheek amazed at its softness. Kelly Marie cooed in approval.

One little hand grasped Annie's finger tightly while two blue eyes studied her face intently. Slowly the baby's eyelids began to droop and she nuzzled comfortably against Annie who watched in awe as this precious bundle fell asleep in her arms. She hummed and rocked, patting the baby's bottom softly to the rhythm.

Children in her future… someday. It could work out.

She spent an hour just holding Kelly Marie, wondering at her perfectly formed little fingers, her beautiful dainty features. When Nancy came downstairs to find Kelly Marie asleep in her arms, Annie looked up at her sister.

"I am so sorry I haven't been around for you this last month or so. I've been very unfair to you by being so absorbed in my own problems. Nancy, she's beautiful, and I'm so glad to meet her." Her eyes watered before she could control them.

"Annie, don't apologize. I understand completely. I've been worried about you." Nancy sat down next to her. "I know how badly you and Mike wanted children. You just started dealing with your miscarriage when you suffered an even bigger loss."

Nancy looked down at her sleeping child. "I didn't know how much to share with you. I want to help you, not make things more painful for you." Nancy hugged her, eyes glistening with tears threatening to spill.

"I'm okay, really. Sitting here holding this beautiful baby makes me realize that children are still within the realm of possibility and someday I may have one or two." She smiled, trying to control her tears. "In the meantime, I'm going to enjoy being Aunt Annie, and spoil this little darling every chance I get." She blinked back the tears filling her eyes.

"Oh, Annie." Nancy wrapped her arm around her, tears flowing from her eyes. "I've been so concerned about you." She sniffled and pulled a tissue out of her pocket. "Have you started writing again?"

Annie smiled. As children, she entertained her younger sister with her newly written stories. And later, as adults, Nancy became her best fan. Her sister understood what an outlet her writing was for her.

"Nothing worth publishing, believe me, but I sit down and write every day. I've gotten back into a routine, fixed up an office area in my room. Now I just have to get back to writing something that the magazine would be interested in. I have a few ideas."

"It'll come. Be patient with yourself. Just keep writing. If you're writing, you're healing." Annie could see the concern in her sister's eyes.

"I'm doin' all right." She reached over and patted Nancy's leg.

"Do you want me to take Kelly? The crib is all ready for her, and she should sleep for a couple of hours."

The two sisters took the sleeping bundle upstairs. The guilt

Lynn Jenssen   *Safe Harbor, Safe Heart*

that weighed Annie down disappeared after talking to Nancy. She hadn't thought about Nancy's concern for her. And she'd healed a little more by holding Kelly. Although her life had veered from her master plan, it wasn't over, and that allowed for all kinds of possibilities. That alone gave her hope.

Aunt Lucy and Uncle Joe arrived with pies galore, and the festive atmosphere intensified as the four women gathered in the kitchen while the two men watched the parades and football together, and the baby slept peacefully upstairs.

Although the celebration was different without Mike, the love and security of her family surrounded her. With dinner over and the kitchen cleaned, the older women sat at the table with a cup of tea, and Nancy went upstairs to nurse the baby. While the others wound down after dinner, Annie paced restlessly.

She missed Eric, that simple. He'd understand the progress she'd made today. She wanted to share it with him. And she wondered about his holiday. Annie dialed the number he'd given her. He answered after only one ring.

"Hi. Annie? Is everything okay? How is your Thanksgiving?" Eric sounded surprised at her call.

"It's so much better than I thought it would be. I've made a new little friend named Kelly Marie. She's beautiful, Eric. Nancy and I talked. We both worried about each other and we had a chance to clear the air. How was Thanksgiving dinner with your Dad?"

"We went to this new restaurant, had a great meal and a good talk. He's been worried about me too and got a chance to see that I'm adjusting. All in all, it was a good day." Eric's voice changed. It was quieter, more intimate. "I didn't expect to hear from you, but I'm really glad you called. I have to tell you that I've been thinking about you, wondering how things were going for you. It helped that the whole Thanksgiving thing was different this year. I wondered if it was hard for you having almost everything the same. Are you really all right?" The concern in Eric's voice brought tears to Annie's eyes. She took a deep breath before she could speak.

"I really am okay. Actually, having everyone here makes me feel loved and part of a family. It's good. But I appreciate being able to talk to you. I wanted to call to share things with you. You understand in a way no one else does. Thank you." *I miss you is what I really want to say, I want to be with you and talk with you.*

"Speaking of thank you... I have one for you too. The card you left on my desk was really special. Thank you." Eric's quiet deep voice sent shivers to her core. Her heart pounded in her ear.

"You're welcome Eric." Although she wanted the conversation to go on forever, she couldn't think of much to say. A strange tongue-tied sensation, but she didn't want to hang up. She wanted to transport herself through the phone lines and be in his arms. *Where did that come from?*

"Well, I suppose I should get off the phone. We usually have card games in the evening, and I can hear the activity gearing up in the living room. I'll see you soon, okay?" She hung onto the phone with both hands.

"Take care, Annie. Thank you for the call."

Just friends? Why did it feel like so much more?

***

The Saturday after Thanksgiving was uncharacteristically warm for the end of November. Annie convinced Nancy to take Kelly Marie for a walk. She planned to stop at Shore Delights to introduce Kelly Marie and Nancy to Eric. He'd heard so much about her family, she wanted him to meet them.

During a short walk along the sheltered harbor road, the air crisp and clean with the warm sun brightening the blue harbor water, Nancy and Annie chatted about Kelly Marie. Annie caught up on all the little things she'd missed over the first month of her niece's life.

Annie was pleased that she'd arranged for Agnes to cover so she could spend extra time with Nancy and the baby. There weren't any cars in front of the restaurant but it wasn't noon, and the lunch rush hadn't begun.

"We can pick up sandwiches here for lunch...it'll save us

having to eat turkey again." Hope filled Nancy's suggestion.

Annie laughed. "You never cared for leftovers, did you? We can get the seafood wraps...you'll love them."

Annie swung open the front door of the restaurant as she and Nancy joked. Agnes stood behind the counter with Eric, her hands on his back, her body leaned seductively into his, as she stood next to him. They seemed to be in their own world. Eric turned at the jingle of the bell above the door. His face colored. Agnes turned too, looking more annoyed than embarrassed.

Agnes and Eric? Her hands all over him? She quelled the need to rip Agnes's hair out. Act normal. Introduce your sister and Kelly, get the sandwiches, and get out.

"Hi Eric. I'd like you to meet my sister, Nancy. And this is my niece Kelly Marie."

Eric came around the counter to shake Nancy's hand; Agnes turned back to the prep counter with a scowl on her face.

"It's nice to meet you, Nancy. And look at this cutie. Kelly Marie, is that your name?" Eric squatted down to eye level with the stroller and Kelly Marie grasped his finger in her tiny hand. "I'm glad you came in." Eric looked up into Annie's eyes, a puzzled look on his face. She sensed tension in him— guilt maybe?

"We thought we'd pick up some seafood wraps. We'll get three to go please." She couldn't help the cool tone in her voice.

"Sure, no problem." Eric watched her, like he tried to read her mind. He seemed taken aback by her brisk attitude toward him. *Well figure it out Eric. Two days ago I felt so close to you and now I see this? Well, it's none of my business... I don't care what goes on between you two. Just don't think you can play with both of us.*

He went back behind the counter and worked on the sandwiches. He seemed to be watching Annie through the corner of his eye. She wondered that he even bothered. Was he worried she'd seen the little play behind the counter?

Annie paid for the wraps and got out the door as fast as she could, no niceties at the cash register—all business. How could she be that wrong about their relationship? Granted, Agnes was a looker, but Eric never seemed like the kind to go after every pretty woman he could.

"That was a quick visit. I thought we'd stay a little longer. Why were you so anxious to get out?"

Don't make me go there, Nancy. She might as well fess up. Nancy had always managed to get right to the heart of things.

"Did you see what was going on when we walked in? I wanted to get out as fast as we could."

"That other waitress coming on strong to Eric? He seemed relieved when we walked in. She didn't though, did she?" Nancy watched her for a reaction. Annie plowed ahead with the stroller.

"You thought Eric looked relieved?" she puzzled as she replayed the scene in her head.

"Yes. His eyes lit up when he saw you. I think the situation irritated him, and maybe embarrassed him that we saw it, but couldn't you see the way he looked at you?"

"Really?" She'd been so wrapped up in what she thought she saw that she missed what her sister apparently had not.

"So...anything going on with this Eric and you?"

"Nancy! We're just good friends." She started walking faster. "He's been a lot of help to me over the past few months. He lost his wife last winter, and it's been good to have someone to share with. We're good friends." Annie looked at Nancy, trying hard to justify her feelings.

"Uh-huh. If that's what you want me to believe...but you didn't appreciate another woman with her hands on your friend." With a smirk on her face she nodded her head like she didn't believe a word she heard.

Kelly Marie, heaven bless her, started to cry, saving Annie from explanations of what she had only started to realize herself. Did she feel more than friendship for Eric? Falling in love?

115

***

Eric got the call at his office on Monday morning. He'd contacted Annie's insurance company several times to find out about her claim. They finally got back to him. It was a bit of a mess, but he needed more answers from Annie before he could get it cleared up for her. He remembered how she'd bolted out the door on Saturday. Damn that Agnes. She hadn't gotten the hint. Not interested. It wasn't the first time she'd come on to him. He ignored it, rather than confront her and hurt her feelings, but now…what did Annie think she saw?

He thought about her all weekend. When she called him at his father's house, something in her voice said she missed him as much as he missed her. He was afraid to hope, but that hadn't stopped him from dreaming.

He called Annie's house. No one answered, and he didn't want to leave a message about insurance on the machine, so he asked her to call him. He thought she'd be home, but obviously she wasn't. Or maybe they had caller ID and she purposely didn't answer the phone.

He wondered about the rest of her weekend. She'd seemed fine with the baby on Saturday. He wanted to talk with her, spend time with her. Now this stupid thing with Agnes seemed to have set things back between them. *I need to get this straightened out. I wonder how she'll react to this insurance mix-up.*

An hour later, the bells of the restaurant door jingled. He looked out his office door and his heart hammered in his chest at the sight of Annie. Then he remembered Saturday's incident, and all the insurance details he had to tell her, and his stomach twisted.

"I got your message on the machine and decided to stop in. I had some errands anyway. What's up?" Annie seemed reserved, cautious—the wall of tension between them thick and tall.

She stood by the door to the office, unwilling to come in and sit down. "It's probably better as a matter of fact. Why don't you grab a seat? I found out some things about your insurance claims that I need to go over with you."

Eric cleared a stack of papers he'd been working on and pulled out a folder, opening it in front of him. He watched her as she took off her coat and put it on the back of a chair. Her face paled, her eyes shiny with unshed tears. Concern filled him as he got up to go around the desk. He put his hand on her arm. He looked into her eyes, trying to break through that wall.

"It's going to work out, I'm sure. It's just going to take a bit longer than normal, I'm afraid." Eric tried to soft step into the situation, speaking in a calming voice.

"Okay. What's going on? What did that letter mean?"

Annie moved away from his touch and dropped in the chair. Eric hesitated then moved back behind his desk.

"That was a standard form letter that simply meant the insurance company wants to review all the facts before they pay off on the claim. That is the car insurance part of it. The company your husband worked for had just switched insurance companies, and they're trying to determine which company is responsible. The exact time of the accident is critical. Unfortunately, it was the switchover date when the accident occurred. But that will get settled. Don't worry about it."

He watched as the little bit of color that had started to return to her face drained out as though someone had pulled the plug. She looked awful. He didn't want to give her the next bit of information, but had to.

"The other thing I found out from the HR department at your husband's company is that his life insurance policy did not name you the beneficiary, it named his parents. Have you heard anything about this from them?"

Annie blew out a long breath, leaned back in the chair, and closed her eyes. Eric watched her.

"It would be just like Mike to forget to switch it over to my name after we got married." She shook her head and looked down at her clinched hands. "His parents were very worried about me and my finances when they came up from Florida when all this happened."

Annie paused to take a deep breath. "They're retired and

just sold their condo up in the Hartford area to move to Florida permanently; they're all set for money."

Her paleness kept his questions gentle. "Would they have said something to you if they received an insurance check?"

She nodded her head.

"Annie do you want a drink of water or something? You okay?"

"No, I'll be all right." She took another deep breath, closed her eyes for a moment, then looked into his. "I have a good relationship with my in-laws. I can't imagine his parents getting an insurance check and not saying anything about it. They'd just turn it over to me. I don't know what to say." Her brow furrowed. "How am I going to call my in-laws and ask them about this?"

"I'll see if I can get any more information. Did you and Mike have mortgage insurance, do you remember?"

"I'm not sure. Mike took care of all that stuff. I feel so dumb not knowing the answers to your questions." Annie looked down at her hands. "I think I have some paperwork in those boxes we brought back with us. I'll check on that. I'm still trying to figure all this out."

"Bring me any papers that look important—annuities, 401K's, anything. I'll make a few more calls on your behalf, and see what happened to the life insurance money. You go home and see what you can find. We'll get this straightened out. Don't worry too much, okay?" He moved around the desk and sat on the front, near Annie. He reached out to take her hands but she shook her head and moved her hands through her hair before he could hold them.

"Annie? Are you okay? I know this has been difficult to deal with this morning but I'm here to help. Annie?"

She closed her eyes and nodded her head. "I'll go look for those papers." She stood up to leave, seeming anxious to get out. He'd watched her try to pull herself together. She struggled into her coat, holding in tears, anger, anxiety. He stood up from his desk and walked Annie to the door. She worked to maintain her composure as he put his arm around her shoulder, turning her into his embrace.

"I know you're upset. We'll get it worked out. It will be all right."

Annie turned her head into his shoulder and sobbed, all signs of composure gone.

"How could he leave me in such a mess? I am so angry with him right now, and I shouldn't be because he didn't know he was going to die, but what am I going to do?"

"You're doing it. You're taking things one step at a time. You've asked for help. We are figuring it out. It's going to take just a little while longer." He lifted her chin with his finger and looked into her eyes. "Annie, I promise you. We will get this straightened out."

"Eric, don't make me any promises. I don't know if I will be able to handle it if you can't keep them." Eric's stomach turned over and his heart banged away. Okay...she's not just talking about insurance here...I've got to explain to her...

Annie sniffled and wiped her eyes and nose with a Kleenex from her pocket. "I'm sorry Eric. I didn't expect this." She tried to pull out of his arms, but he held her close.

"Annie, this is about more than the insurance. You saw something Saturday that looked worse than it was. I want to explain it to you. Will you at least listen?" His heart hammered, but he didn't wait for Annie's answer. She had to listen.

"Agnes has been coming on to me since the day I hired her. Just little comments at first and I ignored them or laughed them off. It's gotten worse, and I don't know how to handle it without hurting her feelings." He scoffed as a thought occurred to him. "I can't even go to the boss and complain about sexual harassment..." He looked into Annie's eyes. Okay, say something—yell, hit me even... just what are you thinking? I need to fix this between us.

Annie stepped back, out of his surrounding arms. She looked down at the tissue in her hand, pulling at it, pausing like she considered her words carefully. "I know we said we are friends, but it shocked me to see Agnes with her hands all over you. It really threw me. Thank you for explaining. I don't know what to tell you to do about it, except to tell her to stop." So cautious, so formal with her words. He fought the urge to shake her, or take her in his arms and kiss her silly. *Tell me what you're feeling. We're more than friends Annie—when are you going to be ready to see that?*

"In terms of all this insurance stuff, I'll be okay," she added. "The house is rented and finances are looking better." She took another step toward the door. "I'll go home and look through those boxes. Mike kept all that kind of stuff together. I'll bring it here as soon as I find anything."

"And I'll go make a few more calls. Let's see where we stand after that. I'll call you if I find out anything too. Okay?"

"Okay. Good-bye Eric." Annie left quickly. *To accomplished the task at hand or to hide the onslaught of tears—was it about the insurance or them?*

He'd get this straightened out as promised. He wanted with all his heart to make this right for her. She didn't need any more grief. And he needed her to trust him again.

***

After a hectic morning at the doctor's office where Sara and Doc hadn't had two seconds to greet each other, Mrs. Biddle, her young son lying listlessly on her shoulder, stopped at Sara's desk to sign the insurance papers. Doc appeared behind her.

"Mrs. Burdick, when you're finished helping Mrs. Biddle, I need to see you in my office." Doc turned and strode back to his office. Sara finished the paperwork and with concern went into Doc's office.

"Doc, what's wrong? You never call me down to your office." Sara worried there'd been a problem with Mrs. Biddle or the young boy.

Doc said nothing but walked past her to close the door. Worry increased.

"I can't stand to see you sitting at that desk when all I want to do is this." He surrounded her with his arms, pulled her tight against his body and devoured her lips. Shock waves

120

ricocheted through her as she responded with her own pent-up desires. It was too long since the night of the storm, and they hadn't been together since. Her arms circled around his waist, her hand caressed his lower back, his tight behind.

Doc pulled his mouth away from hers.

"This isn't helping like I thought. Now I want to drag you upstairs. Maybe we can take a coffee break." He nibbled on her lower lip as she laughed.

"No, we can't do that. You've got sick people waiting to see you." Sara gave him one last kiss and moved away from him, trying to tuck in her shirt.

"I need time with you, Sara. The last week or so, life has interfered with us."

"I know. I'm not ready to go public. I'm not sure Annie is ready to handle having her mother in a relationship."

"I understand your need to keep it quiet. I agree. But I need you too. Can I see you tonight? Come for dinner." His puppy dog eyes did it.

"Annie is working and all of my holiday company is gone. I'd love to have dinner with you." She smiled and gave him a quick kiss on the lips before she opened the door.

"Back to healing the sick…" He followed her out the door, a smile on his face to greet the next patient.

Chapter 15
Undercurrents

Sara primped in front of the mirror, finishing the details on her eye shadow and mascara. One more little splash of perfume between her breasts—naughty girl. A seductive smile graced her lips. She hadn't had this much excitement, literally and figuratively, in her life in a long time. Lord knew, she'd waited patiently for Doc. Well, no more waiting.

The teal silk blouse buttoned to just above her black lace bra highlighted her blue eyes, and gave a hint of the direction she wanted this evening to take. The emergency interlude in his office today made it quite clear that Doc planned the same for tonight too.

She made one last adjustment to her black slacks, turning sideways to get another view in the mirror. Not bad for an old gal. Smiling, she grabbed her purse off the bed, and hurried downstairs to her car.

As she drove the several miles to Doc's house, she recalled some of their conversation the night they'd first made love. He admitted building walls to keep people from getting too close emotionally, but he'd held back details of where he'd been and why he'd kept people at a distance. Something more there. She wanted to get to know him in every way without overwhelming him. What if this didn't work out? They'd still have to work together. Her stomach knotted.

She pulled into Doc's driveway. Life is too short. Go with your heart. She took a deep breath and thought of Doc's arms around her. Yep. Go with your heart.

His front door opened before she could even knock. And there he stood—face freshly shaven, his auburn hair darkened from a shower, and smelling so good. Before the door closed behind her, his arms circled her.

"I didn't think six o'clock was ever going to get here," he

murmured as he nibbled at her ear. "I've missed you."

Sara laughed. "I just left here a few hours ago." Her arms went around him, hands splayed across his muscular back.

"You know that's not what I mean." Doc worked to hold her, kiss her, and get her coat off at the same time. Sara chuckled, gave him a definitive kiss on the lips and pulled away to finish taking off her coat and hang it on the wooden peg near the door.

She turned back toward him and caught him looking her up and down. Warmth filled her almost to a blush.

"Sara, you're beautiful. I hope I can control myself long enough to get through dinner." The sparkle in his green eyes excited her, sending waves of anticipation to her core, rendering her speechless.

"The steaks are marinating, potatoes baking, and the salad is made. Let's have a glass of wine before we start grilling. Okay?" He guided her through the living room to the small sideboard in the dining area where a bottle of white wine was chilling.

They took their glasses to the living room, and as Sara turned to put hers on the coffee table, Doc stopped her by placing his hand on her arm.

"I want to make a toast. To you Sara, for being the special person you are. Thank you."

Sara felt the heat rise to her face. She didn't know what to say.

"You're a special man. I'm happy we've discovered each other." She smiled and clinked glasses, sipping the cool dry wine and staring into his sparkling green eyes.

They sat together on the leather sofa, Doc's arm around her shoulders.

"Tell me how things were over the holiday. I know you were concerned about Annie." His thumb rubbed the back of her neck sending shivers through her, making it difficult to concentrate.

"Annie did better than I expected. She and her sister talked and shared what they'd been feeling, and they both told me separately that they felt good about the talk." Sara turned and met his eyes. "She spent a lot of time with the baby. I know she missed Mike, but I think her relationship with Eric is helping her deal with her loss and begin to rebuild her life."

"Hmm. I haven't seen Eric lately. Maybe I should swing by the restaurant someday this week and see how things are going." Doc smiled at her. "We can get the other side of the story from him. I think Annie is doing him some good too."

"You know Annie may suspect something is going on between us. I haven't said anything to her but she was asking some interesting questions the other day." Sara shook her head. "I didn't exactly lie to her but I let her believe something that isn't true."

"Mrs. Burdick, I'm shocked." She saw the twinkle in his eyes. Teasing her had become one of his favorite sports.

"When she came home after the storm that stranded her and Eric, apparently she had to go through the house resetting all the flashing digital clocks. She found out that the power was out for only a couple of hours at night. She asked point blank if I'd been home that night." Sara, still a bit incredulous that her daughter questioned her, felt her cheeks blushing.

"Are you embarrassed that you stayed the night?" Doc asked quietly. Sara wondered about his thoughts. What had she done by opening up this subject?

She looked him in the eyes. "I don't have any regrets, if that's what you're asking. I told Annie that I stopped here after I put up the sign at the restaurant for Eric. I said we lost power and you didn't think I should go out in the storm and back into a dark house, so I slept over here." Sara picked up her wine glass and took a sip.

"Well, it's the truth—I didn't want you to go out in the storm. I wanted you to stay in bed with me!" Doc chuckled as he nibbled playfully at her earlobe.

"I left that part out." Sara returned the nibbles, catching his lower lip with her teeth. "I'm not sure Annie's ready to handle her mother having a relationship. I've always been there for both of the girls. I don't want her to feel, I don't know, abandoned."

"Sara," Doc pulled away from her to look into her eyes, "you are the most giving, nurturing woman I have ever met. Your daughter knows you're there for her. Has it ever occurred to you that she is handling all of this with the help of other people too?" He smoothed his hand through her hair, holding her head, moving her toward his lips. He created a need in her, right there, right now. It overwhelmed her.

"Doc, you're making me crazy. You know how you were feeling this afternoon? That's what you're doing to me right now."

"And the problem is?" Doc wiggled his eyebrows at her, and went back for more nibbles on her neck, his hands exploring, touching her everywhere.

"Come on Doc, be serious for a minute. What should I do about Annie? She's getting stronger but I don't want to cause a setback."

Doc sat up, keeping his arm around Sara, pulling her close. "I don't think we should deny ourselves happiness because of a what if or a maybe. Just talk to Annie. Tell her we've been seeing each other, and how we feel about each other. Start there and see how she reacts." The wise advisor again.

Sara marveled at how he could go from jokester to advisor so smoothly. He was an incredible man. And how would she describe what they had to Annie? She'd have to think about those words carefully.

"Let's go grill the steaks. Bring your wine. I have a surprise for you while we're cookin'," Doc chuckled as he rose from the couch, pulled Sara up, and handed her the wine glasses.

"What? Come on...no secrets...what are you doing?"

Doc picked up the steaks from the kitchen counter and a portable CD player sitting nearby. He flashed a smile at her, and nodded his head toward the back door. She held it open for him as he carried everything out to the patio, set up the steaks on the grill, and closed the lid. He turned on the CD player.

Nat King Cole's *Unforgettable* filled the crisp late autumn air as he swept her into his arms, held her close and began to dance her around the small wooden deck.

"Steaks are supposed to grill for six minutes per side over a low flame. I figure I have two good slow songs per side of steak...unless you want it well-done!"

She couldn't help it. She started to giggle. "You are the most incredible guy. I've never heard of anyone making grilling steaks romantic."

"Just dance with me."

And she did, snuggled against him, her head on his chest and a smile on her lips. The warmth of his body heated her in the chilly air.

Doc surprised her again after dinner with more music, this time in the living room. He smiled down at her as they held each other close swaying to Patsy Cline's Crazy.

"I never realized how much I like to dance." Sara closed her eyes and luxuriated in the feel of Doc's body moving next to hers, his warmth surrounding her, his scent filling her, his breath warm near her ear.

"It's a socially appropriate way for me to hold you in my arms." Doc's eyes glittered with the intellectual joke, then grew serious. "I love holding you Sara. I love being with you."

"Oh, Doc." A kiss as tender as any she could imagine found her lips. *I love him. I love this incredible man.*

"What else do you like to do besides dance, Mrs. Burdick? I know you like to read and you can fish. What else?" Doc continued to hold her close swaying to the music.

"I love to travel. I got a taste of it after high school, but once I got married we didn't travel too much. After Johnny died and the girls were in college, I decided to start traveling again... for me. What about you, Doc? Do you like to travel?"

Doc moved away from Sara slightly. The music had stopped and he guided her over to the couch. He seemed to be stalling on his answer and his reaction puzzled Sara. What was so difficult about her question?

"I've been to a lot of places in this world, some I enjoyed, some I did not. I guess I like to travel to a certain extent. Where was your favorite place to go?" He kept turning the conversation back to her.

Not letting you off the hook that easy, Doc. "I took a wonderful bus trip to Quebec City. I met some fun people that I've stayed in touch with, and saw beautiful cathedrals, quaint old stone buildings. What's your favorite place, Doc? What's your least favorite place?" Sara picked up her wine and sipped, waiting for his answer.

"I think my favorite place is the Florida Keys. I spent some time down there before I came to the island two years ago. I still stay in touch with friends down there. You should go someday." Doc smiled at her.

"And your least favorite?"

He drew his brows together.

"I suppose I don't actually dislike the places as much as I disliked what I saw happening there. I was a Red Cross doctor for a while, and saw far too much human suffering. I was over in the Afghanistan mess, Africa, the Middle East. I got out as soon as I could. I couldn't handle the waste of human life...on all sides."

"I'm sorry. I didn't mean to upset you. Is that when you went to the Keys, after you left the Red Cross?" Sara stroked her hand over his shoulder.

"No, I bumped around here and there. I've always loved the ocean, so when I got out, I found work at various hospitals in cities along the shore." His brow remained furrowed; she reached up and rubbed out the crease, massaging his forehead.

"Mmm, that feels wonderful." He closed his eyes and Sara circled her fingers around his forehead, through his hair. She loved the way his hair felt through her fingers—thick and soft. She gently held his head and started feathering kisses along his eyebrows, over his forehead and cheeks, moving to his mouth, his lips waiting to meet hers.

"Sara, you're incredible. How did it take me so long to get to really know you?" He pulled her onto his lap. "Let's go upstairs. I don't want to rut around like two teenagers on the couch. I want to do this right. I want us to enjoy each other. I want to make love with you."

Her heart hammered in her chest. Her body tingled from his touches and his words sent waves of warmth through her. She nodded her head, kissed him, slid off his lap, then stood and pulled him by the hand to stand beside her. Together as one, they moved up the stairs to Doc's bedroom, where they'd once before found each other.

***

He knew she had to go home. What would it look like to others if she spent the night? A small close community, and as much as people liked Doc and Sara, there would be gossip. He cared about her too much to ask her to endure that. He needed to find a way to spend more time with her, time for them to be together. He wanted her. He couldn't get enough of her, and it drove him to distraction when she sat in her office. Vivid fantasies of taking her on the desk haunted him.

He paced the living room floor. She'd left not ten minutes ago, and he wanted her again already. He was in trouble. He had fallen hard; it happened before he knew it or could stop it. Now what? He couldn't stand to stop seeing her, but how could he keep seeing her? What the hell to do?

***

What a week. Two weeks before Christmas and Annie knew she had to deal with writing to faraway friends to tell them that Mike had died and that she was working to put the pieces of her life together. Not happy news for a Christmas card but... She'd started writing the Christmas cards individually but just couldn't do it. I'll write it once, get the words right, and print it on my computer as an insert in the cards.

Even for a writer, composing that letter was one piece of hard writing. Her head hurt, her stomach churned, and her fingers tired from addressing the envelopes. And emotionally, she felt even worse.

She'd gotten a call from Mike's parents. They wanted to see her. When could she come to Florida for a visit? How was

128

she holding up? They missed Mike. His mother cried on the phone. Annie couldn't bring herself to ask about insurance money. They hadn't gotten anything. His mother would have said something. Annie promised to call them after Christmas to think about a visit. They understood she needed to get through the holidays.

Monday, her day off, and so far she'd spent it getting the cards ready to mail and talking to Mike's mom. And now—what she'd really been putting off—paying bills. She fidgeted at the dining room table surrounded by the Christmas cards, her bills and her checkbook, calculator at hand. Frustration roiled within her stomach, and her head pounded.

She'd pay December's mortgage and car payment, but the savings were gone. The girls' rent started in January, and the restaurant closed at the end of this month. Things were tight. She wondered if Eric heard any more about the insurance stuff. Having written the last of the checks to go out in the mail, she sat with her head in her hands, trying to massage the headache away.

Annie decided to drive to Shore Delights. Even with the restaurant closed, Eric worked Mondays. She walked through the restaurant and into his office, unceremoniously plopping down into the chair in front of him. He greeted her with a sincere smile that made her stomach flip.

"Okay. Where do I stand with everything? I just got off the phone with my in-laws who want me to come to Florida for Christmas, and I'm sure they don't know anything about an insurance settlement. Do we know anything more?" Annie couldn't hide her mood; she didn't even try.

"As a matter of fact, Mrs. Gee, we do. I was just about to call you." He sounded excited, and Annie started feeling optimistic for the first time in a week.

"You were right. Your in-laws don't know anything about it, because they just moved to Florida. The check was sent registered mail to an address where they used to live and returned to the insurance company. So that explains that part of it."

"Right. Mike's parents sold their house about a year after we got married and moved into a very nice condo. They just sold that and moved to Florida last year. If Mike didn't remember to change names on the policy, I'm sure he didn't change addresses." Annie shook her head, but was relieved to hear this news.

"They finally straightened out the auto insurance part of it too. I don't know the whole story about that but it had to do with the time of the accident and switching companies but that's all resolved. The check is in the mail…as they say."

"Oh Eric, that's the best news. Thank you so much!" Annie crossed the small office and hugged him, relief filling her, lifting the mood of despair and depression threatening to engulf her.

"Now, we need to get things straightened out with your in-laws' address. And we file that small mortgage insurance policy you found in Mike's papers and hopefully in a few weeks you should have enough money to pay off the mortgage and then some. No promises on the timeline, but it looks better."

Annie felt the prick of tears as she looked up into Eric's deep blue eyes. "Thank you so much. I have been totally overwhelmed with things, finances included, and you've taken a huge weight off my shoulders."

"You're welcome, Annie. I'm really glad I could straighten things out for you. I know you've been worried about money. Now between this and the rental, the pressure should be off." He continued to hold her, seeming unwilling to let her go.

The stress of the last week, the upset of having to write her friends about Mike, and now the relief of knowing the insurance stuff was straightened out all combined in her head, and the calm of Eric's arms around her filled Annie with a warm sense of well-being. Very similar to the feeling of waking up in his arms. She gave into it, and enjoyed the peace.

Then came the guilt, so she finally moved away, out of his arms. Too soon to move away, yet too long in his arms. Her feelings warred with each other.

"It's just about lunch time." Eric looked down into her eyes with eagerness. "Why don't you stay and have lunch with me. I have a couple more hours of work here in the office, but I'd love a break." Sincerity shone in his eyes.

"Are you sure? You've been making meals for people all week." Annie didn't want to impose; he was always doing for her. "Why don't you let me make lunch for you? I'd like that!" Annie smiled, took his hand and led him out of the office.

"You sit right here, sir. What can I get you to drink while you decide what to order?" Annie put on her best waitress voice as Eric sat down at a table laughing.

"Okay, miss, but only if you join me. We won't tell the boss you're fraternizing with the customers." Eric made his voice quiet.

"Oh, please don't. He's such an ogre. I'd lose my job!" Sour mood lifted, she enjoyed playing with Eric. "Now, what would you like for lunch?"

"What are you serving?" Eric wiggled his eyebrows suggestively.

"Sorry, with that ogre watching, I'll have to see what I can find in the kitchen."

She returned and they sat together at one of the small tables eating the Caesar salads Annie had whipped up behind the counter. Eric watched her; she'd felt it just as she'd felt the warmth of his arms around her. Her skin tingled at the remembered touch, her stomach twisted as memory of his warm breath on her hair invaded her mind.

"Annie, you said before that you felt overwhelmed with things. Only the financial stuff or is there more?" Eric's eyes reflected the quiet concern in his voice, and made Annie work to control the threatening tears. *He's always so strong and so concerned about me. I'm always the one burdening him.*

"The financial stuff—I paid bills and the savings account is demolished. And I made myself sit and write a note to everyone on our Christmas list about Mike's accident. That was brutal—probably one of the hardest things I've ever had to write. That's where my gray mood came from." Annie played with the last bit of lettuce in her bowl.

"You wrote Christmas cards?" Eric's tone was incredulous. "That's unbelievably strong. I've been beating myself up over not being able to do that. I know I should. We always did them together, with little notes to everyone. I haven't been able to make myself sit down with it." Eric's eyes shone with unshed tears he blinked back.

It shocked Annie. Eric - the pillar of strength when it came to dealing with Cara's death. To see him so torn up about Christmas cards—could she help him in some way? Would he accept her help? How to suggest it? Annie reached for his hand across the table.

"Eric, don't be so tough on yourself. It's been a hard year, and you're entitled to have rough spots too. You've done incredibly well to keep the restaurant going on your own. I saw the impressive way you interacted with the theatre group from the school. I couldn't have done that." Eric shrugged his shoulders.

"Let me help you. You've done so much for me; let me help you find a way to send out cards and stay connected to your friends. They need to know your life's changed... that Cara died. We can work on it together." Annie watched his face, held his hand, and waited.

He looked into her eyes. "You would do that? You just finished telling me it was the hardest thing you've ever had to write, and you would do it again for me?"

"Yes, Eric. I will. Let me help." Determination to get him through this bump in the road filled her. He'd helped her along the bumpy way so many times.

"Maybe tonight? Do you want to come to my house for dinner? Then we could work on it together." He looked so tentative she hurt for him. She knew what he was thinking. The cards were something that he wanted to do, felt he should do, but wanted to avoid too. Yet another reminder of the loss he'd suffered.

"Only under one condition— I bring dinner. I can cook too

you know." Annie smiled at him, trying to get that teasing twinkle in his eyes or a smile on his face. He looked so sad.

He rewarded her efforts and smiled. "That sounds great, Annie." Then the twinkle returned too. "And I won't tell the boss you're fraternizing with the customers." He wiggled his eyebrows at her, and she laughed.

"I'll be there at six." She picked up their plates and brought them back into the kitchen. Eric followed her with the glasses and silverware.

"I'll take care of cleanup. Just leave that in the sink." He stood close to her, reached his arms around her, and turned her toward him. His touch heated her, the scent of him filled her, and her heart hammered in her chest. Slowly his lips lowered to hers, his eyes watching her. Gentle, warm, tender. She melted inside, and moved closer into his arms surrendering to his kiss.

***

All business, with lasagna and laptop in hand, Annie arrived at six sharp at Eric's small seaside bungalow, a one story shingled cottage situated on the ocean side of the island. She'd never been at his house, and had spent the afternoon wondering about this evening and where it would lead.

Memories of the several kisses they'd shared and the feeling of security, peace, and something a little edgier dogged her all afternoon. She wanted to spend time with Eric, be alone with him. If honest with herself, she wanted to be in his arms again, to feel his warm firm lips on hers. And then the guilt that came right after the thoughts of Eric overwhelmed her. The tug of war beat her down, confused her, wore her out.

She slung the shoulder strap from her laptop over her shoulder and rang the doorbell. She heard several quick steps and the door opened; Eric smiled and reached for the lasagna with salad balanced on top.

"Let me help." He closed the door behind her, motioning to the kitchen doorway to the right. Annie stood looking around as Eric placed the food on the counter. The kitchen, a roomy space with light maple cupboards, forest green countertops, and beige flooring opened through a small eat-on counter to a dining area with cushioned wicker chairs and a round glass-top table, a green candle and hurricane lantern as centerpiece.

"Eric, I love your place. It's great." She saw pride in his expression as he looked around the rooms as if seeing it through her eyes.

"We did a lot of work on this place when we first got it. It had been an old retired Navy guy's place, and he clearly hadn't spent much time or energy on it." Eric smiled and seemed to be remembering something. Annie watched as he came back to the present.

"Here. Let me show you the rest." He guided her through the dining area, turning left into the main living area. The room looked out through two large bay windows to the ocean crashing on large boulders at the base of a sizable cliff. A door between the windows led to a deck that stretched the length of the house. The living room walls were paneled in the same light maple. A large stone fireplace occupied most of the far outside wall of the living room. A fire crackled in it, adding to the cozy feeling.

Annie walked to the windows.

"What a great view. I wonder that you ever leave this house."

"Sometimes the memories are just too much."

Eric's mood surprised Annie. So down.

He directed her through another doorway that led back to the small foyer. To the left of the foyer were three doors. Eric opened the one closest to the front door to show a bedroom converted to an office space—a double bed in one corner and a desk and bookshelves in another. The middle door was the bathroom, and the last door was the master bedroom. Maple paneling was throughout the house. The color in the master room came from the matching curtains and bedspread of green leaves with plum-colored flowers and several large plum throw pillows.

As she looked into the master bedroom it struck her that there was only a single bed—a different but similar style to the two dressers. She understood immediately. She couldn't sleep in her large king-size bed after Mike died.

"You're house is beautiful, Eric. Did you put in all the paneling or was that here?" She moved out of the bedroom toward the kitchen.

"It was here but what a mess. We ended up sanding and refinishing the whole house. You can't believe what a job that was!" His smile softened his face, which had been far too serious since she'd arrived.

"Well, it's wonderful." Annie unwrapped the lasagna casserole on the counter. "I just put this together and it needs to cook for half an hour. Why don't I put it in and we can start on the letter before dinner."

"Are you sure you want to do this?" Eric held himself tensely, fidgeting with the aluminum foil off the casserole dish. He looked into Annie's eyes, doubt and concern filled his voice. She knew the dread he experienced, and her heart broke for him. She put the dish in the oven to cook, reached for his hand and led him to a chair in the dining area. As he sat, she moved behind him, hands on his shoulders, massaging the tension that knotted them.

"Relax. We will get through this together, just like you helped me get through so many things. We can make the letter as simple or as detailed as you want. It's totally within your control. And you'll feel better when it's done. Close your eyes a minute and let me work some of these knots out of your shoulders." Annie worked quietly on his shoulders and neck, feeling the tension slowly lessen, his head drooping forward.

She continued to work her fingers along the muscles in his upper back. "What have you thought about saying in this letter? Do you have any ideas?"

Eric lifted his head, circling it around, testing the loose muscles. Annie stopped and moved to a chair next to him, waiting for his answer.

He blew out a long breath. "I know that many of our college friends don't know about Cara. Of course relatives and close friends do and I won't put a letter in their cards. I guess I

135

want to give a few of the details, not dwell on it too long, and tell them that I am trying to stay busy with the restaurant and working at getting my life back on track. This is so hard." He'd taken the flat silver sand dollar out of his pocket and traced the holes with his fingers.

"Okay, that gives us something to go with." Annie pulled out a pad and pencil from the pocket on the side of her laptop case and started writing. "What kind of details do you want to include?" Annie realized she didn't know many of the details of Cara's death. Eric had never talked to her about it in specific terms.

"I guess I want them to know that she found out about the cancer a little more than a year ago, and put her heart into fighting it. She was so brave, and so positive that she could beat it. She died in my arms here at home less than two months after she first got the diagnosis. January thirtieth."

"Oh, Eric." Annie blinked back the tears welling up in her eyes, and focused on writing on her pad. When she looked up at Eric, he stared out the window, tears glistening in his eyes.

He took a deep breath and looked at Annie. "I want this to be brief. Christmas is supposed to be a happy time, and I don't want to belabor the sad news I have to deliver. Cara wouldn't have wanted that either. But I don't want it to look stupid with just a few lines about Cara on a piece of paper."

"Don't worry about that. I can print it out like a small card. I can space it so it looks nice but is still brief. That's the easy part." She smiled and rubbed his arm. He covered her hand with his.

"Thank you. I couldn't do this by myself."

"You're welcome."

He leaned over and lightly touched his lips to hers. She wanted to melt into his arms but she held herself back, enjoying only the softness of his lips on hers. She ended the kiss, and looked down at their joined hands. A deep sigh escaped her before she could control it. God she wanted more.

"Why don't you get us some wine and I'll get my laptop set up. Maybe we can finish this before dinner." Annie tried to return to business though her heart hammered in her chest, drowning out the voice of reason running through her head. That tug-of-war thing again.

Eric took a long time getting the wine, and the dishes set out for dinner. By the time he came back to the table, Annie had started working on the note. He stood reading over her shoulder.

I'm sorry to send sad news along with my Christmas greetings. Last year, we received news that Cara had a very aggressive form of cancer. In spite of her brave spirit and determination to beat it, she died in my arms in late January this past year.

This year has been a very difficult one. I have kept the restaurant open and have been struggling to build a life without Cara.

She was a wonderfully strong beautiful woman who loved life and all of you. Remember her fondly.

Love,
Eric

"How could you hit it so perfectly on the first try?" Tears streamed down his cheeks as he reached for her. She stood and went into his arms, holding him tightly—her hand gently rubbing his back—comforting, soothing, returning what he'd so often given her.

Chapter 16
The Turning Tide

She amazed him. Annie so beautifully expressed how he felt about Cara, explaining her death, but reminding his friends how full of life she'd been. If this was a sample of her writing…

He felt the sting of tears in his eyes as he held Annie. She understood. And she was here... for him. He felt her hands slowly moving across his back. A totally different response came from his body with her light touch…her fingers feathered across that sensitive spot on his back, electrifying him. She couldn't possibly know what it did to him. Cara had always known… and it had been one of her secret messages telling him that she wanted him. Could Annie be sending the same message?

How could he let his thoughts go there? The softness of her body against his, the curves that fit perfectly to him, the smell of strawberry shampoo wafting from her golden hair. His thoughts out of his control… and his body not far behind. He moved away, out of her embrace. Fingering the sand dollar in his pocket, he looked into her eyes.

"I think maybe we ought to get some dinner on the table." He smiled, hoping she couldn't read his thoughts.

"I'll get the lasagna out if you'll get the salad. The bread's ready too." He saw Annie take a deep breath. Did she feel the same desires?

The two of them were quiet at dinner. Annie raised her glass to toast.

"To making it through the holiday season." A sad, but wise smile touched her lips. He clinked his glass to hers and added, "To making it through the holiday season with a friend's help."

"Thank you Eric." She sipped the chilled wine, and looked into his eyes. He took a sip and closed his eyes for a moment. A deep breath helped him relax the muscles knotted again in his neck.

He smiled and teased as he took his first bite, hoping to lighten the atmosphere, lighten his mood. "The lasagna is delicious. I may want the recipe for the restaurant."

"I don't know. It's an old family secret..."

"Hmm, I'll have to figure out a way..." They laughed together and bantered back and forth. The way it usually was between them.

***

Annie poured them each another glass of wine, happy to see Eric smiling. They cleared their plates, putting them in the soapy dishpan in the sink and took their wine glasses into the living room. Eric set his down on the coffee table near the couch and went to the entertainment center. What was he doing? She watched as he slid a VCR tape into the machine and turned on the television.

"This is just a guess but I bet you'll like this." He had a little boy smile on his face. God, he is so cute.

As soon as the music began, Annie knew the show and started laughing.

"How did you know that's my favorite Christmas special?"

He laughed too as he returned to the couch and sat down next to Annie. "Something about the way you've been singing Rudolph the Red-nosed Reindeer around the restaurant tipped me off!"

"It's not the holiday without Rudolph." Annie smiled, snuggled up against Eric on the couch and sipped her wine, ready for the show to begin. She felt him pull her closer and drop his arm around her shoulder. His whole body relaxed next to her. This was good, very good.

One Christmas special ran into another and the wine supply diminished. They giggled their way through two hours of animated holiday shows.

"This must be why I always wanted kids...so I could watch the Christmas specials without looking foolish," Annie giggled as she emptied the bottle of wine into their two glasses.

"You don't look foolish. I think you look beautiful." Eric's matter of fact voice and piercing gaze took Annie by surprise. So serious all of a sudden. As she tried desperately to think of a light comeback, Eric lowered his mouth to hers. Just that suddenly, she was speechless... mindless... breathless. And wanting more. His lips urged hers to open, his tongue exploring, deepening the kiss as none they'd shared before.

He pulled her to him, his firm body against hers. His arms held her close while his hands moved over her, leaving heated paths where they traveled.

The wine mellowed her mind. His wandering touch ignited the explicit thoughts she'd pushed away. She wanted him. What were the reasons she shouldn't do this? Why shouldn't this be happening?

She spoke quietly in his ear. "I don't know if we're ready for this. I want you. I find myself thinking about you a lot, but then I feel guilty. That makes me think this isn't the right time."

Eric lowered his forehead to rest on hers. She could feel him take a deep breath, his arms around her relaxed.

"I know." He lifted his head and looked into her eyes. "But we're still among the living Annie. When is it going to stop hurting? When are we going to be whole again?"

"It will happen, Eric." She melted into his arms, holding him tight to her. Comfort now, passion later. We will happen, maybe not tonight, but we will be together. She knew. They both had more healing to do, but they would be together.

***

Eric planned a quiet Christmas with his father. His dad took Cara's death hard, and worried about his only son, so he was arriving on the last ferry on Christmas Eve to be together for the holidays.

He'd inherited his father's love of cooking and together they created a feast for two. Eric managed to find a lobsterman still pulling pots despite the winter weather, and bought two large lobsters to stuff for dinner. His father put together a hot clam dip to have while the meal cooked.

"Well, it's not your traditional Christmas dinner, but this isn't really a traditional Christmas. I'm glad you're here, Dad. It means a lot to me. Thanks." They didn't often verbalize their feelings for each other, but Eric felt his father's support through this last difficult year.

"I'm glad to be here son and happy you closed the restaurant for the day. I know how lonely it is without Cara. I've been without your mom now for quite a few years, and I'm still not used to it. It takes a while, Eric." A sad smile touched the older man's lips as he stared off.

"Do you ever think about getting married again Dad?" Unsure how much he wanted to share about his feelings for Annie, Eric needed some input. Was he really such a jerk to be with someone else so soon after Cara's death?

"I'd have to find a very special woman; I haven't found her yet." He put the clam dip in the hot oven. "But it's different for me. I had a lot of wonderful years with your mom, raising you and watching you grow. You and Cara didn't have all that time. You still have a lot of life to live. I hope you do find someone else."

For whatever reason, his father's words loosened the tension coiled within him, reassured him that what he felt, what he secretly hoped for, was all right.

***

Eric waited all day for the phone to ring. He wanted to hear from Annie. He knew she'd been apprehensive about spending Christmas at her sister's house. Her mother wouldn't go if she thought Annie would be on the island by herself for Christmas. So, Annie agreed to go. She'd be back tomorrow. He'd make sure he talked to her then.

Eric slept fitfully. When he finally fell asleep, his mind filled with a vague vision. It kept repeating over and over, Cara floating above the whitecaps breaking ashore. He walked the beach, talking to her, but he couldn't hear her words to him.

141

She looked happy and peaceful. He felt relieved. He tried to follow her along the shore, but she kept drifting away, only to return and steer him toward the rocky boundary of the shore. In his dream, he saw Cara hover over a motionless form on the rocks.

Suddenly, Eric's dream shifted from wispy and vague to intensely real. He struggled to get to the figure on the rocks. It took him forever. Moving, running but not getting any closer. He knew. Annie lay slumped over on the rocks. Cara floated above her motioning for Eric to help her. Cara talked to him, but still he couldn't hear her. He watched her lips, trying to read the words she mouthed.

"Nurture love where you find it." He heard it, but what did it mean? He looked up to ask Cara, but she floated away. "Good-bye my love. You can love again, if only you let yourself." Eric watched as Cara's white gown transformed into the waves breaking ashore.

He looked down at the mass at his feet. He no longer struggled to get to it; he was there. He bent down next to her, rolled her over, and lifted her up. Her face pale, her eyes closed. He held her close, her warm breath on his cheek. The only thing warm. Annie—cold and unconscious. He carried her across the rocks and appeared suddenly in his room. He laid her on his bed, talking to her, anxious for her to respond. Doc and others stood around the edge of the room. He watched her, held her hand, whispered to her. He'd found love again, hadn't he? What had Cara said? He fought to remember her words.

Eric awoke in a cold sweat. He reviewed the dream. What did it mean?

He rose to put on his robe, and went out to the living room. He wouldn't be able to sleep again tonight. He stared out the window watching the waves break onshore—reminding him of Cara's white gown—as he tried to decipher the meaning.

Nurture love where you find it...he'd found love, but how to nurture it? Annie hadn't even called him.

***

Annie didn't want to have misgivings about spending

Christmas day with her family. She tried to put on a festive front. But she felt sad, envious, and confused. Sad about the changes in her life, envious of her sister's happiness, and confused about her feelings for Eric—especially confused about her feelings. Was she sad and missing Eric, or just wishing for the same kind of happiness her sister had.

Annie rocked Kelly Marie to sleep after dinner. The gentle motion lulled her as well as the baby; thoughts of Eric filled her mind.

What am I doing? I don't even know how he's feeling about the other night. Hell, I don't know how I'm feeling about the other night. I'm not sorry, but what's next? He's always in my thoughts…is it wrong that we should be together?

Annie watched the baby snuggled in her arms. She looked up as Sara came into the living room.

"She's so precious, Mom. Look how her mouth moves like she's still nursing."

Sara smiled as she said, "They are truly miracles. Someday, Annie, your miracle will come. I have every hope that you'll have a happy life with a husband and children. I know this is still hard to think about, but don't close yourself off to the possibilities."

"I know. A month and a half ago, right after Kelly was born, I had a really hard time about losing my baby and then losing Mike and the possibility of a family. But, I feel as though I'm starting to rebuild my life… slowly, but at least I'm feeling more in control than when everything first happened." She gently stroked the baby's face, then looked up at her mother. "I'm not ready to set any major goals for myself; I'm just trying to take it a little at a time."

"Good. I'm happy to hear that you're feeling more in control. That's important. Just keep working at it." Sara leaned forward in her chair, putting her hand on Annie's arm. "And Annie, don't be afraid to talk to me or lean on me if you need to. I know you've always been the strong independent type, even in your marriage to Mike, but we're all here to help you."

"I know, Mom. I've had a lot to figure out and I don't like

to be a burden. The job at the restaurant helped. Eric's been great and he's a good listener. He's a good friend." She didn't add the rest of her thoughts about Eric.

"I'm glad. Eric is a wonderful man. He's had a hard time this past year too. I think you two are good for each other."

"I think so." Annie thought of him. How is his day going? Maybe I'll call. No, I'll see him tomorrow.

"I'm going to put Kelly in the crib…even though I could hold her like this all night." She smiled down at the peaceful bundle and rose from the rocker.

***

Nancy and Phil had finished cleaning the kitchen. Nancy sat down on the couch next to her mother.

"How's she doing? She seems to be okay, enjoying the baby. Did you get her to talk at all?" Nancy's concern for her older sister was evident.

"She says that she is feeling more in control of things, and that she is rebuilding her life. I'd say she is doing okay. We even talked briefly about someday finding happiness again. I'm hopeful." Sara patted Nancy on the leg. "It's good to be here. Thank you for inviting us. I don't think it would have been good for just the two of us to have Christmas on the island." She shook her head, but then smiled. "Next year's going to be exciting with Kelly. The holidays are so fun when you have little ones."

She remembered her two towheaded beauties in nightgowns racing downstairs on Christmas morning, giggling with excitement as they opened stockings and presents. She wished those kinds of joyful memories for both of her girls. Nancy was well on her way; Sara was hopeful for Annie too.

***

Annie laid the baby in the crib, tucking the covers around her, patting her back to settle her. Kelly snuggled down, shifting a little, but slept through the whole process. Annie stood gazing down at her niece.

Could she really hope to have a child like this someday? Could she ever find another soul mate to share her life? Eric's

144

face immediately came to her mind, startling her. Her thoughts, shifted frequently toward Eric and the possibility of a future for them.

She promised herself more time to think it all through. As she gained control of her life maybe she'd gain control of her wayward thoughts too.

***

The day after Christmas, Eric and his father opened the restaurant. Eric inherited his father's love of food and cooking, and his mother's people skills. He'd packaged that into a successful restaurant business. His father toured the eatery with puffed paternal pride, warming Eric's heart. While he worked in the office, his father set to work preparing his famous minestrone soup, the special for the day. His father had begged.

The doorbell jingled and Eric knew it was Annie without looking.

"Hi there! I'm Eric's father, John. He's in his office. You must be Annie?"

"Yes, I'm Annie. It's nice to meet you, John." She reached across the counter and shook his hand. "Has Eric enlisted your help for the evening shift?" Annie smiled as she joked with his father.

Eric came out of his office as soon as he heard her. The smile that lit Annie's face told volumes about her feelings. She gave him a quick hug. Eric let his hand linger on her waist, though aware that his father watched their whole exchange.

"Merry Christmas! Did you and your dad enjoy your holiday?" Annie smiled and looked up into his eyes.

"We had a nice quiet Christmas, and a great dinner together. He's a good cook too, you know." He smiled back at Annie. "So he's workin' tonight," he said as he winked at her.

"Do you know what you've gotten yourself into, John?" Annie laughed as she set up for the dinner rush.

His dad watched him watch Annie. Had he given too much away when he'd asked his father about loving again? He wanted to get Annie alone, if only for a moment, and a Christmas kiss. Take it slow.

145

***

The dinner rush didn't turn out to be many customers at all, and the trio closed the restaurant by eight-thirty. Annie hadn't talked to Eric alone or sorted out her feelings. It seemed the closer they got, the more confused she felt.

She watched Eric from afar, admiring the way he moved comfortably behind the counter. She remembered waking in his arms the night they were stranded without power. She thought about the many times he listened to her, advised her, and comforted her. He helped her get through the emotional upheaval of cleaning out the house, and straightened out the insurance mess for her.

But the dominant memories were of his kisses, the feel of his body against hers, the passion that grew between them. Was she in love with Eric? The question dogged her. It kept her from falling asleep that night and when she did, her dreams were full of Eric.

***

Sara had wanted to call Doc on Christmas night. Just to hear his voice. But he volunteered at the hospital on the mainland so the emergency room doctors could spend the holiday with their families. Among many things, she admired the way he thought of other people. He was constantly in her thoughts. His past still a mystery to her, he began to tell her things…in little doses.

She couldn't wait to give him her gift. They planned to have their own Christmas celebration several days after Christmas—this evening after returning from Nancy's house. The whole evening to spend with Doc. Anticipation filled her as she dropped her suitcase on her bed, and quickly freshened her make-up. She removed the red envelope from her top dresser drawer. A smile crept over her lips. Their first date…well, it hadn't really been a date, but the beginning of their time together. Fishing. She chuckled to herself. She was the one who got hooked…or maybe it was him… she hoped.

***

Four days. Four damned days without her. He was a lost

cause. In love. Despite that he knew he shouldn't be. Despite that he knew it would hurt again.

She's in my head. Doc paced the floor, waiting for Sara to arrive. No stupid, she's in your heart. Could he live through it again?

She didn't knock; she was just there, and then in his arms. Her perfume intoxicated him, her warm soft lips devoured his, and his head reeled. Passion surrounded them, and he forgot everything—total absorption, complete communion. God, I'm lost… or maybe I'm found.

She slowly withdrew from their kiss, seemingly as unwilling to break the contact as he.

"I've missed you," she whispered against his ear, sending ripples of excitement through his already overloaded system.

"I want you right now but I don't want to seem like a complete Neanderthal and drag you up to my cave." His lips hungrily devoured her.

"I want you too but I have something for you first. I can't wait to see you open it." Sparkling blue eyes danced as she smiled up at him.

"Okay. I have something for you too." He smiled to himself as he thought of his plan, his gift.

He guided her to the leather couch, clicked the remote control for the stereo system, and Christmas music filled the air. A red poinsettia sat on the coffee table with a large green envelope leaning against it. She took a red envelope out of her pocketbook and placed it near the green one.

"It's not quite a Christmas tree, but it is festive looking." The first year in many he'd taken any notice of the holiday.

"You go first; open the envelope. I can't wait to see your face." Sara wiggled in anticipation next to him, her eyes shining with delight as she watched him open the card.

Doc read the card. To the One I Love—the L word. As serious for her as it was for him. He felt a knot develop in his chest as he read the verse and the words she'd written below.

May you be filled with the joy of the season.

147

As you have filled my life with joy.

Love Always,

Sara

Tears threatened and he blinked them back, hugging her so she couldn't see the moisture in his eyes.

An envelope with We've hooked each other written on it lay inside the card. A gift certificate for new surfcasting fishing poles…for both of them.

"Sara, thank you. This will be great."

"I didn't want to pick out the actual poles since I don't know enough about them, but it's how we got started. I thought it appropriate."

He kissed her, touched by the connection to their first date. It'd been years since anyone considered him.

"Now open my gift to you." He handed her the card, and sat back to watch her face. He thought she would like it, but knew it would force their relationship out into the open.

She opened the card and read it. Tears filled her eyes as she looked up into his, unafraid to show the emotion he could only write in the card. She was braver than him.

"I love you too."

Feeling like a coward, he could only kiss her, deeply, tenderly—hoping that could say the words he couldn't.

"Open the other envelope." He watched for her reaction as she read the gift certificate.

"A weekend away in Vermont? Hare Hill Inn? Where is that? How did you find this place? It looks wonderful." He watched as Sara studied the brochure he had tucked in the envelope.

"I found it online at a site for upscale B&B's. It's in northern Vermont and set in a quaint town. There are cross country ski trails, horse drawn sleigh rides, gourmet dining, and Jacuzzis in the rooms. I thought it sounded like a great way for us to spend some quality time together without worrying about appearances. Interested?" Okay, if it's going to be a problem, it'll come out here.

She threw her arms around his neck and kissed him hard

on the lips.

"Of course I'm interested. A weekend with you in a Jacuzzi…" Sara kissed him again, more tenderly this time.

He couldn't help it; he started to laugh.

"What?"

"I don't think we should spend the whole weekend in the Jacuzzi…we'd be awfully pruney by the time we got out. I had other ideas of how we could spend our time."

"Oh, really? Do tell." Sara's eyes gleamed with anticipation.

He took her hand, pulled her up from the couch into his arms. Kissing her teasingly, he started to move her toward the stairs.

He whispered in her ear, "I'd rather show than tell."

Chapter 17
Stormy Seas

Sara lay surrounded by Doc's arms in the afterglow of their lovemaking. Her eyes closed, she heard the steady thump of his heart. Her hand glided through the soft curls of hair on his chest. His hand gently stroked her back, relaxing, soothing, loving.

"You know, Sara, if we're going away for a weekend in Vermont, you're going to have to say something about us to Annie. It would be better to deal with it up front, than try to soft pedal it later. You didn't say anything about us to your family over the Christmas holiday, did you?" His hand continued stroking, as tension moved through her body at the thought of upsetting Annie.

"No. Annie seemed sad. The holidays were hard for her. We talked and she's feeling more in control of her life, but I didn't want to add anything to her worries."

"Do you think it will be such a problem?" he asked quietly.

She shifted her head so she could look into his eyes.

"I'm going to tell her that love comes at different times in your life, and I've been fortunate enough to find it again. I'll see how that goes and move on from there."

Doc raised his eyebrows. "That seems like a bit of a turnaround for you. I thought you were afraid she'd feel abandoned?"

"I guess I heard a note of hope in her voice when we talked about the future. She is healing. It might be good for her to see that you can love more than once in your life." She watched him for a reaction. She'd purposely used the "love" word. He'd written it, but not spoken of it to her. His eyes shuttered closed. Something still existed behind that wall he'd erected. When would they ever get that out in the open? What's going on, Doc? She couldn't read his mind, but she could listen.

She reached her hand up into his soft hair, turning his lips to hers. He came back to her, his attention again focused on her, and not the ghosts of the past that haunted him. If only she could meet them face to face. Sooner or later they had to be dealt with.

***

The restaurant had been closed for a week and Eric paced the floor of the main dining room. He should be in his office taking care of insurance matters, but he couldn't settle. His focus was not on business—insurance or restaurant. He missed Annie. They'd grown close; he enjoyed her company. They were friends and more. He hoped much more. But it wouldn't happen if he didn't see her.

He stared out the window at the winter view of the harbor. The ice floes piled haphazardly onto the shore, the harbor waters calm but gray. He remembered the last time he and Annie were together alone. God, he'd wanted her. He still wanted her. Memories of the strawberry scent of her hair, the salty taste of her lips, and her soft curves against his body assaulted him, leaving him more frustrated than ever. He had to see her.

"Call her you idiot. Call and ask her to come for dinner. Duh!" He strode into his office and picked up the phone.

Annie answered on the first ring, and sounded surprised to hear from him, but the warmth in her tone encouraged him.

"Hi! How are things goin'?" Eric tried to sound casual, but his heart hammered like a teen asking for his first date.

"Good. Eric, I was going to stop down and see how you were doing. Are you enjoying your free time?" She sounded upbeat, perky. Maybe she didn't miss him as much as he missed her.

"It's so quiet here without you around." He couldn't believe it had come out that way…what an idiot.

Her rich laughter bubbled over the phone lines.

"So I'm loud and…"

He laughed with her, "No, you know that's not how I meant it. I've missed you. I'm used to talking to you nearly every day; I even checked the beach to see if you were walking down there so I could bump into you."

She laughed again. "Well, I thought you'd like the time to just close up things and have some quiet time. All you have to do is call."

"That's what I'm doing now. How'd you like to come for dinner tonight?" He held his breath, sure that she'd say yes, but scared she'd say no. Not logical, but he couldn't help it.

"I'd love to. What time and what can I bring?" He could hear the happiness in her voice. His heart hammered in anticipation.

"Just you, and six o'clock. Annie, I'm really glad you can make it." God, did that sound dumb? He took a deep breath and tried to calm down.

"I'm glad too, Eric. I'll see you at six."

***

Annie woke early that morning, determined to revise the rough draft she'd finished for the magazine. After talking to Eric, she worked all morning polishing, rewriting, and checking facts from her notes. By lunchtime she had a good chunk of the article rewritten. She went downstairs to heat up some chowder for herself and her mother. Sara walked into the house as Annie stirred the chowder on the stove.

"I think there might be something here of interest to you!" Sara's singsong voice alerted Annie. Sara handed Annie several envelopes as she came out of the kitchen.

"Do you think it's the insurance check?" She looked at the return address and noted the insurance company's logo.

"You said Eric told you it was in the mail…I think this is it!" Sara watched as her daughter opened the envelope. Annie sat down at the dining table and read the letter that accompanied the check.

"This doesn't in any way make up for Mike's death, but I'm finally dealing with it a little better. This check goes a long way to getting things straightened out financially for me." A tear slid down her cheek, but she quickly swiped it away, willing herself to stay positive and upbeat. "I need to focus on where I'm going instead of where I've been. This will help." She patted the envelope, took a deep breath and exhaled slowly.

"Lunch is almost ready. I'm heating up some chowder for us." Annie changed the subject. "How was your morning?"

"The office was kind of busy. There's a virus going around, so quite a few patients stopped in to see Doc. I'm happy to be home so I can put my feet up." Sara sat at the dining room table across from Annie. "Did your sister call yet? I'm going to her house for a few days at the end of the week. Do you want to come with me?"

"She hasn't called yet, but I think I'm going to stay here. I've made really good progress on my writing and I want to keep going. You go and have a good time with the baby."

"I'll give your sister a call after lunch. Listen, I'm not going to be home for dinner tonight. Are you going to be alright with that?"

"Sure, I'll be fine Mom. Where are you goin'?" Annie watched her mother's face turn slightly pink. What is this about? She waited for the explanation.

"Well, I'm going to have dinner with Doc. He and I are seeing each other. I haven't said anything up until now." Love filled her mother's look. "You're getting stronger, and I'm proud of how you've gotten your life together. You know I'm here for you no matter what, right?"

Her mother's news surprised Annie. Her mother had been by herself for a long time and always attentive to her daughters' needs. But she needed to pay attention to her own needs. Annie hugged her mother.

"Mom, I know I can talk to you anytime. I'm happy that you and Doc are doing things together." Annie chuckled as she added, "And besides, I'm going for dinner tonight at Eric's. He called this morning."

"Oh?" Mom's turn to be surprised.

"We've gotten close and I've missed seeing him. Tonight will be a nice chance to catch up. I can't wait to tell him about the check. He's been such a big help getting that all straightened out." She didn't add about the attraction she felt for Eric, especially since she was still figuring out how to handle it.

By mid-afternoon, she finished her revisions. Though ready to send the article into the magazine, she felt apprehensive after all these months. Annie decided to call the magazine editor that she'd worked with closely before Mike's death.

She took a deep breath and dialed the number. Her heart pounded.

"Hello, Penelope. This is Annie Gee calling."

The editor's voice came across the phone line. "Hi, Annie. How are you? I've been thinking of you."

"Thank you for asking Penelope. I'm okay. Some days are better than others but I'm starting to rebuild my life. In that light, I've finished an article I thought you might be interested in. I'd like to send it in."

"I'd love to see it. In fact, I've just come from an editorial meeting and I have a new project. I'd love to have you look at it because you might be able to help me put together this new column. Send in what you've written and I'll get back to you in a week or two. I'm still developing the project ideas. How does that sound?" Penelope talked fast and Annie worked to contain her excitement and listen to the details. She had a foot in the door and a new opportunity.

Annie's heart hammered as she put down the phone. What a huge step for her—getting back into the swing of things professionally. Her writing block ended and her muse was energized and excited.

She ran upstairs to her office area and pulled out the black binder. Her novel. She'd been thinking about it again. The characters had been making noise in her head, and the plot just kept twisting and turning. She got sucked into the manuscript though she only meant to see where she'd left it before Mike died.

***

"Annie, I'm heading out. Didn't you say you were going to Eric's?"

"Yeah. I'm going to stop in a minute and get ready. Have fun." Annie looked up at her mother standing in the doorway.

"What are you working on so intently?"

"Oh, reworking an old piece."

"I don't know what time I'll be home tonight, but if you're later than me, remember to shut off the outside light."

"Okay—bye Mom." Annie continued typing, the black binder open on the table. She was so totally engrossed, she didn't hear her mother go out and close the door, nor did she hear the phone ring an hour later.

The story all came back to her and the words flowed from her mind onto the computer screen. Her fingers flew across the keys, as scene after scene poured from her liberated muse.

A rhythmic banging momentarily caused her to surface. She ignored it, glancing at the red digits on the clock...eight-thirty-four... she could work for another couple of hours before her mother returned. The pounding continued, interrupting her train of thought. What was that?

She stood and stretched her stiff muscles, opened her bedroom door and ran downstairs to discover the source of the noise. The front door burst open, Eric glancing around and then up at her, a look of desperation on his face.

"Are you all right?" His brow furrowed, his tone loud.

"I'm fine... oh my God, Eric, I totally forgot... I... I got involved in something. I'm sorry." Annie sat down halfway up the stairs, embarrassed at her own oblivion to the date she'd made with him.

"You forgot?" His tone incredulous, his scowl deepened.

"Eric, I didn't mean it like that. I got involved in something and lost track of the time." She moved down the stairs and put her hand out to touch his arm.

He moved away, turning his back on her as he moved to the living room. He spun around.

155

"Do you know how worried I was? I waited until seven figuring… I don't know what… trying not to worry. I tried calling here and there was no answer." He swiped his hand through his hair in frustration.

"I was afraid you'd been in an accident. I checked down at the shore… I drove around looking for you, and saw your mother's car at Doc's. I went tearing in there like a maniac thinking something happened and interrupted what looked like an intimate dinner for two. Your mom said to check here. I've been banging on the door. What were you doing?" He paced the floor in the living room.

He may as well have punched her in the stomach. She nearly doubled over with the need to throw up. How could she have done this to him? She fought to control the tears pricking at the back of her eyes.

Again she approached him, hesitant to touch, but needing the connection.

"Eric I'm so sorry. I didn't mean to worry you. I've had a huge breakthrough with my writing and I got involved. Mom spoke to me before she left and I was just going to do a little more. I got totally absorbed and lost track of everything. Eric?"

As she reached to touch his arm, he scooped her into his arms, holding her tight. She could feel the tension in his body as she wrapped her arms around him. His breath warmed her hair as he leaned his forehead against her.

"Oh, Annie."

She stood quietly in his embrace, guilty that she forgot their dinner, yet exhilarated because of the turnaround in her life. She wanted to share her excitement, tell him about the check in the mail, the call to the editor, even the resurrection of her novel. But she'd blown it. She'd strained whatever had begun between them by her lack of consideration tonight.

"I've ruined things, haven't I?"

"Well, dinner's ruined. I think my heart rate may someday return to normal. I'm sorry if I over-reacted. I was frantically out of control."

"I'm so sorry. Maybe we should call it a night, and try

again another time. I want to make it up to you." Annie moved out of his arms.

"Yeah. Maybe we should." He looked down at the floor as he stuffed his hands in his pockets.

"You okay?"

"Yeah. You?" He looked into her eyes.

"Yeah." What a jerk she was. How could she have done this?

"I'll call you tomorrow." He gave her a quick kiss on the cheek and left.

She went upstairs and cried herself to exhaustion.

***

No phone call the next day... or for days after that. She tried calling him both at home and at the office but there was no answer at either place, any of the times she called. Communication blackout. I really screwed up. That total absorption thing used to get me in trouble with Mike too. Better work on that. But the big question is: how can we get back to where we were before I screwed it up?

***

Eric paced the hospital waiting room anxious to hear the results of his father's tests. He'd gotten a call from his father about a problem with his blood work at his annual physical. The PSA had been very high. More tests. Eric caught the next ferry. He didn't want his father going through any of this alone.

Prostate cancer... cancer again. His mother, Cara, now his father. Memories tumbled in his head, remembering his mother's slow loss of energy, always feeling tired. Then the excruciating pain, lack of appetite, and weight loss—slowly wasting away. The same with Cara, though hers had been very aggressive, very quick. Now his father. God, please let this be okay... let it be a false alarm. I can't lose him to cancer too.

John's physician came through the door and signaled to Eric.

"Your dad asked me to get you before we talk about the results of his tests." The doctor strode quickly down the hallway, Eric hurrying to keep up. His father waited in an

157

examining room for the doctor. The three men sat together, Dr. Robert Knowles explained the findings. Prostate cancer with surgery recommended immediately. With surgery, the success rate for beating this cancer was high. There were other options for treatment but the results were less definitive.

John was adamant. He wanted it done quickly. Get the cancer out of his body. Eric knew why his father reacted this way. Cancer impacted these two men too deeply. There would be no messing around with alternative options. Get it out.

Eric listened as his father made arrangements for surgery scheduled late tomorrow. The voices took on a far-away muted tone as Eric's mind took him back to other doctor's visits. Cara. He struggled to get a full breath; his heartbeat thrummed in his ears, and his vision darkened around the outer edges of his vision. I'm going to pass out if I don't get out of here quickly. Before he could move toward the door, darkness covered him and he floated into the void.

***

A week and a half since she'd forgotten their dinner. No Eric. No sign of him at the restaurant, his house. His car was gone, everything locked up tight. And no word from him.

She sent in her article, worked like a maniac on her novel, not eating or sleeping while the ideas poured from her mind onto paper. Her mother nagged at her periodically to eat, which she did to keep her quiet. But she missed Eric. She worried, but had no idea where he was or how to reach him. Sometimes, she just lay on her bed and cried. What had she done to her best friend?

Her mother knocked on her bedroom door at nearly eleven that night, then opened the door and peeked in.

"I thought you were still awake. I have some news you might be interested in." She'd just come from Doc's.

Annie knew immediately. "Did Doc hear from Eric? Where is he? Is he all right? Mom?"

"Eric called him tonight while I was there. Apparently, his father's had surgery to remove a cancerous tumor, and Eric is there with him. His father's back at his own house now, but

Eric's going to stay with him a little longer to help him while he's recuperating. He asked Doc to check on his house because he left in such a hurry."

"Oh Mom, poor Eric." Annie flopped on her bed.

"I'm surprised he didn't call you."

"Does Doc have his father's number? I'd like to call him. We had a misunderstanding, and I've been trying to get him on the phone for over a week. Can you get his phone number?"

"I'll call Doc and get it for you but it's probably too late to call Eric now. You look tired. Are you going to bed now?"

"I'm going to try. I haven't been sleeping well." Annie yawned and bounced back, lying on top of the covers.

"All right honey. Good night."

***

She called him the next evening. She got the impression he couldn't talk, or didn't want to. She apologized again for missing their dinner. He seemed distant, quiet, worried. Not her normal, upbeat Eric. Though she told him to call if he needed her, she didn't think he would.

Again that night, she cried herself to sleep, dreaming of Eric, her writing, Mike. A confusing jumble, she woke at three o'clock in the morning more tired than when she went to bed. But she couldn't go back to sleep. She got up and sat at her laptop, willing herself back into her story.

She heard her mother get up at seven and make the coffee. She heard the door slam at eight-thirty as her mom left for work. And then she heard nothing more, except the words in her head, tip-tapping onto the computer as fast as her fingers could fly. Finally, fatigue overcame her and she shut the computer down, lay on her bed and slept.

She floated in a warmly lit space, mist blocking her vision. Safe, quiet, calm… security. This place felt right. The mist parted, Mike appeared.

Joy filled her heart… he looked wonderful, handsome as ever, happy. Annie raised her arms to embrace him, but he raised a hand stopping her.

"I'm all right, Annie. You need to move on. Listen to your heart. Keep setting goals and get what you want. Go after it, Annie."

Annie awoke. The dream left her feeling safe and secure yet puzzled by Mike's message. What was she supposed to go after? Eric filled her thoughts. She worried about him. She wanted more details about his father's prognosis. Eric didn't need more hard times.

She missed him. She wanted to see him and tell him about the insurance check. Maybe he would have some ideas about how to best handle her finances, especially now that she actually had some. It certainly opened possibilities for her. She could pay off the house, or she could continue renting it, and let the income pay for the mortgage...she could...the possibilities were overwhelming but exciting too. But mostly, she wanted to make certain he was okay.

She heard her mother come in from work. Annie went downstairs to find Sara looking at a brochure. She peeked over her mother's shoulder and saw a couple in an elegant room in a hot tub.

"Whoa, that looks like fun." Annie rubbed her mother's shoulders, as Sara snapped the brochure closed and turned toward Annie.

"I hope so. I'm going there—Hare Hill Inn—this weekend." The blush on Sara's face was cute.

"Goin' by yourself?" She couldn't help teasing her mother.

"No, Doc and I are going together. His Christmas gift to me." She took a deep breath like she prepared for a battle.

"I'm teasing you Mom. I think it's great. But, um...do we have to have the birth control talk?" She giggled at her mother's deepening blush. That answered the unasked question.

"No, I think I'm past that stage, thank you." She sounded composed, but Annie knew she was rattled. She gave her mother a hug.

"I'm sorry. I'm teasing you. I'm really happy for you. Doc seems like a great guy." She kissed her on the cheek.

"It can happen twice in a lifetime, Annie. Take note." Sara hugged her back and swatted her behind. "And stop teasing your old mother, you brat!"

Laughing, they both went into the kitchen to fix dinner.

***

How dumb could he be? He should have stayed one more day with his father. Then he would have gotten through the anniversary away from their house, away from the memories. Eric was afraid his father would wear himself out trying to prove his fitness. Eric planned to call him every night, and he'd arranged for visiting nurses to help him during the day. What a scare.

And now he was home... by himself... on the anniversary of Cara's death... remembering her in his arms that last day. God, how will I get through this?

He laid his head on the back of the couch and closed his eyes. Annie's face floated through his mind. He should call her. He'd meant to call from his father's but had gotten wrapped up in caring for him.

He needed her. He needed her warmth and friendliness. Hell, who was he kidding? He needed her warmth all right, her warm curves against his. Her quiet understanding and her understated sensuality. He needed her, and he wanted her. Would she come to him? Or had he sabotaged the relationship by not calling.

Well...he couldn't feel any worse. He might as well call and see how bad the damage was.

He picked up the phone and held his breath.

Chapter 18
The Deep, Dark Sea

Eric dialed her number and remembered to breath. What should he say to her? He should have called. He should have talked more when she called Dad's house. She'd tried to talk to him, and get him to talk to her. He'd been too worried about his father. Okay, here goes.

His misery couldn't get any deeper as he listened to the phone ring and ring. Just as he had decided his misery could, in fact, get worse—by her not answering the phone—she picked it up.

"Hello?" She sounded out of breath.

"Hi, Annie? It's Eric." He fidgeted with the stack of mail on the table. "I'm sorry I didn't call sooner. Things have been hectic at Dad's. It's been a rough couple of weeks." He blurted out his excuse. "You sound breathless. Did I catch you at a bad time?"

"No, Eric, I've been so worried about you. When I didn't hear from you, I thought you were mad and didn't want to speak to me." Guilt speared through him at her worry. "Then Doc told Mom about your father, and I worried about both of you. Are you still at your dad's?"

Eric looked around his living room, ghosts filling every corner. Cara peeking in through the windows as they washed them together, Cara fixing flowers for the table. Cara, Cara, Cara. A wave of despair swamped him, his stomach seasick, his head spinning. He tried to breathe, to calm down. He closed his eyes to the ghosts surrounding him but they spun through his head too. Focus. What did she say? I just need her here.

"Annie, I need you to come over tonight…can you?"

"Eric? Are you at your house? Are you sick? What's wrong?"

He could hear the concern in her voice, but he couldn't make himself reassure her. He wasn't okay. He needed her help, her warmth, her sanity. Please come.

"I'm home, Annie. It's a tough night. I need some company, okay?"

"I'll be right over."

The vise around his chest loosened. Air finally filled his lungs. Already she'd helped. "Thanks Annie," and he hung up the phone.

***

Dear God, he sounded awful. More bad news about his father? She'd never heard him so down before. She threw off her old comfortable sweat suit and slipped into a pair of jeans and a fresh turtleneck. She'd been writing when the phone rang. She splashed cold water on her face and ran a brush through her hair, pulling it back in a ponytail.

Within minutes her car zipped toward Eric's house. The night air frigid, her breath steamed the inside of the windshield. Her thoughts raced as she drove the two miles along the shore to Eric's. Why did he sound so miserable? Were there further complications with his dad?

She knocked on the door and heard him call to come in. He sat on the couch in the darkened living room, his head back, eyes closed. He opened them when she came into the room. Sad eyes, tired eyes, looking-for-comfort eyes. Annie threw her jacket on the high-back chair by the living room door and sat next to him on the couch, her hand reaching to touch his hair.

"I'm here, Eric. What's going on?" She stroked her fingers through his hair. His head lolled back on the couch, he again closed his eyes. Dark circles beneath highlighted the red rims.

"I've been so worried about Dad. The prostate cancer and then surgery. He's recovering well, has a great attitude about the whole thing. It's me. I'm the mess."

She reached for his hand. "It's hard, physically and emotionally, to be the caretaker."

"I can't lose him to cancer too. Mom died when I was a teenager, Cara died in my arms, and now, Dad...." His eyes shone with tears and he looked away. "I keep losing the people I love," he whispered, barely speaking the words at all, as though to say them would make them come true.

"Oh, Eric." She sat with her legs under her, circled him with her arms, pulling his head to her shoulder. His breathing hitched, a sob escaping. She rubbed his back, saying nothing, offering quiet solace in her arms. His tense muscles began to relax under her massaging fingers. Her quiet caressing calmed his breathing.

"Tell me about your dad. I know he's had surgery, but what did the doctors say about his prognosis?" Annie continued to hold him until he pulled back to look her in the eyes.

"They got all of it. They think he's going to be fine. They'll monitor him for a while. He's gaining energy every day and insisting that he's okay. I'm the basket case."

"Eric, it's normal to be worried and concerned. But you've handled it. You were there for him, and you helped him get through it. You're a good son."

He shook his head. His eyes held a pained distant look. There had to be more.

"What, Eric? Tell me."

"I should have stayed there until tomorrow. Then I wouldn't be here to face the memories." He gazed around the room as though he watched a scene from another time. "It's the anniversary of her death, Annie." Tears escaped this time, though he seemed oblivious as they rolled down his cheeks.

"Oh, Eric." Annie pulled him close to her, holding him while he let go of the last two weeks' worth of upset and turmoil. She felt the prick of tears that understanding brought, tears for this strong man's sorrow and fear. How could she comfort him? How could she help take away his pain?

She spoke quietly hoping for the right words. "You know, I never met Cara but I know from the way you've talked about her that she was an energetic woman, full of life and love. I think she would be optimistic for your father with that report from the doctors."

Eric nodded, trying to take a deep breath.

"And I think she wouldn't want you to be sad by remembering the day she died. She'd want you to remember all the days she lived and loved instead."

"You're right. She not only wouldn't want me to be sad; she'd be angry with me. It's just with everything else happening..."

"I understand. It feels as though everything is coming down around your head." She smiled ruefully at him. "You've helped me through some of those times. I'm living proof that it gets better."

"I know." Eric took a cleansing breath, and shifted his arm around her shoulders. She leaned against him.

"You're living proof, huh? How's that?" As she looked up at him, she saw the twinkle return to his eyes, though fatigue was there too.

"Things turned around for me, Eric, like you said they would. I've submitted an article to an editor I've worked with before. She sounded happy to hear from me again, and when we talked, she asked for some help with a project she is working on for the magazine. That's a huge foot in the door."

"Annie, that's great." He squeezed her shoulder pulling her closer to him.

"I'm writing again. For so long, I'd been unable to sit and produce anything. My mind wandered and I didn't get anything done. It feels so good to finally get through the block."

She paused, wondering if she should share her secret. "I've never told anyone this." Annie looked up into Eric's eyes. She'd piqued his interest but should she finish her thought? "I'm writing a novel. It's something I've always wanted to do. I started it about ten months ago—before Mike died. I've finally been able to work on it again."

She waited for his reaction. It took a huge leap to trust him with that. Her stomach fluttered. She hadn't even told Mike or her mother when she'd started it. Old childhood wounds from her father's careless comments about her cute little stories kept her from sharing her dream with anyone. But she told Eric.

Because he'd shown his vulnerabilities too?

"Annie. Wow! A novel?" Eric's whole demeanor changed. "I can't imagine the amount of work that is."

She breathed a sigh of joyful relief. She could trust him with her secret.

"I have some other good news." Should she be sharing all of her positives? Wasn't this like rubbing it in?

"Well, come on. Let's hear it. I need to hear that good things happen to good people."

Had he read her mind? His smile totally relaxed his face. He looked more like himself, her Eric.

"The insurance check came in two weeks ago. It's kind of weird. It doesn't bring Mike back, it doesn't replace him. On the other hand, he wouldn't want me to have to worry about finances on top of dealing with his death. I've put it in the bank for now. Maybe you could give me some ideas about managing it well. Would you mind?"

"No, not at all. I'm really happy for you, Annie. Things are looking up for you, both professionally and financially." He leaned over and kissed her forehead.

She lifted her chin so she could look into his eyes. Her lips lingered near his for only a moment. In that instant, she knew he wanted and needed her, as much as she wanted and needed him. His hand gently caressed her cheek as his mouth descended on hers with a passion that washed through her like a wave surge.

Tender, yet aggressive, passionate yet gentle. An interesting mix of good guy and hunk. She couldn't think to analyze it; she could only lose herself in his kisses, his touches, the heat of his muscular body.

The desire he created devastated her. And yet, she craved more.

He pulled her to him. His arms held her close while his hands moved over her, leaving heated paths where they traveled. His lean, hard body against hers reminded Annie of the physicality absent in her life of late. She let herself go; lost the thoughts of halting the onslaught of passion between them.

She could trust him with everything. She spiraled into the vortex of sensation; his touches excited her, his wandering lips blazed a path of heat. His body arched as she ran her fingers along the length of his back, a groan and quick intake of breath coming from his busy lips.

"Good Lord, do you know what you're doing to me?" Eric shifted his body to stand and pulled her up off the couch.

"Annie, I don't know if this is right or wrong for us, but I've been thinking about you, about making love with you, ever since you woke up in my arms two months ago. I want you Annie." He lowered his lips to hers, kissing her tenderly.

She lost herself in the feel of his strong arms around her, languished in the heat he had created pulsing within her. How could she deny him? She wanted him.

"I feel it too, Eric."

"We're still among the living Annie. Stay with me tonight?" She stood within his arms and nodded though her heart thundered, moving with him across the foyer to the guest bedroom.

His hand slid under her turtleneck as his lips devoured hers. She didn't know how they got to the double bed, only that they lay entwined with each other. His hands warm and wandering on her skin, sensitized wherever they roamed. His body just as warm, she slid her hands over his back.

She unbuttoned the first two buttons on his shirt. He stopped her by whipping it up over his head. She moved to do the same with her turtleneck; his hands helped her. She lay back on the pillow, watching him look at her.

Heat filled her as his fingers gently moved the strap of her bra down her shoulder. His lips pushed the white lace fabric away and he caught her breast in his mouth. Shards of electric shock rocketed through her. Her hands stroked his broad bare back. He arched against her as her fingers stroked along the side of his spine.

He moaned, "You've found the spot that drives me wild."

"Really?" She tested to be sure.

He arched again, his lips diving to suckle her, his hands

exploring, pulling her against his hard arousal.

"We've got way too many clothes on here." His fingers fumbled to unfasten the button of her jeans. She reached and undid it quickly, sliding her pants and panties off with one efficient movement. His were off almost as fast.

Naked, skin to skin, heat to heat, entwined legs pulling to further entwine. His mouth devoured her. He shifted to roll on top of her. She pulled him to her, arching her body, willing him to be inside her. And he was. Inside her—where the rhythm of their two bodies became one. Inside her—where sparklers flurried and fireworks exploded. Inside her—where he filled her heart with love.

They lay together as one, floating back from the ecstasy of their lovemaking. She shivered from the chill in the room against the warmth of their heat so he pulled the bedspread over their damp bodies. He slid next to her, feathering sweet kisses over her closed eyes, holding her close.

***

Excitement filled the air. Sara and Doc finally turned onto the northbound highway destined for their weekend getaway. Months had passed since her last trip. Worried about Annie after Mike's death, she cancelled the fall foliage excursion with a travel group. And now, here she sat, listening to the Moody Blues as Doc sang along, driving through the snow-covered hills of Vermont. It was a different journey, and more wonder-filled because of her travel companion.

They took advantage of the quiet couple time on the drive, in short supply for them lately. She valued their time together, though they both complained—too quickly gone and not enough of it. She thought about him all the time...she wanted to be with him all the time. Did he feel the same way? They hadn't discussed the relationship's direction. She worked to curb her concerns. Waiting things out was not her strong suit. But she knew she had to wait for Doc to feel comfortable talking about whatever it was that held him back.

She watched him as he drove and sang. His lack of inhibition was endearing and she smiled as he belted out the

168

chorus along with the boys in the band. His face relaxed despite their long drive. He glanced over as she watched him, winked, and reached for her hand.

"You're smiling. Are you happy, m'dear?" He looked at her again.

"You look so relaxed, and I'm very happy to be getting away for a weekend with you." She leaned over and gave him a peck on the cheek.

He let go of her hand to run his over her leg. "Mrs. Burdick, don't start anything with me in the car. I have to concentrate on driving, and you're making it very hard kissing me like that." His hand slipped higher on her thigh.

She grabbed his wandering hand and laughed. "You better get us there quickly."

"I think this is the exit. Read the directions on that sheet of paper for me please."

She went line by line for the last several miles of turns onto smaller roads until they turned into the parking lot of the quaint B&B covered with a foot of powdery new snow.

A rambling white building, with several sections added on over the years, overlooked the valley below them.

She got out of the car and stretched her travel-weary limbs. It had taken the better part of the day to arrive at their destination. Doc came around the car and wrapped her in his warm embrace. They stood together, absorbing the serenity of the winter scene—the pristine whiteness of the fresh snow, the quiet of the country, and the cold, crisp clean air.

They unloaded their bags and walked the shoveled path to the front entrance. A slim woman with dark hair greeted them at the door and led them to the desk to check in.

"Ben and Sara, it's nice to meet you. I hope you have a wonderful relaxing stay here at the Hare Hill Inn. Anything I can do to make you comfortable, please let me know. My name is Laurie. My husband, Peter and I own the inn. Let me show you to your room, and tell you about dinner." She led them through several common rooms, the first with a fire burning in the fireplace. Wingback chairs, antique side tables, and several colonial settees provided quiet reading spots or conversation areas. A couple at a small table working on a puzzle, looked up and smiled at them as they walked through.

They continued a short distance down the hall that led away from the main building. Each room had a name. Some of the doors were open. As they passed by, Sara peeked in.

"We leave the doors open to rooms that are not occupied for the night so our guests can enjoy the various settings we've put together in each room. The inn is filled with antiques and fun little details. You're welcome to look around." Laurie smiled as she stopped in front of the door to the Cedar Glen. Doc brought their bags in and set them against the wall while Sara stood looking around.

"Oh my, I thought it looked beautiful in the brochure, but it's so much more luxurious in person." She turned, looking from the huge canopy bed dominating the room to the romantic glow of the gas fireplace to the whirlpool tub for two tucked in a corner of the room. The cedar log furniture in the sitting area contained sumptuous navy, green, and maroon plaid cushions, inviting you to curl up with a good book. The king-sized bed covered in the same plaid invited... well, just invited.

"You chose the seven-thirty sitting for dinner. The dining room is through the common area where you entered and to the right. At four-thirty everyday tea and pastries are served in the common rooms, and the lounge is open from lunchtime until eleven at night. Breakfast is in the dining room from six-thirty to nine-thirty every morning. Feel free to look around, enjoy a book from our shelves, or a puzzle or game in the common rooms." The petite brunette turned to leave. "We want you to enjoy your stay with us." She smiled and closed the door.

"This is nice... really nice." Doc seemed pleased with himself. She was impressed too.

"Where do we start? Do you want to unpack, or look around or maybe something a little more romantic?" He slipped his arm around her waist and pulled her close. She wrapped her arms around his neck and nibbled on its warm curve.

"What did you have in mind?"

"Well, why don't I go down to the lounge and get two glasses of wine, and you could see about that Jacuzzi in the corner...and we'll see what happens." He smiled as he nipped her lips, sending shivers of anticipation through her.

"Good plan. But you better get out the door soon or you may not make it at all." He laughed and scooted for the door with a goofy you-can't-catch-me look.

She loved the way they played with each other, a dimension of a relationship she hadn't experienced with her Johnny. He'd been a good man, a good husband, but they each had a role in their marriage. Sexual play hadn't been a part of it for either of them.

Sara turned the water jets on, slipped out of her clothes and into the large forest green tub. Warm soothing bubbles surrounded her and streams of water pulsed against her tired back muscles. She rested her head back, closing her eyes, focusing on the here and now. Doc, or Ben as she had started to think of him, would soon be back. Would he expect her to be in the hot tub already, waiting for him? Anticipation coursed through her, and the bubbles that moments earlier had soothed, now had a scintillating, stimulating effect. A smile touched her lips as she thought of ways to spend the next hour or so with Ben. Where was he anyway?

Half an hour later, Sara wrapped herself in the thick terry robe hanging in the closet. She swiped a pruney hand through her sweat-dampened hair. The reflection she saw in the large mirror over the cedar dresser did not exude relaxation. Concern creased her forehead as she looked at the digital clock on the bedside table. What had happened? She decided to get dressed and go looking for him in the lounge.

The wail of sirens in the distance caused anxiety to pool in her stomach. She quickly finished dressing and rushed out the door and down to the common rooms.

Sara saw Ben rhythmically pumping on the chest of the elderly man lying in the middle of the wide-planked wooden floor. Concentrating. She knelt down opposite Ben, made eye contact as he counted the compressions.

"I'll do the breathing; give me the count."

"Two... three... four..."

She breathed air into the pale man's mouth. Though she'd never joined the ambulance squad, she'd stayed certified in CPR. The crowd that gathered around ceased to exist; Sara focused on the rhythm Ben set for them.

The rescue squad entered the room with their equipment and a stretcher. Soon enough Sara handed off her part of the life-saving technique to a paramedic. Another replaced Ben. He turned to a third EMT and gave a report of what happened and what he'd done.

Finally, he turned searching for Sara. He looked exhausted. His eyes seemed distant and glazed over. He kept the wall up until he had time to process it. Professional but removed. She'd seen it before, in emergency situations at the doctor's office. She looked away and tried not to feel hurt, left out.

A woman stood back in the crowd, surrounded by others, sobbing, alone. She watched the man, now on the stretcher. Sara went to her.

"Are you with him?" Sara gently put her arm around the woman.

"We were here for our thirty-fifth wedding anniversary. His doctor told him to lose weight, change his diet. Will he be okay?" She looked hopefully into Sara's eyes.

"I don't know. The man that worked on him is a doctor, and the paramedics got here quickly. We'll all be saying prayers for both of you."

"Thank you." The woman squeezed Sara's hand before turning to follow the stretcher to the waiting ambulance.

Ben found Sara as the crowd dispersed. "I'm sorry Sara. The guy was choking on an olive when I came into the lounge. I did the Heimlich maneuver, but I think the scare caused him to go into cardiac arrest. He collapsed right here." He took her hands, seeming anxious to explain.

"It's okay, Ben. Don't apologize... you saved his life.

He's in good hands and on his way to the hospital." Sara looked at his pinched face. "Why don't you go get in that hot tub and I'll get the wine. I'll be right there."

"Okay." As he turned and walked toward their room, Sara knew he needed a little time to himself. He's in the medical profession, a healer, a lifesaver. You'd think he would get used to these situations. But it's shaken him. She'd seen determination in his eyes as she had looked across the patient at him. But she'd seen something else too. Fear? Panic?

She ordered the wine and waited as the young bartender filled the order. Maybe Ben would open up. Maybe he'd talk about what she'd seen in his eyes. She hoped she could be patient enough to lead the conversation there, letting him trust her enough to talk. Patience, Sara.

By the time she returned to their room, Ben had taken a shower and changed into clothes for dinner. Okay. Frolic in the hot tub is called off for now. Maybe later. Maybe talk instead. She smiled and handed him a wine glass.

"If it's okay with you, I thought we'd do the Jacuzzi thing a little later. I'm kinda wired right now and just want to relax with you." Ben looked for something from her but she wasn't sure what.

"Of course it's okay. This is going to be a relaxing weekend for both of us, despite how it started. Come on. Let's go sit on the sofa in front of the fire."

She took his wine glass and put them both on the table. She sat behind him, her hands gently massaging his tense shoulders and tight neck. Slowly, the tension drained. She shifted and guided him back to lie with his head in her lap. She continued the tender touches, circling his forehead with her fingers.

"Thank you for your help earlier."

"I'm glad I could help you. You feelin' a little better?" She looked down into his ocean blue-green eyes.

"Yeah. This is the part of doctorin' I'm not so good at... holding someone's life in my hands. What if I'm not good enough? Why should they suffer because of my inabilities?"

Ben sat up, suddenly tense again.

"Ben, you gave that man back his life because of your strength and knowledge…your abilities." Ben's statement astonished Sara. Was this part of what he held back, insecurity about his skill as a doctor? Where had this come from?

"Sometimes it's not enough. Then you wonder if you could do more. Maybe you should have done something differently. I almost gave it all up because of this. It's why I had to get out of the cities, away from the war areas." He took a long hard swallow from his wine glass, as though he wished for something stronger.

"Tell me about the places you've been. I feel like I've known you all my life, yet like I don't know you at all." Sara shifted to work on his shoulders again. Maybe if he relaxed he'd talk more.

"I spent years with the Red Cross overseas. I've worked in Africa and the Far East, India, Thailand. Famines, floods, disasters." He closed his eyes and let his head fall back.

"That must have been tough." Keep him talking.

"Assignments in war zones were the worst, seeing the devastation humans cause each other. A sick and ugly side of mankind. I got out." He shook his head as if the memories still haunted him.

"What did you do when you came back to the States?" She continued to work on his back and shoulders.

"I worked on the East Coast in cities near the ocean. I did ER shifts. Good money, brutal hours… almost as tough on the psyche as a war zone. It's a different kind of ugly in the cities: crime, gang wars, drive-by shootings…" The tension returned in his shoulders. He pulled away from Sara.

"Let's talk about something else. What do you want to do tomorrow?"

She'd felt like he got close to telling her something… about his time in the cities, not the war zones, before he shifted topics.

"I don't know. Maybe some cross country skiing or snowshoeing, a sleigh ride. Let's see what's available. I'm sure there's information at the desk. We can ask on our way to dinner." She smiled at him and caressed his cheek with her hand. "I'll get changed for dinner. Why don't you turn on some music and relax while I get beautiful." She kissed him on the lips and got up off the couch.

"You already are." He caught her hand pulling her back to him.

***

Her lips were his solace, pulling him out of his mood, away from the gravity of cheating death. He should feel wonderful to know he saved that man's life. But it reminded him sometimes you couldn't. You couldn't do enough, you don't know enough, you don't always win over death. He worked to block those thoughts.

Concentrate on her. Warm and soft and wonderful. His Sara. He pulled her soft curves into him, holding her tight, breathing in her scent, tasting the wine on her lips. He loved the way she responded to him. She never pulled back; she wanted him as much as he wanted her.

"Do you have to get ready this minute?" He knew his tone conveyed the message by the way she looked at him...sultry, suggestive, and simmering.

"I think I can spare a moment or two." And it only took that moment for them to pull the covers back on the huge bed. He completely lost himself in her.

Chapter 19
Smooth Sailin'

The delicious food, the superb wine, and the woman sharing his company: beautiful, witty, and sexy beyond belief. After a sumptuous dinner with dessert, and lovemaking in the Jacuzzi, he finally relaxed.

Vacation settled into his system. He lay next to Sara, stroking the smooth soft skin along her back, holding her close under the down comforter in the middle of their huge bed. Her breath feathered across his chest creating warmth more than skin   deep.

"I love the way you feel." He spread little kisses in her hair, silky against his cheek.

"Mmm. You too. And it's wonderful to lie next to you and know I can stay here all night." She smiled up at him. He had to kiss her again, her soft lips so inviting. Tenderly, slowly, gently he moved his lips over hers. Recently sated desires stirred once more.

She moved to snuggle deeper in his embrace, her lips near his ear. "I love you, Ben." Something struck him in the chest. He hadn't heard those words in a decade.

"I love you too."

It was true. And now it was out. He'd fought it; he'd denied it to himself. He wanted to be with this woman on a long-term basis... he wanted her in his life. Saying those four words freed his heart on one plane but... Oh, God. What would it cost him?

***

He'd said it. She hadn't pushed, in fact, she'd held back for months, so he wouldn't feel pressured. She'd actually been patient...until it just slipped out of her mouth. Three little

176

words—and they'd been returned to her. Her heart swelled, a smile crept onto her lips as she nibbled his neck. God, she loved this man.

Twined together, skin to skin, cozy in their down cocoon, they drifted to sleep in each other's arms with words of love held close to their hearts.

***

His heart pounded in his chest, sweat poured from his forehead as he hurried to get to her. He'd heard the crack... it reverberated endlessly in his mind. She lay twisted, unconscious, pale. Just like the last time...

"SARA... no..."

***

She woke to his scream. He sat up in bed, sweating, panting, eyes open but not focused, not seeing her.

"Ben? It's all right Ben, I'm here. What's wrong?" She stroked his back. He turned to look at her, disbelief in his eyes. He shook his head. After a moment, he focused and spoke.

"Sorry I woke you. I had a bad dream." He reached for her, touched her as if he wanted to be sure she was real.

"Are you okay?" She continued to rub his back. "Do you want a drink or something? We've got some cold water in the cooler still." She slipped out of bed and put on the thick terry robe she'd left on the chair earlier. Quickly she found the cooler packed for the ride and got a bottle of spring water. When she returned to the bed, his hand shook as he reached for the water.

Sliding in next to him, sans robe, she pulled him close to her, surrounding him with her arms.

"Do you want to tell me about it?" Massaging, soothing, quieting…she felt his muscles relax.

"Maybe in the light of day, but not now. I just want to hold you." He shifted to take her in his arms. They didn't speak of the dream, but he held her needfully.

Quiet together, the firelight softening the dark, she fell asleep.

***

He couldn't sleep. He lay awake for a long time wondering about his dream, his nightmare. As real as it had been in the past, the only difference, Sara lay in his arms, covered with blood.

His subconscious told him he'd gotten too involved. He'd said he loved her. The spoken words brought with them a certain commitment, at least in his mind. Was that the problem? Look what had happened last time. How would this ever end?

***

Eric felt the warmth of her body against him before he fully awoke. He lay with his eyes closed enjoying the soft curves and smooth skin under his hands. What had he done? Would she be okay with this latest development?

He'd wanted her since the night together on the mainland, and the want got stronger as they spent more time together. Taking it slow (if you could consider this slow) had hardly been easy. So many times he wanted to sweep her up and carry her away. But she had her own circumstances. Had this come too soon for her? He'd know soon enough.

She stirred against him. He sprinkled butterfly kisses in her hair, along her forehead, down to her lips. His hands began to roam, waking her gently.

"Mmm, mornin'." She looked cute trying to make her eyes open.

He smiled. Not a morning person. She struggled to focus on him.

"How ya doin'?" He continued to stroke her back, his hand tracing the sensuous curve of her hip and thigh. She smiled.

"I'm doing fine. The question is *what* are you doin'?" This time her eyes did focus on him.

"Just waking you up."

Her throaty chuckle further heated him. "I guess you are." She shifted, turning toward him, wrapping her arms around him, circling him with warmth, message clear. Definitely okay with last night, and apparently this morning too. All analytical thought ceased, as he turned his full attention to a proper wake-up call.

An hour later, the smell of bacon filled the air as Annie stepped out of the shower. She quickly toweled off and put on the clothes she'd worn to his house. Second thoughts about last night and this morning assailed her as she used Eric's brush to smooth out her freshly washed hair. Six months a widow...what was she doing? She'd never been promiscuous. In fact, Mike had been the only one...until now.

Until Eric. But she wanted him. She wasn't fooling herself about that. And she still wanted him. But was it true emotion or a result of her missing Mike? Was she being fair to Mike's memory? And now what was she going to do? Squaring her shoulders and taking a deep breath, she headed into the kitchen to see if she could help with breakfast, and sort out where they stood.

"Hi! What can I do to help? Smells delicious." She aimed for light and normal sounding, but it felt awkward as hell. She flashed a smile at Eric, hoping he wouldn't see the uncertainty in her eyes. Something in the look he fixed on her face told her he had.

"How about pouring some orange juice and taking care of the toast. I've got coffee brewing, and the bacon is just finished, so I'm ready to do the eggs. How many would you like?" He watched her face. She focused on keeping the smile steady.

"Just one. I'm not much of a breakfast eater and this looks like a feast." She found the glasses in the cupboard near the dishwasher and took out two, then went to the refrigerator to get the juice.

She worked at busying herself making the toast, setting the small dining room table, cleaning crumbs off the counters...anything to avoid looking at Eric. She felt him watching her, although he tried to be subtle about it. What the hell do you say the morning after? This was outside her realm of experience.

Fortunately, the eggs didn't take long to cook, and Eric

had to pay attention to them. He fixed the two plates and brought them to the table, while she fixed their coffees.

When she returned to the table with the two steaming mugs, Eric sat, his gaze down, as if getting ready to say something. Her stomach flopped, and her heart suddenly banged in her chest. She sat, and looked into his eyes. Oh, God. What have I done?

He reached and took her hand, before she could reach for her fork.

"Annie, thank you for coming over last night. I… was a mess and I needed a friend. No. I needed you. I didn't plan for things to happen the way they did. Are you okay?" His eyes steady on hers, filled with concern.

"I think so. I don't have any regrets, if that's what you're asking. I've just never… well, this is just a little awkward. I don't know what you're thinking. Hell, I don't know what I'm thinking." She watched his face for a reaction. He smiled and she let out the breath she'd been holding.

"New territory for me too." His thumb caressed the back of her hand, sending tingles up her arm. She closed her eyes, tried to concentrate on what she wanted, needed to say.

"I'm not sorry we made love. I feel that strongly about you. But I need to go slow. We need to keep talking about things." She opened her eyes to look at him again. He listened.

"I don't want to feel like we rushed into this. And I feel a little guilty. I know what we said last night about still being among the living. But I don't want to feel disloyal to Mike's memory. Know what I mean?" Her heart banged in her chest as she waited for his reaction.

He nodded.

"I've got to get myself back together again, before I can give myself to someone else. I've got to find the me that I am now."

"I know Annie. I'm still struggling with Cara's death too. The year anniversary was just too much to handle alone, especially with all the stuff going on with Dad. We'll take it one step at a time, okay?"

She nodded. He squeezed her hand.

"Let's eat before the eggs get cold." He smiled at her and seemed to relax. She took a breath and relaxed too.

***

After yet another wonderful meal, this one of gourmet pastries and coffeecakes, vegetable-stuffed omelets, and fresh fruits, Sara and Ben changed into warm layers and borrowed the snowshoes available to guests of the Hare Hill Inn. Laurie, the innkeeper, gave them a map of trails leading through the surrounding woods and fields. She also suggested they book a sleigh ride for part of the afternoon. Sara smiled at Ben.

"I've always wanted to do that. We'll be tired from snowshoeing. Let's book it, okay?" She nudged him.

"Sure. Could you set that up for us, Laurie?"

She phoned immediately, wrote down three-thirty on a slip of paper with the directions to Hilltop Farms on it and handed it to Ben.

"I think you'll love it."

Sara hugged him. "I think we will too!" He smiled at her and led her toward the door, the snowshoes slung over his shoulder. Once out the back entrance, they stopped to fasten the large shoes onto their winter boots. Sara adjusted her scarf and hat, grabbed her walking poles and jabbed them into the snow.

"Okay, I'm ready." She watched him finish adjusting his snow shoes.

"Me too. That's where the path starts. It looks like people have gone out ahead of us." He pointed to a groomed path leading away from the inn and into a grove of birch trees, their silvery white bark shimmering in the morning sun.

Sara always enjoyed walking through the woods on the island. This first time on snowshoes seemed like hiking, except it took a bit to get used to the wide shoes. She picked it up with no trouble. Within minutes, she worked up a sweat, and stopped to take her scarf off and stick it in her pocket. Ben followed her and stopped too.

181

"This is beautiful Ben, isn't it?" She took a tissue and wiped her nose.

"So peaceful, untouched." He looked around, then back at her. He's in a quiet mood today, Sara thought. She smiled at him.

"It's not as quiet as I imagined though. The snowshoes crunching through the snow make it loud enough that it's hard to talk without yelling." She put her gloves back on, ready to move on.

"It's nice think time though, here in nature's beauty." She looked at him before she started hiking again. *What is going on, Ben? You've been quiet all morning. And it's not a relaxed quiet.* Tense. But she couldn't ask—at least not here, not yet. Patience. Practice patience.

The mid-morning sun glistened on the ice and snow covering the pine branches, the sounds of birds and crunching snow filled her ears. The crisp cold air nipped at her nose, but the exercise kept her heated. It was a glorious winter day, and she relaxed as she walked. Ben could have his quiet think time, she'd enjoy the outdoors.

They trudged along, setting up a cadence with the snowshoes and walking poles. It was well past noon when they arrived back at the inn. Saturated with sweat from their two mile trek, Sara happily peeled off the drenched layers and slipped into the hot tub that bubbled and waited for them.

Ben joined her in the Jacuzzi with an audible groan of delight. "This is heaven." He laid his head back and closed his eyes. Even in his relaxed state, a furrow line creased his forehead.

"Ben? Is there something bothering you?" She reached up out of the water to smooth the worry line from his forehead, moving her body against his underwater.

"Just a few things, but I'm working my way through it. That hike today helped. It gave me time to clear my head of all the mundane stuff, and focus on the important." He reached his arm under her and pulled her closer to him. His eyes stayed closed but a smile touched his lips.

"And what's that?" Her lips skimmed his wet shoulder, her hand stopped rubbing his forehead and her fingers threaded through his hair.

"You... us... being together." He lowered his lips and gently caressed hers.

"Are you worried about that?" Her heart hammered in fear of the answer. What if he was afraid of a commitment?

"I've been thinking about where our relationship is going. It's serious, Sara. I'm in love with you." Her heart continued to hammer, now with joy.

"It would only be something to worry about if I didn't return your feelings. But I do. I've been afraid to tell you. I wasn't sure how you felt." She kissed him.

"Oh you can be sure. I care about you very much." His mouth descended on hers as he maneuvered her out of her seat, floating through the water to straddle him. Her heart kept up the clamor, blood pulsing in her ears nearly drowning out her moan of ecstasy as they flowed together as one. The water jets pulsed against them in their own water dance, air bubbles sensitizing her skin already excited by her lover's touch. She swam to the edge of ecstasy, floated into the abyss as waves pulsed through her, filling her with joy. She slowly drifted back, Ben's hands held her gently as he too found total release.

A low chuckle rumbled in his chest. He nibbled her neck. "I'm thinking maybe we should have a hot tub put in at home."

Sara chuckled too. "Not a bad idea, Ben."

***

They decided to have the kitchen pack them a light lunch of cheese and crackers and fruit to take with them on the drive to the farm for the sleigh ride. Sara read the directions to Hilltop Farm and Ben navigated along the winding roads plowed barely two cars wide.

Majestic views surrounded them. They pulled into a long dirt driveway and as they crested the hill, it became obvious how the farm had gotten its name. A rambling white farmhouse sat near the road, overlooking large white expanses of snow-covered fields, sloping down a hill toward the tree line. An evergreen forest and fields beyond sloped down to a river. Ben slowed the car to appreciate the breathtaking view. An older gentleman dressed in insulated overalls and layers of flannel and thermal underwear came out of the nearby barn as they pulled to a stop in the driveway.

"Howdy. Name's Jacob Mann. You here from Hare Hill?" He walked to the car with a gait slowed by arthritis and years of farming and cold weather.

"Yes, Laurie called this morning for us. I'm Ben Stephenson and this is Sara. It's nice to meet you." He reached and shook the man's hand. "This is a beautiful place you have here." He looked toward the fields and the view.

A black lab charged out of the barn barking and running circles around Jacob. He chuckled.

"You're some watchdog there, Toby. Come over here and sit down." He slapped his leg and Toby immediately sat by his master's leg watching Ben and Sara. "The sleigh is all hooked up and ready to go. Follow me and we can be on our way. Come on Toby." The old man turned and walked to the far side of the barn. Sara grabbed a blanket from the backseat and followed Ben and Jacob. Two large chestnut workhorses stood together harnessed to the front of a black sleigh. Bells jingled as one shook its mane, delighting Sara. Better than she'd imagined, and they hadn't even gotten into the sleigh yet.

Jacob settled them in the back seat, covering them with extra blankets, and Sara snuggled up to Ben. The sleigh wobbled as Jacob stepped into the driver's seat.

"This is Matilda and Jezabelle. They're Belgian workhorses. Matilda is ten years old, Jez is only six so she's paired with Matilda to learn from her. They work well together," he explained as he put on his heavy work jacket, hat and gloves.

He giddy-upped to the horses and tapped the reins on their broad backs. The bells jingled and Toby raced in front of Matilda and Jezabelle. The sleigh glided smoothly over the snow around the outside of the field.

The clean cold air, Ben's warm body next to her, the

pristine field unspoiled by footprints, and the spectacular views of mountains in the distance filled Sara's senses. Words escaped her, but she looked and smelled and felt, determined to store this moment in her memory to visit often in her mind. Ben smiled as she looked at him. The earlier furrow lines had disappeared. His face held a healthy glow, his eyes sparkled in the sunlight, and his arm wrapped her securely. Love filled her. Life was good.

***

Eric stretched back in his chair after finishing breakfast. He'd love to spend the day with Annie but how to suggest that? She'd warned him about taking it slow. Ah hell, just jump in and ask.

"Do you have any plans for today?" He tried for nonchalance, watching for a reaction.

"Not anything set in stone. I'm almost finished with my book, and I want to have it done by the end of the weekend. What are your plans for the day?" Annie finished the last bite of toast and pushed her plate away.

She smiled at him, waiting for an answer, but he couldn't choke out the words. She took his breath away. Her face glowed, cheeks blushed, and her eyes sparkled at him. She was beautiful, alive; they'd just made love and he couldn't get enough of her. He took a deep breath to calm his overactive libido. It didn't work but he could at least speak.

"I picked up some paint for the lunchroom at the restaurant. It needs freshening up. I thought I'd start it today. Wanna help?" He picked up their plates and cleared them to the kitchen sink. Annie followed with the glasses and coffee cups.

"Sure. I can give you most of the day. I can work on my story tonight and tomorrow. It sounds like fun. I'll swing home, change and meet you there. How's that?" She turned to face him near the sink.

"Great. Thanks, Annie." He leaned over and kissed her because he had to touch her. We wanted to grab her and carry her back into the bedroom.

185

She lingered in the kiss. Was she feeling it too?

"Let me get going before our plans get changed and the painting gets forgotten." Her husky voice sent shivers down his spine hitting him in the groin... she was feeling it too.

A teasing, knowing smile. Then a quick kiss and she grabbed her coat from the chair near the door, where she'd left it last night.

"See you in about half an hour."

"I'll be there." God, she made him feel so alive, so good. That was it... she made him feel alive again, feel love again. It hit him. Love. He watched her through the window over the sink. Her springy step, the sun shining off her blonde hair blowing in the winter breeze, her smile as she turned to get into her car. She spotted him through the window and waved as she started up her car. He watched her drive away. He missed her already.

***

Annie arrived at the restaurant ready to paint— her shapely bottom covered by a pair of worn out jeans, her hair pulled back in a ponytail, with wisps escaping to frame her face, and a large old sweatshirt hiding the treasures within. He couldn't stop looking at her. Maybe painting wasn't such a good idea, maybe they should've stayed in bed all day.

He gave himself a mental shake—chill out, settle down, take a deep breath. If he kept thinking like a randy teenager, he'd scare her away. He watched as she stood with her hands on her hips looking around the room at the project ahead. Does she know how beautiful she is? Cut it out, big boy. Get to work.

"I moved all the furniture away from the walls and threw those old sheets over the stuff closest to that wall. I figured we could start there and work around this way." He pointed to the wall nearest his office and motioned clockwise around the room.

Annie nodded. "Looks like you've got everything set up and ready to go... hand over a roller and let's get started." Annie's smile struck him in the gut. He handed her the paint roller and stripped off his flannel shirt down to just an old t-shirt.

She filled the roller with paint and started spreading it on the wall. "Aren't you going to be cold?"

"No I'm feeling pretty warm already." Isn't that an understatement, Nordsen.

She raised her eyebrows at him as though he was crazy. Shaking her head, she went back to rolling paint on the wall. Did she really have no clue what she did to him?

Eric climbed the small stepladder to work on the top edge. The muted yellow matched what was already in the lunchroom, but the fresh coat of paint brightened the walls and made the room look fresh and clean.

***

Annie watched him out of the corner of her eye as he stood on the ladder stretching to edge the top of the wall with a brush. She wanted to touch his long body, his broad muscular back. Flashes from this morning's encounter popped into her mind as she tried to concentrate on rolling the paint on the wall. He'd taken off that ugly old flannel shirt to show off his body… was he purposely tormenting her? She smiled to herself. Two could play that game.

"Phew, you're right—it's getting hot in here." Annie put the roller down in the tray and moved toward the picture window with the sun streaming through. She crossed her arms and lifted the bottom hem of her sweatshirt up over her head slowly. Her t-shirt rode up exposing her bare back. She thought she heard a noise… a groan from the ladder, but when she turned around Eric faced the wall, painting.

"So… tell me about this book you're writing. I know you said this morning you're almost finished. What's it about?"

His interest surprised but pleased her too. She hadn't shared her book with anyone else, and she talked about it eagerly.

"It's an historical romantic intrigue set in Colonial Boston."

Eric turned and looked at her.

187

"Really? Historical? I didn't know you were interested in history."

"I was never really good at dates and memorizing stuff, but when I went to college, I took the mandatory World Civ class. Fortunately for me, a new young professor taught the class by starting each period in history with a first person experience of the period. It brought you right into their life and times. She talked about what their lives were like, not just the major political and military events of the period. It gave me a different way to think about history. I ended up taking several courses with her."

"I had a high school teacher that got me turned on to history. I like to read stories set in different historical periods. It must take a lot of research to write."

"I've got several really good books about the Colonial period in New England. I have an idea for another book in the same time period, in fact linked to one of the secondary characters in this book. That's why I'm pushing to get this one finished this weekend. I'm so close... and I'm anxious to start on the new one."

Excitement and anticipation filled her. The joy of sharing it with someone special lifted her. He might have temporarily side-tracked her with his question about her book but the sexual tension pooled in her belly pushed her on.

"Hmmm. I missed a spot over here." She slid in front of Eric leaning up from the ladder. She reached to roll the imaginary gap in the paint job, making sure her head and shoulders came into contact with his chest.

She definitely heard the groan this time. Almost a growl as a strong arm swept around her, turning her and pulling her close. She giggled as she put her arms around his neck. He stepped to the bottom of the ladder, throwing his paintbrush on the drop cloth and reached to do the same with her roller. He pulled her close, body to body.

"It took you long enough." She giggled again. He pulled his head up away from the neck he'd been nuzzling, to look into her eyes.

"You've been teasing me… taking off your sweatshirt… your arms are cold! You…" She pulled his mouth to hers before he could finish the sentence. Yes, she'd teased him. She wanted his arms around her again. This morning hadn't been enough… and it occurred to her that going slower as she'd said this morning, probably wasn't possible. She'd fallen hard for this guy, and she was ready to throw up her arms in surrender.

His hot, hungry lips demanded hers. His warm hand slipped under her shirt and worked to release her bra. Nipples tingling in anticipation, she slid her hand along the smooth muscular ridge of his spine. Her fingers feathered outward across the expanse and down the side of his back. He pulled her tight against him, the moan deep in his throat absorbed by their lips pressing together. She loved that spot. She smiled knowingly to herself. But oh dear Lord, he'd found her spots too. She arched toward him because her body demanded it.

He pulled his lips away just long enough to whisper in a husky voice, "Come 'ere… let's go into my office where we can close the door." They couldn't move fast enough. Arms still twined, hands on bare skin, they moved as one into Eric's office. He kicked the door shut with his foot as his lips descended on hers again. His tongue explored, her hand stroked his back. He kissed along her jaw to her ear.

"Annie, I want you." He whispered as his tongue traced the outline of her lobe, sending shivers through her body.

"We just made love this morning, and I can't believe how much I want you again. Right now." She turned and nipped at his ear, then stopped to kiss it, running her fingers through his thick blond hair. "What are we going to do?"

"Well let's think outside the box here." He smiled down at her and brought his lips to hers. He nudged her gently back against his desk, sliding her bottom up on the front. He moved between her legs as she wrapped them around him, his arousal evident.

"Think this'll work?" he whispered as he shifted, rubbing against her, sending shock waves through her. She was ready for him, wanting him with an intensity that surprised her.

"We've got too many clothes on," she giggled as she remembered the line from last night.

A chuckle rumbled in his chest. "That's quite a problem for us. Let's see what we can do to solve it." He slid her off the desk, reached between them, unfastening the button and zipper of her jeans. He slipped his hand inside, groaning again as he met the wet warmth of her. He slid her jeans and panties off, all the way down her legs, his hands creating a tingle of anticipation on the journey.

Excitement raced through her, pulsing to her core. A moan escaped her lips as she felt him travel back up her legs with his lips. She leaned back onto the desk, pulling him with her.

"Eric, come here. Get inside me. You're drivin' me wild." His lips ravaged hers. She reached down and unfastened his jeans. He quickly freed himself to move against her, heat to heat, as she lifted and wrapped her legs around him. He surged into her, filling her, driving her pulsing warmth with his own rhythmic passion. Together they crested the wave of ecstasy, body surfing back to shore in each other's arms.

Annie giggled.

"What?" He smiled down into her eyes.

"I thought you said painting, not panting."

He laughed. "Oops. My mistake." She laughed too. He kissed her. A comfortable kiss, a possessive kiss, a kiss with a common future between them.

They separated and put themselves back together as they teased light-heartedly.

"So, okay, first panting, then painting? Think we should go back out there and see where we left off?" Annie smiled as she opened the door to the office. Eric pushed things back in order on his desk and turned to look at her, a twinkle of laughter in his eyes.

"I don't think I'm ever going to be able to work at this desk again without remembering…"

"…thinking outside the box?" Annie finished for him.

***

The rest of the day passed quickly as they returned to the lunchroom-painting project and finished the walls by mid-afternoon. They still had the curtains down and the tables covered with drop clothes, but Eric decided to put it all back together after the walls were dry. He'd come back tomorrow and clean up, rearranging the furniture then.

"I know I've taken up most of your day but I wondered if you'd like dinner tonight at my house. I'd love to fix something for us." Eric knew she wanted to write but he hoped to spend more time with her.

"I really wanted to get some writing done. I'm so close to finished..." He could see that she was torn. His heart hammered. There was hope.

"How's this for an idea?" He moved close to her taking her into his arms. "I'll make something that we can heat up whenever you're ready. You come over at whatever time you finish...even if it's really late. We'll have dinner when you get there, and maybe you could spend the night?" He kissed her then—a soft kiss, a familiar kiss, a kiss with the promise of more. He looked into her eyes, hoping for the reply he wanted to hear.

"What are you serving?"

"Chef's delight."

"A new menu item."

"It's only for one special customer..."He smiled.

Just the twinkle in her eye told him volumes.

Chapter 20
Rip Currents

Annie lingered over her morning coffee, watching Eric move around his kitchen, cleaning the last of the breakfast dishes. Mentally she returned to last night when she'd finished the last word in the last sentence of her last chapter. She'd written The End with such a feeling of satisfaction, completion, accomplishment. They'd celebrated together. Eric made a lasagna dinner, ready for her even though it was nine o'clock before they actually sat down to eat.

He asked about her goals, her dreams. That had been enlightening for her. She surprised herself. Her goal had always been to write for a magazine, full-time, not freelance like now. But her story, her book, took hold of her mind, occupying her thoughts with twists and turns, the characters taking on a life of their own. The open and creative process was different from the writing she did for the magazine, and that enthralled her. She was hooked.

She knew now, whatever she did, wherever she ended up, she wanted to write fiction. The End was not the end, it was the beginning. And she'd shared it with Eric last night. He'd listened, nodded, smiled, and asked questions that showed he cared. He told her he was proud of her for going after her dreams, following her heart. And then they'd made love, and fell asleep in each other's arms.

She rose from the table with her empty coffee cup and walked to the sink where Eric stood washing the frying pan. She put the cup in the water and wrapped her arms around his slim waist, laying her head against his back.

"Thank you for a wonderful weekend." She closed her eyes and savored the moment.

"You're welcome. But this is no fair. My hands are all

wet. If you're going to accost the dishwasher, at least let him dry his hands so he can accost back." Annie giggled as she completely released Eric and reached for the nearby dishtowel. She handed it to him and then spread her arms.

"Accost away!" She squealed as Eric grabbed her and swung her around in a circle. His eyes sparkled with laughter as he slowed and lowered his lips to hers. He pulled her body close to his—a familiar fit over the last several days.

"I really do need to go. And you were going to put the lunchroom together, remember?" She kissed his lips once more before moving out of his embrace.

"I'll call you later this afternoon. We'll figure something out for dinner. Maybe watch a movie?" He looked at her with such tenderness in his eyes.

"Okay". She picked up the large black leather overnight bag she'd left near the front door. "Bye."

"Bye."

She didn't want to leave but she took a deep breath and started the car, looking up to see Eric waving in the window, and smiled. Scary as it was, love was also freeing. She felt free from the crushing sadness that had overshadowed her life for the past six months. Mike would want her to be happy, go after her dreams, live. An inner peace filled her at the thought. Yes, it was okay to love again.

Annie walked into the quiet house. She'd left the porch light on last night, and flipped it off now. She set her bag down by the stairs and on her way into the kitchen saw the light on the answering machine flashing.

"Maybe Mom called from Vermont." She pressed the play button.

"Hello, Annie. This is Penelope Gilbright at the magazine. We definitely want your article, but that's not the main reason I called. I have a position here at the magazine I'd like to talk to you about. I just got authorization for it today, and I know this is very short notice, but wondered if you could be in New York on Monday. I'll give you my home phone so we can set this up. I'll be around all weekend. Call me."

Annie quickly scribbled down the number. A job at the magazine? Oh my God. She'd wanted this forever. Okay, breathe. Calm down. What should she say? What did she need to ask?

She plunked down in the nearby chair, her knees collapsing beneath her. Mentally, she went through a conversation with Penelope, trying to sound calm and professional, and writerly…whatever that was. She took a deep breath and dialed the number.

"Hello?"

"Hello, Penelope. This is Annie Gee. I have a message from you on my machine."

"Oh Annie. I'm so glad you called back. I was afraid you were away for the weekend or something. I know this is short notice and I'm so sorry, but I wanted to give you first shot at this position. You're perfect for the job. The problem is that the senior editor who approves it is going on vacation for two weeks, leaving Thursday. Is a Monday meeting possible for you? I want to leave a day or two leeway for Shawn, the editor. What do you think?"

"Well, yes. I'm definitely interested. I can leave here this afternoon and take a commuter train into the city in the morning. What exactly is this job you're thinking of?"

"It's a monthly byline for a column of your own. It fits perfectly with your style and the topics you write about— issues dealing with young marrieds, professionals, trying to make it all work. We can talk about the format and the specific topics when you come in. I immediately thought of you, and fortunately I had your recent article to show as a sample. The editorial team loved it."

"Thank you, Penelope. I'm flattered. I'll be there tomorrow. I'm not sure what time because I don't know the train schedule yet, but I'll say mid-morning. Can we leave it that open?"

"Great. I'm glad you can do this on such short notice. I'll leave word at the front desk that you'll be coming in and to buzz me. You have the address, right?"

"Yes, I'm all set. I'll see you tomorrow then! Thank you."

She hung up the phone. A squeal of delight escaped in spite of herself. She called Eric—no answer at either the house or the restaurant. She jumped up and ran to the stairs, grabbing the overnight bag, and raced upstairs to unpack and pack. Hotel room... train schedule... the ferry schedule...what to wear?

She threw the bag on her bed... and spun around. Where to start? Okay, take a deep breath and make a list. She sat at her desk and quickly jotted down details.

***

Hours later, Annie sat in a hotel room in Stamford, CT. She traveled by car that far and the hotel was near the train station. She planned to commute in, meet with Penelope, and travel back to the island by Monday night. The only thing bothering her now, besides a nervous stomach, was that she hadn't gotten in touch with Eric before she left. He'd be worried if he didn't hear from her. She tried to call again, but there still was no answer. Unfortunately, one down side to living on the island was poor cell phone coverage. No towers, no coverage. She and Mike had been in touch constantly, but her cell phone was next to useless on the island.

She knew Eric had planned to work at the restaurant, but she missed him when she stopped there on the way to the boat. She left a note on the door, and she'd try calling him tonight. She'd left a note for her mother too, just in case they got back on Monday before her.

She took out her laptop and set it up on the desk in the room. She'd take advantage of some good writing time. Hunger, rather than nerves, now rumbled in her stomach, and Annie glanced at the room service menu. Something quick to eat, and then write. Good plan. She dialed the number, ordered a bowl of chowder and a turkey sandwich, and sat at the desk.

She cleared her mind and put her fingers to the keys where they took on a mind of their own, putting thought to word to keystrokes without conscious effort. Half an hour later the knock from room service roused her from her creative trance. She answered the door, tipped well, and quickly changed into her nightshirt while munching on chips from the sandwich plate. Her mind raced as the story unfolded within, and she quickly returned to the keys, anxious to get it down.

She glanced at the clock at the corner of her laptop. Seven-thirty. She tried calling Eric again. Busy. Probably talking to his dad.

She finished half the sandwich and dove back into the story. The ease with which the words flowed from her mind amazed her. Granted, this was a very rough draft of her next manuscript, but it was all right there, ready to be harvested. It was ten o'clock the next time she came up for air. A lump sat in the pit of her stomach because she'd forgotten to call Eric. She called again.

She let it ring and ring. No answer? Where could he be? If she could just leave a message... Why the hell didn't he have an answering machine?

**

After an early breakfast, and a play in the Jacuzzi, Sara and Ben explored the small town with its eclectic shops geared toward the winter ski tourist trade. They returned to Hare Hill to bundle up after lunch and rent snowmobiles. Laurie recommended a rental outfit just over the mountain at an old farm. A series of trails cut through the woods and large fields hooked into a maze of old logging roads. People raved about it when they returned to the Inn.

The young man who got them all situated on the two silver machines handed Ben a walkie-talkie.

"These things break down fairly often, but are easy to fix if you know what you're doing. We find it's better for us to come out to you, than for you to have to trek back into us. Just radio. All the trails are marked with names."

Ben slipped it into his left parka pocket and turned the key on his machine.

"Ready?" He looked at Sara. She sat straddling the snowmobile, helmet on her head, and scarf wrapped around her neck. He could see the smile on her lips through the gear.

She gave him a thumbs up and pushed the throttle with her thumb. The engine raced and the snowmobile took off; he zipped after her trying to keep up. The woman was a speed demon. Thank God she wore a helmet on that head of hers.

They flew across the open field, snow fan tailing out behind them. Whoops of delight from the lead machine caught in the wind. He chuckled as he saw her sway the machine back and forth in the pristine white. Her joie de vive evident in everything they'd done this weekend was one more reason he loved her. Memories flashed as he raced to follow the speed fiend. Splashing in the hot tub, tickling on the bed, singing jingle bells in time to the horses' rhythm on the sleigh ride. He chuckled and shook his head. Oh, how he loved her.

Sara slowed the pace as they headed for the logging trail at the end of the field. The fifteen-foot-wide road sat on a raised bed, the sides sloping away to a swampy wooded area populated with mountain laurel, mixed sapling trees and evergreens. Ledge outcroppings dotted the landscape as well. Apparently comfortable now with the new terrain, Sara sped up ahead of him.

He concentrated on the trail. A terror-filled scream snapped his attention to the silver bullet careening out of control—rolling, plummeting down the embankment. Teal blue and black flew through the air in slow motion, landing with a sharp snap. He dove off his snowmobile scrambling down the short slope, his anguished scream echoing in the silent woods. Already a sickening bright red pool stained the clean whiteness around Sara's body.

Panic paralyzed him. The blood. So much blood—like before. Her face pale, pasty grey-white. He swallowed his need to vomit.

She opened her eyes and looked into his. How can she look so calm? The calm before death... she knows she dying and ...

"Ben, my leg."

A deep breath and his medical training kicked in, though

the ball of panic in the pit of his stomach burned. The puddle of blood increased at an alarming rate though mere seconds had elapsed since he'd gotten to her.

He ripped away her torn pant leg. A dead branch skewered through her leg had lacerated her femoral artery. She'd bleed to death in minutes. Without pause, he pulled off his right glove, reached his finger and thumb into the wound to pinch shut the main artery feeding the leg. He needed to get her to a hospital, no—to surgery—fast. If she didn't die, she stood a serious chance of losing her leg.

"Sara, baby, I need you to lie still. I know it hurts. I'm calling for help. Stay with me."

She nodded, her eyes steady on his.

He pulled the walkie-talkie from his pocket and radioed the rental station.

"This is Doc Stephenson. I have a seriously injured woman several hundred yards from the field on Logger's Load Road. I need a rescue sled out to us immediately, and an ambulance at the nearest loading spot. She's critical. Hurry."

She closed her eyes. The panic that had been roiling in his stomach exploded through his system. His heart hammered, his vision blurred with tears, and his voice shook as he sobbed.

"Sara, don't do this to me. I've just started to live again because of you. Damn it. Don't you leave me, covered in your blood, like Marcie did. We have too much to do together... too many years of loving left... don't you leave me." He lowered his head, pinching the gaping artery with his right hand, wiping his eyes on the sleeve of his left arm.

Her eyes fluttered and opened, deep-ocean blue against her pale cheeks. "Who's Marcie?"

Surprise stopped him at first, but he had to answer her. "The woman I was going to marry ten years ago."

She nodded and closed her eyes again.

"Sara, do you hurt anywhere else? Your head, your back? Don't try to move, just take an inventory... where does it hurt?" He wanted to keep her talking, keep her awake.

"Everywhere is sore but there is a searing white hot pain in my leg."

"I know, baby. I know. I hear the sled coming for us. We're going to get you to the hospital. Just hang on for me, baby, okay?"

She nodded, her eyes still closed. "Why was there blood?"

He didn't want to tell her but knew he had to. "You've lacerated your femoral artery. We need to get you into a hospital so we can close it up." She nodded, then shook her head. What did she mean?

Her eyes opened. "Marcie? Why so much blood?"

"Don't do this now." He closed his eyes and turned his head, lowered.

"Ben? That's what it's been about. Tell me."

The sound of a snowmobile in the distance gave him hope. But he knew he had to tell her what she asked. He had to face it.

"I was on the midnight shift at the ER where we both worked. She was going off duty, went out the doors and got caught in the crossfire of a drive-by between two rival gangs, one of which was dropping off a wounded member. She was shot in the head and died in my arms, covered in her blood. I couldn't save her." His heart banged in his chest not for the memory of Marcie, but for his reality now, his Sara.

She reached her hand to touch his cheek. "I'm not going to die Ben. You are saving me." She closed her eyes as a tear slid down her cheek. His were free flowing when the rescue sled arrived moments later. He could only pray she'd spoken the truth.

***

With great efficiency several members of the Volunteer Ambulance and Rescue loaded Sara onto the sled, Ben holding the artery in her leg closed the whole way. They packaged them on together, knowing that Ben could not release his hold or Sara would surely bleed to death. Right now they were fighting to not only save her life, but also her leg.

Within five minutes they traveled to the edge of the field where an ambulance waited, its lights flashing. Three more paramedics met them, helping to move her to the ambulance. Soon situated in the ambulance, they raced for the hospital as one of the paramedics started an IV. They knew their stuff, but Ben would be her overseeing doctor. Everything had to go right, but even then, she could still lose the leg. He couldn't think about what that would do to her. She had to come out of this whole.

His arm shook from exhaustion, his hands sticky from her blood. She'd not regained consciousness since they'd talked. Could she hear him? He had to try.

"Sara, you are a brave, strong woman. You are going to come out of this with no problems. Keep that thought in your head. And hold it in your heart. I love you. I need you in my life. I want you to be my wife. You'll want to be waking up to take care of the details Sara, cause it's going to happen."

No response from her. She was the grey-white of someone in shock. Her vital statistics deteriorated, her blood pressure low from the loss of blood. He concentrated to stay in his medical state of mind. Panic and despair hovered, waiting to invade. For now, he kept the memories they'd created this weekend at bay…both their lives depended on it.

Though it seemed like it took an hour, it was five short minutes until the ambulance reached the regional hospital in town. He'd maintained constant pressure on the severed artery, though his fingers had nearly gone numb. They'd clamp it soon and get her into surgery. Would they let him observe? He couldn't leave her.

Around him the ER staff bustled efficiently to stabilize Sara's condition. When they clamped off the artery above his fingers he couldn't move them. He reported all the details of the accident to Dr. Tournier, the ER doctor in charge.

"One of the top surgeons in the area is on staff here. We deal with a lot of winter sport injuries. He'll be on the case. He's prepping for OR now. We've got to get her up there."

Ben leaned down and kissed Sara's clammy forehead.

"You come back to me. I'll be right here waiting for you." Tears blurred his vision as he watched her being wheeled through the doors to the operating suite.

"Okay." He took a deep breath. Exhaustion hit him. He looked into the younger doctor's dark brown eyes. "After I've cleaned up and called her family, will I be able to scrub and observe?"

"We're a teaching hospital, so we have an observation room. You're welcome to watch from there. I'll let the nurses know. Someone will help you out."

Ben saw compassion in the man's eyes. "Thank you."

The doctor nodded, turned and spoke with a nurse at the nurses' station then picked up the phone on the desk. The grey-haired nurse came over to Ben, and gently touched his elbow. Her grandmotherly manner calmed him.

"Doctor, we have a physician's lounge that I'll show you to so you can clean up. I can get you a scrub set if you'd like. And there's a phone there so you'll have some privacy." She led him down a hallway to several rooms. Some couches and chairs were clustered around a TV in the first room. Two young interns sat eating at a table. There was a locker room with sinks and towels, a shower stall and lockers. A third room had several cots with pillows and blankets stacked on each. The nurse opened a cabinet and took out a set of scrubs for him. She smiled. "Professional courtesy."

He managed a smile. "Thank you. Once I'm cleaned up, Dr. Tournier said I'd be able to observe."

"I'll take you there myself. Just come back to the nurses' station when you're ready."

"Thank you so much."

He sat for a moment after she left. What would he do if... He couldn't let himself go there. He needed to focus on what he needed to do. Call her girls. Annie would be easy to get in touch with, and she could call Nancy.

He reached for the phone and dialed Sara's home phone. It rang and rang, the answering machine finally picking up. He couldn't leave this as a message. He'd try Eric. It might be better if Eric were with her when she found out about her mother anyway. He dialed his young friend's house. No answer there, and no machine. Now what? He called information and got the number for Eric's insurance office at the restaurant.

He finally got through to him. He sounded winded on the phone.

"Eric, I'm trying to get in touch with Annie. Is she with you there?"

"No. I'm here cleaning up from our painting project yesterday. She should be home."

"I tried and there was no answer. Listen, Eric, her mom's been badly hurt and she's on her way to the operating room now. I want to get up there to observe. Will you tell Annie? She needs to get up here. It's serious."

"Doc? What happened?"

"Snowmobile accident—she severed the femoral artery. I held it shut and got help, but she's lost a lot of blood. She's not out of the woods. She could lose the leg."

"Oh my God. I'll tell Annie and drive her up. I don't want her to be alone with this. Where are you staying?"

Doc gave him the name of the inn, the name of the hospital, and asked him to call Nancy too.

"I'll take care of everything here. You hang in there, pal." Doc knew the concern he now heard was directed at him too.

"I will Eric. See you when you get here. Thank you." He hung up the phone, and rushed to shower and get into the scrubs so he could be in the observation room as soon as possible.

Anxiety, concern, despair—fear pooled in the pit of his stomach. Tears washed down his cheeks as the shower spray washed Sara's blood from his hands and arms. *She has to make it. She's given me back my life. She is my life.*

***

Eric called Annie. She had to be home. No answer, just the machine.

"Annie this is Eric. Call me as soon as you get this." Where could she be? Down at the beach? She'll be a mess when she hears about her mother. It's my turn to be there for her.

He quickly looked around the lunchroom. He'd put everything back in place before the telephone call from Doc. He had to call Nancy too; her number was at his house from Thanksgiving. First go check the beach, then go home for that number. Hopefully Annie would be home by then. Had she gone out to run errands?

A paper whipped by him as he closed the storm door. We'll have to do a spring clean-up outside once the weather gets better. He chided himself as he headed for his SUV and to the shore to search for Annie.

He swung down the winding road leading to the beach where he'd first met—found—Annie. Barren gray winter trees lined one side of the road. The other opened to a small nine-hole golf course, then to the shore.

The grey-blue waters were rough this afternoon but not the worst he'd ever seen. White caps dotted the offshore waters as the wind pushed the ocean onshore, waves crashing on the rocky point at the end of the beach. He pulled into the small dirt parking lot. No car. He got out and checked to see if she walked further down the beach. Buffeted by the wind, he saw only empty shoreline in the dusk of early evening.

The beginning nudge of concern became tension between his shoulder blades as he drove back toward home. He searched for her sports car as he passed the post office, the grocery store. As he came to the road leading to Sara Burdick's house, he turned quickly. I'll check at her house before I go find Nancy's number at home. No car. The tension banded up his neck as he sped toward home. I've got to find her. Poor Doc. Poor Sara. I've got to get Annie up there.

He ran into his house dashing for his telephone book. If the number was anywhere, it would be there. He rifled through the multitude of paper scraps stored in the front of the book, mentally scolding himself. It's not here. Great... can't find Annie... can't find Nancy's number. Maybe the number's at Annie's house. When she gets back, I'll be waiting. The worry increased as the minutes ticked by. He ran back to his car, hoping that when he pulled into Sara's driveway, Annie's car would be there.

It wasn't. His head throbbed from the tension traveling up his neck. He shouldn't barge into Annie's house, but had to get in touch with Nancy and Annie too. He remembered seeing a list of numbers by the kitchen phone, when he'd been there months ago, helping Annie.

The sun had set, and the house was dark. Though the front door was locked, the deck doors around back were unlocked. Thank God. He flicked on lights as he moved through the house toward the kitchen. The list of numbers was tacked to the wall. He picked up the phone and took a deep breath planning what he needed to say. What should he say about Annie?

He noticed a paper on the table in Annie's handwriting. He walked over and read it.

Mom- If you get home and I'm not here, it's because I've gone to New York City. I got a call about a job—writing! Doing what I've always dreamed of doing. I'll fill you in when I get home...hopefully Monday night. Love, Annie

Eric landed in a dining room chair. She'd never said anything about a job in New York City. She never even called him. Hurt and betrayal speared him in the chest; he couldn't breathe.

New York City? What the hell? And what kind of a relationship could they have if she lived in the city? *Why didn't she tell me?* Angry tears ran down his cheeks unchecked. He took a breath, swiped away the dampness on his cheeks, and dialed Nancy's number.

"Hello, Nancy? This is Eric Nordsen, on the island. I have some bad news I need to tell you."

He passed along the details he knew. Through a haze, he heard himself tell Nancy that he was trying to get in touch with Annie but he thought she was off-island. He would drive her to Vermont when she returned. Nancy would drive up as soon as her husband got home. Eric hung up the phone.

Numb, dead inside...again. He'd lost her; he'd just found her and now she was gone. Gone to New York to follow her dream of writing. Last night when she'd shared her dreams, he had no idea they would take her away from him. It was all too clear, she needed to follow her dreams. Obviously, he wasn't in them.

Chapter 21
Caught in the Undertow

Cold pressed against her. Was she in cold flowing water? Sara struggled to make sense of the sensations, but her mind drifted away from that purpose. It floated just as her body did. The cold surrounded her, yet she wasn't uncomfortable. Odd, but security and calmness filled her.

A prickle of doubt. Something about lots of blood, and maybe her head. She focused on her head. It didn't hurt. Her leg hurt though, sharp hot pain. She had the odd sensation of not being able to use it, not being able to move at all. Well, that was okay. She was too tired. She didn't want to move, she just wanted to rest.

Something sounded soothing. She strained to hear it. A voice, a calming deep voice. What was it saying? She thought he said something about plans. Plans? What plans? Too confusing; she floated back into relaxation.

"Hold this in your heart. I love you." Ben's voice. He loves me. Yes, he said it. I love you too. She couldn't make her mouth move to say the words. Strangest thing… and her leg was hurting again… but it was warmer now, the warmth wrapped around her.

The sensations of weightlessness, floating, and drifting converged; she tired of struggling to the surface. She let go and relaxed into a deep sleep. She glided over the snow-covered field in the horse drawn sleigh, snuggled next to Ben, relaxing and calming. She took a deep breath of the fresh air but it had a funny smell, sweet and perfumed.

Something to plan? Maybe later, too tired now. Someone's talking again, she wanted to go back to sleep. Mmm, someone rubbed her head, talking, trying to wake her up? Why couldn't she just sleep? So tired…

***

The back of his fingers stroked her cheek as his other hand held hers laden with IV tubes and tape. He watched her face, her eyelids for any movement.

"Sara, baby, I'm here with you. You're doing fine. Open your eyes. I want to see your beautiful eyes looking at me. Come on Sara, wake up. I love you."

What else could he say to her? Please just wake up. I need you. Better to keep the desperation and worry out of your voice. Stay calm.

Eager to see her eyelids flutter open, he was just as anxious for the next twenty-four hours to pass, the critical time period to determine if he'd gotten her to the hospital in time to save not just her life, but her leg too. He laid his head on her shoulder and closed his eyes as the monitors beeped the rhythm of her heart. He hadn't prayed in a long time. Please God, let her be okay.

He'd watched the surgery from the observation deck, joining the team in the recovery room to get a full report. The surgeon had been cautiously optimistic. He'd told Ben what he already knew...the next twenty-four hours... They could only wait, monitor, and pray. Ben was already doing all three.

"Come on Sara. It's time to wake up. You're out of surgery. They stitched up your leg and now it's time to wake up. Come on baby, open your eyes." He slid his fingers over her soft hair, her pale cheek.

The knot in his stomach had lessened slightly when she made it through surgery, but concern and fear still gnawed at him at her delay in waking from the anesthesia. What if she had a head injury they hadn't found? What if there were internal injuries too? They'd all been so focused on the life threatening severed artery that they could've overlooked something else. God, what would he do if...

The nurse came in to check her vital statistics and wrote them on the clipboard hanging from the bottom rail of her bed. Then she looked up at him.

"Are you okay? Do you want a soda or a coffee?" Concern

touched her voice. Was she worried about him because she knew the patient wasn't doing well? He shook his head unwilling to trust his voice. He turned his attention back to Sara, looking for any sign that she was coming out of it. Nothing.

"Sara, you have to wake up. We have only begun to do the things we have to share. You know, the first thing we're going to do, once you feel well enough, is get married. I don't want to be engaged... I don't want to sneak time together. I want you with me all the time, through everything. You are too important to me to let this wait. So you have to wake up and tell me yes. Say you'll marry me." Ben watched. She had to hear him. Wake up. Had he failed her? He hated knowing all the things that could go wrong...but if he wasn't a doctor, would he have been able to save her in the woods? Would he even know her... his whole life would be different.

"Sara, come on baby, wake up." He leaned down and kissed her. A wayward tear slipped down his cheek and onto hers. He wiped it away with his finger, again tenderly stroking her smooth skin.

He heard the nurses talking outside the recovery room to someone trying to come in. He saw a young woman holding a baby, a man standing next to her talking at the nurses' station. He immediately recognized the family resemblance to Sara and Annie. Nancy... this must be her daughter. Of course. Eric had called her. Where were Eric and Annie? Why hadn't they all come up together?

The nurse came in to speak to him. Not standard practice to let the family into the recovery room. He stayed because of his professional status.

"Doctor Stephenson, could you come out and talk to Mrs. Burdick's daughter and let her know you've seen her mother."

"I'll be right out." He patted Sara's shoulder and gently placed her hand on the side of the bed. "I'll be right outside. Nancy is here. I'm going to tell her what a crazy driver you are, so you better wake up and defend yourself." He'd try that approach... still no reaction. The worry continued to gnaw at his insides.

What would he tell her daughter?

***

Butterflies jitterbugged in Annie's stomach as she stood at the receptionist's desk waiting to enter Penelope Gilbright's office. She'd met her once before, spoken with her numerous times on the phone, but never for anything this big. She took a deep breath, trying to slow the butterflies to a ballroom waltz.

The office door opened and Penelope's welcoming smile and outstretched hand helped to calm her.

"Annie, I am so glad you could make it on such short notice. I honestly don't know if I could have done that! Thank you." Her firm, warm handshake lowered Annie's anxiety another notch.

Penelope's office was not big but had several padded chairs sitting in front of a large matching oak table, with stacks of papers neatly arranged on one end. A small brass clock, pictures of a man with two children and various desk accessories sat on the other side. Penelope guided Annie toward a chair and took the other one, in front of the desk.

Penelope reached to the pile of papers and took the top clipped pile. Annie recognized it as her article. The butterflies picked up the beat. She folded her hands in her lap to keep from wringing them.

"First, can I offer you a coffee, or soda, water?"

Annie shook her head and smiled. "I'm all set, thanks."

"I want to tell you how happy the editorial staff is to get something from you. The pieces you've contributed in the past have always been top notch. We were very sorry about your loss and certainly understood your need to take some time off. It's nice to have you back."

"Thank you. It's good to be back to writing again. It gives me focus, keeps me centered. I have good days and bad days, but I'm working through it."

"Well, this article is definitely up to your past standard and we'd like to run it in one of the spring issues. But that's not the main reason I wanted to see you. We've always done business by mail and phone. This project I have in mind is a little different, and I wanted to have a chance to sit with you and talk, get your ideas about it."

"Okay. What exactly are we talking about? You said on the phone something about a monthly column?"

"Our magazine targets the young professional woman. Your articles speak to just that target group on issues important to them. We'd like to set up a monthly column where we can deal with readers' concerns around a specific issue. We thought we'd solicit letters/emails from readers about specific areas of concern, give them to you, and let you research that issue and come back with an article the next month. Sort of an advice column, but with a researched article to deal with the specific issue. Is this making sense?"

Annie's head spun with ideas. Excitement bubbled, and the butterflies jigged. She couldn't keep from smiling her enthusiasm.

"Yes, it's something I've often thought about, but I had no way of getting the initial letters, the readers' issues. This is great. I am definitely interested." Her heart hammered at the thought that her dreams were finally being realized. Something she'd always wanted was being handed to her. She'd have the security of a monthly paycheck, and be able to work in the field she loved. A deeper voice whispered that she'd still be able to write her novels too.

"I have notes from the editorial staff meetings that involve ideas or issues you could start with, but the specific topics will be up to you to choose and pitch at our monthly organizational meetings. You'd have to know several months in advance since we would have to solicit letters in an earlier edition. The timing will get worked out a bit more specifically as we go along, I'm sure." Penelope reached for a manila folder and handed it to her.

Annie's mind raced with ideas, questions, plans.

"This is so exciting. Where do we start?" She opened the folder to see typed notes concerning her column with possible topics listed.

"We thought we'd run an advertisement next to this article and introduce you as a new member of our staff. We'll put the first topic in that introduction as a way of starting up reader interest and correspondence. What do you think?" Penelope lifted Annie's article from her lap and returned it to her desk.

Annie nodded as she thought about everything they'd talked about. Several concerns kept popping up as she listened to Penelope. She knew she needed to address them up front; the butterflies dancing in her stomach picked up speed.

"I think that's a great way to introduce me and the issues I'll be working on. I have a few things I'm wondering about. When do you plan to start this?"

"Well, we left that a little flexible. I wanted to give you some leeway for moving and finding a place. We'd like to definitely have it up and running by the June issue, but we'd go earlier if we can." Penelope looked hopefully at Annie.

A spear of panic shot through her. Moving, finding a place? I don't want to live in the city. Is that a prerequisite? I want to stay on the island. I write well there. I don't want to leave all that I have there.

How could this work out? The job opportunity of a lifetime, something she'd always dreamed of, yet she didn't want to give up what was between Eric and her. Couldn't she have both?

"Well, I'd like to think outside the box on the whole housing thing. I really like where I am right now. I wonder if I need to be living in or near the city. With internet and fax machines, phone conferencing, could we work something out so I could work from the island? I could come in for meetings or conferences as needed." Annie mentally held her breath.

What if they couldn't come to an understanding? Was she willing to risk this dream job for the sake of something that could happen with Eric? Was she willing to risk what had begun between them for the sake of the dream job? She held onto the folder in her lap to keep from wringing her hands. She couldn't believe she was negotiating.

Penelope's brow scowled as she rose from her chair and

moved across the office to a small coffee maker. She seemed to be thinking as she poured herself a cup of coffee. Annie watched Penelope. Fear that she'd blown the whole package gnawed in her stomach. Her father's voice reverberated through her head... no one successful lives on the island full time. To be successful you have to leave the island. Why was she remembering that now?

The petite brunette in the Ann Taylor classic navy suit crossed the room to sit behind her desk. Annie's heart hammered. Was Penelope going to tell her that she'd get back to her? What had she done?

Penelope took a form from one of the folders on her desk and handed it to Annie.

"This is the contract for your article. It's the standard one we've used before." Annie took the contract. A sick feeling in her stomach, as though the butterflies had all died, lodged in her stomach. She couldn't look at Penelope. She tried to read the contract but her eyes refused to focus on the words.

"I think the long distance arrangement could work. There isn't any big reason you have to work here. We could provide the office technology for you to work from home. We can set up a system for getting mail to you though most of it will be Internet."

Annie looked up from the contract into Penelope's eyes. They shone warm and smiling. She'd taken the chance, spoken up, and it worked.

"Oh, wonderful. I'm so excited." She smiled at Penelope.

"Finish looking over the contract and I'll get the senior editor. He's due to leave on vacation later this week and he's the one who has final approval. I want you to meet him. I'll brief him on the long distance set-up we've talked about and bring him back with me." Penelope rose from her desk and left her office.

A huge sigh of relief escaped Annie's lips. She thought she'd screwed up the biggest chance in her career. Although the deal wasn't officially done, it seemed solid. The butterflies lightly danced as she signed the contract selling her original article to the magazine. What else would be agreed to today?

A tall elderly man with white hair and bright blue eyes strode into the office followed by Penelope. Annie rose from her seat to take his extended hand.

"Shawn McDonough. Nice to meet you, Ms. Gee."

She nodded her head and looked up at the tall energetic man.

"It's a pleasure to meet you, Mr. McDonough."

He pulled the extra chair to face hers and motioned for her to sit. Penelope slipped around her desk and sat in the chair behind the desk.

"Penelope tells me you're willing to do the monthly column for us. I'm delighted. I've liked your style with each article you've sent us and you'll be a valuable addition to our magazine staff."

He paused, and the butterflies in her stomach jitterbugged to the beat of her heart pounding in her chest.

"Let's talk about this work setup you were speaking about to Penelope."

Annie's heartbeat continued to hammer. *Oh God. Here it comes. I'm going to have to choose. Eric or the job. What am I going to do?*

"We could set up an office at your home with a fax machine, computer with Internet, conference calling, copier. In fact, we'll run an email address for you so readers can contact you by either email or regular mail." He nodded to Penelope who jotted it down. "We have to see you at least once a month at our planning meeting for each issue. There might be other special projects we'd like you to work on... as things come up. Think it's a go?"

Annie nodded. "Absolutely."

Her heart pumped so loud she feared she wouldn't hear Mr. McDonough. She could have the job and Eric too.

"Mr. McDonough, I'm delighted. Thank you." This man was high energy, and had a vision of what he wanted from her...and he'd liked her writing. Excitement about the job and pride that her work was so highly respected created a warm glow throughout her, just the confidence builder she needed.

"Penelope, why don't you take Ms. Gee out to lunch and I'll ask Sylvia to make the changes we'll need in the contract. After lunch, Annie can sign it and get all the paperwork done with Human Resources." He smiled as he stood up, reaching to shake her hand again.

"Thank you again, Mr. McDonough. I appreciate this opportunity." She couldn't believe her good fortune.

Penelope rose and walked to a coat hook as Shawn McDonough showed himself out. Annie took the cue and put her jacket on as well. Minutes later, she and Penelope walked out of the elevator chatting like two people who knew they'd be friends.

At the small Italian café down the block they had no trouble getting a table. The staff seemed to know Penelope. She was friendly and talkative, sharing a story about one of her daughters in nursery school as they waited for their lunch to arrive. The butterflies in Annie's stomach slowed down the pace. Penelope's effervescent personality warmed her, as though she'd known this woman for years.

Through lunch they shared small talk about their lives and families, finding similarities in the things they liked to do with their spare time.

"Besides writing articles, I've started dabbling with fiction. Annie almost bit her tongue to keep from telling Penelope, but the words bubbled out before she could stop them. "In fact, I've just finished my first novel."

"Really? Finishing a novel is hardly dabbling! What's it about?" Penelope leaned forward.

I can't believe I'm telling her about this. She'd only just told Eric about her book, and now she was talking about it with Penelope?

As soon as she started talking, all the emotion she felt for her story surfaced as she explained the plot and characters. Penelope listened with interest.

"Annie, I know your style and I think you are a wonderful writer. I have a good friend who is an editor at a publishing house. I haven't ever done this before, but if you can get me a copy of your manuscript, I would be willing to see if she'd look at it for you. I'm supposed to see her this weekend. Can you get it to me overnight?"

"Really? I can't believe this. I printed the whole story out for one final read-through while I was traveling down on the train. It's in my briefcase. If you promise to tell her it's rough, I could leave it with you today. I'd love to have someone in the business look at it."

Two hours later, Annie sat on the commuter train back to Stanford. She put her head back on the seat, trying to relax. She tried calling Eric at his house without luck. She couldn't wait to share it all with Eric and her mom this evening. How could so many wonderful things happen to her within the last forty-eight hours? Making love with Eric, having her dream job just fall into her lap, and giving her manuscript to an editor. The butterflies in her stomach had been dancing the happy dance since leaving Penelope's office. Life couldn't get much better.

***

Annie pulled into the parking lot to catch the evening ferry, filled with relief and happiness. Tired but excited by all that had happened, she was surprised to see Eric get out of his car parked by the freight office and walk toward her car in line for the ferry. She couldn't wait to share all her news.

What's he doing on this side? Did something come up at the office... or with his dad? I hope everything's okay. He doesn't look good, he looks angry.

She got out of the car to greet him. His dark scowl kept her from going into his arms like she wanted. "Eric, what are you doing here? I'm surprised to see you."

Thunderclouds roiled, ready to burst over his head; she'd never seen him like this. What was wrong?

"You need to take your car to the overnight parking garage and I'll meet you there. I have some bad news for you but let's get on the road first." He moved to return to his car but her hand on his arm stopped him.

"Eric, what?" Panic sliced through her heart.

"Doc called last night. Your mother was in a snowmobile accident, and you need to get up there fast. Get in your car and drive to the parking garage and I'll fill you in on the details while we're traveling."

Her heart thundered in her ears. Her vision darkened around the edges, and she swayed, grabbing the open car door for support. He moved in and caught her around the waist. His touch was heaven, a lifeline in a raging sea. He moved her into the seat of the car and away from his warmth. She reached to catch his hand as he moved away.

"Eric?" She looked into his eyes. Sorrow, loss, sadness. Oh God, had her mother...?

Eric squatted down to talk to her. "Annie. Take a deep breath. I'm sorry to hit you with it like this but I tried to reach you. Doc called last night; your mom was in surgery. He said it's serious. I want to get you up there. Nancy is already there. She left last night. Take another breath and let's move your car." His tone had gentled, and his eyes were sympathetic.

Annie took another deep breath. "Okay, let's go. I'll be all right. Follow me to the garage?"

He nodded and moved off to his car. She shut the door and pulled her car down the road to the parking garage. Her mind raced with all of the possibilities. She feared the worst, and tears immediately pricked her eyes. Could she face another devastating loss? Please God, let her be okay.

She pulled into the first parking space, Eric right behind her. She got her overnight bag out of the back seat, locked the doors and got into Eric's SUV. She looked over at him.

"Okay. Tell me everything you know. What happened?"

He seemed to be holding himself under tight control. It must be really bad. She tried to prepare herself. He looked straight ahead at the road and started driving, quickly maneuvering his way out of the garage.

"Doc called my house late yesterday afternoon... around four-thirty or so. He said that he tried to call you at the house but there was no answer. He didn't have Nancy's number with him and needed to get in touch with both of you. Your mom was in a snowmobile accident and severed the main artery in her leg. She lost quite a bit of blood. Apparently, Doc managed to get to her, pinch the artery shut, and call for help. They got her to the hospital and into surgery. He called before he went to observe the surgery. He hasn't called back. I don't know how she is."

He quickly glanced at her and took a deep breath. "He said it was bad. He said to get you and your sister up there." He paused. Annie continued to watch him staring straight ahead as tears filled her eyes and her heart hammered.

"Did you get in touch with Nancy? Is she there?"

Eric nodded. "I thought you gave me the number when you were at her house for the holidays, but I couldn't find it. I went to your house and found it by the phone in the kitchen. I called her from there. I saw the note you left for your mother. That's how I knew to meet you over here. It certainly wasn't because of any information you chose to share with me." And then silence.

The final sentence he'd spoken hit as deeply as all the rest of the information he'd given her so far. Hurt and betrayal resonated in his tone.

She needed to throw up.

"Eric...I tried calling you in the afternoon and again last night. I left a note for you down at the restaurant on my way to the ferry. I thought I'd get to talk to you last night but the line was busy." She reached to touch his arm. He did not look at her, did not respond to her touch. She pulled her hand away from him. The rejection stung.

He's being a jerk. I need him. I tried to tell him about New York but I couldn't reach him. I just want to feel his arms around me. What if Mom's not all right? I need him to help me be strong. Doesn't he know how important he is to me?

"I was probably at the shop in the afternoon, but I was home all evening. I might have been on the phone with Nancy, or my dad. You could have tried again. I expected to hear from you. I thought we were doing dinner or something." He continued to stare ahead at the road, not even looking her way.

Was that why he was so mad... I didn't go there for dinner? That doesn't seem right.

"Eric, I had a message on the machine when I got home from your house from the editor in New York. The magazine wanted me to come into the city to talk about a new project they have. They want me on staff." Excitement filled her voice.

"That's great Annie. Just great. You go have a wonderful life in the city. Maybe I'll see you sometime when you're down visiting your mother." The sarcasm oozed from his tone of voice, only outdone by the pain in his eyes as he quickly glanced over at her.

Tears appeared from nowhere; her stomach threatened to empty, and she couldn't focus on anything... her mother, Eric... everything suddenly spiraled out of control. How could this be happening?

"Eric, listen to me. I have to explain things to you."

"No Annie. You don't owe me any explanations. It's all pretty clear. I don't want to talk about anything. I don't want to listen to your explanations. I told Doc I'd get you up there. He's a good, loyal friend so I'll do that for him. But that's it." He raised his hand as she started to speak and shook his head.

The car lurched forward as he suddenly accelerated. He reached and turned the volume up on the radio.

He didn't want to listen; he made that very clear.

She turned away from him, staring out the window. Fine. Let him have his tantrum. He'll have to listen sooner or later. It's five hours in the car.

She reached for the volume control and turned down the music. "What exactly do you know about the accident and my mother?" She shifted her body toward Eric.

He glanced over at her, a look of disdain in his eyes.

"I told you everything I know about it. Snowmobile accident, severed the artery in her leg and Doc kept her from bleeding to death. Transported to the nearest hospital, surgery as we talked. Doc didn't know if she was going to make it, didn't know if they could save the leg, and didn't mention any other injuries. He was very worried about her and wanted to get back to her. That's how people in love act. They don't want to be away from each other. Now, I've told you all I know. Leave me alone so I can concentrate on getting you there."

"Why are you being so awful to me?" Tears ran freely down her cheeks.

Her only answer was the volume being turned up on the radio again.

Chapter 22
Crashing Breakers

Thank God we're here. I can't take many more tears. God, please let Sara be okay. Doc was so frantic on the phone. Eric glanced over at the back of Annie's head, turned away from him, looking out the window. That's how she'd spent most of the four and a half hour ride here. He couldn't blame her. He'd outdone himself in the jerk department; he'd been awful to her.

It's better this way. Now she can go off to New York without ties keeping her on the island, reminding her of the past. He'd told her she needed to move on, pursue her dreams, follow her heart. That was the rub...she was following her heart and it led her away from him. Unfortunately, his heart was breaking...again.

He pulled into the hospital parking near the main entrance. She bolted out the door before he'd even turned off the engine.

That's all right. Let her go ahead. She needs to find out about her mother... and get away from me. I hope Sara's all right. Annie doesn't need any more heartache.

He slowly unfolded himself out of the SUV, stretching his legs, loosening the cricks and cramps from long hours of driving. He laughed at himself...his body was sore, but his heart ached. The body would stretch itself out and be fine. He didn't hold out the same prognosis for his heart. She was going away—leaving him. He'd just found her. He locked the car and walked toward the hospital, apprehensive of the news they might hear.

He spoke to the woman at the front desk asking for Sara Burdick's room. She directed him to the blue elevators, second floor, Room 245. He waited for the elevator. Obviously, Annie had already gotten this information and rode up ahead of him. He took the elevator to the second floor and stepped out. Room

245 was several doors to the right. Doc stood outside the door, looking in, smiling. Eric breathed a sigh of relief. Sara must be okay. Doc wouldn't have left her side if she wasn't.

Doc shook his hand, and clapped him on the back.

"Thank you for all your help getting the girls here, Eric. I panicked last night when I called you. I can't imagine getting in touch with them if it hadn't been for you. Thanks."

Eric put his hand on Doc's shoulder. "I take it everything's okay. She came through the surgery okay?"

Doc nodded. "She gave me a scare. She took a long time waking from the anesthesia. I was afraid there could be other injuries. Late last night she finally came around. Today's better, though she's in quite a bit of pain. Tomorrow they'll test to be sure the leg tissue is viable. It looks good."

"I'm glad we got up here. Annie's pretty upset. She was away for the day and I met her on the mainland and drove her up."

"She's fortunate you were there for her. Come on in and say hi to Sara. I'm sure she'll want to see you too." Doc guided him into Sara's room before he could object. Annie moved away from him and wouldn't make eye contact. He could feel the tension; he wondered if anyone else did.

Sara glanced from Eric to Annie and back to Eric. She raised her arms to pull him into a hug.

"Thank you for bringing my Annie to me. I'm sorry to have given all of you such a scare. I guess I'm not cut out to be a speed demon."

"We're just glad you're okay." Eric smiled and stepped back from the bedside.

"Yes, Mrs. Burdick. I think you'd better stick to the sleigh rides from now on." Ben wiggled her big toe on her good leg.

"Only if I'm assured of your company, Dr. Stephenson." She smiled coyly at him.

"Absolutely."

Eric watched his friend flirting with Sara. They both deserved happiness, and it was obvious they were in love. It was a bittersweet thought that came into his head. They both found a second chance at love. Mine's moving to New York.

He moved away from the bedside, leaving Nancy and Annie and Doc to the fore. He watched from outside as the two sisters talked and laughed with their mother and Doc. Down the hall, he could see a small waiting room with soda machines and chairs. He walked down, put money in a machine and punched a button.

Caffeine. He'd decided somewhere along the way that as soon as he knew everything was all right with Sara, he'd leave Annie there and drive back home. He didn't need to be here with this family. It wasn't ever going to be his. And his melancholy state of mind wouldn't do anyone any good.

His stomach churned as he thought about Annie. Her soft skin, the way she breathed when she slept, the feel of her wonderful lips on him. *Stop this. Just stop thinking about her. It's got to be over.*

He took a long swallow from the cold can of soda. What was he going to do? How would he get through this? How could he walk away from her so that she'd pursue her dream?

Annie walked down the hallway toward him. She didn't look happy— determination covered her face, her eyes glittering with challenge.

"Doc has offered us their room at the inn. Nancy and her husband are staying there too. I haven't said anything to anyone about our... problems. They all think we're friends. I'm willing to try this for tonight if you are. I don't want to add to Mom or Doc's worries."

"Maybe I should head back tonight. It's what I'd planned to do." He wasn't looking forward to spending the night in the same room with Annie. Or maybe that was the problem. He would very much like to spend the night with Annie but knew it would only make things harder in the end.

"Don't be stupid. If you're going to leave, at least do it with a good night's sleep behind you. You're exhausted."

She was right... and he hated that. He was having trouble staying angry with her. She'd been so pathetic on the ride up, so anxious about her mother, and now she thought about him.

"Are you sure?"

"I'll be fine." What was it he saw in her eyes? Sadness, determination, hope? He wasn't sure. He wasn't sure about anything right now. His whole life had turned upside down. Sleep sounded good. Maybe things would be clearer in the morning.

He nodded. "Okay. I'll stay."

She turned on her heel and walked back to the room. He returned more slowly, sipping the soda, wondering how he would make it through the night. What had he gotten himself into?

***

Anxious to have Sara to himself, Ben thought they would never leave. He and Sara had to talk. Late last night when she finally woke from the anesthesia, so groggy, he couldn't talk. Today, Nancy and her husband were there most of the day, and Sara had slept. They were happy to see Eric and Annie, though they seemed frazzled and edgy. The long drive and the uncertainty of Sara's condition took a toll. He'd talk to Eric tomorrow.

The nurse finished taking Sara's vitals and recorded them. They looked good. He checked her chart himself. She'd scolded him of course, but he just smiled and continued studying it. She'd been extremely lucky. Lucky he'd been with her, lucky he'd been able to hold the artery closed, and lucky there was a hospital so close. Another ten minutes could have cost her the leg. Tomorrow they'd do the tests to make sure blood flow had returned to all areas of her leg, but it looked good. His doctor's instinct told him that she was out of the woods. Relief filled him. Now he had something else to worry about.

The nurse checked the dressing on her leg, settled her in for the night, and left. Finally. He sat on the edge of Sara's bed, and took her hands in his.

"Sara, do you remember anything I said to you while you were in and out of consciousness? Anything I said while we were alone in the woods, waiting for help?"

"Everything is pretty blurry. Why?" She looked puzzled, her brow furrowed and her eyes studied his face.

"I asked you something and I'm still waiting for an answer. I guess I'm going to have to ask you again." He couldn't contain the smile that escaped and sat on his lips.

"Ben? What are you up to? That twinkle in your eye always scares me." She smiled now too.

"I asked you to marry me. I don't want any engagement. I want us to be married—now. As soon as possible." He lifted her hands to his lips and tenderly kissed them. "What do you say? Will you be my wife?" He watched the emotions cross her face. Surprise, happiness, love. He knew before she said it.

"Oh Ben. Yes, I'll marry you. But right away? Here? Really?"

He nodded. "I'm going to talk to the hospital chaplain right now if he's in. Your family's here, Eric too. Who else do we need? We can have a party later on the island. But I don't want to wait." He leaned forward and kissed her lips. "Okay?" Again he read her response on her face, and he smiled.

"Yes. I don't need a big wedding. I just need you. Go see if you can find the chaplain. Do I at least get to change out of my hospital gown?" She laughed with him, filling him with joy as he hurried out of the room.

***

Married in a hospital room? Sounded like something out of a soap opera… but she wasn't the dying heroine. She knew that. She felt fine, except for the terrible ache in her leg. That was her only concern. What if they hadn't gotten here in time? What if she did end up losing the leg? She didn't want to saddle Ben with a handicapped wife. They'd have to talk about that.

And where had this big turn-around in his thinking come from? She worked to remember the accident. He'd asked her if she remembered what he'd said to her. It was really blurry. All that would come to her was something about blood and her head. But she didn't have a head injury. What was that? Snippets of words and images kaleidoscoped in her mind,

224

nothing clear. She'd have to ask Ben for details. Maybe then things would start making sense.

An hour later, he returned, beaming from ear to ear. He'd met with the chaplain. He'd had blood drawn for a blood test and the lab rushed it. The chaplain thought he could get a special waiver from a judge friend of his and would let them know after speaking with his friend.

Things moved fast, but she needed to slow it down. They needed to talk. She reached for his hand, and motioned for him to sit on the edge of her bed.

"I know you're really excited about this, and I am too. But I need to know some things first. And I need to tell you about some concerns I have."

She watched his expression change from total euphoria to anxious concern.

"What? Baby, did I push you too hard? Is this too fast? Are you having doubts about us?" Panic edged into his voice as the questions progressed.

"No, Ben, just listen to me for a minute. I want to marry you. I love you. I have no doubts about us. But I'm wondering about some things. What happened during the accident to make you so eager to get married? What did I miss?"

Ben took a deep breath and exhaled. He looked into her eyes, suddenly very serious.

"I held you in my arms; we were both covered with your blood. I promised myself and you and God above, that if we made it through this, that I would marry you as fast as I could get you to agree. I lost one love. She died in my arms covered with blood. The scene was too reminiscent. I told you about it as we waited for help, but you were in shock and probably don't remember."

"Did your fiancée die of a head wound?" Pieces began to fit together in her mind.

"Yes. Why?"

"I remember something about a head injury and lots of blood. I couldn't figure it out since my head didn't hurt. Now it makes sense."

"I've shut down for all these years. Now, with you, I've started to feel again, to be alive. When I held you, trying to save you, you were saving me too." He looked down at their joined hands. "You saved my life, made it worth living again. I don't want to be separated from you anymore. We have lots of living, lots of loving to do. I want to get started." He leaned down and kissed her. His kiss, gentle and tender, filled with love and longing, brought tears to her eyes.

"Ben, what if I lose the leg? I don't want to be a burden on you. I don't want…"

"Stop." He held up their joined hands between them. "Look. Together. We are together. We can deal with anything—together. In my professional opinion, your leg looks good and I think it is going to heal well. In my personal opinion, it doesn't matter because we will deal with it together."

Tears continued to stream down her cheeks. She couldn't help it. This beautiful man was hers. "I love you Ben." She put her arms around his neck. He reached to embrace her.

"I love you too Sara." He held her, gently stroking her hair. "We're gonna be all right."

***

What had she been thinking? Agreeing to spend the night at the inn in the same room with Eric. She must be out of her mind. He didn't speak to her for practically the whole ride up, and what he did say was laced with sarcasm and anger.

He wouldn't listen to her in the car, she was sure he wouldn't listen to her now. Probably crazy, but she'd at least try to talk with him.

Why is he being such a jerk? I tried to call him, I left him a note at the restaurant… what else could I have done? And I'll be damned if I'll share all my good news with him while he's being such an idiot.

Annie stewed all the way back to the inn. Nancy rode with them since Phil took the baby back early. Nancy chatted away while Annie made noncommittal noises every once in a while. Eric kept his eyes focused forward, concentrating on the road.

226

He kept himself out of the conversation.Once at the inn, Nancy introduced them to Laurie who immediately asked how their mom was doing, concern evident in her voice. She showed Annie and Eric to the Cedar Glen and took Annie's hand in hers.

"If there is anything you need, or any way that we can help, please don't hesitate to let me know. Your mom and Ben are special people. They saved a man who had a heart attack in our front room. Now it's our turn to do for them. You let me know." She squeezed Annie's hand and nodded, leaving them alone in the room.

Eric took off his jacket and threw it on the cedar log chair. He arranged the pillows on the couch, took off his shoes and laid down.

"I'll sleep here tonight. You get the bed." His arm covered his eyes, as though he would sleep right away.

"Okay, fine. You can sleep wherever you want. But I'd like to know what your problem is. I understand you being upset about not knowing where I was, but I legitimately tried to get in touch with you several times. We missed each other. Can't you get over it?"

"I'm over that. I'm sorry I was so upset with you at the ferry, and in the car. I just realized that this weekend was a mistake for both of us, and I'm angry at myself for letting it happen." He kept his arm over his eyes so she couldn't see them, couldn't read them.

Her gut twisted at his words. They hurt. She thought their lovemaking meant something special, that it meant as much to him as it had to her. She had wanted it. Why was he doing this? Something didn't ring true.

"I don't agree. I don't think it was a mistake; I'm sorry you feel that way. I don't understand the big turn-around." Her legs felt weak, and tears began to blur her vision. She dropped down on the foot of the bed before her legs gave out on her, fighting to hold back the tears.

"Let's say you're not the person I thought you were, and I don't think we should continue our physical relationship." He hadn't looked at her.

"Fine. I guess we don't have much of anything else to talk about. You've made it very clear how you feel. Good night." She wished she could slam a door, throw something, scream. She wouldn't give him the satisfaction. She wouldn't let him see her tears, and she wouldn't let him see her broken heart. Damn him.

She took her bag and slipped into the large bathroom, quietly closing the door behind her. She stood for a moment with her back against the door, her eyes closed, trying to calm down. Anger and hurt twisted her stomach into knots.

He wasn't talking, not really. He took potshots, trying to push her away. It didn't make sense. Mr. Supportive, Mr. Caring? So out of character. How can I get to him? I've got to find out what's in his head.

It came to her. Talk about out of character. But the need to shock him was strong. A smile came to her lips as she slipped her travel weary body out of her clothes. Whatever it takes. A nice long soak in the Jacuzzi might do the trick.

Eric sat with his elbows on his knees and his head in his hands as she opened the bathroom door and strolled to the hot tub, naked as a newborn babe. She turned on the jets and slowly stepped over the side, sitting where she could see him out of the corner of her eye.

"Oh, this is what I needed. I am so tired and stiff from the long ride…and all the stress of worrying about Mom. Oh, this is great!" She moaned for emphasis and stretched out, resting her head back and closing her eyes. She didn't need to keep them open. She'd seen the look on his face. Wants to end the physical relationship? Right! I don't think so, Eric. I don't think you're being at all honest.

One more little sigh of delight escaped her.

"Maybe you should think about relaxing in the hot tub. You must be stiff… from the drive." Oh my God, I can't believe I just said that… She opened her eyes, trying for an innocent look.

His face was stone pale, his eyes wide and, what was that

look? Hunger? She'd never known such feminine power; it surprised her. He stood quickly, whipping his turtleneck sweater off over his head, his pants shed in the next swift movement.

Oh my. She'd wanted to get a reaction from him and quite apparently, she had. He stalked to the Jacuzzi, stepped in, and sank into the seat next to her, reaching for her before he was even in the water.

He pulled her hard against him.

"You're right. I am a bit stiff. Maybe you could help me relax." His voice husky and harsh, angry but pleading too.

What is going on in your head, Eric? She didn't understand him at this moment, but abandoned all thought of trying as his mouth ravished hers. She could only follow where her heart led her—into his arms, into his heart.

Chapter 23
Still Waters

Sara wanted something nice to wear today, her wedding day. Ben left her while he took care of a few things. She picked up the phone on her bedside table and dialed the inn, leaving a message for Annie. There were no phones in the inn's rooms, but Laurie said she would give Annie the message right away.

She laid her head back on the pillow. My wedding day. Who would ever have thought... She smiled to herself. Serenity filled her. She'd been given another chance. To love and be loved. She was very lucky, not just that Ben had saved her, but that he loved her, and they would be together.

She wished for a second chance for Annie too. She'd heard how Annie's voice changed when she talked about Eric. She'd watched Annie's face light up when he called on the phone. Wouldn't that be wonderful... for both of them... although the tension between them last night...

Hopefully, Annie would come to the hospital a little early and bring her an outfit. She hoped to get a chance to talk to Annie about second chances.

She lay back and closed her eyes. What would the girls think about her surprise wedding? They'll be happy for me.

Happy dreams filled her mind as she dozed. Images of Ben as he fished from the shore casting into the surf, the feel of his arms around her as he held her, and the taste of his lips, tender and loving drifted through her dreams.

"Mom?"

Annie stood next to her bed with several pieces of clothing draped over her arm.

"I wasn't sure from your message what you wanted me to bring. What's going on that you want to be dressed up?"

"I'm getting married." Sara watched as Annie's face

reflected surprise then happiness. She smiled as her daughter's arms surrounded her in a hug.

"Mom, I'm so happy for you. But why today? Don't you two want to wait until you get back to the island?"

"We want to be together and all the important people we want at the wedding are right here. So we're doing it today."

"Oh, Mom." Annie hugged her again.

"Where's Eric?" Sara watched as several emotions crossed Annie's face. She blushed, then lowered her eyes.

"He's still at the inn. He said he'd get a ride over here with Nancy and Phil and the baby."

"Are things okay between you two? It seemed a bit tense in here yesterday." She wanted to shake her daughter and say, "tell me what's happening," but Annie was a grown woman.

"Things are okay for now. He was a little upset with me yesterday." Her eyes were down again.

Sara knew that meant she wasn't getting the whole story, but she also knew not to push. "If you need to talk…"

"I know Mom. I'm okay. Where's Doc? Did he sleep here in the chair?" Annie laid the clothes she'd been holding on the edge of the bed.

"No. He finally went down to the staff lounge and stretched out there for a little while. They've been wonderful to us here. Annie, he's going to be part of the family. Call him Ben."

Annie smiled and nodded. "So, what can I do to help you get ready? How is this all going to happen?"

"I'm not sure about all the details. Ben's working some things out this morning. I know the hospital chaplain will marry us, I think late morning or early afternoon but I'm not sure. Ben's off doing I don't know what. 'A few things to do' he told me!" She smiled remembering his excitement when he'd gotten the call from the chaplain saying the license went through. She shook her head. "He's quite a guy."

"Mom, why don't I get you your washcloth and makeup and stuff. I'm going to run downstairs to the gift shop and see if I can get one of those disposable cameras."

"Good idea. Hopefully by the time you get back, I'll be organized and beautiful." Sara kissed her daughter and watched her hurry out the door, set on a mission.

***

On the way down in the elevator, Annie made a mental list of the things she wanted to get for her mother at the gift shop. Something old, something new, something borrowed, something blue. Her outfit would be the something old, something new... maybe she could find some nice earrings in the gift shop. Something borrowed... hmm... Annie fingered the gold chain she was wearing. That would work. Something blue... she'd have to keep her eyes open in the gift shop. And flowers... maybe a bouquet of roses. And the camera... ideas bombarded her busy brain as she waited impatiently for the elevator to travel to the first floor.

Finally arriving at the gift shop, she saw a rack of handmade earrings. A beautiful pair of blue lapis ovals jumped out at her. They were simple but elegant. These will take care of new and blue. Great. She took it as a good omen that she'd found them so quickly. Now flowers and the camera.

As she stood waiting to speak to the elderly woman behind the counter, she overheard the conversation between the woman and her supervisor.

"We only have what's left in the cooler to sell. Only the pre-made arrangements, no individual stems left. He bought us out!"

A niggle of concern struck her. Could they mean no flowers? That's what it sounds like. What will I do? Maybe find a flower shop in town... but I don't know this town at all... oh please...

The woman with white hair and the pink volunteer smock came over to the counter to wait on her.

"Do you have any of those disposable cameras?"

"We don't have much of a selection but we do have a few over there by the magazine rack." The woman pointed and Annie moved in that direction.

"And I'd like to get a small bouquet of roses, white if you

232

have them. Wrapped so they can be held, if you can."

"I'm sorry miss. The only flowers we have are what you see in the cooler, already made into arrangements."

"I can't buy even a single white rose?" Annie tried to think of other options. Her mother had to have flowers at her wedding.

"I'm sorry. Normally it wouldn't be a problem, but this morning, a man came through here and bought all the roses we had... they're being delivered to one of the rooms now."

Annie smiled. "Would it be Room 245?"

"Yes! How did you know?" The woman looked surprised.

"He's quite a guy...that's what my mother told me. Okay then, I guess I'll be getting the camera and the earrings. We're having a wedding upstairs. It seems the flowers have been taken care of."

"Oh how nice. The man who was in this morning must have been the groom. He was just so excited." The older woman twittered as she peeled the price tag off the earring box and carefully punched in the numbers on the cash register.

Annie paid for her purchases, anxious to get upstairs to help her mom get ready. As she waited at the elevator, Eric came and stood next to her.

"Nancy and Phil already went upstairs. I wanted to call my dad and check on him. He didn't know I came up here."

"Oh. There's some interesting news from Room 245." Annie watched Eric. They'd slept together last night in the big king-sized bed, but things were very strained this morning when they got up. She tried to read his eyes; where did they stand with each other?

"Is everything okay?" Concern etched creases in his forehead. She tamped down the urge to reach her fingers up and smooth the creases away, afraid he'd reject her.

She smiled. "Everything is more than okay. Ben and Mom are getting married today." She watched the shock and then approval register on his face.

"Well, good for them. They love each other and they're going to be together—no matter what. That's the way it should be." Did she detect a tone of sarcasm? His eyes held a hard steely look as they met hers. He was driving her mad with his little remarks…why couldn't they just talk and get it all out in the open?

The elevator door opened before she could say any more and the opportunity to push him to open up lost. He quickly got off the elevator. Was he afraid to be near her? What was going on? They seemed to be back to yesterday when nothing but anger and tension existed between them. She took a deep breath and stepped into her mother's room, mentally setting aside the upset with Eric.

The scent of roses hit her. The room overflowed. Sara sat up in bed with a huge smile. Annie went over and kissed her.

"You look beautiful Mom… and the roses. I tried to get you a bouquet to hold and go figure—they were all sold out."

Sara motioned to the bedside table where a small bouquet of roses and daisies sat. "I told you he's quite a guy."

Annie smiled. Warmth filled her at seeing her mother's happiness. She looked over at Eric. He watched her, making her stomach flip-flop. She wanted to feel his arm around her, and enjoy this happiness together. Instead he'd erected barriers between them. She didn't know why… or how to knock them down. Last night only made things worse.

Nancy fussed with flowers, trying to find room for all the vases full of roses. Kelly Marie gurgled and cooed in Phil's arms.

Sara's doctor walked into the room and stopped, surprise registering on his face. "Well, well, what have we got going on here? I heard a rumor. Is it true? Is there a wedding planned and I wasn't invited?" Dr. Tournier grinned as Sara blushed.

"We hardly had time to send out engraved invitations, but you most certainly are invited." Sara chuckled, "I just don't know what time to tell you."

"It seems the groom left a note at the desk that there will be a wedding in Room 245 at eleven o'clock and anyone who would like to witness the ceremony was welcome to come. And the head nurse gave me strict instructions to get through with my rounds so I can be here." He chuckled as he lifted her hand to feel her pulse.

"We'll all just step outside Mom." Annie shooed the small group out the door just in time to see Doc rushing off the elevator headed for Sara's room, a smile beaming from his face.

"The doctor is in there with her now."

"Good, I made it back in time. I wanted to be here to see what he had to say. I think it looks fine, but we want to hear his good words too." Ben stepped into the room to Sara's side immediately reaching for her hand. Annie caught a glimpse at the look exchanged between them. Pure beautiful love and devotion. Happiness filled Annie, although she fought to squash the pang of envy that crept into her heart uninvited.

Tears pricked at her eyes. A relationship like that had seemed so possible with Eric a few short days ago, now it seemed like it would never be. What happened? How could things change so drastically? And how could he make love to her like he did last night, and yet be so cold and distant today? She tried not to think about it. *I want to be happy for Mom. I need to leave all the upset with Eric alone for now... until I have time to figure out what's wrong and what I'm gonna do. I just wish I could share this happiness with him. He looks so miserable...*

When they all stepped out in the hall, Eric removed himself. He walked to the small sitting room down the hall. She watched him, head hung down, no spring in his step. She followed him after a few moments. Maybe they could get things worked out.

"Eric?" She spoke tentatively, hoping he'd listen.

He turned and stared at her, his eyes shuttered against her read.

"What Annie?" He turned away from her, his back heaving as he let out a deep breath.

"First, thank you for letting me take your car this morning. When I got that message from Laurie, I couldn't help but worry about Mom, even though she just asked for clothes."

"You're welcome."

"I just wondered... well, we didn't get a chance to talk this morning, and I wondered if we could talk now." She moved around him so that she could see his face, try to see what he was thinking.

"Annie, I don't know what we have to talk about. I don't know what to say." He wouldn't meet her look and moved away from her as though he was afraid of her touch.

"I don't know what's happened between us to cause this tension and upset. I understand that you were worried about me when you couldn't find me. I explained to you that I tried to call you several times, and left you a note... but I feel like there is more to it than that. I can't fix it, if I don't know what it is."

"You can't fix it Annie. It's done. I'm sorry about last night. I shouldn't have, we shouldn't have... well... I meant to sleep on the couch. Let's just leave it."

"Eric?" Her stomach twisted at his hurtful words.

"I'm driving home after the ceremony. I told Doc I'd be here to share his happiness. He's been a good friend to me and stuck by me in some really bad times, and I want to be here for him in his good times too. But beyond that, I have to leave. I'm glad your mom is going to be okay. I'm sure you can get a ride back with your sister and Phil." He turned and walked out of the waiting room and down the hall.

Annie reached for a chair and fell into it. He dismissed everything growing between them, just like that. No explanation. She fought the tears that sprang to her eyes. Damn him. Why is he being such a jerk? There was nothing she could do, at least not now, not here. But it wasn't over, not by a long shot.

She took a deep breath, stood, and marched back down the hall to await a wedding.

***

She asked him to leave. To step outside while she talked to her doctor? I'm your doctor. What is going on here?

He knew he stood there with his jaw dropped. Dr. Tournier

looked at him with sympathy, compassion, brotherly bewilderment at the female of the species. The doctor shrugged his shoulders and nodded his head.

Okay, he'd step outside, humor her, but not happily.

He put on a professional face, trying to look as normal as possible. He didn't want to worry the girls, or show his upset to the world.

"What did the doctor say?" Nancy stepped forward anxiously, voicing the question that they all waited to have answered.

"I stepped out to give your mom a little privacy. I think things look good, but we'll hear from the doctor soon enough. In the meantime, I'm sure you've all heard about our plans for today?" He looked at the nodding heads, smiles on all faces, making eye contact with Eric.

"You are full of surprises, Doc." Eric winked at him. A good friend, Ben could think of no one he'd rather have here for him.

"Come for a walk with me Eric. I need your help." He motioned his head toward the waiting room at the end of the hall, and the younger man fell into step next to him.

"What can I do for you?" Concern etched a line in Eric's brow.

"I'm glad you're here. I can't think of anyone I'd rather have as a best man at my wedding. Will you stand up for me?"

"Of course, I'd be honored. I am going to leave after the ceremony though. It's a long drive back, and I want to try and make the night boat back to the island."

"Sure. There isn't going to be any big reception with dancing and dinner. We'll save the party 'til my bride can dance." He patted Eric on the back.

"How are you doin'? You've had a wild few days. You okay?" Eric looked him in the eyes.

The professional face slipped. He could share with this man how it felt to hold the woman you love in your arms, and wonder if you'll have the rest of your lives together. "She scared me. I thought I lost her. When I saw all the blood..." He shook his head, afraid the image would stay in his mind forever.

"You saved her, Doc. She's going to be fine. And she's going to be your wife. You have lots of years ahead of you. You are a lucky man."

The look in the younger man's eyes... was it sorrow, regret. Oh, what an idiot I am. Of course he's thinking of Cara... "I'm sorry. I didn't mean to remind you of Cara."

"No. It's okay. How lucky you are to have found love, and to be able to be together with that person. Second chances don't always work out. I'm happy yours is going to." They'd reached the waiting room, and Eric slid into a chair. Doc pulled another one around to face Eric.

"Thanks. I thought things between you and Annie were— how to say it—developing? I was happy for you two. What's happened?"

"Too much I'm afraid. I've managed to make things really difficult for myself but... it's the way it has to be. Things were developing. But now they're not. Let's just say we are going our separate ways. Or she's going her separate way." He rubbed his hands over his face. "I don't really want to talk about it now. I'd much rather just be here to enjoy your day. I'll be fine."

"Hmm. We'll talk about all this when I get back to the island though. I want to know what's going on... what happened... okay?" He watched the young man struggling to hold it together. He hadn't seen this man look so hurt and lost since the week after Cara died. He couldn't imagine what had occurred between Annie and Eric.

"Yeah. We should probably get back down the hall. The doctor's just come out of the room and Nancy's pointing down here. I think they're looking for you."

His heart hammered as he rose and strode quickly down the hall. Was something wrong? Did Sara need him?

The smile on Dr. Tournier's face did wonders to relieve his worries. "How is she?"

"She's ready to be a bride, I'd say. She asked me to send

you back in… alone. I'll be back for the ceremony at eleven."
He patted Ben's shoulder and hurried off down the hall.

Ben peeked in Sara's room. She sat up in bed, waiting for
him. She smiled. The upset he'd felt at being dismissed from
her room dissipated. He couldn't stay mad at her. God she's
beautiful. He closed the door behind him and went to her,
taking the hand she reached out for him. Soft, warm… just like
the rest of her.

"I saw the hurt look on your face when I asked you to
leave. Don't be upset. I had some things I needed to ask the
doctor… privately. I'll explain later. But he said the same
things you did. Everything looks good. It seems like there is no
leakage from the sutures and the tissue color all the way down
the leg indicates that blood flow is good. There, I remembered
it all for you." She smiled.

It warmed his soul. His arms were around her without
conscious thought. "I am so happy. So relieved."

"You aren't mad at me?" She pulled away to look into his
eyes.

"No. I was a little hurt but you said you'd explain later,
and I trust you. I'm sure you have a good reason. I'm okay."
He nodded at her and pulled her close. Joy filled him just
holding her. He breathed in the scent of her mixed with the
scent of the roses. He kissed her soft lips gently, and moved
away from her.

"So, let's tell everyone the good report and then we can
plan the rest of this wedding." Her radiant smile brought tears
to his eyes. His bride.

***

She didn't need the white dress and all the trappings; she
had what was truly important—the man she loved, her family
around her, and her future. She'd lain in bed this morning, after
Ben had buzzed off to do things and thought about how truly
lucky she was. She could have very easily bled to death out in
the woods. She could have lost her second chance at love.
Tears flowed. Tears of joy, tears of relief, tears of thanks.

And now with the scent of roses filling the room, her

family stood around the bed and Ben stood next to her. The chaplain had just arrived and staff members filled in the spaces near the door. She waited for one more person—Dr. Tournier. She wouldn't let them start without him.

"Who are we having as witnesses?" The chaplain took the marriage certificate out of an envelope. Ben stepped forward and signaled for Eric to join him. Sara waved for Annie to come to the bedside table where the chaplain waited.

"Who woulda thought the weekend would end up like this?" Ben winked at her and smiled, an intimate smile between the two of them.

"You're full of surprises, Ben. I hope I can keep up with you!" She squeezed his hand. Her heartbeat quickened when she thought of the surprise she planned. *Where is Dr. Tournier? He promised he would be here.* She glanced at the wall clock. Exactly eleven. Her stomach fluttered with butterflies.

She watched as first Annie, then Eric signed the document. They shifted away from each other, very aware of avoiding each other's personal space. *Odd. No eye contact.* Sara looked over them to Ben. He read her bewildered look and shrugged. He saw it too, but had no explanation. *She'd ask Annie later.*

She looked at her daughter. Her blonde hair flowed loosely over the turquoise cowl neck sweater. Color blushed her cheeks, and her eyes shone with tears. She watched as Annie watched Eric sign the document. *Were the tears somehow about him?* Annie looked away before Eric could see her, and Sara reached her hand out to stop him from turning.

"Thank you for being here Eric, and being a witness for us. That makes it even more special." She saw Annie collect herself out of the corner of her eye. When she turned to speak to Annie, Eric ducked away from the bed, toward the crowd gathering.

"And thank you Annie." She reached over and gave Annie's hand a squeeze. "You okay?" she added quietly. A quick nod was all she got for a response. *Grown up or not, I'm going to have to do a little interrogating soon.*

"Okay are we ready to get started?" The chaplain looked

toward her. Ben moved next to the bed to take her hand.

"Here I am Mrs. Burdick. Did you think I would forget?" Dr. Tournier moved through the crowd of staff at the door and entered the room. He stepped in between Ben and Sara. She watched Ben's face scowl in puzzlement. Sara moved the covers off her legs, and with Dr. Tournier's help, swung her legs off the side of the bed. She gingerly stood up, keeping most of her weight on her good leg, but touching down with the injured leg.

"Sara, what are you doing? Are you sure she should be doing this?" Ben immediately moved to her side taking her arm.

She looked up at him. "I'm fine. I wanted to stand by the man who is going to be my husband. Surprise," she smiled into his eyes. "Now I'm ready." She nodded at the chaplain, then at Dr. Tournier who stepped back from the couple. Ben had a grip on her arm like he was afraid she'd fall over any moment. She turned to him, loosened the grip, and held his hands with hers. "I'm okay Ben. I practiced this morning. So... let's get married."

Rev. Roberts opened his book and started the ceremony. Annie and Eric stood behind them, Nancy and Phil nearby with Kelly Marie gurgling through the vows. Family, friends, and staff members watched as Ben Stephenson promised to cherish her, Sara Burdick, for the rest of their days. Joy sang through her as she promised to love and honor this wonderful man all the days of our lives.

Music started playing from the CD player Ben had brought in earlier. Phil manned the buttons. John Denver's voice resonated through the room; Follow Me had been one of the songs they listened to on the drive north. Now it would forever be one of their special songs.

Tears pricked at the back of Sara's eyes. He'd thought of everything. She squeezed his hand and looked at his face. He mouthed the words of the song, as though he sang it for her. When the song ended, he leaned into a tender kiss.

"I love you."

"I love you too Ben."

Reverend Roberts reached into his pocket and produced two simple gold bands. He handed the larger to her, the smaller to Ben. As they exchanged rings, symbolizing their unending love for each other, Sara saw Eric out of the corner of her eye, wiping a tear from his. She and Ben slipped the rings on each other's fingers, kissed, and held hands. They turned to face the crowd gathered as Reverend Roberts announced them as Dr. and Mrs. Stephenson.

Sara looked at her girls, Nancy beaming as she held a sleeping baby, and Annie, with tears in her eyes, looking not at them, but at Eric.

***

She wanted to be happy for her mother, and she was. But right now, the need to have a good cry almost overwhelmed her, and she certainly couldn't break down in front of this crowd of well-wishers. She took a deep breath and tried to swallow the tears threatening to swallow her. She struggled to keep a smile on her face. *I've got to get out of here...just for a few minutes.* She made her way to the door. The ceremony was over and people milled around to speak to the happy couple. She slipped into the empty room next door for a minute. *Just until I get myself calmed down. Damn him! What's he looking so sad about? He's the one being a jerk.*

She covered her face with her hands, closing her eyes. Just think about Mom and Ben. They looked so happy...so in love. She took another deep breath, and wiped her eyes with her fingers, opening them to see Eric standing in the doorway looking at her. Gut punch... again.

"Are you okay?" He stepped into the room, closer to her.

"No. I'm not. It was tough standing there watching my mother and Doc finding their chance at happiness, while all the time wondering about us and what happened. I don't understand Eric. I really don't get it." She was tired. And she wanted answers.

"I was wrong to call you the other night, and I shouldn't have taken you to bed, had sex with you. It's too soon, and it

242

wasn't right of me. And last night just made it harder. I'm sorry. I think it will be better if we don't see each other anymore."

Another gut punch. She leaned against the wall and closed her eyes, shaking her head. Disbelief filled her. Something isn't ringing true here. He's not telling me the truth. Why not?

"I don't understand Eric." She opened her eyes and really looked at his face. Pained. Hurt. He looked awful. Why?

"It's time for you to move on, Annie. You have great opportunities ahead of you, and you need to go after them. Go after your dreams. I wish you nothing but happiness and good luck in your future. Good-bye Annie." He turned and walked out.

She had her cry then. She couldn't stop the tears. He'd walked out. He'd dismissed what had started between them. He'd said good-bye with a finality that crushed her.

The tears did nothing to wash away the hurt. That had cut too deep.

Chapter 24
Man Overboard

A week later, after getting his bride home to the island, Ben finally found himself outside Eric's office door at the restaurant. Eric's SUV was the only car parked outside so Ben knew they'd have a little privacy. Something had definitely been going on with that boy in Vermont, and he had a sneaking suspicion it had to do with love. Not that he had such a great track record in matters of the heart... he'd only recently rediscovered his.

He peeked through the partially open office door. Eric sat with his hands holding his head, elbows on the desk, eyes closed. He obviously hadn't heard the bells jingle as the front door opened. Ben knocked.

The young man looked up. Dark circles under red-rimmed eyes, pale coloring, disheveled hair. Damn, he looked like crap.

"Oh. Hi Doc." Eric ran his hands through his hair as if to straighten it. He didn't seem eager for company.

"Hello yourself. We just got back to the island and I wanted to talk about a couple of things with you. You open for business?" He slid into the chair facing the desk, settled in and got comfortable. Ready for a nice long talk. Yep. Looks like the boy needs to talk.

"Ah, sure. What can I do for you?" Eric shuffled some papers around, trying to organize. He set the stack of papers on the side, and met Doc's eyes. "Is this really business or can we just talk?"

"Business can wait. You look like you need to talk. What's going on?" He settled back. He knew from experience that Eric was forthcoming with his feelings once he started talking. He just needed a prod. "You didn't seem too happy in Vermont."

"I was happy for you and Sara. It's great to see you two

together. You deserve to be happy." Eric looked at him and
then fidgeted with the metal sand dollar in his hand.

"We all deserve love and happiness in our lives Eric. So
tell me what's keeping it out of yours."

The look that Eric pierced him with verified he'd hit it on
the head. Love troubles. Annie.

"I've lost another one, Doc. Every woman I've ever loved,
leaves me. Well. At least this one didn't die like my mother
and Cara. But she's still gone."

"Explain it to me. I'm missing info here."

"I fell in love with Annie. It's been happening for a while.
We both fought it but... we spent the weekend together. It felt
so right. I thought for her too. When she went home Sunday
morning, we planned to get in touch later and maybe have
dinner. The next thing I know I'm getting a call from you
saying you can't reach her. I couldn't find her either. I looked
all over... the beach, downtown, her house. I was frantic. No
car. No Annie." He took a deep breath and exhaled. His face
paled as he spoke. "I was scared to death something happened
to her."

Ben watched as Eric continued to fidget with the
paperweight... like worry beads. "How did you find her?"

"I decided to call Nancy. I thought I had the number at
home, but couldn't find it, so I went to Annie's house. I'd seen
a list of numbers by the phone in the kitchen. It was there. So
was a note to her mother. She'd left the island to go to New
York. She got a job with a magazine. Don't you think this
would be something you should mention to the guy you
supposedly care about? Who you've just spent the weekend
making passionate love with?" He shook his head, then swiped
his hand through his hair. "I don't know. Maybe I was asking
for too much, too soon. I thought she felt the same way I did. I
thought..."

"How did you know she got a job in New York?"

"The note said she got a call from her editor in New York
and they had a job offer for her. She went down to talk to them
about it. It's what she's always wanted."

"So how did you hook up with her to drive her to Vermont if she was in New York?"

"I went over on the noon boat, parked my car in the ferry parking lot, and waited for her."

"Eric. You didn't know when she was coming back?"

"No. I just figured I'd wait."

It was his turn to shake his head. This boy has it bad.

"So, when she got to the ferry, what happened?"

"I told her about her mom. She almost passed out. I feel bad about that. I kind of hit her with it without thinking about how it sounded." He paused. "We parked her car in the garage and I drove her up."

"Well you had five hours in the car. Didn't you talk things out?"

Eric hung his head like a little boy caught doing something wrong. "I was so angry and hurt with her just leaving without telling me... we didn't talk... much. I don't really know all the details about her job even. She shut down after a while." He shook his head. "No, we didn't talk."

"So... you're just going to let it end?" Bad choice, Eric. Don't give up. There's more there than you even know.

"I don't think I have much choice. She's always wanted to write for a magazine. She deserves to have a fresh start and go after what she's always wanted, always dreamed of. I can't see us having a long distance relationship. I need to let her go. I have to get over her." He leaned back in his office chair and closed his eyes, rubbing the bridge of his nose trying to massage away the stress.

Ben shook his head again. What was he going to do with this boy? He'd found love a second time, and just threw it away.

"I'm not sure I understand why you have to let her go? Have you talked to her about all this?"

"Sorta... in Vermont... before I left."

"And she agrees?"

Again he looked sheepish. "Well, no. I just said goodbye and left her."

"And how are you doin' since you got back?" Eric looked miserable to Ben's practiced eye.

"I miss her like crazy. I can't get anything done. I haven't even felt like leaving the house. She's in my head, all the time."

"Maybe you should call her and try talking. I'm not so sure it needs to be over."

"I want her to have her dream job. She needs to go to New York and start her life over. I'm afraid if I see her, I'll want to make love to her and never let her go. It'll just be harder. I already made that mistake once."

"Well, if you need to talk, you know where to find me. Except that's going to change too. Sara and I have decided to live at her house and renovate mine. We're having plans drawn up to expand the office area and have an apartment upstairs. Actually I'm here to talk to you about insurance stuff."

"Okay. What can I do for you?"

He'd managed to get part of the story from Eric, and now they could get on with business. Sara had had a long talk last night with Annie before she left today to go to Florida. Ben couldn't wait to get home and compare notes. Maybe between the two of them, they'd be able to figure out what was going on, or not going on, between Annie and Eric. Lord knows, they both looked miserable.

***

After visiting Mike's parents for two weeks, Annie returned from Florida with a tan and a mission. She'd figured out what she wanted her life to be, and she had a plan to get it. Mike's parents received the life insurance settlement from his company. They'd signed it over to her. Touched that they wanted her to have it, it relieved her money troubles and allowed her to start this new phase of her life. Mike's parents had been wonderful. They listened with excitement about her new job, suggesting topics and ways to research. She told them about her plans to stay on the island; they encouraged her.

She called the one and only real estate agency on the island and told them what she wanted. Within two weeks of returning from Florida, Annie owned a house on the island, the old Prichard place.

Now she stood in the middle of the empty living room, looking out through the four double hung windows that formed the eastern wall. The house sat up on a hill looking east over the harbor and Eric's restaurant. The view was spectacular and the price was reasonable because so much work needed to be done. Mrs. Pritchard lived there alone for many years until she'd been moved to a nursing home on the mainland. Upon her death, the empty unused house had been sold and her estate split by numerous distant relatives. Annie'd love this place and turn it into a home.

The morning sun shone through the windows, streaked and dirty as they were, across a hardwood floor to the fireplace on the adjacent wall. Everything needed cleaning but she could see in her mind's eye what it would look like after hard work and elbow grease. And she was ready. It was hers.

Pride and satisfaction filled her. Yep. It was what she wanted...well, it wasn't everything, but it was a step in the right direction. The rest of her dream... she was going to start working on that—on him—soon... as soon as the house was ready.

That determination fired her, pushing her to unload the bucket, mop, and cleaning supplies from her car and get started. Mom and Ben volunteered to help after office hours this afternoon. She'd have a good showing for them when they got there.

She filled the bucket with water and cleaned the walls, the floor, and the windows. She emptied bucket after bucket of dirty water down the kitchen sink.

She dreamed as she scrubbed. Tow-headed children laughing as they romped on the floor with their dad, tall muscular blond... that same tall blond with the ocean blue eyes making love with her by the fireplace...the two of them cooking together in the kitchen...

Maybe I'm nuts. The last time we were together he hardly talked to me. And I've bought a house, set up my professional life, and have a repertoire of dreams all centered on him. Well, he told me to go after my dreams... she smiled. Ben said he looked terrible and was pretty sure Eric didn't know she'd bought this house. Good. Now that it was hers, she'd have to go check out the local insurance agent. She smiled as she scrubbed.

***

Sara was surprised to see how much Annie had accomplished by the time they arrived. The living room was finished, the office scrubbed, and the kitchen started. Such a nice place for her. And ready soon. Sara remembered the conversation with Annie upon her return from Florida. She'd feared Annie would return depressed and sad from seeing Mike's parents, but instead she arrived invigorated and determined. She'd made a plan and things were going accordingly. A mother's pride filled her. Her baby was going to be all right.

"Ben, could you help me move some of my things in tomorrow? I have furniture and office stuff being delivered here too. I think I can be moved in by the day after tomorrow." Her face beamed with optimism.

"Sure I can help. Your mom can supervise though. I don't want her lifting anything. Sara, you sit down."

"Yes dear." She smiled and rolled her eyes at Annie. He'd been so over-protective since she'd gotten out of the hospital. Almost five weeks since the accident, the cut had healed, but Ben wasn't taking any chances. She'd have to get him to loosen up a bit. Maybe after Annie moved out, they could talk about getting that Jacuzzi. She had just the spot for it out back on the deck. She smiled at the thought.

"Annie, I can paper the drawers for you if you want... or wash the windows... that's not too strenuous." She winked at her daughter.

"Miss Sara B., are you making fun of me?" Ben turned around from his job of washing the wall and smiled at her. He dropped the sponge and scooped her up swinging her around in his arms. A squeal escaped her lips before he covered them with his. "I'm just trying to take care of my bride." He smiled down at her. "Go easy ma'am." He lowered her to her feet and slapped her bottom.

"You're so fresh," she laughed and danced out of his way. "Get that sponge and go back to work."

"Slave driver!"

They laughed as the three of them worked to finish cleaning the kitchen. By early evening, it sparkled. As Ben carried out several bags of garbage, Sara spoke quietly to her daughter. "Have you seen Eric?"

"No. I want to have the house done, and be able to invite him for dinner and see if we can get back on the right foot."

"Ben says he looks terrible. He hasn't seen him like this since Cara died."

"I know Mom. That's why I'm hurrying to get in here. And I want to give you two newlyweds some privacy too!"

"Oh you… come on. Let's go home and get some dinner." She put her arm around her daughter's waist and gave her a squeeze. Givin' her newlywed mom some privacy… who woulda thought?

***

Eric sat on a weather-beaten log at the high tide mark. He'd left his house because memories of Annie there with him, working in the kitchen with him, sitting with him on the couch, haunted him. He'd had to close the door to the spare bedroom. He couldn't stop thinking about what they'd done there. *My life is a mess. I can't get her out of my mind.*

So he'd gone to the restaurant. She was there too. In the dining room, painting the lunch room, in his office, on his desk…

She was everywhere. He couldn't get rid of the picture in his mind of her standing in the empty hospital room, tears streaming down her cheeks. And he'd left her. Turned and walked away from the only thing that mattered to him, because she mattered to him.

Sitting on the log didn't work for him. He needed the weather to be battering him, the waves and surf pounding; he needed nature's fury to help rid him of this mood.

Nature wasn't cooperating. The water was calm; the rhythmic sound of the gently breaking waves filled the air. A fog hung over the shore, the foghorn sounded warning of rocks ahead to sailors. It should have been a peaceful calming walk for him. It only added to his gloom.

He had walked the rocks toward the lighthouse thousands of times. Miles and miles over the past year—miles for Cara, and now miles for Annie.

He turned around and walked back toward his SUV. He'd have to pull it together since it was nearly time to re-open the restaurant for the summer. He'd need to get a whole new staff in there. Annie wouldn't even be around to train anyone.

Oh well. I've done it before. I can do it again.

His toe caught on something and his foot landed between two rocks and wedged tight—stuck. He pitched forward, landing hard, his knee twisted as he fell. Pain seared through him. He worked to get his foot free, each motion sending new shards of sharp pain up his leg. Sweat broke out on his face despite the cool temperature. His stomach roiled with the pain. Even if he managed to get the foot free, how was he going to get back to his car? He lay on the rocks and closed his eyes, blackness enveloped him.

***

Ah. Finished. Three days' worth of deliveries, moving boxes from Mom's house, arranging furniture in her new house, making it finally livable. Granted, she still had several rooms upstairs to work on, but her room and the bathroom upstairs were done, and the rooms downstairs, especially her office, were beautiful. New furniture, new appliances, and all of her office equipment had been delivered and installed.

She stood and looked around. Her house. Her home. It felt right. Satisfaction filled her as she walked from room to room through the downstairs. She stood next to her desk and fingered the heart shaped glass paperweight from Mike. He'd be proud of her. She missed him. She loved him. But she worked hard to make a new life for herself. A warmth filled her. He approved.

Now, her first night and she couldn't wait to work in her kitchen, work in her office, live in her home. Mom brought over a small casserole for dinner, so she decided to walk on the beach before she got dinner ready. Lord knew, her muscles were tired and sore from the heavy work she'd done to get moved in. It would feel good to stretch them out. She threw on her light jacket and walked out the door. The beach, their beach was not far away.

It was a peaceful walk. The temperature was cool, with a mist in the air from fog, the foghorn sounded in the distance. It was a melancholy sound, but it also gave her a sense of security. You knew it was there to protect you. Warn you of dangers, guide you to a safe harbor in a storm. She laughed at her philosophical thoughts. *It's a lighthouse for Pete's sake. Your writer's mind is going off again.*

As she walked into the parking lot of the beach, she saw Eric's vehicle. Should she stop and turn around? She hadn't planned to run into Eric until tomorrow or the next day when she would go and talk to him about insurance. That had been her plan.

Maybe she should try and talk to him here. It worked for them in the past. She thought about him. Actually, she'd thought of little else besides Eric and the house. Time to confront him? He needed a good shake. He needed to be yelled at.

No Annie, yelling will not get you what you want. Tell him how you feel; you need to tell him about your plan.

She looked down the rocky shore hoping to see the now familiar silhouette of the man she'd come to love. Nothing. She glanced in the other direction, wondering if maybe he'd gone around the bend to the next inlet. Large rocks jutted out into the water. Walking would be hard going; climbing over the rocks would be the way you'd need to go. No sign of him there.

The fog shifted in clouds passing over the water and shore. As she walked, the sound of the gentle waves soothed her. Maybe Eric walked farther down the shore and she'd see him walking out of the mist and then into her arms. He filled her thoughts. She'd missed him so much these last weeks. She'd had a lot to keep her busy. But he was always with her. It wasn't over. She was determined to set it straight... set him straight. Anger, loneliness, determination, love, passion—how was it possible to feel all of these emotions without bursting?

She walked slowly on the sandy beach below the rocks. The tide was out and the waves gently lapped the shore with plenty of beach at her disposal. The fog hindered her view of the long stretch of seashore she knew was ahead of her.

The sun neared the horizon. Not wanting to return home in the dark, she headed back, walking along the rounded rocks at the top of the beach. The fog shifted in the distance, and twenty feet ahead of her, on the rocks, lay something that looked like a jacket...red like the one Eric wore.

Fear and panic sliced through her like a knife. She ran along the beach and up onto the rocks. She'd seen Eric's truck but not Eric.

"Eric?" She knelt down next to him, touching him gently. "Eric, are you okay?" His eyes were closed, his body twisted, and his foot caught at an odd angle.

"Eric, wake up. I'm here. I'll help you."

His eyes fluttered. "Annie? Is that you?" He lifted his hand to his head, a bluish bump was forming on his forehead. He closed his eyes and opened them again.

"What happened? You're foot's wedged between these two rocks."

"I guess I got stuck and went down."

"If I move this rock away, can you get your foot out?"

"Yeah. It hurts like hell but I'll get it out. Be careful." He winced as she moved the rock and he pulled his leg free with both hands supporting the injured limb.

His face was pale. He sat on the rocks.

"If I help you, do you think you can make it to your truck?" Annie saw the pain on his face. He was such a big man. How could she support him? She'd have to find a way.

"I don't think I'm going to be able to put any weight on it.

Maybe you should go into town for help."

"I don't want to leave you here. Wait. I have an idea…give me your keys."

He reached in his pocket and handed his keys to her. Their fingers touched and the shock of electricity that flowed through them startled and excited her. It was still there—the electricity, the spark, the connection.

She moved quickly across the rocks, almost ran, being careful not to fall or miss a step. She got into his SUV, started it up and put it in four-wheel drive. She drove along the top level of rocks, flattened by other off-road drivers, to within five feet of where Eric sat.

He shimmied over the rocks on his hands and his bottom. She helped him stand, keeping the weight off his leg. Both his knee and ankle were swelling up fast. She helped him maneuver into the passenger seat. Once inside, he collapsed against the back, closing his eyes. His face was white with pain. She could see him take several deep breaths. Trying to control the pain? Trying to regain composure?

She got back in the driver's seat and started the engine, moving quickly to get off the rocks and to Ben's office.

"Thanks Annie. I don't know what I would have done if you hadn't come along. Are you visiting your Mom and Doc?"

Annie kept her eyes on the road. Dusk had fallen and the fog affected the visibility on the road too. "I've been back and forth." She wasn't giving him any information yet. A plan began to develop in her mind, but she'd wait and make sure he was going to be okay.

Before she knew it, they were at the office. She quickly dialed Ben on the emergency phone outside the office. He'd be there in less than five minutes.

She checked on Eric through the window. His eyes were closed, a pained expression on his face. She paced while she waited for Ben. How could she make this work? It was as though the fates that led him to find her on the beach months ago had worked to help her find him there tonight. It's where it had all started for them. Could it be what they needed to fix the rift between them? Could they find each other again?

Ben arrived and opened the building. He directed Annie to a wheelchair from the storage room while he looked at Eric's injured leg. Together they helped him out of the car and into the chair, Ben pushing him and Annie holding the doors open.

She paced in the waiting room while Ben examined Eric. She wanted to be there to hear the diagnosis, but what right did she have? She wanted to be there to hold his hand, smooth back the hair from his forehead, kiss away the hurt. She wanted.

She decided. She'd never acted so forward, so bold... but she'd never had so much to lose. She went into the examining room as though she belonged there, took his hand and turned to Ben.

"How is he? What did you find?" She almost laughed at the stunned look she got from Eric. He stared at her... speechless.

"Well, he's got a good bump on the head, a badly sprained ankle and a twisted knee. Nothing's broken. We'll have to keep an eye on the knee. He may have damaged ligaments. He shouldn't put any weight on that leg for a few days at least."

"I'll make sure he stays off it. Can you give me a hand getting him back in the car? Do you want him to use crutches?"

"Yes. There are a few pairs in that closet over there." Ben pointed her toward the storage closet in the corner of the room.

"I want him to keep ice on both the knee and the ankle, off and on for the next twenty-four to forty-eight hours. And here is some pain medication in case he needs it." Ben finished bandaging the ankle, and handed her a bottle with half a dozen pills in it. "They may make him sleepy."

"Annie, you're not going to take care of me. I'll be fine. You have to get back to New York, to your job."

She looked at him. Let him think that for a little while longer, just until I get him home. "I'm not going to argue about it. Let me help you get back to the car."

He grimaced as he moved off the examining table. The crutches helped, but it seemed any motion caused him pain. His face was white. He looked as though he might pass out. She ran ahead to open the doors. Ben followed behind.

"Eric, I'll stop by tomorrow to see how you're doing. It's going to take a few days before the swelling goes down enough to tell what you've done to that knee. Call me if you need anything."

"I can't believe I did this. How many times have I walked on the beach?" Annie could hear the disgust in his voice.

Annie opened the door to Eric's SUV. It was a painful process to get him in. Bending the knee caused a groan of agony from Eric that made her stomach turn. Hold it together Annie. You can't get sick from his pain. You've got to be the strong one.

Ben finished helping Eric while she ran around to the driver's side and got in, starting the car. She turned on the heat and the headlights; she remembered one more thing she wanted to tell Ben. She got out of the car and went around to him, as he was closing the door on Eric's side.

"I'm taking him to my house. He can sleep on the couch, and maybe we can finally get some things straightened out. I don't think he knows that I bought it; he asked if I was back visiting you and Mom."

"She told me that you didn't want him to know so I haven't said anything. He's been pretty miserable. I'd say it's time to put him out of his misery." He smiled as he winked.

She laughed and nodded. A little pang of guilt stabbed at her heart; maybe she should have told Eric that she planned to stay on the island and work from there. But damn it, he hadn't given her a chance. He hadn't trusted her feelings for him. He'd walked away. And he had been miserable... and so had she. Time to put them both out of their misery.

Chapter 25
The Calm Before the Storm

Eric laid his head back on the car seat and closed his eyes. His leg hurt like nothing he'd ever felt before. He concentrated on trying to put Annie out of his mind. That only added to his pain. She was everywhere. Thank God she'd been on the beach. Thank God for Annie. Seeing her was killing him, yet he couldn't get enough of her. He was an addict, wanting to quit but not able to stay away.

She'd left the car running and gotten out to talk to Ben. Probably getting instructions. She opened the door and climbed in the driver's seat, her fresh scent filled his head, memories of their weekend together swirled through his mind. His heart raced. He kept his eyes closed.

Just get me home so I can take that pain medication and lay down. His entire leg throbbed. Every bump in the road reverberated through his body. He held his body tense, trying to cushion the leg. He moaned.

"I'm trying to be careful. I know you're in pain. We're almost there." Annie's voice soothed him.

"I've never had anything hurt this bad in my life."

"Just keep your eyes closed and try to relax. It's going to be okay."

God he wanted to believe that... but how could anything be okay without her in his life? A wave of self-pity gut-punched him. He'd been miserable for the last six weeks without her. Days went by when he didn't even leave his house. Insurance business was light, and the restaurant was closed. Cara would have called it moping. He didn't know what Annie would have called it. He called it his life.

And now her fresh scent, the musical sound of her voice,

even the rhythm of her breathing filled his senses reminding him of all he'd lost. The throb of his leg was a hangnail compared to the painful throb of his heart.

The car pulled to a stop. He hadn't been paying attention to the ride and was surprised to be home so soon. He opened his eyes and shifted his weight ready to get out of the car.

"Where are we? What are we doing here?" Puzzled by a house he'd never seen before, he looked into her eyes. Mistake. He saw yearning, he saw love, he saw that he was going to have to hurt her again when she went back to New York. Why couldn't she understand that a long distance relationship wasn't going to work?

She didn't answer him. She turned off the car and walked around to his side of the car. She opened the door to help him out.

"Annie, what are you doing? I need to get home. What the hell is going on?"

"Come on. Here are your crutches. I'll answer all of your questions as soon as you get inside and sit down. We need to get that leg elevated and put ice on it."

She avoided his questions. His leg throbbed with pain so that must be why it wasn't making sense.

She'd pulled close to the porch. One step up, across ten feet of covered porch, and one more step up into the house. For the life of him, he couldn't figure out why they were here. Just concentrate on getting up the step with these damn crutches.

She held the door open wide. He maneuvered up the step and into a wide central hallway, stairs to the second floor set back and to the left. The smell of paint and cleaner and new furniture assailed him. She moved into the room and turned on a floor lamp. A polished hardwood floor, cream walls, warm maroon and green stuffed couches, a large stone hearth and the front wall of windows invited him, surrounded him, soothed him. *The pain must really be getting to me.*

"Annie?"

"Welcome to my home, Eric. Here let's get you comfortable on this couch. We need to get you off that leg."

She moved toward him, guiding him to the nearby couch. Good thing her hand was on his back, he could fall over at any minute. Her home...did she say her home? What about New York? What the hell was going on?

He sat quickly—pain exploded up his leg, a curse escaped his breath, confusion filled his head. Annie moved to help him shift his leg onto the couch and put pillows behind his back. He reached up and took her hand. Soft, warm, gentle. Like the rest of her.

"Sit down and tell me what is going on...please?"

"I will. Let me go get you some water so you can take the pain medication, a bag of ice for your knee, and then I'll explain everything." She let go of his hand and left. He wanted her back near him. Just the touch of her hand relieved his pain. She was his remedy, his cure.

She returned with a glass of water, the bottle of pills from Ben and a plastic bag filled with ice. She handed him the pills, waiting with the water while he opened the bottle. She arranged the ice on his knee and stood near the couch, near him.

He looked up into her eyes. He saw strength, love, humor. He was lost in those eyes. He didn't want to ever look away. "Come, sit here next to me and tell me." He patted the couch next to his hip.

Instead she sat in an overstuffed chair of forest green, her legs curled under her. He felt her reserve. The distance between them seemed enormous. Was she trying to stay away from him? He'd hurt her at the hospital; the memory of her tear-streaked face haunted him every minute of the last six weeks.

"I told Ben I'd bring you here because it will be easier for me to take care of you here rather than running back and forth to your house. He's going to stop by tomorrow." She seemed to be avoiding his real question... What is going on?

"Annie, when I left you in Vermont, you were going to take a job in New York. I thought you came to the island to visit your mom. Did the job fall through? What's the story with this house? What is going on?" Maybe it was the pain, or the pain medication, but he seemed to be missing a big piece of the puzzle. He couldn't think to figure it out; she had all his senses dancing at high alert and his brain functioning like oatmeal. Great.

***

She should take pity on him; he was in pain and totally confused... and frustrated with her evasive answers. Or she could make him suffer a little more, for all the pain he'd caused her by not communicating what he was really feeling in Vermont. She could let him wallow in confusion just a little more... but she wasn't like that. Her heart went out to him. It took all her strength to sit in the chair instead of next to him on the couch. She wanted to hold him in her arms, sooth his pain... and hers too. It was time.

"Eric, do you remember I once told you that I admired the way you negotiated with your bosses in the insurance company to let you have a different work arrangement so that you and Cara could go after the dream of owning a restaurant here? I told you I like the way you think outside the box." She felt the color rise in her cheeks as images of one interlude of thinking outside the box on Eric's office desk flitted through her mind. Her heart hammered.

He nodded; his eyes watched her face but he said nothing.

"I found myself sitting in the editor's office in New York having just heard my dream job being offered to me and I was disappointed. I wasn't sure I wanted to take it." She looked down at her folded hands. This was harder than she thought it'd be.

"You deserve to have that job. You should go after what you want. What happened?"

"Well, that's the thing. I thought I wanted the big magazine job and life in the city. My dad had always said you couldn't be successful and live your life on an island. I think that was his way of making sure I didn't limit myself to what the island had to offer. But I discovered my own definition of successful, and I think I can be successful here."

"What do you mean you thought you wanted the magazine

job?" He shook his head.

Poor guy, it really wasn't sinking in. She'd spell it all out for him. "Sitting in that office, I realized what I wanted. I wanted the job—writing a monthly column on issues surrounding young married couples—and I wanted to be here on the island too. No wait, that's not entirely truthful. I wanted to stay on the island and be with you." She took a deep breath, trying to calm her hammering heart. "I thought we had a good start at a new relationship and I wasn't willing to give that up for the job in New York."

"So you didn't take the job?" His eyes were huge with wonder and concern. "How are you affording this house? How are you going to be able to live?" He glanced around the living room.

His reaction did nothing to reassure her. Why wasn't he saying anything about their relationship?

"I took the job…but I negotiated a little before I did. I can think outside the box too. I pulled an Eric Nordsen move."

He looked at her, confusion covering his face. "I don't understand."

"E-mail, Fax, and phone conferencing. They set up an office here for me. I don't have to be in the New York office to write. I have to travel there several times a month for meetings, and it may be more often if there are special projects, but I can do almost everything here. I'll still have time to work on my novel; I may even have time to help at the restaurant, if you still want me. I went after what I really want, the way I want it." She smiled as she thought of what she wanted the most. He lay on her couch. And he still didn't get it.

"I'm impressed. But how did you get this place? I know you got some insurance money but it couldn't be enough for a house." He shook his head, his brows gathered.

"You know that Mike's parents wanted me to go to Florida over Christmas. I couldn't face that over the holidays. After I got back from Vermont, and I was sure Mom was okay, I arranged to spend a couple of weeks with them. They were wonderful. I already knew about my job, and I told them I wanted to stay on the island. I also told them about my writing...novels I mean. They are both avid readers and were so proud and supportive, excited really. And they encouraged me to go after my dream."

"I'm glad you're working that into your plan. I know how important it is to you."

"They got the insurance check from Mike's company. They were absolutely adamant about giving it to me. They insisted it's what he would have wanted. So I took it and the money from the car insurance, along with a small loan, and bought this place. I have the house on the mainland that is mortgage free and rented, and just a small monthly payment on this house. I have enough income from the mainland house and my job to live very comfortably, and the time and space to write."

"You have worked it all out." He looked down at his hands, his shoulders drooped.

Why did he look so sad? Now she was confused. He'd said he was happy for her, yet his tone and his face filled with disappointment and sadness.

He hadn't reacted to her statement about their relationship. What had she done? She needed to get out of the room...she needed to think. Had she assumed too much about their relationship? Had she made all these huge life decisions based on a false assumption? Her stomach twisted. She felt like throwing up.

"I'll be right back Eric. I have something to do in the kitchen." She bolted out of the room.

She leaned against the gleaming new stove, its heat warming the chill that settled over her. "What if he doesn't want me in his life?" She whispered the question, not even wanting to hear it asked out loud. Tears threatened, as they had so often lately. She fought to control them.

She opened the refrigerator and took out the casserole her mother had made for her and put it in the preheated oven. She took a deep breath. Time to regroup here. They could talk about other things, maybe watch some TV while dinner heated up. She needed to keep it light. She needed more time to figure this out.

She walked slowly back to the living room. She glanced in her office as she walked by the doorway. It was dark but the light from the hallway shone in. It was organized and orderly. She remembered the satisfaction that morning as she set up all the equipment the way she wanted it. She looked at the freshly painted walls in the entry hall, turned and walked into the living room with all the beautiful new furniture. All of it meant nothing if she couldn't have the one thing she wanted most of all.

***

He lay with his eyes closed. The pain medication kicked in. His knee didn't throb if he didn't move it. The ankle had only a dull ache. Unfortunately, the pills had no effect on the pain in his heart.

He was an idiot. He'd been so wrapped up in the hurt he'd felt by Annie not telling him about her job interview, he'd felt so left out and abandoned that he'd totally blown it with her. He treated her badly on the drive to Vermont, and he'd been even worse at the hospital. And he'd been selfish enough to make love with her one last time at the inn, knowing that she was leaving for New York... except now she lived here instead of the city. How could he possibly see her around town and stay away from her? She'd never forgive him. He couldn't forgive himself.

Somehow, he'd make her understand. He'd been frantic when he couldn't find her anywhere. Then furious and hurt when he found out she'd left without a call. He pushed her away because of his hurt. And he'd been miserable since he left her in Vermont. And now... he'd be amazed if she forgave him. But he needed her... wanted her... in his life.

She walked back into the living room. He could take the coward's way out and pretend he was asleep. She was so considerate, she'd let him sleep. You're already an idiot, don't make it worse. He opened his eyes. She looked so sad. Her shoulders drooped, her eyes downcast.

"Annie? Are you alright?" He watched her try to paste a slight smile on her face.

"I'm okay. Mom made a casserole and I just put it in. We could watch some television until dinner's ready if you want." Her sad eyes focused on him.

"Okay. If that's what you want." He watched her shake her head slowly.

"It's not, but I don't know how to get there from here." She shrugged her shoulders.

"What do you mean?"

"I want us to talk... really talk... like we used to. Just talk to me Eric." She flipped her hands out to the sides in frustration as she moved to sit in the overstuffed chair. He reached his hand for hers as she walked by. It was warm, strong... just like her. He pulled her to sit down next to him as he lay with his leg elevated on the couch.

"I'm afraid, Annie."

"Afraid to talk?" Her tone was incredulous.

"Afraid that I'm too much of an idiot for you to care about me anymore. I am so sorry Annie. I was awful to you. I hurt you. I didn't listen to you, and I pushed you away. I was afraid that I'd lost another love in my life. I couldn't handle it so I pushed you away." His heart hammered but he had to do this. He had to try.

"Why did you think you'd lost another love?"

"That weekend together was unbelievable. I thought there could be a future for us... when we were both ready. When I got the call from Doc about your mom, and I couldn't find you, I was frantic. I searched all over the island." He twined his fingers with hers.

"Then I went to your house and found the note you'd written to your mother about your dream job. You left for New York without a word to me." He paused to take a deep breath. He had to continue. He needed her to understand and forgive.

"I knew you needed to go after that job. After all you've been through, you deserve to have what you've always wanted. On one hand, I didn't want to stand in your way. On the other hand, I was crushed that I didn't mean enough to you to share it with me. So I pushed you away." He looked down at their hands joined together. He had to finish this. Not the idiot anymore.

"I've been miserable. There have been days when I didn't even get out of bed. Everything at home reminds me of you, everything at the restaurant reminds me of you... I can't even walk the beach without thinking of you." He watched her face. He reached to stroke her cheek with his fingers. "Annie, I love you. I want you in my life."

She reached up and held his hand against her cheek and closed her eyes. Would she say the words he needed to hear from her?

"I love you too Eric." She leaned down and touched her soft lips to his. It was a gentle tender kiss. He moved his hand through her silky hair and pulled her closer, deepening the kiss.

"I've missed you. I feel like we have so much to catch up on." She pulled her mouth away and rested her head on his chest.

"Come back here. We have to get caught up on this too." He took her mouth again. He couldn't get enough of her; his arms held her close as he devoured her lips. He shifted his body to get closer to her, hold her body against his.

"SSSS..." A stab of pain shot through his leg.

"Are you okay?" Concern creased her forehead. She moved away.

"I just twisted my knee the wrong way. Maybe we should cool it for a while. Just lay here next to me and talk. Tell me about your new job, the house, everything." He stroked his hand down her back as she lay next to him, and she began to talk. The sound of her voice soothed his aches, especially the one in his heart. He'd been forgiven. His Annie was back.

***

"Do you think they're okay? I can't believe you let her take him back to her house. Was he hurt badly? Maybe I should call and make sure she's okay. She's been so emotional lately. I'm sure it's everything that's been going on between them, but I worry about her." Sara paced as she interrogated Ben.

"Sara, calm down. Annie's a big girl and she has everything under control. Based on the twinkle in her eye when she told me she was taking him to her house, they'll be fine. Maybe they'll finally talk and get rid of all the nonsense standing between them." He reached for her and pulled her onto his lap. She melted into him without reservation.

"We're alone in the house, Mrs. Stephenson." He circled his fingertips over her back as he covered her lips with his.

"So we are." She smiled at him. His heart hammered in his chest. It took only a smile from her to set him on fire. She was incredible, this wife of his.

"I have something I want to show you upstairs." He tried to nibble her lips but she chuckled.

"Oh I bet you do," she answered with a deep sensuous laugh.

"You might be surprised." He winked at her. He knew what she was thinking, and they'd get to that. But he did have a surprise upstairs for her. He'd gotten the quote for the deck and hot tub job in the mail today.

"Dinner's going to be ready in half an hour." She stood and pulled him up next to her.

"Half an hour's plenty of time." He put his arm around her and walked with her to the stairs.

***

Annie fixed their plates in the kitchen and carried them to the living room. Fortunately her mom had sent over a shepherd's pie. Her stomach had been bothering her all day—mashed potatoes and hamburger might be mild enough to sit right. Nerves had been wreaking havoc with her this whole week. Must be all the new house stuff, and Eric. Maybe now things would settle down.

She took a deep breath as she loaded their plates onto a tray to carry into the living room. New furniture or not, they ate on the coffee table. The dining room furniture hadn't arrived yet, and she didn't want Eric to move around much.

They sat together on the couch, side by side, enjoying the meal, and talking … finally talking the way they used to.

"Annie, thanks for being on the beach today. I don't know what I would have done." He'd finished his dinner and pushed the plate away. He looked into her eyes.

"Seems like we're even. You saved me from the rocks, and now I've saved you too. That beach is treacherous. Maybe we should stop going there." She smiled at him. She'd missed the verbal play back and forth with him.

"No, but I think we should go there together. It's a special place for me. It's where I first met you and first kissed you. It's where you found me and let me back into your life."

Her heart swelled with love. He was so incredible to think about a beach that way… all in terms of their relationship. He leaned over and kissed her slowly, gently.

"I've missed you Annie."

"I've missed you too."

"When were you going to tell me you were back on the island?" He sat back on the couch and circled his arm around her shoulders.

"My master plan was to get everything set up here, then come to your office for homeowner's insurance. I was going to invite you to my new home and wow you with a wonderful meal, explain my job plan and see if you still wanted help at the restaurant. I hoped we would make up and resume where we left off."

He teased. "You had it all figured out. What if I didn't cooperate?"

"Then I'd just have to rescue you from those treacherous rocks and serve you shepherd's pie." She laughed as she turned to fake punch him in the stomach. He grabbed her wrist and pulled her toward him, wrapping his other arm around her. His firm muscles flexed as she was held against them. He lowered his lips to hers for a long deep kiss—six weeks of pent up passion bubbled between them waiting to be released. Oh, how she wanted him.

"Eric, how is your leg feeling?" She touched his thigh.

"Better. The pain medication has kicked in. Why?" He had a puzzled look on his face.

"I wondered if you wanted to see the rest of the house. Are you up for it?"

He smiled. "I'd love the grand tour. I can't believe how quickly you were able to get everything done."

"Things are slow for the contractors right now, and it was a small job for them. Once I got things cleaned up a bit, JG Builders came in and painted the walls and refinished the floors. Come on. I'll show you."

She stood and offered him a hand. "Be careful."

He managed to get up off the couch and reached for his crutches. He maneuvered his way toward the hallway.

Across the entry hall was another double doorway leading to a room almost identical to the living room without the fireplace. She entered first to turn on several lights. She looked around with pride. A large desk was the central piece of furniture, but several comfortable chairs sat near the front wall of windows that mirrored the ones in the living room.

"The morning sun in here is wonderful. I think it's going to be a great place to write." She liked this room the best. "It feels comfortable to me; this whole house feels like home." She wanted him to understand. "It was amazing when I first walked into the house, dirty and in disrepair, I could see what it could be and picture myself here."

He nodded. "It fits you. I love the office, Annie. It's so big, functional and comfortable."

His words of praise filled her with pride. She'd worked hard to pull this place together. She guided him through a door to the kitchen. New appliances, white painted cupboards and new green and white flooring had modernized the old kitchen. An oak pedestal table sat in the back corner near two large windows that looked out to the back yard. To the right was a doorway to the back entry and a small bathroom. To the left was the doorway to the dining room. Annie stood in the dining room doorway.

"This room's not finished yet. The furniture is supposed to

be delivered soon. I focused more on the office and living room to start with. Upstairs isn't all done yet either. Just my room and the master bathroom are finished. Do you want to see upstairs? Do you think you can do the stairs with the crutches?"

"Let's try. How many bedrooms?" He moved up the stairs without much difficulty on the crutches.

"Four big bedrooms, master bath and a shared bathroom. The ceilings are high and there's good closet space. The master bedroom and the other front room have wonderful views of the harbor." And it was hers. She still couldn't believe her good luck at finding it right as she had decided to look for a house on the island. It was as though someone had been watching over her.

"It's bigger than it looks. These rooms are great, Annie" He had looked at the two smaller rooms toward the back of the house and the common bath. He slowly walked back toward the stairs, and her bedroom.

"Mine's the largest of the four; the bathroom is through there." She stood in her room and pointed to the door at the right. The green and cream bathroom and yellow bedroom set a beautiful background for the comforter of yellow and light green floral print covering her bed. Several small throw rugs picked up the color theme and accented the dark hardwood floors.

"You've got to be proud of what you've done." He came up next to her and put his arm around her. "I'm proud of you." He lowered his lips to hers filling her with a longing she'd been trying to forget for six long weeks. She needed him.

His fingers roamed her back, his slightest touch sending chills of delight through her. He moved to pull her close and hold her tight. She realized through a haze of desire that he was balancing on his good leg, his crutches under his arms and his arms around her. He needed to get off that leg.

"Eric, come and sit on the bed. You're balancing on one leg. That's not good."

"Only if you'll come and sit next to me." He smiled. She

couldn't help smiling back as she moved toward the bed with him.

They sat on the edge of the bed, suddenly awkward with each other.

Eric cleared his throat. "I think I should probably put my leg up on the bed." He scooted back so he leaned up against the headboard.

"Should I put a pillow under your knee?"

"No. Just come here and make me forget about it," he whispered, sending shivers up her spine.

She crawled next to him and whispered, "If I do this, does it make you forget?" She traced her tongue around his lips. She feathered kisses along his jaw to his ear. She nipped his ear lobe. "I know we need to be careful of your leg, but maybe if we both think outside the box…" She whispered her idea in his ear. His excitement was obvious as he pulled her down next to him on the bed. His gentle hands roamed her curves, his mouth traveled over her neck, her face, her lips.

"Let me make you more comfortable." She unbuttoned his shirt and ran her hands over his chest on the way to slipping it off his shoulders.

"Okay, but you look very warm in that sweater. Let me help you out of it." She lifted her arms so he could take it over her head. "You are so beautiful." He traced his finger along the lacey top of her bra. Her breasts tingled at his trailing touch.

"Let me help you get your pants off. I don't want to hurt you."

He chuckled, "You're killing me right now."

She looked up at him quickly, afraid she had hurt his leg. His eyes were looking at her breasts brimming out of top of the bra.

She smiled. "Patience, my dear. Let me help you then you can help me."

Chapter 26
Safe Harbor, Safe Heart

She woke early, the sun streaming through the east windows. Her first night in her new house and they'd spent it together. It felt so right. She lay in the crook of his arm after their lovemaking, and knew she was home. The pale yellow walls soaked up the sunlight, as if saving it for a cloudy day. Warm and comfortable, snuggled against the man she loved, she smiled. Life was good. Gently sliding away from Eric and out of bed, she put her robe and slippers on and went down to make coffee and enjoy the early morning in her new office.

She'd been working on her first column for the last week or so, but with the house details, furniture deliveries, and moving, the deadline had snuck up on her. She was due to fax it by tomorrow, and she had a lot of polishing to do on it yet. The first staff meeting was on Friday. She wanted to make a good impression and had several ideas for her next column already lined up.

She sipped on coffee as she sat at the desk editing her article. A loud thump from upstairs and what sounded like a muffled curse caused her to jump out of her chair.

"Eric? Are you okay?" She hurried for the stairs.

"Annie, I hate to ask but could you help me?" Eric's voice sounded distressed.

She ran up the stairs. What happened? Eric sat on the bed with his jeans halfway up his legs and the pair of crutches lying on the floor near the bed.

"What's that saying about putting your pants on one leg at a time?" He smiled up at her sheepishly. "It's a little harder when one leg won't bend, and you can only stand on one leg. And then I dropped the damn crutches." He shook his head in self-disgust.

Annie chuckled with him. "Why didn't you call me? I would've helped you."

He laughed again. "Yeh, that would be a pretty smooth morning-after line, 'That was great last night honey, but can you help me get my pants on?' Real macho."

"Oh stop it. I hope we're beyond that." She bent down and pulled the pant leg gently over his wrapped ankle and his swollen knee. He worked the other leg into the pants. As he stood to finish pulling them up, Annie stood nearby to hold him steady. Once he finished snapping and zipping, he reached around her and pulled her close.

"Thanks. Now, how about a proper good morning?" He kissed her tenderly stirring her yet again. "How long have you been up?"

"Um, about an hour. Coffee's on and I have some bagels and cream cheese. How does that sound?"

"Sounds good. I think I can even handle fixing it, if you have stuff to do."

"I do. I'm trying to get this first article finished for tomorrow. And I have a meeting at the end of this week so I need to have some ideas ready for that too."

"I'm going to try to drive home after breakfast. I don't want to be in your way if you have work to do." He reached to stroke her hair.

"Oh. I hoped you'd stay around for a while. I like having you here and I want to be able to help you." Her stomach twisted. She didn't want him to leave.

"Annie, I don't want you to have to take care of me. I'll be able to manage... it'll just take me longer. I don't want you to worry about me."

"I'll worry more if you are home alone... and Ben said he would stop by here to check on you today."

"Let's get breakfast and we can figure it out. Okay?" He rubbed his hand up and down her back. It was a familiar, comfortable touch.

"Okay. Be careful on the stairs." She went down in front of him watching his every move.

He drove her crazy. He wouldn't sit down at the kitchen table and let her fix breakfast for him, too determined to do it himself. He did consent to let her move the coffee mug from the counter to the table. He admitted it was a little difficult to manage with crutches.

"How about if we go to your house together, and the office too if you want, and we can pack up some things for you to do here, get some fresh clothes and then we can go to the store. I have some food here but I haven't stocked the cupboards yet. You could give me a hand with that. What about it?"

"Why not wait and see what Doc has to say?" He was tough. Could he just go with the flow? She shook her head. She'd make sure she was present when Ben examined the leg; she'd talk to him about it.

She nodded as she sipped her coffee. The first cup hadn't agreed with her. This went down a little better. The bagel helped settle her stomach too.

"So tell me about your week. You said you have a meeting on Friday. Are you nervous?" Eric spread cream cheese on his bagel as he spoke.

"I am a little just because it's all new. I'm sure once I get there and start to know people on the staff it'll be easier. I want to make a good impression so I'd like to have a few ideas already developed for them to look at. That's what I plan to work on this afternoon. This morning is just to finish editing the article that's already written."

"I love the way your eyes light up when you talk about your writing. How's your book?" He took a sip of coffee.

"I don't think I ever told you. When I was in New York, it came out in conversation with Penelope that I had just finished a manuscript. I described it to her, and she asked to show it to a friend who's an editor for a publishing house. I haven't heard anything yet. I don't expect to soon but it's a step in the right direction anyway."

Eric had stopped his hand in mid-air listening to her.

"Annie, that's great. I can't believe you didn't tell me." He looked sheepish and apologetic and miserable all at once.

273

"Forget I said that. I wasn't exactly being supportive at that point, was I?"

"No. You weren't in a listening mood, but we're past that now. Remember?"

He smiled and touched her cheek with the back of his fingers. "Yes, I remember."

She reached up and took his hand in hers. Just to be able to sit and hold hands with him at the breakfast table filled her with joy.

"Listen, what time will you be getting back on Friday night? I have a meeting on the mainland in the afternoon. Maybe I could meet your train and take you out to dinner before the late boat back. Will that work?"

"The train schedule is in the office but I think it gets in around four-thirty. Let me check. I'm going to run upstairs and get changed before Ben gets here. Want another cup of coffee?" She rose with her half empty cup of coffee and plate.

"If you don't mind." He smiled at her. "Aren't you going to have another cup?"

"I've already had my limit. My stomach's not feeling too great so I'll just go easy on it today." She filled his coffee cup and set the sugar and cream on the table for him. "I'll be down in a few minutes." She hurried out of the kitchen. Her stomach was twisting and churning. Beads of sweat formed on her forehead.

It was cooler upstairs, and she splashed her face with cool water. *Oh, that's a little better. This must be a touch of a stomach bug. Great. I hope I'm better by Friday.*

She took a quick shower and changed into a comfortable navy blue sweatsuit. There, that feels better. She heard voices in the living room, took a deep breath and went downstairs. Eric sat on the couch with his pant leg rolled up over his ankle. Ben bent over, holding the ankle gently. He poked and moved it, feeling all sides as he did.

"It looks much better today. Some of the swelling has gone down. You kept ice on it, didn't you?"

"Annie was good about changing the ice bags. My knee

isn't as swollen today either."

"Great. I want you to keep all weight off this leg for a few more days. At least today and tomorrow. You gonna stay here?" Doc looked eye to eye with Eric. It seemed to Annie that there was an unspoken question there.

She stepped in. "Of course he's staying here. I'd just have to worry twice as much if he were home by himself." Doc nodded.

"Good. Your mom'll be happy to hear you're taking good care of him too."

"We're going to go to his house and get some of his things, I'll run in and do a quick pick-up at the grocery store, then come back here and get that leg up and iced. What do you think, Ben?" She stood with her hands on her hips just daring Eric to object.

"Sounds perfect, Annie. He'll be good as new with you watching over him." Ben smiled. She knew he saw what was going on here. He'd go home and tell her mother, and then maybe she'd stop worrying about her.

She turned to Eric. "Why don't we go over to your house now while it's still early and you haven't been on the leg too long." He nodded. Apparently he isn't fighting it. Good.

"I'll give you a hand getting out to the car." Ben winked at Annie as he moved to help Eric off the couch.

"What do you think of Annie's new house, Eric?"

"It's wonderful. She's done a lot with it already. I'm surprised I didn't hear anything about this house being sold." Eric glared at Doc. Annie just watched the exchange with interest.

Ben shrugged his shoulders. "You weren't in much of a talking mood the few times I saw you. Didn't want to bother you."

Eric just shook his head. "I'm doing much better now, thank you." He smiled at his friend who handed him the crutches and helped him with his jacket. Annie grabbed the keys from the table in the entry. "Eric, can we take your car? I think it'll be easier for you to get in and out."

"That's fine."

Ben helped Eric get into the SUV with a minimum of pain. Annie got in the driver's side and started the car. It was April but the wind blew into the harbor, and a chill was in the air. They wound down the long driveway hill, the view of the harbor disappearing behind the trees.

As they drove through town and out on the shore road to Eric's house, Annie noticed the trees beginning to bud and the lawns beginning to green. "I love spring. Everything is beginning anew. It's such a hopeful season. Oh look, the daffodils are out over there."

Annie pointed to a patch of bright yellow flowers planted against a stone wall in front of a weathered Cape. "They have to be one of my favorite flowers." She smiled and looked at Eric. His lips smiled but his mind seemed to be elsewhere. She continued enjoying the signs of spring to herself.

When they arrived at Eric's house, he got out of the car and hobbled up the walkway to the porch stairs. He took the stairs one at a time, slowly. Annie went ahead and opened the door, waiting for him. His face was pale, but he didn't say anything.

"Annie, I'm going to sit on the bed and tell you where things are, okay? I think it'll be easier if I just have a couple pairs of sweatpants. They're in that bottom drawer." He directed and Annie found his clothes, a couple of books he wanted to read, and several folders of papers on the kitchen table.

"Anything else?" Annie put the stack of clothes in a large blue gym bag hanging in the closet.

"I need to go do something. Will you check the stuff in the refrigerator? Let's take anything that will spoil and use it at your place. Check the freezer too. See if there's anything in there you feel like having for dinner." He smiled at her, but he seemed preoccupied.

She went into the kitchen and opened the refrigerator: milk, eggs, leftover stir-fry, an open bottle of wine, and a carton of orange juice. She looked in the tall closet in the hall and found a cooler to carry it all. Then she looked in the freezer for something for dinner. Nothing really appealed to her. Food just wasn't a good topic for thought these days. She had to shake this bug.

She finally settled on a package of two Cornish hens. They'd had those on one of their first evenings together. If all else failed, she could make a good soup. Maybe that would cure her unsettled stomach.

She slung the gym bag over her shoulder and carried the cooler to the door.

"Eric, you ready to go?" She looked around but didn't see him.

"Annie, I'm out here. I'm all set if you are." He was sitting in the passenger's seat of the car. She carried everything out, closed the door behind her and loaded the food and clothes into the back of the SUV.

"I didn't hear you go out. Okay, off to the store." She told him what she had taken from the refrigerator and freezer as they headed back along the shore road to the center of town.

"Annie, my leg is really throbbing and I haven't taken the pain medication yet this morning. I think I'll just stay in the car while you shop if that's okay."

"Sure. I'll be quick." She smiled trying to keep it upbeat. The pain paled his face. She wanted to get him back home. That sounded so natural to her... home.

She hurried through the store and ten minutes and four bags later she loaded the groceries into the car. Finally, she pulled up the long hill to stop close to her covered porch. Eric hadn't said much since leaving his house. What was on his mind?

"I'm sorry I'm not much help. I do have one thing for you though." He had gotten out of the car and opened the back door. He reached down onto the floor of the back seat and pulled out a bunch of daffodils. He handed them to her. "Happy spring Annie. Thank you for everything." He kissed her, lingering on her lips.

Her heart flip-flopped in her chest. Tears sprang to her

eyes. Why was she crying?

"Eric, they're lovely." She wiped the tears in her eyes. "Where did you get them?"

"Cara had a patch of them that she loved. Every spring, she'd wait anxiously for them to blossom. I know she'd want you to enjoy them too."

She hugged him, holding him close so he couldn't see the tears running down her cheeks.

"They're still with us, aren't they?" She looked up at him, the tears flowing freely.

"Good memories of the past bring good hopes for the future." He looked out over the harbor deep in thought. He looked down at her, and wiped the tears from her cheek. "Let's get inside. It's still chilly out." He maneuvered the stair and porch, while Annie grabbed some of the groceries from the back of the car.

"Since you're carrying things in, I'll put them away in the kitchen." He found a large jar, placed the daffodils in it and set it in the middle of the oak table. Annie made several trips back and forth to the car and finally plopped down in the chair at the table.

"Whew, I'm tired."

"Why don't you get settled in the office? I'll make a pot of coffee for us and call you when it's ready."

"That sounds good." Anxious to finish her work, she disappeared into her office as Eric finished putting away the groceries and leftovers from his house.

***

She'd complained about her stomach several times over last night and this morning. It could just be a little virus bothering her. Or maybe all the stress she'd been under lately. New job, new house, stupid boyfriend... he chastised himself for his part in her stress. He planned to work at making her life easier from here on out. Maybe he'd call and make reservations at a nice restaurant for Friday night.

Eric found the coffee and managed to hobble around to put things away in the kitchen. He found all the ingredients he needed to make a minestrone soup and quickly put it together to simmer for lunch. If she insists on taking care of me, I'm going to take care of her too. The thought warmed him. He looked around the kitchen, through to the dining room, down the hallway to the entry. She'd done amazing things in six weeks. No wonder she was stressed. But now that they were together again, he could help her, share with her, and support her.

Relief enveloped him. She'd forgiven him and never given up on him. For her to make major decisions to be here on the island told him exactly how much she cared for him. And that she loved the island. And that she was healing.

Was she ready for the next thing he wanted to throw at her? He should probably give her more time, take it slow. That would be the hard part. Because of Cara's death, Doc nearly losing Sara, and his scare of Annie being out of his life, he'd gotten philosophical about life partners. If you're meant to be together, don't waste time on the trivial. Just be together.

He shook himself out of his contemplation. The coffee brewed. He'd love to be able to deliver a mug to Annie but didn't think he could manage it on crutches. He tentatively put his foot on the floor, testing a little weight on it. It hurt a little. He tried to take a step using one crutch to support most of his weight on the right leg. Not bad. He smiled to himself.

He filled a mug with coffee, fixing it the way she liked it. Carefully he maneuvered through the door of her office. She looked up and smiled at the sight of the coffee, then realized that he was walking with it.

"Don't yell at me. I just wanted to try out my leg and wait on you a little."

She jumped up from her desk. He handed her the coffee but wrapped his other arm around her to hold her close.

"Are you okay? How's your leg?" She spoke quietly, concern in her eyes as she looked up at him.

"It's okay. I couldn't do that for long, and I'm going to go put it up and read for a while. But first I need this." He kissed her...long and lingering, pulling her body against his. Her soft curves melded to him, her lips parted. The desire to sweep her up in his arms filled him.

"Maybe a little later we could go take a nap together," he whispered into her ear. He took a little nibble while there.

"I'm sure I'll be exhausted after I finish this. I'll come get you." She kissed him and pulled away to set the coffee on her desk. She turned back. "Do you need anything in the living room?"

"I'm all set. Soup is simmering on the stove for lunch." He smiled down at her. Did she know how beautiful she was? He kissed her quickly and moved to the door.

"Get back to work so you can get exhausted!" He turned and winked as she chuckled.

"I'll do my best!"

***

His stay stretched for the rest of the week. He cheated more and more with his leg and by the end of the week he lost the crutches. He knew he could have gone home after that first night, but he didn't want to, and Annie made it obvious she wanted him to stay. On Friday morning he got up early with Annie. He watched as she packed several folders in her briefcase and an apple and bottle of water in her large shoulder bag.

"I'll drive you down to the ferry and then head over to my house. I have a few things to organize before my meeting this afternoon. I'll meet you at the train station around four-thirty."

"Okay, that sounds good."

He thought about his real plan while she continued packing up. He'd called and made reservations at one of the finest restaurants in the area. He planned to stop and do some jewelry shopping before his meeting. He'd thought of nothing but their relationship this week. He wanted Annie in his life in a permanent way. He wanted to marry her, take care of her, be with her.

But was she ready? It hadn't been a year since her husband's death. She'd taken huge strides toward getting her life organized and pulled together. Her new job and her house made her happy. Was she ready to let him into her life…permanently? That made his stomach clench, his heart hammer, his palms sweat. What if she wasn't? Wouldn't it be better to keep the status quo? Should he push it with a ring? He needed to take the risk. Life was too short…

The ring reminded him of Annie—beautiful, simple but stylish. He pictured it on her finger—a square, blue sapphire with smaller square cut diamonds on each side.

He put the jewelry box in his pocket. Tonight at dinner…

The afternoon flew by with several meetings at the office. The partners were happy. Having an insurance agent on the island increased their visibility and their business. Eric was pleased too. He looked at his watch—four twenty-seven. He'd be late picking her up. He quickly collected his things, made his good-byes and rushed to the train station, only minutes away.

As he pulled around the corner to park outside the train station, an ambulance pulled up, siren blaring, lights flashing. As an EMT he could offer help if needed, but if it was for a transport to the hospital they always had enough personnel in the ambulance. He walked in behind the technicians.

He looked around for Annie. A group of people gathered around several uniformed men, one kneeling down next to a woman on the floor… Annie.

He raced through the crowd. "What happened? Annie? Annie—wake up." His heart hammered so that all he heard was the rushing of his own blood.

The EMTs tried to move in and remove him from their work area.

"Look—I'm an EMT and her boyfriend. I came to pick her up. What happened? Who called this in?"

A security guard stepped forward. "She got off the four-twenty-five from New York and looked a little wobbly and dropped right there. I didn't want to move her. We called it in."

"Any medical conditions we should know about?" one of the EMTs asked Eric.

"Not that I know of." He was scared. The EMT hat had

fallen off and he was civilian Eric, watching them move the woman he loved to a stretcher, taking her vital signs. She looked pasty pale.

"We're going to transport her to the hospital. You might want to follow us there." The young attendant looked at him sympathetically.

"Absolutely."

As quick as they moved, it wasn't fast enough. He wanted her there and taken care of. He wanted her to regain consciousness. Why hadn't she woken up yet? What the hell was going on?

His mind raced with questions as he pulled up next to the ambulance at the emergency room entrance. He was next to her when they brought her in. He stayed as the ER doctor examined her.

They started an IV, took blood, and hooked her up to monitors. Within minutes, her eyelids fluttered.

"Annie? Can you hear me? Open your eyes." Eric held the hand without the tubes attached.

"You're in the hospital, ma'am. My name is Dr. Grant. You passed out at the train station. We're getting you fixed up here. How are you feeling?

"I don't know what happened. I felt a little dizzy then it all went black."

"Annie, did you have anything to eat today?" Eric watched as she closed her eyes.

"I had that apple I packed but that was this morning on the ferry. I've been busy or in meetings all day. And my stomach hasn't felt that great." Annie looked to him for understanding. He squeezed her hand.

"Doctor, she's been complaining lately of flu-like symptoms—nausea, fatigue—we thought she might have a touch of the flu. Could she be dehydrated? Would that make her pass out?"

"Well, her blood sugar was low when she came in. The IV will take care of both low sugar and dehydration. We ran some other tests to be sure. I want you to relax and let this bottle of fluid get into you and hopefully by then I'll have some results for you."

His stomach twisted into a knot. Tests... hospital... results... just to be sure. He'd heard it before. And she'd died. Come to think of it, she'd had the same sort of symptoms in the beginning too. Nauseous, tired, dizzy, weak.

His head began to spin. He couldn't lose Annie. Not fair. How could the Fates take her away, just after he'd found her? He looked down at her. She'd closed her eyes, resting. Her color started to come back, but she looked so vulnerable.

He had to get out. The hospital smell clawed at him, the paging system ringing in his ears. He leaned down and kissed her on the cheek.

"Annie, I'm going to go find some bottled water. I'll be right back. You rest." She nodded her head.

Once outside the room, he bolted for the automatic doors leading to the outside. He needed the fresh air. He needed to think. Breathe and think. She's got cancer too. That's it. Why is this happening? I want to marry her, spend the rest of our lives together, but I want more than a few months, a year with her.

He sat on the cement wall outside the emergency room doors. Thoughts spun through his head, emotions churned in his stomach. It made him nauseous. He stopped at the soda machine in the entry and got a bottle of water. He touched the ring box in his pocket.

I should ask her to marry me now. If she gets the results back before I ask her, she'll say she doesn't want to burden my life, she doesn't want to put me through it again. But I want her for as long as I can have her.

He finished the bottle of water, nodded his head with determination. That's what he'd do. Go ask her now.

He'd been gone a mere ten minutes but as he rounded the corner into the emergency room, and headed toward Exam Room Two, he saw Dr. Grant standing next to Annie who sat up on the side of the table. The doctor shook her hand, and Eric arrived in time to hear him finish talking to her.

"You don't have to make the appointment immediately, but you should get set up with the doctor within the next month. He'll want to set up a schedule of appointments."

Annie nodded. She looked in shock. *He's already told her. She'll never agree to marry me now. It doesn't matter what it is. I want to spend whatever time is left…I want to be with her. I want us to be together.*

Eric stepped into the room. The doctor turned and shook his hand. "She's all set for now. I'm sure she'll fill you in. Take good care of her." Then he smiled, nodded at Annie and left.

"What's going on, Annie?" He took her hand.

"He said I could go. I'd rather wait until we have a little privacy. Let's talk about it in the car, okay?" Her eyes looked glazed over as if she tried to process the news.

"Okay. I'm parked right outside." He took her arm and held her close. Once to the car, he opened the passenger's side and carefully helped her in. She looked at him with an odd look on her face.

"Did the doctor talk to you?" she asked as he got into the driver's seat.

"No. But Annie, I want to ask you something before you tell me everything that's going on. I wanted to wait until dinner tonight, but now I want to do it before we get there." He turned toward her and took her hand.

"Eric, what is it?"

"Annie, I want us to be together. I love you. This past week felt right." His heart thundered but he raced on to keep her from objecting. "I want to make it permanent. Annie, will you marry me?" He tried to quiet himself, take a deep breath, but everything focused on her. *Please say yes.*

"Eric, are you sure the doctor didn't say anything to you?" Her eyes were wide.

"Annie, it doesn't matter what the doctor said. I love you and I want to be with you for as long as we have. I heard him say you'll need to set up a schedule of appointments. I know what Cara went through. I'll be there for you. We've got to try to beat this." She couldn't deny them the time.

"What? Eric what are you talking about?"

"It dawned on me as I listened to the doctor, and then sat outside getting some fresh air, that you've had the same symptoms as Cara when it first started with…"

"Oh my… Eric stop. Listen to me. I don't have cancer. I don't have any life-threatening disease." She smiled and reached for his hand. "Although it will be life-altering."

"Okay, I'm totally lost. What are you talking about?"

"I'm going to be fine… in about seven and a half months. I'm pregnant."

His jaw drop; his stomach somersaulted, then it hit him… a baby. He reached his arms around her and pulled her close.

"Oh Annie, I love you. I am so happy. Relief filled his voice. "Wait! You haven't answered my question. Will you marry me?" He looked into her eyes, and saw the answer sparkling there in her tears.

"Yes, Eric. I would be honored to be your wife. I love you." She kissed him, her soft lips caressing his.

He struggled to maintain control. He wanted to surround her with his arms and hold her and make love with her and …

Instead he reached into his coat pocket for the little box. Things hadn't gone according to his plan, but since when does life go as planned? The important thing—they had each other, their love, and now, their future.

He opened the lid and showed her the ring. "I planned to ask you tonight at dinner. I got this in the hope that you'd say yes." He took the ring out and put it on her finger.

"Oh Eric, I love it."

He kissed her again. "Let's get some dinner. I made reservations. Let's see if we can still get in. We have a lot to talk about."

***

At dinner, they talked, planned, laughed. They celebrated. After a peaceful ferry ride back to the island, Annie asked Eric to pull down to their spot… their beach.

They got out of the car and stood on the rocks entwined in

each other's arms, listening to the gentle sound of surf on the shore.

Annie took a deep breath of the crisp salt air.

"It's going to be a good life, Eric. We're both blessed to have had deep abiding love once, and to have found it again, with each other." She knew it was right. Some might say it was too soon after Mike's death. She'd come to understand that each minute of life is precious, to be cherished and spent with those you love. She wanted to spend every moment celebrating life, celebrating love.

He kissed her, sending waves of passion through her body and soul.

"I love you, Eric."

"I love you too, Annie. We're going to be happy."

They stood together watching the waves, and though there was no fog, no violent sea spray, they watched a white mist move along the shore toward the distant lighthouse that tonight sat silent. Cara and Mike, Eric and Annie.

Epilogue
Passion in Port

The sounds of Eric playing with eighteen- month-old Kristoff in the living room created a joyful distraction to Annie as she put the finishing touches on the latest article .

The editorial staff had been delighted with the work-at-home arrangement. Annie was even more delighted. She had the best of all worlds: quality time with her loving husband and their beautiful towhead toddler, her dream career, and time to write the novels she loved.

She stood and stretched as she waited for the fax machine to finish transmitting to New York. She rubbed her hand over her abdomen. Though not far along, her belly started to show her condition.

She watched from the archway as her two boys rough tumbled in the living room. If truth be known, Eric got the worst of it as young Kristoff ran and jumped on Daddy lying on the floor. Giggles and squeals filled the air.

The doorbell rang. Annie opened the door. A large box had been delivered to the front porch.

"Don't lift that. I'll get it." Eric appeared on the spot to prevent her from doing anything strenuous. He'd been just as attentive with this pregnancy as with the first.

"Oh, it's from your publisher. I bet it's your book." They quickly pulled the flaps open. "Annie, look at it. It's great. I am so proud of you," he beamed as he took his wife in his arms. "And the second one isn't far behind. It'll be released right around the time the baby is born."

"I am so blessed. Think how different our life is from the day we first met. You've been my safe harbor through all the storms of life."

"And you mine. I love you Annie." He nibbled at her ear reminding her of the passion to be found in this safe harbor.

About the Author

Raised on a small island off the coast of New England, Lynn Jenssen infuses her writing - women's fiction, and contemporary romance - with characters that live and laugh and love in small-town communities by the ocean. Lynn Jenssen now lives in Rhode Island with her romantic hero husband, Bill, on a small family farm. With two grown sons, two wonderful daughter-in-laws, several joyful grandchildren, and three siblings with extended families, she appreciates the variety of relationships woven into a family fabric. When she isn't writing or working, she loves to cook, swim, or go for walks – while letting her muse run wild!

You can contact her on her website: www.lynnjenssen.com
or email her: lynnjenssen@aol.com

Turn the page for a sneak peak from

Mystical Connections

by Christine Mazurk,

author of
Identity: Sisters of Spirit Anthology
Passion's Race

-

Mystical Connections

Chapter 1

Jenna Nichols paced in front of the large picture window in her office, excitement mixing with a pinch of nerves in the pit of her stomach. She stopped to stare at the bay, trying to calm herself. The San Francisco fog had dissipated not more than thirty minutes ago. The vast body of water, now tranquil.

Though Jenna looked forward to promoting her newest release, a knot of trepidation fluttered through her, making it difficult to breathe. Book reviewer, Carla Wren, known for her no-nonsense approach to interviewing, did only exclusives. Her agent, Kira, pulled some strings to book this.

Why was she so nervous? Was it that Carla was late or was it a sign? Her morning run along the Embarcadero to the Golden Gate Bridge didn't ease her stress, and pacing now didn't help.

She knew the characters better than anyone. No one else could describe her story better than she. After all, they were her creation—or her channel to the special revelations sent for her to share with the world. A sharp knock at the door pulled her attention, and she turned to greet the journalist.

The door opened, and in stepped a younger, much hunkier, and oh-so-sexy version of Kevin Bacon. His blue eyes stopped her in her tracks like lasers cutting through steel.

"Ms. Nichols?" His top lip lifted to one side as he smiled, though his eyes remained cool. He sauntered over. "I'm here to discuss your new book, *Destiny's Power*."

She glanced up at the man before her. Light brown, finger-combed hair lazily framed his lean face, as his electric blue eyes flicked over her body. She wore a simple pants suit of black and cream over a solid black tank, but for a moment, she felt naked.

Her pulse skipped, and she felt a sizzle of warmth shimmy down her spine. When his gaze zeroed in on her face, she swore he looked straight through to her soul.

"I was expecting Ms. Wren." Her tongue tripped over the syllables, and heat kissed her cheeks.

"Yes. Unfortunately, on her drive here, she got side-swiped, landed her in the hospital. They sent me in her place." He reached out to shake hands. "I'm Aidan Scott. Can't say I'm happy about this assignment, but you want to get started?"

His hand swallowed hers, his long tapered fingers tightening around her flesh. His skin felt warm against hers, but still, she shivered.

"Oh," she sputtered. "Was she injured?"

"Carla's banged up pretty bad, but she'll live."

She edged back, reclaimed her hand. "That's good to hear. Shall we sit?" She indicated the two over-stuffed chairs in the corner. "Can I get you anything before we begin?"

"No." He flipped open his note pad, the one he pulled from the inside pocket of his dark blazer. The tee shirt underneath exactly matched his eyes. From his messenger bag, he took out a small hand-held recorder. Placing it in the center of the table, he hovered his finger above the buttons. "You don't mind if I record this, do you?"

She held her breath as she walked over to sit down. It helped steady her nerves. "Not at all." She leveled her voice to sound calm.

He punched the button, poised his pen, and launched. "How old are you, Ms. Nichols?"

"Twenty-two." She sat back and crossed her legs.

"And you've written how many books?"

"Seven."

"And what exactly do you write about in all of your infinite wisdom and experience?"

The hair at the back of her neck bristled, and goose flesh skimmed her arms. Yeah, he was eye candy, the kind that left a sour taste in her mouth.

"That depends," she replied.

"On what?"

"What comes to me." How could she say it without appearing *out* there? "I dream the theme and research from there. Some stories beg for center stage."

"Oh, come on. Maybe you'd like airport security to shake magic sticks and chant to keep the world safe?"

She jerked back, his taunt like a punch to her gut. Folding her arms over her chest, she sank back into the cushion of the chair and eyed him.

"Have you read *Destiny's Power*, Mr. Scott?"

He shook his head, and his lip curled back like a rabid dog. "I don't read romance."

Her hand dropped and tensed against her thigh; she imagined his throat beneath her fingertips. She held her anger but pushed back. "Maybe you should; it might soften your edges."

What an arrogant clown.

His expression shifted, but only for an instant, a darkening of his irises, and the quick slant of an eyebrow. That smirk he first used when he introduced himself took over.

In one quick movement, he stood, picking up the recorder. With a snap of the switch, he strode to the door. Over his shoulder he stated, "I take it we're done."

"Yes, why don't you run along and do your homework. Call me when you're ready to talk like an adult."

Too late, she pressed her lips together. Her words hung suspended in the room, an awkward silence following.

He shrugged, but the look on his face said plenty.

She cringed as he exited her office, the door clicking shut with a sickening reality. She blew the interview.

*   *   *

Shaken to the core, her stupidity choking her, Jenna grabbed her handbag and headed through the office. Only the wide-eyed stares of her staff slowed her footsteps until she reached the door to the elevator. She held her breath, this time to disguise her rapid breathing. When she released it, she announced, "I'm going for coffee and a short walk to plot the next story. Anyone want anything?"

"Oh, I'd love a black and white cookie," Erin, her publicist answered, "and a latte." She lifted the phone and plastered it to her ear.

"Nothing for me," said Lindsay. Jenna's second pair of eyes for her manuscripts allowed her hot-pink pen to hover over the stack of papers in front of her, but regarded Jenna with curiosity. "Have you plotted the next book?"

"Not yet, but I'm working with something," she replied, ready to bolt.

"Bring back a few of Anya's creations; they're yummy," Justin added, while his fingers danced over the keyboard. He worked magic on her web site, running daily stats, and updating the content of each page on a bi-weekly basis. He even fed her ideas for her Blog, monitoring the comments as they posted.

Missy, her assistant, must have stepped out, which was a relief, because she wouldn't know the journalist had left only moments after arriving.

She sighed when the elevator doors finally closed.

As she stepped onto the sidewalk, the sun hit her full in the face, and reality dawned, causing her to gasp. Oh my God. The end of a successful career for her meant the unemployment line for her staff. By not controlling her tongue, she damaged more than her own life.

She thought of the ripple effect. Her agent would kill her, probably drive to some close-by ghost town, bury her body, and send out a press release that stated she'd wed a rock star and dropped off the face of the earth. Who would care? Only her parents, she realized with dismay.

By uttering those snide comments, she threw a towel in the middle of the ring, yanking her reputation out of the competition, proving she was a young and unprofessional idiot, one who had little regard for her career, because his expression suggested an unflattering portrait of her as an author.

She stepped into the haven of Brews B'neath the Bridge, the scent of freshly roasted beans easing her tension. She drew in a deep breath, almost tasting the rich Colombian blend. As she made her way to the counter, a very beautiful young girl greeted her.

"Hey, Jenna, the usual?" Her striking blue eyes suddenly reminded her of the predator stalking her career.

The comparison jolted her, and she blinked in surprise. "Oh, hey, Anya. Yeah, the usual."

Blue eyes were common, but she feared the sight of them would now remind her only of this disastrous interview. She must find a way to resolve her dilemma. She couldn't allow a jaded reporter to ruin what she'd worked so hard to make credible. "Everything happened for a reason." Her need to know "why" served as the foundation of her stories.

"Your vanilla latte," Anya's soft voice brought her back.

"Thanks. Do you have any samples to share? My staff adores your creations." The girl loved to bake, and the owner of the shop allowed her to give out samples and sell some of her treats.

"I'll box them up for you."

"Thanks. I'll swing back by in a bit."

A brisk walk on the Embarcadero would help Jenna think. She slipped through the crowd, edging to the right, sipping on her drink. The crisp air carried a slight scent of brine; the sun warmed her skin. The clear blue sky reminded her of those eyes that now haunted her.

Had her angst about the interview with Carla Wren been nerves or instinct? Because then *he* showed up. Had Carla's accident steered Aidan to her? And if so, why? Was his presence a detour to her success? Or could she be a catalyst in his life?

As she pondered, a crumpled piece of paper blew past her. Detesting litter, she ran after it. She caught it with the tip of her Santana pump then reached down to grab it. She carried it with her, searching for a trash can as she continued her walk.

Her thoughts returned to Aidan Scott. What was his deal? Why would he want to provoke her? Was his heart black enough to want to discredit her, make her look silly?

Or had she derailed herself by taking his bait?

Her plan to share her next story possibility, show how her process worked, using the old building from her dream the other night as the starting point, evaporated as soon as they opened their mouths. She ran him off with her impulsiveness—something that had gotten her in trouble before. When would she learn?

Turning to head back, Jenna spied a garbage bin and stopped to discard her trash. She hesitated. Curiosity made her smooth open the balled-up flyer. The building from her dream. She dropped onto a nearby bench. Another sign.

Her stories started this way: a dream, a few signals, followed by research to see where it led her. The clues linked to a person who recently entered or would soon enter her life, an energy inexplicable to the average man, though together they formed a Universal connection.

As she looked at the flyer, she felt the familiar tingle. "Historic building transformed to contemporary lofts on sale now! Located on Montgomery Street between Washington and Jackson. They're going fast."

Was this building her next story?

Where to start? What to search for? Questions rallied for attention in her brain. Without realizing it, she got up and changed direction, heading west, her need to see the building pulling her.

When she got there, she stood across the street, absorbing the lines of character the building portrayed. The historic value preserved on the outside, yet, she imagined, the insides as newly recreated. Wide open spaces with large picture windows that allowed sunlight to pour in and pool on the floors. She closed her eyes and pictured a light airy loft.

Opening her eyes, she continued to study the building, waiting for some plot idea to morph, now sure of a story.

Then the solution hit her.

Invite the clown to join in on her research.

Made in the USA
San Bernardino, CA
06 July 2014